THE NIGHT BAZAAR

ELEVEN HAUNTING TALES OF FORBIDDEN WISHES AND DANGEROUS DESIRES

EDITED BY

LENORE HART

NORTHAMPTON HOUSE PRESS

Cover design by Naia Poyer.
Cover photos: silk dancer © tBoyan/iStock Photo; moon mask © 1Photodiva/iStock Photo; pomegranate © ValentynVolkov/iStock Photo; market background © Grandfailure/iStock Photo.

ISBN 978-1-937997-78-6
Library of Congress Control Number: 2016951953

THE NIGHT BAZAAR

CONTENTS

We must not look at Goblin Men,
We must not buy their fruits
Who knows upon what soil they fed
Their hungry thirsty roots?

—Christina Rosetti, *Goblin Market*, 1862

An Invitation to the Bazaar

You will not find us on your own, no matter how long or how far you search. We only come to you: with a tap on the shoulder, an elegantly engraved invitation, cryptic calligraphy on parchment, or perhaps one pale, slender hand beckoning from an alleyway.

We either choose you, or we don't.

The first mention of the Night Bazaar in Western literature can be found in a passage from the 1518 edition of *Confessionale Seu Manuale Confessorum* by Johannes Nider, a volume printed by Pierre Gaudoul in Paris. The author mentions a mysterious marketplace which appeared in St. Mark's Square in Venice, at the stroke of midnight in 1348. This "bazaare nuctornalis" featured secretive, cunning merchants from the East plying exotic goods displayed in brocade-covered stalls. Its vanishing coincided with the arrival of *yersinia pestis*, the Black Death or Plague, in Europe. There is a possible previous reference, too, in the writings of the Mad Arab Abdul Al-Hazred, poet of Sana'a, around 700 C.E.

Since then, mentions of a "Midnight Bazaar" or "Night Market" appear in other obscure and controversial works from around the world. The marketplace they describe appears for one week only in the same city . . . as it did in Paris, in 1796 . . . London, in 1888 . . . Berlin, in 1933 . . . San Francisco, in 1906 . . . but never in precisely the same venue for any of those consecutive nights, and never again in the same city.

The common elements are these: the Bazaar opens at midnight. It closes before dawn. The stalls and booths within are filled with an amazing variety of goods, few new, but all of impeccable quality. These include quite rare or antique oddities, all of interesting origin. In curtained alcoves certain services are also rendered, including various forms of tattooing, piercing, costuming, elective surgery, elaborate leather, pottery, and *papier-maché* masks, herbal and alchemical treatments; in short, every imaginable sort of body art and alteration. And of course the palm reading, Tarot, tea leaf-reading, and water-, glass-, and crystal-gazing one would naturally expect.

The booths and narrow alleyways are filled with modern (and possibly not-so-modern) strolling jongleurs, freaks, charlatans, mountebanks, prostitutes, dancers, and other entertainers. Money-changers and masked vendors offer ready loans on a wide array of forms of security (tangible and otherwise), as well as queer or ancient *objets d'art*, curiosities, and vintage musical and medical instruments. Barkers tout various arcane and legally-prohibited "Highly Serious Games of Chance and Skill." The mingled scents of opium, perfume, tobacco, greasepaint, incense, plastic explosive, alcohol, and sex always permeate the heavy, intoxicating air.

In sum, whatever is odd, questionable, and averse to the light of day can be discovered, and rented or purchased, somewhere at the Night Bazaar.

But it cannot be *found*. The Bazaar finds you. Then, at the end of the appointed week, it folds its tents and steals off into the night. To someday appear elsewhere . . . or perhaps elsewhen.

But for that fleeting moment it will be your conduit: to romance, to madness, to truth, to honesty, to finally admitting the darkest desires of your heart. Oh yes, you will yearn to attend, before even grasping precisely what it is you pine for.

No matter. We know what you want.

Do not attend, though, if you are timid or faint of heart. Nor if you truly value respectability or piety. (If, on the other hand, you merely use their appearance to mask your own ends, then . . . welcome.) No, it is best for the weak to ignore the whispered come-on, the anonymous text message, the beckoning hand. And to set aside the invitation.

No need to burn it. For you will discover, when you look again, that it has already disappeared.

The question is, will you be brave enough to step through our doorway?

Let's find out.

Come forward, gentle citizen. Cease slumbering on while the Bazaar unfolds in the dark and secret basements of your City. Rise from that warm fusty bed and stroll with new determination past all those glowing plate-glass windows full of overpriced goods that, once acquired, inevitably disappoint. Step off the curb—looking both ways first, of course—and cross with the light. Past the subway entrances and steam grates and deserted stalls of knock-off purses and polyester pashminas and plastic Statue of Liberty souvenirs. Through the smoky lingering ghosts of halal food carts and portable sausage grills. Past the poor wretched ones who huddle in doorways with hands outstretched to take any bills or coins you might deign to dispense before hurrying on your way.

Have you ever looked back to see if their gazes follow? If they are perhaps making some vague, mysterious gesture at your retreating back?

I was once like you, though that was long ago. Since joining the Bazaar I have lived in many places, under many names, and in various guises suited to the role at hand: equestrienne, croupier, spy, mistress of ceremonies, dominatrix, purveyor of fortunes. You may call me Madam Vera. Lady Truth. The name I've assumed most often, for I think it suits me best. The truth and I are both ageless, and so very hard to hold onto.

But I digress.

Once invited, walk on across town, carefully following whispered directions, or a silent guide, or with GPS in hand, until you reach our latest venue. As I mentioned, the Bazaar is never in the same place two nights running, so it will be impossible to find us again. In any case, most of the Invited find one night is quite enough.

So abandon your fears and foolish expectations. The reality is more enticing, and far more disturbing.

Step in, step closer, and view our wares! Mysterious antiquities, cast-off white elephants, curious contraptions crafted of vintage wood, rusted steel, or engraved silver. Wander the crowded, twisted aisles and inspect satin-draped booths, billowing silk tents, ebony and mahogany tables displaying strange, even seemingly useless goods. Do not fail to also investigate the comely or malformed purveyors who offer unusual services—from the benignly ordinary to the wildly erotic—behind a hanging tapestry or a clacking, beaded curtain. By all means, immerse yourself in our world.

But are you the contemplator, or the contemplated? A patronizing spectator . . . or perhaps someone has chalked a tell-tale mark upon your back.

Do you recognize any of us yet? Perhaps you only recognize what we sell: Everything which cannot be had elsewhere. All that is forbidden. Everything you've read about but thought had long since passed away, or perhaps never existed. How wrong you were! Here before you is Wish Fulfillment . . . with its price attached, of course. For we at the Bazaar, though preternaturally understanding and permissive, must live as well.

At least, those of us who still lay claim to that mode of existence.

Ah. It appears you have already spotted something you desire, no? But don't head off that way, not just yet. There's no rush.

You have all night.

All night—but not a moment more.

Mind your step as we walk from one aisle to the next. There are blind corners here, and sometimes boisterous, unruly crowds converge. Also the Invited have an unfortunate tendency to litter the floor with kebab wrappers, used love philters, or small trinkets that in the end did not satisfy. Sometimes, disappointed, they may foolishly discard a charm or an amulet they have failed to apply properly. Or an item whose term of use has ended.

Here, for example . . . on the floor by the Games of Serious Chance and Skill concession, lies a wallet-sized card with a photo of a commuter train. A New Jersey Transit weekly rail pass. However, in the corner of this one is a demi-lune mask, our logo. So it was purchased here at the Bazaar. The bearer must have changed his mind about his destination, though. Or perhaps he merely missed the last train. . . .

WEEKLY PASS

Jim Scheers

Monday

David was starting to suspect the big guy wasn't a real train conductor. For one thing, the uniform didn't fit. The seams of his blue shirt strained across wide shoulders and the sleeves didn't reach past those thick wrists. And even though they were in Penn Station, he didn't seem sure where he was going. But David couldn't turn back now. They were several levels below the main concourse—they'd gone down at least four flights of steps—but after following the man through a series of dank cinder-block corridors, moving in and out of the sickly blue light cast by fluorescent bulbs hidden in the pipe work overhead, he'd completely lost his way.

Only a short while ago he'd been up on the concourse with all the other weary suits who'd worked way too late into the evening again. Sitting on a metal bench, staring mindlessly at a wad of gum squashed into a grimy pink coin on the tile floor between his shoes.

Then the conductor had appeared, standing over him. A large man with a ponderous belly and a face like a plump, white pillow. He'd bent slightly to look David in the face, waiting for him to return the gaze before he spoke.

"You work late a lot."

Was that a question or a statement? David had never been comfortable with small talk, even with co-workers he'd known for a decade. But staring up at the passive face, he'd thought this must be someone he knew. From when or where he couldn't recall, but he was instantly sure this was a friend he could trust.

"Yeah. Well . . ." he had shrugged. "There's not much reason to rush home."

"I know a better place to pass your time. If you'd like to follow me."

So he had trailed him across the concourse to a dented metal door marked AUTHORIZED EMPLOYEES ONLY.

But now, following the broad, sloping shoulders down yet another flight of stained concrete steps, he realized this conductor's wide leather accessory belt was empty. No hole punch. No pad of tickets. He'd been commuting long enough to know that was odd.

The conductor finally stopped at the entrance to a wider corridor, glanced left and right, then let out a sigh of relief. He turned, round face lit by the weak glow from a flickering light bulb far above them in the ductwork. David was sure now he'd made a mistake coming down here. He'd never met this fellow before. He didn't recognize him at all.

"Look." He tried to make his tone firm. "It's getting late. I have to go back. People—my family—will wonder where I am."

This wasn't true. He lived by himself in a one-bedroom in Somerset with venetian blinds and bare white walls. He talked to his parents in Lakewood once a week every Friday evening. He had no friends.

"You want to go back?" The conductor shook his head, disbelieving. His eyes were so deeply set in that plump face, David couldn't tell what color they were. Just two dark glimmers, like water at the bottom of a well. Behind him, from down the corridor, came a murmur of voices. The occasional muted thump of hammers on wood. The conductor stepped into the corridor, then beckoned with a resigned wave of the hand.

David didn't move.

"You've come this far, sir." The man had dropped the familiarity he'd affected upstairs. He spoke courteously, though the tone was sullen and weary. That much was like a real train conductor. "Might as well look around."

"At what? It's too dark to see."

"Give your eyes a moment to adjust, sir."

David blinked a few times, then followed him through the entrance into the broad tunnel that seem to stretch much too far into the darkness. A vaulted ceiling arched overhead. He smelled smoke—heavy, woodsy smoke, like a campfire—and incense. Then, gradually, other scents, like dozens of spices all mixed together. Uneven rows of torches were racked into holes in the wall, extending along both sides of the corridor, all the way to distant shadows where the tunnel abruptly turned. The orange glow of flames flickered across long wooden tables and tents draped with velvet and brocades. People hurried past in both directions, some with sacks slung over their shoulders. Others, empty-handed, hunched, eyes darting to and fro, were peeking into the tents or pausing to pick over the tables.

"Welcome to the Bazaar," the conductor said. David followed him as he paced down the aisles, listing the wares in a bored monotone, like someone counting an inventory. " . . . all sorts of talismans, for protection, for great strength, sexual potency, ancient ivory spurs, ancient surgical implements—those are cursed, just so you know—and services, too . . . fortune telling, assisted suicide, assisted homicide, all kinds of sexual favors . . ."

At last the conductor fell silent. He turned to David and raised his shoulders in a lazy shrug. "Anything appeal?"

"I don't want any of that stuff," David said. "I'm not interested in super-powers or antique magical spurs."

The man frowned. "I wouldn't have been sent up for you for no reason. There must be something."

David bowed his head, considering. His whole life he'd gone with the flow. High school to college to an internship to a regular office job. Like riding a greased slide on a playground. Always the path of least resistance. His so-called friends were just people from the office. The only women he'd dated were from there too, or the office next door. He'd always wondered: *What if I tried something totally different?* A real life where he actually *chose*, instead of accepting whatever came along. But then he'd get home each night at eight or nine, or sometimes ten o'clock, and eat frozen Thai in front of the TV, so wiped out he couldn't remember what he'd been daydreaming, let alone get up and do something about it. He'd always stayed on the same course, never taking that first step to change anything.

The conductor cast his head back and watched the smoke from the torches curling up toward the ceiling. Finally he let out a quick cough. "What is it you *want*, sir?"

David took a deep breath, then exhaled. "A different life. I want options."

The conductor stared, mouth hanging open. Maybe he was thinking.

David shifted his feet impatiently. "You have anything like that?"

The conductor looked to the ceiling again, then nodded slowly. "Sure. This way."

***

After navigating once again through the now-crowded aisles—where did all these people come from? Had they been "summoned" like him?—they reached a narrow stall draped with dark russet tapestry. The conductor parted this and poked his head inside. Then he held it open and told David to step inside.

An emaciated old man, wrapped in pale robes all the way up to his chin, sat at a small wooden table lit by a single candle. "Please." He pointed to the empty chair opposite.

David sat and the conductor withdrew, closing the curtain behind him. The old man slid the candle to the side so David could see his face clearly. The hollow cheeks and brittle, reed-thin wrists made him think of skeletons, but the skin was perfectly smooth. Except for the wrinkle of a few veins across a freshly-shaven scalp, which glistened in the candle's flickering glow. He smiled at David, gray eyes placid.

"There is a doctor, a 'psychologist,' I believe he is called." The old man's voice carried the measured pacing and private-school archness of a British aristocrat, but not the accent. "From a few decades earlier in this time. He has been discredited since, perhaps unfairly . . ."

As David's eyes adjusted to the dimness, he saw that three walls of the stall were lined with bookcases, but all the shelves were empty.

"This doctor, he wrote once that 'action' . . ." The old man raised one crooked finger for emphasis. "'*Action* is the dead end of possibility.'" He smiled again, as if savoring the phrase.

"OK . . ." David said. "And why are you telling me this?"

The man made a slight bow, lowering his chin. "My apologies. This is the United States, of course. Down to the business, as you say."

* * *

A short time later, the conductor led David out of the bazaar and up winding stairways that led to the station, though he couldn't tell if it was the same stairs they'd taken before. His legs were numb from walking, his eyes gritty and dry from the smoking torches.

The concourse was empty except for, here and there, a janitor mopping the floors. They paid no attention when David and the conductor came out of the service entrance and went to the nearest ATM, then the next one, and the next. David would never have thought he'd hand over that much money to a stranger. But within the course of their brief conversation, the old man had recited the details of David's life so succinctly, so clearly and clinically, he had no doubt this was the only person who truly could change his life.

He handed the last withdrawal to the conductor, who tucked the bills into the inner pocket of his jacket and then handed over a cream-colored envelope. David ran his fingertips over the thick linen stock. He'd never seen paper like this before. The back flap was sealed with a blob of red wax, impressed with the imprint of a carnival mask in the curved shape of a waning moon.

By now the conductor looked as weary as David felt. Gray shadows ringed his eyes. "Sorry about the little push before," he muttered.

David frowned. "The what?"

"When I came up to get you. You thought I was an old friend."

"Yeah. I did, for a little while."

The man nodded ruefully. "Short-term enchantment. Nothing harmful, just so you know. The old lady casts it on me every time they send me out." He shrugged. "Not how I'd do things. But I'm not one who makes the decisions."

David was too exhausted to ask what that meant. He turned to leave, then realized. "Crap. I missed the last train."

"Car's waiting outside." The conductor pointed to a set of stairs leading up to street level. "Fare's been taken care of."

David settled into the back of the yellow cab and told the driver his home address. It would be a long ride. Along 8th Avenue taxis rushed past, horns beeping, and drunk men in suits leaned on each other as they stumbled along the sidewalk. A typical late night in the city. He'd thought somehow things would look different, or he'd feel different. He pulled out the envelope again. The paper was thick and rough as burlap, stiff as cardboard. He worked a fingernail underneath the wax seal and opened it. Inside was a wallet-sized card with a photo of a commuter train and, smaller, in the upper right corner, that same quarter moon mask. A NJ Transit weekly rail pass. The kind you can get at any station in New Jersey. He slumped back in his seat, defeated.

He'd been scammed.

***

Tuesday

On the train into the city the next morning, when the conductor came by—a real one this time, in a neatly buttoned uniform and stiff cap pulled down to the eyebrows—David flashed his new rail pass, expecting some acknowledgement. Maybe this guy was part of the Bazaar, too. Maybe the pass only looked like an ordinary rail pass and he needed to use it first to unlock its power, like calling to activate a credit card.

But the official simply punched the pass with barely a glance and moved on.

At work, David was too embarrassed to tell anyone about the con. And by whom would he say he'd been scammed? No names had been exchanged. And how would he direct the police through that impossible maze of corridors and stairwells? On his lunch break, while everyone else was out, he Googled *night bazaar*—a phrase the conductor had used—but found only a tourist destination in China.

That evening, on the way home, he settled into a seat on the crowded train and watched the walls and fluorescent lights of the underground tunnel flicker black white black white. Then the windows suddenly brightened, opening onto rail yards and buildings the color of soot and a blue late summer evening sky streaked with pink clouds.

The door to the rail car swung open. "All tickets, all passes!"

David straightened. It was the "conductor" from last night, in the same too-small, ill-fitting uniform, working his way down the aisle, checking passes and punching tickets with lazy deliberation.

When he reached for the pass David said, "I need to talk to your boss."

The conductor blinked. "Who's that, sir?"

"You know."

The conductor's dull black eyes stared blankly down, but he said nothing.

"Or I could have the police meet me at my stop." Everyone was staring now. Nobody talked to conductors, except for the occasional greeting or passing comment about the weather. The man punched David's pass with a sluggish squeeze and handed it back.

"Ipswich!" he called out as he walked away. "Next stop, Ipswich!"

David clenched his jaw. What could he do now? The train slowed and its horn sounded. The conductor sauntered back down the aisle and stood by the open door. "Ipswich!" he shouted, louder this time. No passengers rose from their seats. No one else seemed to even notice the train had stopped. In fact, no one was casting sidelong glances at him anymore, as if they'd forgotten what had just happened.

Then David realized: there was no Ipswich station on this line.

"Ipswich this stop, sir." The conductor was staring directly at him, nodding as if in reassurance.

David rose. The fat man stepped aside to let him exit. "Enjoy your evening," he said in a weary monotone, and closed the door behind him.

He stepped out into warm evening air. The station was a square, small brick building, its narrow, tidy parking lot ringed by elms. Streetlights reflected off car windshields. Beyond the lot ran an avenue lined with tiny shops, their windows aglow beneath striped red-and-white awnings. Cafes with tables and chairs on the sidewalk. All the places had their doors open, and voices and laughter drifted across the avenue. A young woman was walking across the lot, heading in his direction. Simple white blouse and snug jeans tucked into short brown boots. Her hips swung like a pendulum, blonde curly hair bouncing with each step.

A tremor ran through David's body, as if the ground beneath his feet had buckled. *Why am I here? Who is this woman? I'm alone. No one's met me at a station in years.* A troubling thought flickered: *I don't belong here. My home is someplace else, a different stop. An apartment complex. Bare white walls, Venetian blinds.* But as she approached those vague images evaporated. He knew this place. Knew those cafes, and that her second-floor apartment was around the corner. Its bedroom window looked down on the back door of an Indian place where late at night the cooks sat on overturned plastic milk crates and smoked cigarettes.

He knew her name. "Lisa," he said.

She smiled. He remembered that sweetly bemused expression, as if she were always holding back a laugh, and the blue eyes. But he was still startled—as he always was—by how clear and bright they were.

"Hey, stranger," she said.

They kissed quickly on the lips and hugged. She drew back and frowned at him. "You OK?"

"Yeah, I'm fine now." He rubbed his eyes. "I had the strangest feeling for a second there. Like I was supposed to be somewhere else."

"Wow." She smirked. "You're already looking for an excuse to go home?"

"No! Not at all." He laughed and put an arm around her as they walked down the avenue. "I'm glad I'm here." He nodded toward a Spanish restaurant with white-stucco walls and arched doorways. The one they'd gone to several times before. "Olvido's?"

She nodded. "Olvido's."

Over beers and a plate of chicken quesadillas, they caught up. It had been two months since their last date. "Well, seven weeks," she said.

He wasn't sure why in the end things never quite seemed to work between them. Because just now it felt easy and comfortable sitting at this tiny round table in the far corner of the bar, leaning into each other as they talked. Lisa smiling, cheeks flushed from two beers, the lights from the bar casting highlights in her hair. He looked into her eyes as he spoke, as if by focusing only on them he could silence the nagging sense of disconnection when he'd stepped off the train.

The beer helped. So did the way she leaned into him when they left the bar. He wrapped an arm around her and pulled her close. She slid one hand down his spine, pressing a warm palm into the small of his back.

Back at the apartment, he sat at the foot of her bed. The place was a cramped one-bedroom over a store, but it seemed cozier than at their last date. Lots of house plants and scented candles in glass jars, throw pillows everywhere. After a few fumbling tries, he untied his shoes.

She lifted her blouse, but then lowered it, squinting at him in that way people do when they're concentrating on not being drunk. "Just so you know. I'm not . . . not going to put up with this forever. You have to make up your mind."

He nodded. "I know."

"I want something real. I don't have all day."

"I know."

"So, starting tonight, this is strictly a limited-time offer."

He took a deep breath, still holding one shoe. "OK." He didn't want to talk about this right now.

"Tick. Tick. Tick." She waited.

"OK," he said. "I get it."

* * *

Wednesday

As he was stepping out of the shower the next morning she knocked on the door and poked her head in. "I made coffee." She was wearing his wrinkled dress shirt from last night.

"Thanks. I'm going to need that for work."

"You're going in?"

"Why do you sound surprised?"

She shrugged. "I thought we could hang for a little bit. At least go in late."

"Oh, well . . . I don't know." He dried off, hung the towel on a hook on the back of the bathroom door, then pulled on briefs and undershirt, never once looking over at her. He hadn't taken any time off all year. Nobody in the office would care if he came in late, but he wasn't ready for the long talk he knew they must eventually have.

"Just a thought." She sighed. "You can have this shirt back, or your blue one is still in my closet."

"You kept it?"

"Yep. Thought you were coming right back. I even ironed it for you." She flashed a wry half-smile then turned away and went back to the bedroom. She sat on the bed, bare legs stretched out, coffee mug cradled in both hands. He found his shirt from the last visit in the back of her closet and slipped it on, then put on his pants.

"Sorry I can't stick around," he said. "I have to be in on time today."

"It's fine."

He knew she wasn't going to ask when he'd be coming back. "Can you hand me my wallet over there?"

She picked it up from the nightstand and glanced at the cards in the clear laminate wallet sleeve. "What kind of pass is this?"

"It's, uh—a weekly."

She laughed. "Why don't you get a monthly like everybody else? Tourists get weeklies."

"I don't know."

"Wow. You can't even commit to a renewable rail pass?"

"Why pay for a whole month when I might not need it?" He fumbled for a more reasonable explanation. Why *did* he have a weekly pass? He didn't recall buying it. "You know . . . I might not need it next week. Things change . . ."

She held out the wallet, her gaze on his face. Without any makeup she looked like a pale and sleepy teenager. "You've had this job forever. You've been taking this train forever. Nothing's going to change."

* * *

But I can change, he told himself, sitting in his beige upholstered cubicle, staring down his laptop screen, struggling to reword another horrible promotional draft from their latest client. *SourceTech Inc. provides an array of diverse solutions and state-of-the-art services to enable cost-saving efficiencies.* If he kept hesitating with Lisa—advancing, then withdrawing for weeks, months at a time—he would lose her. Amazing he hadn't already.

He liked, as they said in the office, to keep his options open. It wasn't that he couldn't make decisions. What disturbed him was thinking of all the other options that had been sacrificed once a decision had been made. Each decision was a hallway full of doors slamming shut on all those other possibilities. The finality of it frightened him.

But last night had been perfect. Why let that go?

On the train that evening, he stared at the slumped shoulders of the woman in front of him. The man beside her was asleep and lightly snoring, head cast back, a crumpled newspaper in his lap. For once David felt energetic. The weight of the workday had slipped off, because he'd made a decision. He felt brave. He couldn't wait to see Lisa's face and tell her.

Forty minutes into the train ride, he waved down the conductor when he walked by.

"Hey, did we pass Ipswich?"

The conductor cocked his head. "Where?"

"Ipswich."

The man shook his head. He was heavyset, with thick, broad hands the size of frying pans and dark circles under his eyes. The stiff brim of his conductor's hat was pushed back to the top of his forehead. A somewhat familiar face. He must've worked this line before. "No stop there." The uniform jacket barely fit him. He kept tugging on the sleeves to get them past his thick wrists.

"I got off at Ipswich yesterday."

"Not on this line, sir."

David leaned forward. "But this is the only line I ever take."

"Sorry. Don't know what to tell you." The conductor walked away, swaying with the rock of the train. "*Dunsmore*! Dunsmore. Next stop."

David must've gotten on the wrong train, distracted thinking about Lisa. He'd never heard of Dunsmore. But he got off there anyway. He could catch a train going back and figure out how to switch lines to Ipswich.

He stood on the platform and looked around. This station had a sprawling asphalt parking lot packed with cars. There must be a major highway nearby. He could hear the whoosh of speeding traffic.

A ripple of confusion unsettled him. *Why am I here? I was going to meet a woman. At a different station, though.* But no, this was his station. He always got off at this stop.

He lowered his head and blinked a few times. When he looked up, a hand was waving to him behind the windshield of a blue minivan. He knew that van. They'd bought it used from Kowalski Honda a year after they got married. He'd had to trade in his Corolla for it.

As David walked over, Joanne leaned out the window. Joanne. His wife had a slender face and short-cropped dark hair. "Hurry up, slowpoke," she called. "We're going to get stuck in traffic."

He got in and she threw the van into reverse. He twisted to look in the backseat. "Hello, sweetheart. How was school?"

Their daughter had just started fourth grade. She looked like tiny royalty strapped into the van's big padded captain's chair. "It was boring."

"She's fibbing." Joanne smirked in the rear-view mirror. "Somebody got in a little trouble today with Mrs. Galindo, didn't you? She was a Chatty Kathy with her girlfriends."

Katie frowned. "I was only talking because they talked to me first."

"Take Roosevelt instead of the highway," David said. "You'll miss most of the traffic that way."

"I know."

At dinner he talked about work and she talked about her job at the insurance company, until their daughter sighed and said, "Can I be excused now?" In a few minutes they heard SpongeBob SquarePants from the living room and he and Joanne were alone at the table, not saying anything. David lowered his head and stared at the vegetable lasagna.

After a few minutes, Joanne got up without a word and went upstairs to talk to her mom on the phone. He put the dishes in the washer and scrubbed out the baked-on lasagna still stuck to the pan. Then he stood in the doorway to the living room, drying his hands on a dishtowel, watching Katie seated cross-legged in front of the TV.

"Daddy, listen." She turned off the cartoon and pulled out the violin case they'd rented from her school. "I'm in the recital tomorrow."

She tucked the violin beneath her chin, took a breath, then drew the bow across the strings. Her tongue was clamped between her teeth, one eyebrow raised. The same expression Joanne wore when sewing. Katie's gaze was fixed on her fingers as they picked across the strings, as if she could guide the notes through sheer concentration. David was fascinated. Her entire focus was on creating the song. Nothing else mattered. How could someone be like that? He had no idea if she was any good for her age, but her determination was beautiful.

"That was great, sweetheart," he said.

Later, after tucking Katie in, he went to the master bedroom and changed into cotton pajama bottoms and an old Giants t-shirt. Joanne was brushing her teeth in the bathroom. He climbed into bed and pulled the covers up.

She sat down on her side turned halfway to face him. "Katie has her class recital tomorrow afternoon."

"Oh, yeah. She told me."

"Are you going?"

"I have to work."

She turned away. "You could take the day off. You never take time off. Or work from home, maybe."

He sighed. "I can't."

Slumped back against the headboard, she looked tired. He wanted to put his arms around her. "I don't know what's bothering you," she said. "And I can only guess because I know you don't know how to tell me. So I just want to say, I know our life isn't perfect. But we could get through this if you're willing to do the work."

He stared up at the ceiling. "It feels like all I do is work."

She lowered her gaze, like a curtain coming down. "You know that's not what I mean."

***

Thursday

David stared at his screen, struggling to rewrite the sentence that began: *SourceTech Inc.'s diverse solutions and state-of-the-art services enable a diverse array of . . .* The longer he stared, the less sense the words made. He thought about last night. Why hadn't he reached out for her? He'd wanted to. Why *couldn't* he? Their whole marriage he'd been half-involved, never fully committed to anything they did together. Always hindered by the feeling he should be somewhere else, or should've made a different choice. But *this* was the life he'd chosen.

Those doubts were just vague, pointless daydreams. Why couldn't he focus on the here and now? His daughter knew how to do that when she played violin, and she was only nine.

Then it hit him: Katie's recital was this afternoon. "Crap," he said aloud. He'd missed it. He'd thought maybe to leave at lunchtime and catch it. But of course he'd lost track of time. Why hadn't he stayed home like Joanne asked? Why go into the office, just as he always did? Mindlessly, without a second thought.

But it isn't too late to fix this, he thought, sitting in the train at the end of the workday, gazing out at the factories and sludge-filled swamps speeding by. From now on, he wouldn't miss out again on anything Katie did. He'd focus, stop thinking about all the other possible paths. Devote himself to what he had now, before he lost everything.

But the train kept going. There was no stop for Dunsmore. Did he get on the wrong one? At Thornton, a place he'd never heard of, the conductor nodded at him. He rose and hesitantly stepped off.

The parking lot here was a band of crumbling pavement with no lines painted on it. Farther down a single-lane road stood a plain wooden building with a blue-neon sign in the plate-glass window. FREDDY'S TAVERN.

As David waited on the platform he got an image—as convincing as a memory—that someone was coming to take him home. A dark-haired woman behind the wheel of a mini-van, their round-faced daughter in the back seat. But that had never happened. Even when he was married—years ago—his wife never picked him up at the station. And they had a son, not a daughter.

A few minutes passed. Idiot, he thought. He descended the creaking wooden steps and set off down the road, chuckling ruefully. What the hell had he been thinking? He was alone.

No one's ever coming to get you.

The moment he entered Freddy's, Tommy behind the bar said, "There he is," and reached for a bottle of Grey Goose.

David hitched up onto his usual stool. "How's it going, Tom?"

The bartender was tall and lean with round glasses and an indifferent stare. He put the tall vodka and tonic in front of David and glanced at the wide-screen in the corner. "Tell you after kick-off."

By the time the game came on, the bar had filled up. Guys in blue Giants caps and women in football jerseys far too big for them. David floated along, lifted on a crashing tide of voices and vodka. During commercial breaks he started chatting with the woman next to him—or maybe she started chatting first. She was dressed casually, or at least to give that impression—a white Dominic Cruz jersey and wavy blond hair pulled back in a ponytail. But her makeup was perfect, and she kept touching the back of her head to check the ponytail and adjusting the knot she had cinched in the bottom of the jersey to accentuate her narrow waist.

They kept talking, even when the game was on. "Are you married?" she asked.

"Divorced."

"Same here. Kids?"

"A son," David replied.

She had two girls, both teenagers, alternately manic or morose. "Never can tell which mood'll pop up." She grimaced. "The kitchen table's like a minefield every morning."

He talked about Brandon. Not how he was now, a sullen nineteen, but back when he was a child, perpetually curious and inquisitive, always going to David for answers. For a time, always trusting what Daddy told him.

A few drinks in, the usual bitter silence began to muffle his thoughts. It happened every time he thought about his son. Brandon's resentment crippled him, left David staggering and stumbling through life, too lame to face any social interaction. As if failure as a father was some sort of physical disfigurement. The conversation sputtered down to a dribble of half-hearted comments about the game.

At last, the woman slid off her stool and gave him a weary, disappointed smile, "Have a nice life." She adjusted the knot of her jersey, pulling it down just so, and tottered back to her friends at the other end of the bar.

David settled up with Tom, then rose, but he had to brace his palms on the smooth, worn wood of the bar for a moment. The game was still on. Cheers bounced off the walls.

He walked home along the cracked, uneven sidewalk. The trees looked frozen beneath the streetlights, leaves too motionless. He stumbled but caught himself and straightened with a deep breath, hands on hips, then continued on. No one else was out, but television commercials and muffled voices drifted across the front yards. A boy yelled, "*Mom*! Are you even *listening*?"

His shuffling footsteps echoed down the street. I need to change my life before it's too late, he thought. Before I'm just another anonymous loner in a bar. And he *could* change. He had a good job, some money saved, plenty of free time.

The windows of the houses he passed—some lit blue with a flat screen's light, others glowing a muted yellow behind curtains—were like display cases in a department store. Look at all the possible lives to be had. A sense of purpose stirred in him. The last few strides that took him to his dark front yard were determined, confident.

Alongside all the well-tended little cottages along the street, his looked sullen and withdrawn. The light over the front door had burned out. The trees needed pruning, their branches hung low over the windows so that the entire façade seemed to be scowling. Fine. That was the first thing he'd do: call out from work tomorrow—for once in his life—and clean up the stupid yard. And then somehow convince his son to come over. Fix him dinner—good plain steak and mashed potatoes, no beer, no alcohol at all—and they could sit and watch football or something. He could show Brandon. *Look. Look how much better I am now.*

He tripped on the front steps in the dark, stubbing his toe. "Shit," he muttered, then gingerly opened the screen door. The bottom hinge had come loose during a storm a year ago . . . no, three years ago . . . and he'd never fixed it. Open the door gently every time or else it would pull free from its last remaining hinge. Each time he entered the house, he told himself: Got to fix that. But he never did.

David unlocked the inner door and stepped inside. The screen swung shut behind him with a clatter, like the flat of a hand smacking a metal table. Then, with a long screech, it swung back, dangling crookedly from the one top hinge.

Idiot, he thought. *Who are you kidding? You'll never change.*

***

Friday

David sat slumped on a metal bench on the Penn Station concourse with the other weary office drones. He checked his watch—fifteen minutes before the next train—then lowered his head and sighed. A wad of pink gum was squashed into a grimy coin on the floor between his shoes. He felt a sudden dislocation, and remembered another moment like this—but how long ago? It felt like decades. Some man, a conductor, had approached him.

Slowly, the memories surfaced. Lisa's quick, flashing smile, her bright blue eyes alight. Joanne's weary slouch. Determined little Katie and her violin. Brandon—a voice too bitter for his age, on the other end of a telephone line. The images overlapped, and emotions flooded his heart: desire, doubt, love, self-loathing, compassion. And always—always—regret.

He bent over and rubbed his eyes. Which one was his real life? How did this all start? Where was his home now? Where could he go?

The conductor. David took out his wallet and removed a weekly rail pass. He recalled a smoke-filled catacomb. The smell of burning tar. A thin old man with a gaze piercing as a searchlight. David fingered the pass: nothing unusual about it. But this little card had somehow been the start of everything. He bent, elbows on knees, the pass creased in one clenched fist, and concentrated. Sifting through layers of memories.

***

He was still holding the pass as the 6:22 train barreled from the tunnels of Penn Station and over the petrol-stinking swamps of north Jersey. The conductor ambled down the aisle, checking everyone's fares.

A mound of a man with a trudging gait like a weary soldier's march.

It was him.

Every seat was filled, so it was a few minutes before the conductor reached him. David looked up and searched the round placid face. The conductor nodded in recognition.

"You have to take me back." David leaned forward intently, shoulders hunched. "Back to that place."

The conductor paused, a quick blink the only indication of surprise. "It's moved on, sir," he said quietly.

"Where? Is it still in the city?"

"For now, yes. But I wouldn't know where exactly. Doesn't matter anyway."

"Why not?"

"It's Friday." The conductor extended a hand. "Your pass?"

David shook his head. "But it didn't work. Whatever it was supposed to do, it didn't work."

The conductor bent until his round head blocked out the overhead lights. "Sorry, I can't help with that. My job's just to get you all to wherever you're supposed to be." He extended the hand again. "Your pass, sir?"

David didn't move or answer him. He didn't know what to do.

The conductor straightened with a sigh. "Keep it then. Nothing but a bookmark after today."

David slumped back in his seat. He handed over the pass and looked up helplessly. "Where will it take me this time?"

The man tucked the pass into his shirt pocket. "That I don't know."

"You said 'you all.' So there are others like me?"

The conductor continued down the aisle without another word.

The train stopped at Rahway, then Metuchen, then New Brunswick. All the normal stations. People disembarked in large, weary groups. At the next stop, only one person got off. At the next two, the same thing happened. No announcements blared over the loudspeaker. Instead, before each stop, the conductor approached someone. That person rose and went to the door, then stepped off the train like a high-diver at the edge of a diving board. No one else on the train but David seemed to notice this.

The first was a woman in a dark suit. She descended to the platform, then stood there, outside the open door, head swiveling left and right, arms wrapped around herself tightly, as if unwilling to move away.

The next was a young man in shirtsleeves. At the top step, he said aloud, "Here goes," and hopped off. He strode confidently across the platform, arms swinging. Then stopped, looked around, and put both hands to his head.

The old man who stepped off next immediately turned to get back on the train just as it pulled away, but was too late.

The car was now empty except for David. From beside the door, the conductor called to him, "Evandale next."

But when the train stopped, he stayed in his seat.

"Evandale, this stop."

David glanced out the window, but all that was visible in the dusk was a streetlight and the barred window of a ticket office. He didn't move.

The conductor sighed and tugged at the sleeves of his ill-fitting jacket, first the left sleeve, next the right, then came down the aisle, hands clenched at his side. David wondered if the man was capable of violence. He had the flabby bulk of a former boxer, the casual fearlessness of someone who'd survived a few battles. But he also seemed lazy, too uninterested to actually throw a punch. All the wonders and strangeness this guy must've seen at that bazaar, and the only emotion clear on his face was boredom. The only thing that seemed to propel him through his perpetual weariness, shuffling from task to task, was some dogged aura of responsibility. He was a worker. Nothing more.

"This *is* your stop, sir."

David glanced out again. God knows what he would step into if he got off this time. No, he would stay here. They'd have to take him back to the bazaar then. He stared up into the conductor's dull black eyes and shook his head.

The conductor went to the engineer's booth in the corner, opened the door, leaned in and said a few words. Then he sat down with an exhausted huff on one of the passenger seats at the far end of the car. The train sped on, its walls shuddering. An hour passed. The streetlights that occasionally zipped past gradually gave way to a continuous darkness. David called out, "So, are we going back then?"

The conductor didn't respond. His head lolled back, cap askew. He let out a deep, rumbling snore.

The train slowed. The car swayed then pitched forward as the brakes were applied. With a hydraulic wheeze, they stopped. The conductor grunted, rose, and adjusted his cap. Then, apparently realizing how pointless the disguise was now, he tossed it onto an empty seat, and threw David an indifferent glance. "Final stop."

David stayed in his seat.

The conductor sighed. He shook his head, then shouted down the length of the rail car, "There are *no more stops*!" He slid open the door, lumbered down the steps, then hopped to the ground, landing with a grunt.

David tried to look outside but the windows were black mirrors. He could see only the reflection of himself, the rows of empty seats. He rose and went to the door. There was no platform here to step onto. He had to clutch both metal handholds in the doorframe and half-jump, half-lower himself down to the gravel track bed.

The conductor stood watching his progress, hands loose at his sides.

Crickets chirped far off. David felt the lingering heat of the day on the back of his neck. He planted his feet and looked around. They were in a field of tall, straw-colored grass. Wheat, maybe? On the horizon, along a low hill, a forest of tall pines was silhouetted by moonlight, trees pitching in the wind like the masts of tall ships.

"What's this place? Where's the damn bazaar?"

"There's no bazaar for you. There are no more stops."

David turned to look at him. "I want to go back."

He shook his head with the familiar sullen tolerance. "Week's over, sir. You're done."

A breeze whispered across the field and the stalks of grain bowed with a soft rustle. David noticed a white glow just beyond the edge of the hill. He pointed. "What'is that?"

"Supposed to be another station past those trees."

"Where does it go? Will it take me back to the city?"

"Couldn't tell you."

"Look." David reached into his pants pocket. "I know my pass expired. But I can pay for a ticket back. I have cash."

"I'm not going back into the city." The conductor walked over the rail car, gripped the handhold inside the door frame, and hauled himself up to the first step. "Where we're going, you can't come."

"Please." David withdrew all the cash in his wallet and held out a wad of bills.

The conductor stared down, as if noticing him for the first time. Something flickered behind his dull eyes, like a match lit in darkness. A scowl creased his brow.

"I have to try again," David said.

The conductor's face twisted in a sudden palsy of anger. His jaw worked up and down several times before he finally spoke. "*Every* night—you had your chance. But *every* morning—you got back on the goddamned train." He barked out his words as if he were choking on them. "So tell me, *sir*—just how many chances do you think you *deserve*?"

The man's glare was so hateful David took a step back. An eternity of injustice and failure and regret haunted that dark stare. The conductor took a deep breath, then let out a deep, shuddering sigh. David could see the anger and hate wasn't directed entirely at him. This man was someone who, unlike him, had lived a life instead of gliding through the motions. Who, unlike himself, had tried for something real but then stumbled somewhere—or was misled or deceived—and now found himself in this bizarre servitude. How long had he been indentured like this? How long before it had worn him down, ground his body to a shambling hulk, frayed and desiccated his will? He wasn't a worker. He was a slave.

"I'm sorry," David said, but his voice was lost in the hiss of the brake releasing. The train lurched, rumbled, and slowly pulled away. The conductor still stood balanced on the bottom step, body swaying with the swaying of the train. He raised a hand. David couldn't tell if he was bidding him farewell or motioning for him to continue on over the hill.

The train withdrew into the darkness as if swallowed up. The chorus of crickets rose to a din. David set off across the field, eyes on the hill in the distance. Tall, dry stalks crackled underfoot. The soles of his leather dress shoes slipped on the uneven ground. Gnats whirled about his face. He cast off his laptop bag, then his sports jacket. A train whistle moaned, far away. He quickened his pace, arms swinging. His shirt collar grew wet with sweat.

I can start again. Do it right this time. No matter what happens next, accept it. Without delay. Make a choice. Any choice. Wherever the next train dropped him—there had to be another station, it couldn't end like this—whatever his destination, whatever life it offered, he would stay. He would say yes, and let all the doors on all the other possible lives shut behind him.

Stumbling through the endless tangle of grass and weeds, he repeated this, like a prayer, hoping that when he stepped off at that new station, he would remember.

The Bazaar offers curious objects from around the world, handcrafted by artisans with special skills. And some with special . . . intentions.

We all wear masks sometimes to hide our true identities, or to forget inhibitions. To be held blameless. It is traditional in some cultures to wear masks at annual celebrations: fantastic pieces of folk artistry with beautiful or frightening human or animal features. Wearing them helps preserve the old ways, traditions of an ancient time and place.

For instance, take this brightly-painted vejigante *mask from the Caribbean. Worn by dancers to become someone else as they march through the streets at an annual festival in Loiza, Puerto Rico. But sometimes even simple-looking objects may be imbued with sophisticated talents. They may not only conceal or empower, but take the wearer to another place. Even another time. Where they can then make history . . . or preserve it.*

VISTA ETERNA

Dania Ramos

Sal first sensed his sister Katrina's presence as he was climbing the four flights to his Brooklyn apartment on Tuesday evening. Ever since infancy they'd shared what they called "twin sense." So it was no surprise when she pounced and hugged him the second he entered the apartment, before his laptop bag even slid to the floor.

"Hey, little brother!" Katrina liked to remind him every chance she got that she was a whole eight and a half minutes older.

He grinned and hung his gray peacoat on the back of the door. "Sebastian let you in?"

"In all his Nordic glory." She tossed long dark brown curls over one shoulder of her coral wrap sweater. "Wish he was *my* neighbor with the spare key."

"Oh, yeah?" Sal raised an eyebrow. "What about Malcolm?"

She grimaced. "The jerk broke up with me to take a travel-blog gig in Europe."

"Not good enough for you anyway." He sauntered over to the tiny kitchenette, grabbed two craft beers from the fridge, and popped the caps. "Try this. It's local." He handed her a bottle and raised his high. "To tomorrow."

She grinned and mirrored him. "Right. Happy birthday to us." They clinked bottles and sank onto stools by the counter. "If only Ma and Pa were here."

Sal smiled wistfully. "Yeah . . . if only."

Their parents had died in a car accident ten years earlier. The twins, only twenty at the time, had each coped in their own way. Sal threw himself into history studies. Katrina had backpacked across Europe, and her travel bug remained. Sal often joked that she spent more time subletting her Orlando studio apartment than living in it. These days, she did freelance editing, which allowed time for global volunteer work.

"Wow. Thirty." She sipped more beer. "Thought at least one of us would be married by now."

Sal took a long swig. "I never get past the third date. That's romance in the city for you." He didn't mention how exhausted the adjunct professor grind at NYU left him. Not to mention how broke. "Anyway, I'm so busy. Research for the book is nuts."

"Oh?" A blank stare. "Still that one about, um, Native American pets?"

Sal rolled his eyes. "Indigenous animals of Latin America."

She shrugged. "Right. That's basically what I said."

He sighed. "Don't worry. I don't expect you to actually read it."

"You just think I won't understand it." She poked his arm. "But I'm down for googling arcane words, thou pretentious one."

"I only use arcane language in a proper historical context." He ignored her giggles, feeling stuffy and now, somehow, older. "Anyway, you'd understand it fine. But I know you're not interested."

"For God's sake!" She slammed her bottle on the counter. "I'll read your goddamn Pan-American animal kingdom opus before anyone else does."

"Opus?" Sal snorted. He got up and opened the fridge again. "Hardly the right word."

She pushed away a hand in disgust. "Do you have to be right about *everything*?"

He opened a cardboard takeout container. "Not everything. For instance, there's this leftover Chow Fun." He sniffed, then winced at the pungent stench.

They stared at each other a second, then burst into laughter. Katrina fanned away spoiled-chicken fumes. "Eew. Trying to kill me with noxious poultry gas?"

"Man, that's ripe." He tossed the container in the trash. "Let's go out instead."

"Now there's a plan." She leaned both elbows on the counter. "Hey, after dinner, we can check out this underground fair. Sebastian went last night. Highly recommended." She fished a business card from the back pocket of her jeans and slid it across the counter.

www.NightBazaarNYC.com

Sal frowned down at it, silently cursing his neighbor. "Dunno. Got a ton of papers to grade."

"But I already checked out the website." She grinned, clearly proud to have the inside scoop for once. "It's a funky pop-up market at some abandoned subway platform."

"The old City Hall station?" That caught his interest. "The one deserted in the forties. What's it called, a . . . phantom? No—ghost station, that's it."

"Seriously," she said. "You even *know* about the long-lost secret train station?"

"Some colleagues took a tour." He dropped the card on the counter. "Pretty sure you need a membership to the Transit Museum to get in, though."

"Unless you know the password to the protected link with secret instructions on how to secretly get in." Katrina flipped over the card to flash a single word: `ENTRY.` She wiggled her eyebrows. "Come on. Let's end our twenties with a big adventure."

***

After a late dinner in Little Italy, the twins walked to the Brooklyn Bridge-City Hall station and waited for the Downtown 6. Katrina half expected they'd be the only ones boarding at the last official southbound stop. But by the time the train arrived, a dozen people were huddled near the seventh car, exactly as the instructions on www.NightBazaarNYC.com had stated.

The *ding dong* sounded. Doors slid open. A few passengers exiting the train whizzed by as the twins stepped on. The intercom boomed, "*Last downtown stop. Next stop Brooklyn Bridge-City Hall on the uptown platform.*"

The twins sat right alongside the conductor, a sturdy middle-aged man with copper skin, a white beard, and a thin silvery braid that hung to the middle of his back. "Well, well." He winked. "Guess I'll be making an extra stop at the old City Hall station. Fifth group of the night headed there. My co-workers and I are keeping track. Usually zip right through that old platform, but not tonight. Ask me, the best part of working the 6 train is riding through the old City Hall loop. The architecture, it's quite a sight."

"Neo-Romanesque, right?" Sal asked.

The conductor raised his eyebrows. "Indeed. You an architect?"

Sal shook his head. "It was featured in a podcast on WNYC. Fascinating stuff."

Katrina watched her brother stifle a yawn. He looked more exhausted than fascinated. Obviously, the poor guy needed a break. Why not use her low-budget-travel expertise to score discount tickets for a little vacation? It'd be nice to visit their great-aunt. She lived in the mountains of Puerto Rico, their parents' homeland. Back when they were kids, Tía Berta had always been elated to host family in the quaint inn she kept at the edge of the famous rainforest, El Yunque.

"Hey, Sal?" Katrina smiled. "How about spending a few days with Tía Berta? Just like old times."

He shot her a sideways glance. "You know things are rough there right now."

She knew all about the current situation in Puerto Rico, even though it wasn't really covered on the mainstream online news sites. . . . *unprecedented debt . . . staggering unemployment rates . . . cuts to education and public service . . . federally-appointed financial oversight board . . . failing healthcare system. . . .*

. . .the latest mosquito-borne virus. . . .

During a phone call a couple months earlier Tía Berta had admitted business was slow. She feared it would only get worse. Katrina wanted to help, but how? At least by visiting they could show support. Why didn't Sal see that? "So you're going to let economics stop you from seeing family?"

"That's not it." He sighed. "I can't just drop everything mid-semester."

"Okay, sure." She shrugged. "We'll go during the holiday break."

He shook his head. "Not if I want to finish my manuscript. But you seem really into it. You should go."

She forced a smile. "Maybe." Oh well. So much for that.

The train slowed. The recorded *ding dong* sounded, the doors slid open. Their conductor winked again and threw a goodbye salute.

The passengers stepped onto the dim platform, apparently knowing to head toward the far right as instructed by the website. Katrina spotted a glowing green rectangle located within the tiled mosaic that spelled out CITY HALL. The others crowded around as she reached out and pressed the illuminated tile hard. A few feet to their left the wall receded, sliding inward, unveiling an entrance pulsating with colored light and percussive rhythm.

"Wow. Looks like the right place." A sibling adventure, just like old times. She couldn't suppress a grin as she stepped through the secret passageway, into the bazaar.

***

This midnight marketplace went on as far as Sal could see, with row after row of offbeat merchandise and services. Booths with hand-stitched clothing, tooled leather bags, posters of otherworldly cartoonish aliens, skulls, scary clowns. In one section a vendor was selling preserved bottled animal organs. The next aisle over held a digital photo booth where visitors were piling in two or three at a time to take a picture with wax statues of various famous cryptids—Loch Ness Monster, Bigfoot, a chupacabra. At least he thought they were wax. Had that Jersey Devil just winked at him?

Still, silver hookahs, legendary monsters, and hand-embroidered belts weren't enough to distract him from the nagging sense he should be at home working. He wandered ahead, leaving Katrina chatting with an Asian woman selling beaded jewelry of every shape, color, and astrological significance. Down one aisle he stopped to sample a concoction called The Smoothie of Life, reputed to cure everything from heartburn to hair loss. After one whiff of the putrid gray-green liquid he decided against even a sip.

As he turned away to toss it into a nearby trash can he thought, Maybe Kat is right. I *am* always working now.

He'd actually been aching to return to Puerto Rico for years. The real reason for his reluctance had nothing to do with its current crisis. But going back to Tía Berta's parador, where they used to stay as a family, would be too painful. Even a decade after their parents' deaths.

His hip struck the corner of a table draped with embroidered silk. "Ouch," he muttered, stepping back.

A teenage girl with long black hair and olive skin was sitting behind a small sign: TABLE OF DESTINY. She closed her book and glanced up, one eyebrow raised.

He chuckled. "So *this* is where you find fate? I've always wondered."

She had piercing brown eyes and was pretty despite the scowl. She took a slow, deliberate sip from a large plastic cup half-full of The

Smoothie of Life, and eyed him up and down. Something about her seemed oddly familiar. Not a former student. He would've remembered that intensity, the old-soul wisdom in her gaze.

"Know what you want yet?" she asked.

He shrugged. "Just looking. Thanks." He perused terracotta pottery, artwork made of feathers, hand-woven straw baskets. He picked up a mask, recognizing the style—half of a hollowed-out coconut shell painted in three differing sections. The colors were chipped and worn: yellow, turquoise, red. Triangular holes served as the eyes. A crude slit suggested the mouth. Four long white horns protruded from each side. Thin leather straps formed a web across the back to hold it securely on the wearer's head.

With that uncanny ability Katrina had to find him no matter where he was, she suddenly rushed up and poked his ribs. "Ooh, a *vejigante*! This one looks kinda decrepit, though. Ancient. Not like the masks Tía Berta has on the walls of the inn. Remember when you took one down and broke it?"

Was anything more annoying than a sister? "I just wanted to see how it was made." He glared at her, embarrassed. "Besides, I fixed it."

"Yeah, right. You glued that horn back on so crooked the poor mask looked drunk." She squinted at the one in his hands and snorted. "Sort of like this one."

"They're not supposed to be pretty. Whole point is to frighten people."

Katrina turned to the girl behind the table. "Has my brother the professor schooled you in the history of the vejigante? Its Spanish origins. The Catholic church. The Moors. And, oh, by the way, he knows everything ever recorded about the history and cultures of mankind."

The girl didn't crack a smile. "You're brother and sister?"

Katrina threw an arm around Sal and leaned her head on his shoulder. "Twins. Obviously I'm the pretty one."

"Of course." There was a hint of recognition in the girl's voice. "I mean . . . now I see it."

"Hey, this is authentic." Sal rapped the hard colorful face lightly with his knuckles. "Coconut shell is the traditional mask-making material of the indigenous Taíno."

The vendor nodded. "Most likely crafted for the Saint James Festival in Loíza."

He nodded, impressed. "In the northeast. So you're familiar with the traditions."

"I know the origin of every item on this table." Her mouth twisted as if she was trying not to smirk. "I also know you're taking that mask with you."

He shifted uneasily and looked down at it. A tingle like an electric current ran up both arms when he traced one rough-edged eyehole cut into the brown shell. He couldn't shake a haunting sensation he was expected someplace, to do . . . something. But where, and what?

"Uh, Sal?" Katrina cleared her throat. "Would you stop acting possessed? You're freaking me out."

He didn't look up. "Sorry. But this feels . . . I dunno. Weird. Like it's trying to tell me something."

"Oh, sure." Kat wiggled her fingers at it. "The mask is spe-e-e-aking to yo-o-o-u."

Shit, he thought. *I shouldn't have said anything. She doesn't understand me. She never will.*

"Whatever happens, we've survived this long," the vendor told him in a low voice. "You must always remember that." Her scowl was gone, replaced by a slight, knowing smile. "Meanwhile, enjoy the view."

***

Katrina turned away for a moment to yawn and rub her eyes, so it wouldn't seem rude. She'd had enough of this strange market. Nothing here she wanted, and she was freezing. The cute wrap sweater didn't cut it for a chilly New York autumn. "Hey Sal, I'm beat. We should head home." She turned back to her brother.

But he was no longer standing next to her. What the hell? "Hey. You see where my brother went?" she asked the vendor.

The girl shrugged. "He left." She was rearranging other items to fill the spot where the mask had been. A tile seahorse mosaic, a telescoping tower carved from a single piece of wood.

Katrina rolled her eyes. "Uh, yeah. That's why I'm asking." She glanced down the aisle one way, then the other. But she'd only turned away for a moment. He was playing a joke on her. "Okay! You got me." She glanced at the bright embroidered curtains behind the girl. "He's hiding back there, right?"

"No, I mean he's *gone*," the vendor said. "If he were still here, wouldn't you sense him?"

"How do you know about that?" Katrina stepped back, alarmed. Now that she thought about it, she *didn't* feel him nearby. Either her twin sense had failed, or the creepy girl was right—he was gone. She dug her cell from her purse and tapped his speed dial with shaking hands. It went straight to voicemail. She hit END.

The vendor was still staring. "Your destinies are very different."

"Oh really. How would you know?" Katrina gritted her teeth. "What the hell is this place, some kind of cult recruitment center?"

"No. Just an entry point." The girl stood. "Come back here, behind the table. This leads to the answers you seek." She held the backdrop cloth aside.

Katrina rolled her eyes. God, what a hokey line. Obviously Sal and this smirking teenager had conspired to pull a trick on her. Fine, she'd play along. Anything to make him relax and have a little fun for a change.

She stepped behind the table and through the colorful drapes, expecting Sal to leap out. Instead, the only thing in front of her was an unpainted plywood partition. "What the hell. Hey," she called to the girl. "There's nothing back here. Where's—"

In a flash of white light, all sight and sound vanished. She managed to scream once before her entire body stiffened, then seized. For a moment gravity lost its hold, and the world spun as if she'd just boarded a planet-sized Tilt-A-Whirl.

My organs are liquefying, she thought. *My head's gonna snap off.*

She landed painfully on all fours, rough concrete beneath hands and knees. She gagged, sick with vertigo, then looked around.

She was on the floor of a pastel green porch, overlooking a lushly-planted yard. At least gravity was back. But why was it so *hot*? She tore off her sweater. Somewhere, through an open window, a radio was blaring an advertisement in Spanish. She sucked in warm hibiscus-scented air. "Well, we sure aren't in Brooklyn anymore, Katrina," she whispered.

Something creaked overhead. She stiffened warily. Looking up, in the soft early morning light she made out a hand-painted sign attached to the awning of the porch: PARADOR VISTA ETERNA. But . . . that was her great-aunt's inn. In Puerto Rico.

"What the effing hell," she whispered.

* * *

Sal lay on his back, sweating in his gray wool peacoat, dry brown palm fronds crunching beneath him. Sunlight glinted here and there through a dense canopy of lush tropical trees. The humidity was stifling. And where was his sister? What had happened to the bazaar?

He sat abruptly to yank off the stifling coat and long sleeve oxford, stripping down to white undershirt. "Kat! Hey Kat, where are you?"

No answer.

He called until his throat was sore, until he could no longer out-shout the noises around him. The creaking of bamboo stalks. The shrill, raucous cries of bright-feathered birds. A chorus of other unseen animals, all combined into an outdoor symphony. One he'd experienced as a boy, when visiting Tía Berta in Puerto Rico. The entire family had ventured up the mountain into the tropical rainforest then.

Could this be El Yunque? No, that was crazy.

Years ago, his great-aunt had taught him about the great rainforest. About how before the native population had been killed off by the Spanish, the Taíno people had believed the towering, majestic landscape was home to Yúcahu, the god of fertility. Well, no wonder. The air was pure, the forest teeming with life. The mountain had made such an impression on him as a boy that he'd included an entire chapter in his current manuscript about the Puerto Rican parrot, an endangered species living in El Yunque.

And yet, now he felt completely out of place. Alone and scared. There wasn't a public walking trail or a signpost in sight. No Tía Berta to lead the way. He closed his eyes, wishing it all was a dream. Hoping soon he'd simply wake up in Brooklyn to a chorus of wailing ambulances, the familiar squeal of subway line brakes.

Something small, fast, and light scurried up his left leg. "Aaah!" He flailed at his jeans, flinging off a small green lizard which landed on a massive tree trunk and scurried to the other side, out of sight. Only then did he recall there were no poisonous animals or deadly predators in El Yunque, and feel foolish. Plenty else to worry about, though. Like how the hell did he get here? Maybe he'd had a blackout and somehow bought a plane ticket . . . no, that didn't make sense. Katrina had been with him. How long would it take to find a way out—let alone get in touch with her?

Well, duh. He dug out his phone. Which was dead. "Dammit." He shoved the cell back into his pocket. OK, he needed a plan. He'd hike down the mountainside, find a trail leading back to the visitors' center. Call Kat, then hop on the first plane home—

Someone yelled from behind him, an inarticulate shout of alarm.

He flinched, then whirled to see who it was. A bearded guy with tousled brown hair was kneeling a few yards away. The stranger clutched at his face, eyes wide with terror, staring at Sal. "What have you done?" he accused in Spanish. "Why do you bring me here?"

Sal froze. He could've sworn this guy hadn't been there a moment ago. Surely he would've noticed that traditional bright-red vejigante costume with the wide, flowing sleeves, amongst all the green of the rainforest. "Please," he replied, in Spanish. "You've mistaken me for someone else."

The man lifted one trembling arm and jabbed a finger at Sal's face. "Then how is it you wear the mask?"

Sal had forgotten about that. "Oh. Sorry." He slid it off over his head. "I didn't intend to frighten you."

Just then he felt a familiar tug at his core. *Twin sense? But that's impossible!* He glanced around, trying not to take his eyes off the stranger for too long. Kat was nowhere in sight. He must've imagined the sensation, mere wishful thinking. But one thing was certain: this stranger was real. Yet he'd appeared out of nowhere.

"I don't understand what has happened." The man shook his head. "I was preparing for the festival. But when I pulled the mask down over my face, all was silent. There came a tremendous light. I had to close my eyes. And when I open them, I am here in the jungle. And you are there. Wearing *my* mask!"

Sal swallowed hard. "Perhaps it only looks similar—"

"Was it a spell? Is that how you brought me here? For you must be a witch, in such strange garments." The man snatched up a heavy fallen branch and pointed it before him like a weapon. "I shall kill you, *brujo*!"

* * *

As Katrina sat on the porch floor of the parador, contradictory emotions swirled like a hurricane in her chest. Fear, yes. But also a strong sense of homecoming. She'd felt the same as a kid each time her family had visited the island: As connected to this place as she was to her brother.

Oh God. *Sal. He was right beside me, back at the bazaar. Then he simply . . . wasn't.*

And then she . . . hands shaking, Katrina took the balled-up sweater from her lap and wiped away tears.

A rooster crowed beneath an old jeep parked in the carport several yards away. The bird clucked a few times as if scolding her, and crowed again.

"¡Basta, Pepito!" An elderly woman with mahogany skin and short gray curls stepped out onto the porch, stomping and shouting to shoo the noisy rooster away.

"Tía Berta!" Katrina jumped up to wrap her arms around her great-aunt. "God, how I've missed you."

"Dios mío!" Tía Berta held her at arm's length. "Nena, why you didn't tell me you were coming?" She grabbed a tissue from the deep pocket of a long housedress and blotted Katrina's tears. "¿Pero qué pasó?"

If only she *could* explain what had happened. "No se." She turned up her palms. If she told her aunt, it would sound crazy. She stared out at the glorious view of the coast, the ocean sparkling in the distance. "Sal's missing. We were at a bazaar in New York City. One minute he was right next to me, holding a mask. Kind of like the ones on your walls. Only this one was really—"

Tía Berta's eyes widened. "—Old?"

Katrina nodded. "Yeah. For some reason he couldn't stop staring at it."

Tía Berta took her by the arm and quickly steered her inside, through a small room with a couple of sofas, past a coffeemaker and an old television. Katrina felt comforted by the familiar scents of the parador—coffee, lemon cleaner, and the clear plastic covers that protected the upholstered furniture from the muddy feet of younger guests. The colorful vejigante masks on the walls felt like old friends looking down to greet her.

When Katrina and Sal had been kids, their great-aunt had often told them stories of the inn, which had belonged to the family for generations. For many decades people had come from all over the world to spend a night or two at the edge of the rainforest. Tía Berta always took great pride in being a top-notch innkeeper.

"Don't you need to prepare breakfast soon?" Katrina asked.

"Ay, no." Tía Berta sighed. "Not a single guest last night."

Her great-aunt's sad look and slumped shoulders tugged at Katrina's heart. So it was true. Business was bad.

They continued through the immaculate dining area and large kitchen, finally arriving at a heavy wooden door Katrina knew well. It led to the mysterious studio that had always been kept locked whenever the twins were visiting. Katrina and Sal had spent countless hours plotting to sneak into the forbidden room. She felt a twinge of guilt at finally entering the mysterious space without him. "You're letting me in el estudio?"

"Bueno, it's finally time." Tía Berta pulled out a set of keys from her housedress pocket and unlocked the antique wrought iron latch. With a grunt of effort, she swung the door open.

She led Katrina into a room whose white plaster walls were hung with masks, paintings, and photos. An old mahogany drafting table was cluttered with paint brushes, colored pencils, and stacks of drawing paper. Each sheet was a sketch of a costume or mask, or jumpers with fabric wings stretching from wrists to ankles.

"Besides running el parador, craftwork was always the true calling in our family. On my side, anyway. Your tío, descanse en paz, wanted nothing to do with any of it. Wouldn't even go to la fiesta de Santiago Apóstol."

Katrina nodded. "Oh, right. The Festival of Saint James."

The keys jingled in Tía Berta's hand as she pointed to a framed photo on the closest wall. "That's it, there." The image was of a group of bomba dancers, the women in traditional long white ruffled skirts and white turbans, the men in loose white guayabera shirts. Other people were also marching in the street, some in white suits and straw pava hats, others clad in bright-colored midriff-baring dresses, with flowers in their hair. And some, of course, wearing masks.

"Pero, Tía." Katrina shook her head. "What does this room have to do with Sal?"

"What's on the walls? Nada. *These* masks are simply works of art." Her great-aunt gently laid a hand on her arm. "But your great-great-great grandfather Genaro—mi bisabuelo—once kept a very special mask hidden in here."

Katrina's throat tightened. "A vejigante. The kind Sal wore? At the bazaar last night."

Tía Berta nodded. "Back in eighteen sixty-seven a young man came to this house looking for Genaro. He asked him to repair and restore a mask brought down from the rainforest. The young man also entrusted him with the secret of the mask's origin and power. You see..." She paused, biting her lip, staring intently at Katrina as if carefully considering what she ought to say next. "It was, well . . . enchanted, you might say. And based on what I know of the spell, when Salvador placed the mask on his face, he would've been teleported into the depths of the rainforest."

"No. That's impossible," Katrina whispered. Yet hadn't Sal disappeared after doing exactly that? And suddenly here she was with her great-aunt in Puerto Rico, after simply passing through a curtain at that strange bazaar.

"I know it sounds unbelievable, but it's true." Tía Berta said. "Back in eighteen sixty-seven, nine years before El Yunque was declared a reserve, a greedy man named Reynaldo Méndez plotted to plunder the rainforest for personal gain. Jíbaros living in the mountains learned of his scheme and decided to fight back with a custom the locals knew well."

Katrina swallowed hard. "The vejigante mask."

"The jíbaros placed a spell on Mendez's mask to forever tie it to the rainforest." Her great-aunt sighed. "On the morning of the festival procession, the men planned to leave him stranded in the very place he sought to destroy. The Spaniard indeed went missing that morning, never to be heard from again. Soon after, our ancestor— "

"Genaro?" Katrina asked.

"Si, si." Tía Berta waved a hand. "He kept the enchanted mask safe in this room for several years, until the young man returned to retrieve it."

Katrina frowned. "Yet somehow, a hundred fifty years later, it ended up in New York City."

Her aunt gasped. "*Nueva York*?"

The entire story came pouring out of Katrina with barely a pause for breath. The bazaar, Sal vanishing, crossing through the curtain on the advice of a strange girl sucking down puke-green juice. "I swear, Tía, she couldn't have been even twenty. But her eyes, they were . . . so old."

The older woman narrowed her eyes. "Do you think she knew of the mask's powers?"

Katrina shrugged. "Could be. Maybe she's some kind of, I don't know . . . teleportation expert? Because the next thing I knew, I was flung onto your front porch."

"Perhaps," Tia Berta said.

"OK then." Katrina clapped once. She knew what to do now. "Since teleportation is real now—crazy as it sounds—finding Sal should be possible, too. You said the mask takes people to El Yunque, so I'll just hike every inch until—"

"You won't find him there." Tía Berta took a deep breath. "The mask also sent him to . . . the date of the festival procession Mendez was supposed to attend."

"But . . . but you said that was way back in eighteen . . . wait." Katrina blinked rapidly. "Are you telling me that my brother is . . . is . . ."

"He has traveled to July twenty-fifth, eighteen sixty-seven."

"No. That can't be. It can't!" It would mean Sal was lost to her forever. That he was not only dead, but had been for over a hundred and fifty years.

"Ay Dios." Tía Berta made the sign of the cross and tossed a kiss up to God. "I've kept this secret so long. My mother told me. Her mother passed it down to her, that a woman in our family would seek answers only to be found here, in the rainforest." With the same set of keys she unlocked a drawer in the old drawing desk. She carefully lifted out a yellowed sheet of paper. "This letter is for you."

"For me, here? But . . . are you sure?" Katrina took the brittle old paper with a trembling hand. The words written there were faded. But she would recognize her brother's messy chicken-scratch scrawl anywhere.

Kat,

If you're reading this it means you've come searching for me. You MUST stop looking now. I know going on alone will be one of the hardest things you'll ever have to do, but we survived losing Ma and Pa. You'll get through this too.

I hope you'll forgive me for leaving without warning, and for not returning. But I came to realize there was something I alone could do. And in order to do it, I made the choice to never return. I've always admired how you volunteer so much time to make a difference in the lives of complete strangers. I guess you inspired me to do the same here.

Please go back to your own life. Live it well, for me. You have no idea how much I miss you. And that I will always WANT to be with you again. But I must stay here, where I'm needed even more.

Love you always,
Sal

"So you see, it was Sal who brought the mask to Genaro." Tía Berta sighed.

Katrina turned from her aunt, wiping away fresh tears. As she looked down at the desktop she realized there were other items on it she hadn't noticed before. Sal's cell phone. His old wallet, the one with his initials embossed in the leather. But now for some reason the leather looked crumbly and ancient, the plastic faded and corroded. Had all these things really come from . . . the *past?* God, it seemed too ridiculous. But what else could the letter mean? Which meant Sal was still up in El Yunque, somewhere. Well, wherever — or whenever—she'd track him down. Forget this going-on-alone stuff.

"We need a plan, Tía. How do we find him?"

"Ay, nena, don't you see?" The older woman shook her head sadly. "You're not supposed to."

Katrina crumpled the paper in one fist. "But he's my brother! Our parents are gone. The hell with that." She shoved letter, wallet, and cell phone into her purse. Before this moment she'd never dared speak back to an elder. But that was before she'd received a letter from her own brother written over a century ago. Polite manners be damned, now.

She grabbed up her great-aunt's keys from where they lay on the desk. Surely one would start the jeep out in the carport. "I'm searching for him, Tía. With or without you."

* * *

Brujo? Witch. The tugging in Sal's gut returned. It felt so much like

Kat's presence he almost called out her name. But he didn't want to do anything the stranger wielding a large branch might misinterpret as threatening. "N-no, I'm not a witch. Just here to enjoy nature, that's all. I got lost. Know where I can find the trail leading back to the entrance?"

The other man scowled. "What entrance?"

Sal cleared his throat. "The main gate by the visitor's center?"

The man threw his head back and laughed. "What in the name of God are you saying? You are in the wilderness." He cocked his head and smirked. "Ah, now I see. You must be with them. I had heard a team was coming to count trees, or some such nonsense."

Sal pressed a hand to his chest. His heart was racing like a released spring too tightly wound. "Uh . . . no, I'm not. I don't even—"

"This land has lain fallow for far too long. It is going to waste." The man curled his lip, baring a gap in his teeth. "But I shall change that. And no Corps of Forestry will get in the way."

Sal's knees buckled and he barely caught himself. "Excuse me. I'm feeling a bit disoriented." He knew about the Corps of Forestry, Spanish men who had been sent across the Atlantic to Puerto Rico for a conservation project. But that had been back in the nineteenth century, when the island was still a colony of Spain.

"Oh, but where are my manners? I have not introduced myself." The stranger stepped toward Sal, still pointing the branch. "Reynaldo Méndez, proprietor, held in high esteem by the Crown. I have plans for this mountain, and an entire faction along the northeastern shore is to work with me. Once the royal court understands the fortune to be had they'll follow our recommendations." He looked Sal up and down dismissively. "And common visitors will certainly *not* be welcome."

Sal inhaled slowly, trying to stay calm. To think. But there was no denying the truth any more. The mask had not only transported him far away from the bazaar, it had sent him to a whole other freaking *time*. He exhaled, trying to push down the terrifying idea he might never see his sister again. He'd only imagined her presence, of course. In truth, he was alone. Except for this crazy Spaniard who was plotting the destruction of El Yunque.

He stared nervously at the jagged point of the branch only a couple of feet away, aimed at his face. For the first time in his life he was being threatened with bodily harm. He'd never even gotten into a fistfight in elementary school. Always he'd been the ignored kid, tucked away in a corner, nose in a book. "This is a misunderstanding. I swear I didn't bring you here."

"You still take me, a righteous Christian, for a fool. Well, this is what I think of your pitiful sorcery." Méndez lunged, thrusting the pointed branch at Sal's face.

He ducked left and managed to dodge the tip. Méndez stumbled past him, tripped over a root, and fell. He screamed and cursed, lying on the ground. The branch had broken in two. One end had pierced the cloth of the jumpsuit . . . and the Spaniard's belly.

Incredibly, he staggered up again to tackle Sal, who shoved him away. The coppery scent of blood filled the air as Méndez fell again, writhing and howling on the ground.

Instinctively, Sal patted his pockets for his cell phone, to dial 911, before the absurdity of that hit him. "God, how stupid can I be," he chided himself. "How useless. "

He didn't dare pull out the branch. There was no way to know what arteries or organs it had damaged on the way in. Instead he knelt and tore off a swath of the red material from one sleeve of the man's costume, to make a pressure bandage. Méndez screamed as Sal wrapped the cloth around him. The wrenching pull under his own ribcage expanded. Not sympathy pains. He felt sure now it *was* the presence of his sister. The sense was so strong he expected her to burst from the trees any minute, and come running to help.

I guess I'm losing my mind, he thought. Well then, screw it. Might as well go with the insanity.

Méndez's wails faded to whimpers. Sal pressed his weight against the bandaged gash to stop the bleeding. "I don't think he's going to make it, Kat," he said to the air before him. "God, I wish you were here! Wherever . . . whenever here is. All your travels . . . I bet you'd know what to do."

The body beneath his hands went limp. Silent.

"Kat!" Sal leapt up, horrified. "Oh God, I've killed him. What should I do?" He grabbed the mask, smearing it with bloody fingerprints, and clutched it to his chest. As if that would help! He shouted up at the trees, "What do I *do?*"

The only answer that came back was the disparaging squawks of dozens of bright green Puerto Rican parrots. A handful burst from the treetops, the undersides of their wings flashing bluer than the sky above. It felt as if his very core was being pulled with them into a whirling vortex, an air current too strong to resist.

The world went white.

* * *

Katrina clutched the jeep's scorching steering wheel tighter, even though it burned her palms. The hot, humid air flowing in through the windows did nothing to dry the sweat on her face as they approached the official entrance gate of El Yunque National Forest. Tía Berta waved at the park ranger from the passenger seat as Kat drove on through. The impressive white triangular rooftops of the visitor center stood off to their right. When the twins were eight, Sal had wandered off and disappeared, scaring their parents. Her twin sense had led her right to the Puerto Rican parrot exhibit, where he stood gaping at the displays. She'd always taken the shared perception for granted. But this search might not be as simple.

Anyway, she first had to trigger the sense, somehow. She tried to envision her brother's tan face, his cocky smirk. To hear his low, pleased laugh. The only sensation that came was like butterfly wings brushing the inside of her stomach as she rounded a curve, tall bushes rushing by on either side of the jeep. What if this turned out to be like trying to control your heartbeat, or make your hair grow faster? Still, she had to try. The alternative was unthinkable.

Oh, Sal. Why'd you have to put on that damned mask? Her face flushed hot. *This never would've happened if you—*

There it was. As if the emotion had sparked a connection. Sal was coming to her now like a faint beacon, a warm ray of light.

She pulled into the next parking area and spotted a sign leading to the trailhead. She glanced over at Tía Berta. Back at the parador her aunt had insisted on changing out of her housedress and into a blouse and skirt, but in the rush she'd left wearing flimsy, slip-on sandals.

"You can't hike in chanclas, Tía."

Tía Berta smiled gently. "I'll stay here and pray for you kids."

"We'll be back soon," Katrina said firmly, trying to steady the quaver in her voice. She pecked a kiss at her aunt's cheek and started up the trail, weaving through groups of meandering tourists. Following the pull she plunged off into the forest, tramping up slick, steep terrain, leaping over roots and fallen trees, ducking low-hanging vines. Splashing once across a small natural pool, leaving her sneakers sodden, her jeans wet to the knees.

The first hint she'd felt in the car gradually turned into a magnetic pull in her belly, one that dragged her along at a rapid clip. She followed eagerly, as if this were her Northern Star, until she burst through a clump of wide, fan-shaped leaves, expecting to find her brother there.

No Sal.

She closed her eyes, panting, and paused to catch her breath. A glowing orb appeared behind her lids. Pulses of color radiated from the amorphous shape. Not just colors . . . emotions. A flood of fear, sadness, and desperation surged through her. Twin perception had always been limited to merely feeling certain the other was nearby. Now it seemed she'd entered her brother's mind, his emotions.

"Sal!" She opened her eyes. The shape was gone, but he still felt close. "Sal, where are you?" Holding so still she barely breathed, Katrina shut her eyes again. The colorful form reappeared, accompanied by the same disturbing panic. She took a few steps and flung her arms out, groping at thin air, until finally her hands landed on something warm and solid and alive.

"Yes!" When she looked again her fingers were outlined in light. *Sal.* She wrapped her arms tight around his glowing presence until, with a bright white flash, her brother materialized in her arms.

"Who's there?" He jerked away, throwing her to one side. "What do you want?"

His reaction startled Kat, but she was agile enough to regain her footing. "Sal," she said, weeping. "I thought I'd never see you again."

He turned toward her, looking dazed. He let the mask fall onto a flowering bush. "Just a hallucination," he muttered, as if talking to himself. "Focus on the problem at hand!"

"Sal!"

"What? " he said unwillingly, not looking directly at her. He turned in a complete circle and mumbled, "Where'd he go?"

"Who?"

From a distant part of the trail came faint voices, the laughter of hikers, the recorded notes of a popular song. Sal cocked his head, listening intently. His expression slowly grew incredulous as he gazed up at the trees. "The parrots are gone. And that . . . that *music*. Is it really you, Kat?"

"It's me. You're back in the twenty-first century, where you belong."

"But . . . how can I be here?"

She laughed. "Me! I brought you back. The twin sense, we can actually control it. It's connected to emotions, I think. Which we both must be full of right now." She noticed a sticky red substance on her fingers. Not dirt. More like . . . blood? She looked closer at Sal. "Hey. You're hurt!"

"No. I'm okay. This blood . . . it's not mine."

"Are you sure?" She searched each arm for a wound. "My God, it's everywhere." He was still gripping the mask, which was also splotched with blood. "There's something you should know about that thing. It's . . . well, enchanted, Tía Berta says."

"So what the man said was true." Sal looked down at it. "This did belong to him. When you pulled me through time . . . like the blood on my hands . . . it traveled with me. "

Katrina shook her head. "Who? What the hell are you talking about?"

"Reynaldo Méndez."

Katrina gasped. During the ride over, she'd made her poor great-aunt repeat the story of the mask and the spell it had worked on Méndez. "But he's the guy who plotted to destroy the forest."

Sal frowned. "How'd you know that?"

"Tía Berta said . . . long story." She held a hand up. "Wait. Are you saying you met this man?"

"Yes. Right here." He pointed behind him. "Only it was back then. His body stayed in—"

"—Eighteen sixty-seven. July twenty-fifth. The Saint James Festival."

"Yes." Sal nodded. "He was wearing the vejigante costume. Told me he was getting ready—"

"—for the procession. I know. But he disappeared!" She took a deep breath. "The mask sent him to the mountain. He never returned to the village."

"Yes. Never returned," Sal whispered. "Because of me." His bloody hands trembled.

She met her brother's tormented gaze. A bolt of overwhelming guilt and shame slammed into her. "Oh." She clapped a hand to her mouth. "Oh no."

"It was an accident. Méndez came after me with a weapon." He choked back sobs. "But I didn't . . .I didn't mean to—"

"—kill him," she finished softly. "So it's his blood on you."

"But this isn't over! He said there were others who would come to destroy the forest." Sal glanced down at the mask. "I have to go back now."

"What!" She stepped in front of him. "Are you insane? I just found you. We're going back to the parador, right now."

"But there are consequences, Kat."

"For killing a man from the past?" She jabbed a finger into his chest. "Yes. There definitely *are*. But thanks to me, you've just gotten a free pass from having to pay them."

"No. Not that. It's what will happen to this land." Sal held his head. "See? You've never understood—"

Katrina gritted her teeth, tears slicking her face. "I understood enough to find you." She dug the letter from her purse. "Across *time*. I found you. Me! Even though you asked me not to look." She pressed the paper into his chest. A spark of light flared when the paper touched him.

"Aah! No!" Sal faded from sight, then stumbled back into view as the sheet fluttered away to settle on a rotting log beside the path. "What just happened? Did you see it too?"

"You . . . uh, vanished." She blinked. "For like maybe a second."

He narrowed his eyes. "That's all you saw?"

"Yeah. Why? Did you go back in time again?"

"No, not back. It was. . . ." He paused and shivered, as if the temperature had suddenly dropped. "Never mind." He crouched to read the yellowing letter. " 'You must stop the search.' It *is* my handwriting. But where'd you get this?"

She shifted her feet and her sneakers squelched. "In the back room of el parador." She dug into her purse and fished out his wallet and cell phone. "You left these, too."

"But they look so old. Could they really be mine?" He passed a hand above the items. A thin blue electric current rose from each into the center of his palm. Another white flash. Once again he vanished for a moment. "No!" He returned again, fully corporeal, but looking shaken. "I can't touch these again. Keep them *away*."

"What's going on?" She ran over to the log and snatched up the old letter. "Why do you flicker out like a dying light bulb whenever you're near your own things?"

"Because they only exist here. With you. Now." His brown eyes seemed to be pleading with her to accept what he said. "Whatever happened to lead to this moment has already been set in motion. Don't you see? It means I *have* to go back."

Raindrops fell, cool and light as mist on Katrina's skin. "But you've already done your part! The evil Reynaldo dude is dead. Plot averted, forest saved. Right?"

Sal shook his head. "Méndez told me there's a ring of men along the northern coast, all in on the scheme. They could still pull off their plan to end forest conservation if they aren't stopped."

"And what . . . you're the big savior?" Katrina laughed in his face. "Get over yourself, Sal. I'm sure that back in eighteen sixty-seven there were plenty of good guys on the island perfectly capable of handling the situation."

"Of course. Probably. Maybe. But isn't this our fight, too? I mean, it affects our people, our history. If I can help the cause in any way . . . talk about deforestation and how to avoid it, from a future perspective, well." He took a long breath. "We know the situation on the island today is dire, remember? Imagine how much worse it'd be if Méndez's guys had actually pulled off their scheme. The place called El Yunque, where we stand right now . . . it wouldn't have survived." Sal grimaced. The streaks of blood and rainwater made his face look for a moment strange, even a bit frightening. "There's a reason the Taínos believed this forest was the island's source of life."

"Oh please. It's just a mountain!" The rain fell harder, smacking the leaves, stirring the animals in the trees to hoot and caw, as if jeering at them. She shouted over the din, "There's no deity on a throne up there!"

"If you think the traditional beliefs are nonsense, fine." He flung both arms out. "But you can't argue with science. This rainforest means life or death for the island's ecosystem."

"Oh, so now you're a scientist too?" She'd had enough of his know-it-all bullshit. "You're making this part up. You just want an excuse to go back to the nineteenth century because you're too cowardly to stay in the present one with me!"

Sal was silent for a moment. "What makes you think I'm running to the past because the present is too painful?"

"All those strong, confused emotions," she said, "I *felt* them, searching for you."

"Well, I've just killed a man." He exhaled. "Maybe that's the terror you feel inside me."

"Maybe. But it's time to deal with what happened even before that. You've never gotten over losing Ma and Dad."

He blinked. "Have you?"

"I'm talking about *you*— " Her voice cracked. "Not m-me. You."

He wrapped his arms around her. "I miss them too, Kat."

"No," she wailed. "You can't leave me. I'll be alone!" As she wept, water trickled from the hollow of the mask. *If I take it, he can't return to the past again.* She reached around and clutched at the coconut shell.

The moment she touched its coarse hard surface she winced, blinded by an intense light. Her fingertips felt scorched, as if she'd tried to snatch up a red-hot ember. She forced her eyes open again, just a slit.

Before her lay a lifeless, arid mountain landscape. The soil was a uniform, dusty brown. Not a single tree grew to block the blazing sun. A place of silence so eerie she couldn't bear to look at it. She squinted harder against the haze. In the distance stood rows of abandoned plantations. The broken walls of former mills and factories. But no people.

Except . . . what were those slivers of white at her feet, littering the dry, cracked soil? "Oh my God," she whispered. *Bones.* She swallowed back sour bile. Of animals, or of people? Whichever, they'd clearly been there a long time. This barren moonscape was no rainforest. This was not her Puerto Rico. But then where was she, exactly? How had she come here?

The mask. This disturbing vista had appeared when she touched it. She could no longer see the mask, yet the hard surface of the painted shell, slippery with rain, was still cool against her hand. How was that possible? Could she be in two different times at once?

Sal had disappeared once after he'd touched the letter, and again when he went for the wallet and cell phone case. Each time he'd seemed distressed upon his reappearance. No wonder, if this hell was what he'd seen. The possible alternate reality.

This isn't another time. It is what El Yunque will become if Sal is not there to help make sure conservation efforts happen, back then.

"No!" She yelled, tearing her hands away from the mask. Suddenly she was back in the forest, looking up at the sky, grateful for the rain-wet leaves that dripped on her face, the lively chatter of birds, the endless, pattering rain. The whole magnificent, endless green canopy.

She swallowed hard. "I saw it, Sal. What will happen if you don't go back to finish what you've started." When he lifted his head to meet her gaze she could feel a difference in him. The panic was gone. He had made his decision.

"You know what? You were right." His smile trembled a bit. He reached out and took her hand. "Absolutely right to come find me. Now we can say a real goodbye."

She took a deep breath. "The girl at the bazaar said it first. To me. Our destinies are different."

"Only as different as you choose." He pulled her to him, tight. "I'll always miss you. I'll always love you."

"Me too." She wiped her nose on the back of a hand and then laid her head on his shoulder. "Happy birthday, little brother."

He kissed her forehead and stepped back. "Happy birthday, Kat."

She watched him slide the enchanted mask down over his face again. Her beloved Sal vanished. The imaginary string that still connected them tugged at her now, as it always had, but she didn't reach out. Instead she turned away and trudged back to the trail, stopping once at the clear, natural pool to rinse her face, still salty with tears despite the rain. To wash away what was left of Mendez's blood. She didn't want to frighten Tía Berta, or to be suspected by one of the rangers of some crime.

Gradually the rain shower subsided and warm sunlight slid in between the tall trees. As crushed as she felt at this moment, she was exactly where she was supposed to be—in this spot, on this mountain, on her island. It was still a peaceful, beautiful sanctuary.

Our destinies are different. But only as different as I choose them to be.

Yes. Of course. Her choice was as clear as the cool water she'd splashed on her face earlier. She thought of her aunt's worried, anxious face. Of the empty parador, no longer full of happy visitors to the forest. Right now, somewhere in time, Sal was fighting for the island's past. Well then, she would fight for its future.

When Katrina reached the Jeep she fell into Tía Berta's embrace.

"What is it?" her aunt exclaimed. "Dios mío. What's happened? "

"I'm coming home," she told her. "Here. To Puerto Rico."

We have more for sale here than oddities, antiquities, vintage costumes, and curious baubles, of course. Some offerings may be less tangible to the casual observer. The ordinary services to be had at the Bazaar are pleasant but unremarkable: hot stone massages, tea leaf readings, palm readings, Tarot and water, glass, and crystal gazing to herbal treatments. In the more erotically-themed areas, shops like The Body Artistic offer internal and external tattooing, piercing, elective surgery, herbal and alchemical treatments, and every sort of body art or alteration which can be purchased. The Invited will also find any number of erotic provisions in Adult Wares . . . and we are all adults, here.

But there are also more arcane services, some of so delicate a nature I prefer to always oversee them myself. . . .

FRIENDS OF VERA

Gregory Fletcher

Had we come to the end of a conversation, or a business transaction, or even a shared moment between strangers, the old woman's "goodbye" might not have grabbed me the way it did. I shot to my feet as if she had actually said *hello*. By then she was past me, stopped at the curb, shoulders hunched forward as she waited to cross Ninth Avenue.

My nightly walk often led me to this prized bench in the middle of a pedestrian island, where time and thoughts were cradled by the white noise of the surrounding traffic. At fifty-eight years old, my sitting and drifting off had become the familiar intermission before the walk home ended the day, and then to bed.

The same sort of farewell had brought me back to earth many times before. But it was usually Jeff's baritone I heard. His ghostly goodbye sometimes still whispered me back to the present, and reality, even though a heart attack had taken the man himself away twenty-seven years earlier.

Tonight's parting word, however, had come from a tall angular woman whose graying red hair was braided and coiled into a tight bun. Her long skirt was a rich dark-paisley tapestry of crushed velvet. Her blouse looked like expensive Egyptian cotton, skillfully hand-woven. Despite the aging body, there was something graceful about her still. Perhaps she'd been a ballerina in her youth, back in the 1960s. How odd, though, that this stranger had greeted me with "goodbye." In all the hours I've sat people watching, my gazing and daydreaming had always kept me near-invisible. Or so I'd thought.

"Um . . . hello?" I called after her.

Her uneven hips twisted as she turned to look back. The eye contact convinced me we must've met before. Her lips relaxed, curved, almost smiled. But she turned away and continued walking west, without looking back.

Intrigued, I couldn't help but follow at a distance.

The farther west she headed, the fewer businesses were active on the street level. Some former stores had been boarded up, abandoned, sprayed with graffiti. Even the paving had been neglected. Old cobblestones from yesteryear had begun to rise up through the asphalt more and more.

I wasn't alone. Others seemed to be following, too. Old and young, male and female, black, white, Asians, Latinos—somehow we'd all been bewitched by this eccentric old woman. Or perhaps by the midnight moon.

She stopped in front of a large plain brick building. Not residential, perhaps a warehouse left over from the former meat packing district. She turned to us and smiled faintly, as if pleased with the dozens of admirers who were texting and taking photos of her and the building behind her. With a graceful sweep of an arm she bade us enter. Then turned and went in an unmarked door.

I hesitated on the cobblestoned street. Most of the others did not.

"Who is she?" I asked a passerby whose hairless pale skin was covered in green and brown camouflage tattoos. No reply. He continued past me toward the door. Maybe I wasn't supposed to have been able to see him.

"What group is this?" I asked a small woman who wore so many wooden chokers her elongated neck seemed held extra high. She didn't respond either, although once she brushed past I wasn't sure she could've turned her head my way anyhow.

Finally, with my third query, a transgender person wearing a man's suit and bowtie bowed and answered ever so politely, "Friends of Vera."

"Thank you," I said, more baffled than ever. I've been a Friend of Bill W. for almost sixteen years. It was my New Century's resolution. And despite the plague I'd survived throughout the 1980s and 90s, I've remained a true and loyal member of Friends of Dorothy. But Friends of Vera . . . which secret community was this?

The knobby handle of a walking cane tapped my arm. When I glanced over, a French beret was whipped off. A lush mane of dark purple hair fell to shoulder length. "Excuse me, sir," the older man said. "Friend of Vera?"

"Um, yes, we just met." Then, wishing to match Vera's mystery, I said, "Goodbye," and turned away and headed to the door, following the others downstairs.

A couple levels down, aisles of wall-to-wall booths lined the basement. Pipe-and-drape scaffolding had apparently been the construction method of choice. Some booths were private. Others stood open for all to see. Around me, different body parts were being pierced, tattooed, clamped, tickled, spanked, and worshipped. The person with purple hair headed straight for a three-foot tall platform covered with a lubricated pad. Teams of naked bodies were being dropped, twisted, and pinned by muscular rivals who appeared both menacing and lustful. A little person, wearing a striped suit and top hat with BOOKIE painted on the front and back, roamed among the onlookers taking bets.

Even the enclosed booths were not completely private. Certain sounds issued from each, making it all too obvious what must be going on inside. Role-playing, at the first one I strolled past. Light torture inside the second. And at a third booth, screams and laughter from . . . well, perhaps a water-balloon fight? But when a middle-aged woman stepped out, she wasn't dripping wet. Instead she was splattered from head to toe with something darker . . . possibly a food fight? Oh, Hell no. The foul stench pushed me away so quickly, I collided with a barker at the next booth.

"Welcome to Celebrity Orgasm," said the tall young man.

I couldn't believe my eyes. "Ashton Kutcher?"

"At your service. We've also got Brad Pitt with us tonight. The *young* Brad Pitt. But he's occupied at the moment. Or perhaps you might prefer Madonna?"

"Uh . . . no, thanks."

"Good call. She's not the *young* Madonna."

"Unlike a Virgin?"

"More like a Cougar, touched for the millionth time."

Just as I was going to confess to Ashton that he'd been at the top of my list of sexiest celebs for decades, he ruined it with one last offer. "We also have another celebrity classic available at this very moment, but not for long."

"Brando?" I guessed, then quickly corrected myself. "A *young* Marlon Brando, that is?"

He shook his head. "Try again."

"James Dean?"

He smiled as if he knew I'd never guess. "No. The classic 1930s Buckwheat."

My eyes widened. "From 'The Little Rascals?'"

He leaned closer. "The price is higher, but he's worth every penny."

"Good God," I blurted. "Surely you mean an *older* Buckwheat?"

"No, *young*. Just as he always looked."

I felt the blood drain from my face, and from other places, too. Not Ashton's intention, presumably. "Well, if this is what Friends of Vera is about, then no thanks." I turned away and hurried off, back toward the entrance.

That's when I saw the tall, angular Vera again, across two aisles. She was just stepping inside an enclosed booth. I changed course and walked her way.

Oddly enough, her booth had no entrance marked, no signage hung. And no sounds came from inside. I ran a hand along the hanging drapery, which was beautifully embroidered with Byzantine patterns. Some of the repeating shapes seemed to writhe, to coil and uncoil. Or were my eyes playing tricks? But after two passes, I still couldn't find an entrance.

"Hello?" I considered knocking, but on what? I felt for an upright, finally located some solid internal framework and rapped on it.

No one responded.

Just when I was about to walk away a middle-aged woman approached the booth. She stopped a few feet from me, but didn't look my way. She simply waited. When I tried to make eye contact she lifted the back of her scarf and draped it over her Afro like a monk's hood.

"Excuse me. What goes on inside?" I asked, jerking a thumb back at the booth before us.

She tapped her voice box and shook her head.

Oh, a mute. Just my luck. We stood, silently facing the hanging drapery for a few more minutes. The fabric was expertly woven, the linked, repeating triangles and squares clearly stitched by hand. "Exquisite cloth, isn't it?" I said, hoping to get some kind of a reaction from the women beside me.

She didn't look my way or give any acknowledgement whatsoever. Maybe she was deaf, too.

At last the drapes parted. Vera stepped through. Her cool green eyes gave both of us a sharp once-over. Then she gestured for the woman to step inside. I thought to complain, *I was here first.* Before my mouth was even open, Vera held up those long graceful fingers to stop me.

"But . . . is there a sign-up or reservation list?" I didn't want to be pushy, but as she stepped inside, I added, "Wait. Please. You said 'goodbye' to me on the street. Do you recall?"

"Yes. Goodbye." This time she clearly meant it. Even though up on the street she'd clearly meant something else. Jeff's goodbyes over the last twenty-seven years could never be taken as literal, either. Sometimes his meant, "Focus." Or, "No." Or even simply, "Go to bed."

Before she twitched the curtain closed I saw the silent woman who had stepped inside was unwrapping her scarf. I realized it was identical to Vera's.

I waited, but didn't hear anything. After what felt like a long while I walked away to browse around the bazaar, avoiding the Celebrity Orgasm. Still, nothing interested me like Vera's mysterious booth. Something about that rich, one-of-a-kind fabric that enclosed her space seemed to call to me.

A stranger bounced his eyebrows at me in the same comically suggestive way Jeff used to do. I walked past him and imagined finding Jeff somewhere here, whispering *Come here often?* I smiled at the thought of us even being together in a place like this. When he'd laugh it always revealed his slightly crooked bottom teeth, which I found as cute as his dimpled chin. I could hear myself asking him, *Did you know such places existed?*

No response, as usual.

Guess I haven't been very surprising lately. Boring, in fact. Sorry.

Still no response, even in my mind.

I felt like egging his spirit on to say something more than the same old "goodbye." So I continued our talk. I'm fairly sure it was not out loud.

No, I don't miss our membership to MOMA or our season tickets at Lincoln Center. I'm bored with films and books. I've heard enough stories to last a lifetime.

I could imagine Jeff using his brown, sad-puppy eyes to look sorry for me. Had the cloud that'd been hovering these past twenty-seven years finally turned me into a sad little man?

"*Goodbye.*"

The terse farewell jolted me back again. The bazaar buzzed all around me with voices. But whose had it been this time? Not Jeff's. Nor Vera's. I turned in a complete circle, then looked toward the exit. There was the deaf mute, headed for the stairwell. I followed.

Up on the street, I spotted her hailing a taxi. A yellow cab stopped on the other side of the street, facing the opposite direction. She started across, but froze halfway. An SUV was heading straight for her, the young driver's face illuminated by the glow of a cell phone screen.

I gasped, "Look out!"

Behind me, a pedestrian screamed.

The texting driver looked up just in time to yank the steering wheel right. The SUV jumped the curb and slammed into a street sign. On impact, the air bag inflated, slamming the driver's phone into her face, knocking her out cold.

The taxi driver sped off, perhaps worried the accident could be blamed on him. The deaf mute stood stiffly in the middle of the street. I rushed to her. "May I help?"

She turned her head to look at the unconscious driver, where other pedestrians had come to her aid. "Let's get out of the street." I took her arm gently. "Someone is already calling 911."

"I can't." She pointed down at her shoes. One high heel was caught, wedged between two cobblestones.

I refrained from commenting on the fact that she was no longer deaf or mute.

Cars crept past. I knelt, wrapped both hands around her shoe, and yanked hard. Once, twice. It came free at last.

She sighed, clearly much relieved. "You're a saint."

I grinned. "Really. Saint Todd?"

She tilted her head, reconsidering. "Hmm. Maybe not."

As we walked to the safe haven of the far sidewalk, I wondered if she had recognized me from inside, earlier. If so, she didn't let on. "I have a train to catch."

Not at all what I had been hoping to hear. "You might have better luck finding a cab at the intersection. I'm walking that way."

She hesitated, then nodded. We walked on together.

There were so many things I wanted to ask. *Why did you pretend to be deaf and mute? What strange rites or arcane services go on in Vera's booth? Is it merely a coincidence that your scarves match?* But I couldn't find quite the right words, or maybe just the nerve. Even so, there was something calming about her presence. Something comfortable about our mutual silence.

At the intersection I hailed a cab. "You take the first one."

"Let me drop you somewhere," she said. "It's the least I can do."

As our taxi sped up Tenth Avenue, a tear ran down her cheek. I dug a packet of tissues from my jacket and offered one. She smiled as if impressed with my continued gallantry, then blotted underneath her eyes.

For the first time during a taxi ride I hated that the driver was catching every single green light. I wanted more time, not speed. "I hope we can do this again," I said, and felt my face heat. I sounded ridiculous. Which part: sharing a taxi? Or almost getting hit by a car?

But she only turned her head and gave me a long look that seemed to say, *I know what you meant.*

The cab turned onto my street and stopped in front of my place. When I opened the door and stepped out, she scooted over to look up and admire the building. "Nice brownstone. All yours?"

"Just the third floor. I'd be happy to show it off. Is there a later train you can take? I'd love to hear about, well . . . so many things."

She frowned a little and then reached for the door. "I wish I could." She closed it, but lowered the window. "Thank you so much. For everything."

"Please, if you have a few minutes, let's share a pot of tea. You're totally safe with me. I'm gay. Or was. *Is*. Okay, now I am sounding crazy."

Her smile revealed a charming little space between her two front teeth. There was something about our crossing paths. I felt certain we were destined to be friends. She laid a hand on mine, which was gripping the door as if I could somehow hold the cab in place and keep it from speeding off.

"I know I can trust you," she said. "Can you trust me?"

"Yes, of course."

Her face seemed to soften. But in the next moment she simply sat back against the seat and said, "Driver. Penn Station."

The cab sped off.

* * *

"Goodbye," Jeff's voice whispered in my ear the next morning. I was sitting under his tree in the back garden. I reached up and touched the memorial plaque fastened to it.

JEFF TOWNSEND 1958-1989

I'd just been fantasizing. Imagine what he would've said about my meeting Vera, and . . . damn it, I couldn't believe I hadn't asked for the woman's name.

My hand cradled Jeff's smiling, framed photo. It had hung on the tree for the whole twenty-seven years since he died. The waterproofed frame was holding tight despite its age. Jeff was so thin in that shot, taken the year he'd passed, thanks to an extreme-cardio health kick. In fact he'd become addicted to running. As had Jim Fixx, the author of *The Complete Book of Running*, who'd dropped dead from a heart attack at fifty-two—while running! Five years later, Jeff died from the same thing, at age thirty-one.

Being fit wasn't at all what most gay men were dying from at that time. Jeff's family, who had never acknowledged me as his partner even after our six years together, merely sounded relieved at the news. They hadn't flown up for the memorial, but his mother did telephone to speak with me for the very first time.

"Heart disease doesn't run in our family," she'd said flatly in an Oklahoma twang. "But I'll take it. I sure will take it. At least now no one can say my boy died from . . . you know."

When I didn't respond, she'd actually surprised me. "I take it you're okay? I reckon if Jeff was, then you are, too?" When I agreed, she simply said, "Well, good for you." And then had hung up.

Oh yes, goody for me, I thought. When the love of my life died I had been at an estate sale, eating a Country Sausage Biscuit Platter for breakfast. The one of us who'd cared least about his health had outlived the one who'd cared the most. And I hadn't worked out in a gym since.

My heart's been breaking for twenty-seven years, but it was not yet attacking.

***

The front buzzer woke me from a nap Saturday afternoon. When I came down the FedEx driver wanted a signature. The package was addressed to "Saint Todd." Evidently I *could* trust Monique Thorpes of 312 Nicole Mews, Princeton, New Jersey. I zipped open the package and found her scarf—the same design as Vera's. When I flung it open to admire, though, it wasn't a scarf at all, simply a narrow strip of fabric. The same heavy brocade woven in classic Byzantine geometric shapes that had draped Vera's booth.

I searched Facebook and found Monique Thorpes of Princeton. She must've been online because my friend request was accepted immediately. I scrolled through her Timeline. As the photos got older, her beautiful Afro got shorter and shorter until it was completely buzzed, reminiscent of a young Whitney Houston from the mid-1980s.

Received the package, I messaged her. *I take it the scarf is my invitation to Vera's booth. Any details to share?*

No answer. She'd apparently just gone off line. Oh well, bad timing.

As I rolled up the cloth, I heard the crinkle of paper within. I felt around and found a rectangular pocket with a tiny hidden zipper. Inside was a folded sheet with terse but specific instructions.

> *To assure yourself of an invitation to Vera's booth, be sure to wear the fabric.*
>
> *P.S. Bring $5000 in cash.*

The price tag floored me. I had to sit down before my knees gave way. I hadn't noticed anything this extravagant being sold at the Night Bazaar. I reread Monique's instructions. But what exactly would I be purchasing? I turned the note over, but the back was blank. Astounding that more detailed instructions hadn't been included, or at least a clue as to what I would receive for all that money. Or was the price tag supposed to dissuade me? If so, perhaps I wasn't the typical Night

Bazaar patron. Whenever I perceived a thing had value and exclusivity, it had only intrigued me all the more. Now I felt certain. Whatever was inside that booth, I wanted it.

At Chase Bank, the teller examined the withdrawal slip I passed under the window. As she checked my account on her screen, she whispered, "So, like . . . is everything cool with you right now?"

I raised one eyebrow. "Oh. You mean because I want all that in cash? Yes, fine."

"It's just . . . I see you've never taken out such a large amount before and, well . . . "She blushed. "Let's forget I said anything. Which denominations would you like?"

"Hundreds, please. And actually I appreciate your asking."

She placed a stack of bills in the automatic counter, then ran it again. "Alrighty then. That's five thousand even."

Back home I downloaded the app for Facebook onto my cell and searched my notifications for the invitation to join the Secret Facebook Group, *Friends of Vera*.

Found it! Now I was an official member with thousands of others, from all around the world. Monique's note said Vera sightings could be posted as early as 11:30 P.M., so I was dressed and ready to go by ten. I taped the envelope of cash to my undershirt, which seemed safer than carrying a wad of bills in a pocket.

I had assumed the bazaar would be located in the same building as before, but Monique's note explained it never met twice in the same place. And that it only lasted for seven nights. According to the note, we'd met on night four, so there were only three left before it folded its tents and moved on to wherever.

I checked my phone for any sightings. Nothing yet at a quarter to eleven.

To think I had been part of a Vera sighting on the fourth night and hadn't even realized it. I wrapped the long strip of soft embroidered fabric around my neck and imagined I was standing in front of her booth. This time, those long skinny fingers would beckon me inside.

"Goodbye," Jeff's voice whispered next to my ear.

I jumped up to check the envelope taped to my undershirt. Still there. While waiting for a posting, I'd apparently fallen asleep in the front foyer sitting on its red shellacked Art Deco bench. I checked my phone again. Several earlier postings had narrowed the location to a basement in the Bronx. But rushing uptown at 3 A.M. with 5K taped to my chest didn't sound like the wisest idea. Luckily, two more nights remained.

I slept in most of Sunday, intentionally. I got up at one point to email the manager of my store and let him know I wouldn't be in on Monday. A last-minute estate sale or a sudden lead on a new lot of antiques was not uncommon. In fact it was the usual explanation I gave whenever I wanted to take some time off. Not that I needed an excuse any more. Six years ago I'd bought the store from the previous owner.

By midnight I was sure to be still up and wide awake, this time ready to travel to any far-flung borough the Night Bazaar might beckon from.

At 11:40, sightings of Vera started coming in along West 125th Street. Fifteen minutes later the location was posted: 128th Street, west of Broadway. The photos looked like a new building still under construction. I rushed out to catch the number 1 train.

When I arrived at the 125th Street Station, where the 1 train shot over the street for several blocks, a large construction site stretched west toward the Hudson. I headed down the stairs to Broadway and north to the deserted stretch of 128th Street. A sign announcing the future north campus of Columbia University was attached to an unattended gate. I couldn't help but admire the connections Vera must have, with people and places all around the world.

Taking one more look at the most recent posted photo, I found an unmarked steel door and headed down the stairs to the basement. Amazing how similar the set-up looked to the time before. I found Vera's booth again on the third aisle, and pulled the fabric from my book bag. This time, instead of wrapping it around my neck as a scarf, I wore it as a Fly plaid, the over-the-shoulder drape that usually accompanied a kilt. Then I stood nearby and waited patiently.

After ten minutes Vera parted the curtain. She stepped out and eyed the fabric that hung to my knees on either side. Her nod and half-smile clearly approved of my fashion sense. At last she uttered the two words I had been hoping to hear. "Come inside."

We sat at a small round wrought-iron table with a travertine top, set up on an Iranian rug woven in the walled-garden pattern. The silk and wool looked soft and worn, the rose and pale green dyes muted by age. I was relieved not to see any Tarot cards or crystal balls. For five grand, I expected more than kitsch clichés.

She pointed at the fabric over my shoulder and held out a palm. I pulled the cloth off and handed it to her. She ran her fingers along the inside to the hidden zipper. When she found the pocket empty, she looked up sharply, eyes narrowed.

Ah, of course. The money. I reached inside my shirt and pulled out the taped envelope. She nodded curtly and said, "Excuse me for a moment." Then she went out . . . to count the cash, presumably.

When she returned she presented me with a large elegant leather-bound menu. "Everything is in order now. Let's begin."

With . . . food? I gave her a look as if to say, *I don't normally eat at this time of night.*

"If you don't see exactly what you want, simply write it in." She slid a tortoise shell Mont Blanc pen across the table.

"But for when? Surely not tonight."

"Certainly not. I'll need at least a few days notice to prepare. Depending of course on your requests."

Had I really just purchased a catered affair? Plenty of great dishes were listed on the menu. I checked all my favorites: Lobster bisque, Waldorf salad, Kobe Filet Mignon, baked sweet potato, grilled asparagus, and white corn-on-the-cob. Then a thought struck me. I looked up at her. "How many will be coming to this shindig?"

"Oh, just you, my dear." Those long fingers circled and fluttered in an old-fashioned, feminine way. It was fun seeing this coy, flirtatious other side. "Please continue."

I added Lobster Mac-and-Cheese, pumpkin pie, dark chocolate truffles, and . . . oh, what the heck . . . S'mores. I'd never be able to consume all this, but I was determined to get my money's worth.

I turned the page and discovered a roster of fine wines. I circled the perfect vintage for each course. The next page listed favorite music choices, both by artists and titles. The following page offered pre-and post-dinner activities: meditation, hot stone massage, Hatha or Kundalini yoga, and more. I was tempted to write in *Celebrity Orgasm with Ashton Kutcher*, but somehow it didn't seem to go with the rest of the menu.

Next, the offerings of after-dinner drinks. Then came smokes of every imaginable kind: from Cuban Romeo y Julietas to medicinal marijuana to more illegal substances. The next page mentioned after-dinner dancing.

"Oh, but with whom?" I asked, smiling.

She didn't respond but both eyebrows rose.

"Will I have the pleasure of dancing with you?"

There was warmth in her eyes I hadn't noticed before. She laughed and ran a finger down the checklist to help find my ideal partner. Can you guess whose name was listed? When I circled *Ashton*, she didn't bat an eye. The head of the Night Bazaar clearly understood the power of synergy.

Next came Live Solo Performance. I was to choose a singer or an instrumentalist. All the names looked tantalizingly familiar. "How in the world do you do all this for five grand?"

She frowned. "I don't. That is merely the deposit."

"Oh," I murmured, thinking, *What!* "And can you tell me the balance I'll owe on the day of the event?"

She shrugged. "Ten more."

I wanted to scream, *Are you freaking kidding me! A 15K catered affair for one?* Surely I was missing something here. But when she eyed the menu again sternly, I obediently turned the page.

Ah. Finally. There it was, in the not-so-fine print: Cremated or Buried? Open or Closed Casket? Public or Private Viewing? Religious or Secular? Next came a full page of memorial service choices. One could request a Facebook announcement and informative posts on any other social media. A video or slideshow could be created and uploaded. Not only those arrangements, but also options for shutting down utilities, closing all financial accounts, execution of a last will and testament, the careful boxing up of all personal effects, payment of bequests and charitable donations or personal mailings, death certificates, announcement cards—my God, there wasn't a single post mortem detail omitted.

I was speechless. My throat was so dry it clicked when I swallowed. I wiped sweaty palms down my slacks and tried to ask if she was kidding. But I couldn't talk because my stomach was actually quivering. I looked around surreptitiously for the exit point in the drapes. Though by then I felt so turned around I had no idea in which direction I ought to run.

Vera set a chilled water bottle in front of me, and a moist towelette packet. I downed half the bottle and wiped my face with the mint-scented towelette while she waited.

At last she broke the silence. "No worries, my dear. After all, you're still alive, no? So don't concern yourself about when. Just think about how."

I shrugged. This was what I'd wanted for so long. Yet I had no idea.

"Hmm. Well, let's start with . . ." She stopped a moment to study me.

The suspense was about to kill me without any additional charge. "Yes, with what?"

"With or without pain?" The level gaze said she wasn't teasing.

"That's an easy one. I tend to be old-fashioned when it comes to dying. How about in my sleep?"

"Ah, like my dearly departed husband, God rest his soul. I can do that."

"And I wouldn't want it to be thought I'd committed suicide."

Her expression shifted, as if she'd taken offense at some slur on her talents. She tapped the book to indicate I should turn to the last page.

There they were, the Final Choices: Heart Attack, Brain Aneurism, Stroke, Accident? Then: while Sleeping, Working, Dancing, Following an Important Event?

"It's up to you, sweet bird. The goodbye celebration is all about choices. Including the when. So which do you choose?"

I took a deep breath and looked down at my menu again.

***

When I finally got home it was just after 5:30 A.M. I checked Facebook to see if Monique had responded to my last message.

I felt disappointed to see that she hadn't.

I sent another message, inviting her to visit next Sunday. I proposed brunch and a matinee of an Off-Broadway play. I could envision us getting together once a month. I hoped my newfound enthusiasm wouldn't put her off.

I awoke in the early afternoon. Still no reply from Monique. I sent another message. *Maybe you prefer a foreign film to a play? Or perhaps a Broadway musical? Something serious or silly? Your choice! Hope to see you soon.*

I wondered where in the process with Vera she was. Just because she'd acquired a way out didn't mean she had to act on it. Like insurance. A plan purchased for peace of mind. One that need never be redeemed.

At work, I kept busy for a couple days catching up on orders, then made arrangements to scout an important estate sale in Savannah. I even contemplated a side visit to Princeton. Not exactly on the way, of course. Not even the same direction on the compass. Worse yet, I didn't want to cause a scene. I could hear Monique saying, *How dare you! Who do you think you are? My life is none of your business.*

And she'd be right, too. For all I knew, she was terminally ill and trying to say goodbye as gracefully as possible. Who was I to interfere? But for the first time in this century, I really wanted to give of myself. To be a good friend to someone.

***

"Goodbye," Jeff's voice whispered.

I opened my eyes and found myself sitting against his tree. Why were his haunting words always so final? Why not just *goodnight* or *till later*?

"I'm sick of your goodbyes!" I hadn't meant to snap at his spirit, to push away his benevolent energy, but enough was enough. "Please, Jeff, not goodbye. *Goodnight*."

I returned upstairs. When I climbed into bed, I still had no idea whether or not I would be meeting Monique this Sunday. Couldn't she simply respond with a curt yes or no? I used to be busy, too, but could always manage to RSVP to an invitation.

In the morning, dressed and ready for work, I clicked onto Facebook. A youthful photo of Monique complete with winning smile had posted to my News Feed. I clicked on the image and a slideshow began. The header scrolled. IN MEMORY OF MONIQUE THORPES, 1965-2016. A quiet Philip Glass piece accompanied a few dozen photos.

I fell back into my desk chair and muttered, "No."

I watched it again.

And then again.

From the comments posted, no one had seen this coming. A niece commented, *Aunt Monique passed peacefully in her sleep. God must've had urgent plans for her, to take my auntie at 51 years young.* Many more grieving, loving comments followed. Out of 117 Facebook friends, I seemed to have been the only one who knew the truth about her sudden demise.

I kept wondering what she'd chosen for her final evening. I reached for the strip of fabric Vera had returned to me and wrapped it around my neck several times, exactly as Monique had worn it.

Suddenly I craved a Mimosa. I went into the kitchen to see if I had the OJ. What was missing, of course, was the champagne. How could one crave a drink so badly after sixteen years of sobriety? Yet I felt certain I could survive it once without falling off the wagon. I wanted to toast Monique. To hold up a glass of Veuve Clicquot and drink to her life. A celebration. Two or three toasts at most. Even if I drank all morning long, the entire godforsaken bottle, didn't she deserve the attention?

The focus? The apology? Because somehow I had failed her. I'd tried to show her someone cared. But too late. Far too late.

"God damn it!" I snatched up a Majolica ashtray and flung it at the wall. It shattered with a satisfying crash. The thing hadn't been used since I'd gone clean and sober to mark the millennium, anyhow.

I took a deep breath and acknowledged the truth: Every single day I craved a drink. But I'd always been able to resist temptation before. I undressed and got back in bed. If I went out, it would be too easy to walk into a bar. To toast Monique's life. To admit how jealous I was of her, that she'd gotten up the nerve to check out. On her own terms. To finally be the one to say goodbye.

"Goodbye," Jeff whispered.

"Yes, damn it, goodbye," I yelled. "You got to leave early, too. How nice for you both." I squeezed the pillow over my head. So sick and tired of hearing his smug, endless farewells. "Jesus, Jeff," I mumbled into the memory foam pillow. "Walk into the light. Move on. Stop torturing me!"

And then a new thought came to mind. I sat up and gasped, tearing the strip of material from around my neck, staring at it as if for the very first time. My body bounded out of bed with purpose, almost with a mind of its own. I rushed to the hall closet and started pulling things out: boxes, boots, storage containers. Even as I wondered what I was looking for, I was unbolting the front door and just noticing the shovel clutched in one hand. My eyes acknowledging that, yes, I was still only wearing my underclothes. Rushing down the stairs and wondering, *Where am I going?*

Bracing one bare sole, I jammed the blade of the shovel into the dirt. Still trying to figure out why I was digging frantically in the back garden, prying up the sod in front of Jeff's tree, stepping on that blade over and over, going deeper, scooping up more and more dirt. Digging as if that lone gasp had filled me with the energy to work faster than I could mentally keep up with. Sweating, throwing clods left and right, a few feet down hitting something. Dropping to my knees, digging madly with bare hands, clawing up the dirt surrounding the urn. Forcing my fingernails down along its edges until I was able to lift it out.

The rose marble was just as it had looked when the urn was handed to me at the funeral home, wrapped with a length of cloth. As I swatted the dirt away, I remembered thinking, *How classy to present it wrapped up with fabric instead of in a plain cardboard box.* I'd never questioned that, or unwrapped it, as if this were the way all cremation urns were presented. I'd buried it whole, and planted Jeff's memorial tree nearby.

With the urn cradled in my lap, I pulled the fabric from around it. The cloth was frail, the colors faded with time, damp from the buried earth. I stood and let it unreel, falling open to the ground, knowing what I would find. The same fabric that had draped Vera's booth. The same that had made up Monique's scarf.

I squeezed the material from one end to the other. When I felt the length of the hidden zipper, paper crinkled inside. My knees buckled and I landed on them in the dirt. I slipped out a folded piece of paper. It shook with the trembling of my hands. The writing was Jeff's; I'd recognize his elegant scrawl anywhere.

So he hadn't passed from a heart attack brought on by exertion. His supposed addiction to running was a ruse. He was sick, HIV positive, which had meant a fast and ugly demise back in the 1980s. The bruise I'd discovered on his back one morning as he toweled off after a shower? It wasn't from ducking underneath a tree branch on an earlier run, as he'd told me. The night sweats were not from a bout of flu. The sore in his mouth not a burn from too-hot soup. His digestive problems were not a new sensitivity to garlic. The purple scab on his leg wasn't the result of tripping while running, but Kaposi's Sarcoma.

I'd wanted to believe those lies.

Back then, too many of our friends had collapsed. Endless hospital visits became our daily routine, along with constant, vigorous hand washing. And spoon-feeding, bathing, cooling down, warming up, shopping, cooking, cleaning, calling more friends, cajoling families to visit before it was too late, organizing another funeral, another memorial service, packing up possessions, clearing away another life—what could his letter tell me now that I hadn't already known?

How much ugliness and death can one endure? his note declared.

Of course. Had he wanted to spare me going through it all yet again?

Yes. Jeff had been saving me.

If things were reversed, I knew I couldn't emotionally survive. I would weep for you for endless years to come.

As I have done, anyway, despite his efforts.

Goodbye.

There it was. That first "goodbye." The one I'd been hearing for twenty-seven years. Now the meaning was clear. It had always been a last, literal farewell.

With one email to Vera I could say goodbye, too. And then . . . my oh my, what an evening would ensue. What power. To be one who gets to say goodbye. To finally *end* all the goodbyes, forever.

I knelt there in the dirt for an eternity, though it might have been only minutes. Until at last my head seemed clear. Until the heaviness of despair lifted. Evaporated like sun-struck mist.

"But not yet," I said aloud, without planning to. "Not yet."

I reburied Jeff's urn. Then returned upstairs to shower and dress. At todaytix.com I purchased an orchestra seat for the Broadway musical *An American in Paris*. Next, I opened an account with OkCupid. After creating a profile and answering dozens of questions, I felt ready to meet whoever my answers might attract. The hope of new friends and, perhaps even dating again, if I was lucky, made me notice the grim aubergine walls in the foyer. Way too dark for greeting a guest. I needed a quick trip to MOMA, where I always used to discover new ideas, new designs and colors for redecorating. Why not go right now?

As I passed the mailboxes at the front entrance to the brownstone, I stopped to stare at the label with Jeff's name. It had remained there above mine all these years, a reminder of what I'd lost. I'd never been able to remove it, and let him go. But now, in one fell swoop, I reached out and peeled off the curling, faded sticker above mine.

Finally, it was time. I was the one who had to say it out loud.

"Goodbye," I whispered.

A few aisles over stands one of our most popular booths: The Vanishing Hat: A Realm of Famous, Infamous, and Unheard-Of Magick. Here the aficionado, the professional, and the novice may find all the tools, implements, trappings, props, and costumes ever dreamed of by the conjurer. Also quaint souvenirs of shocking and as-yet unheard-of crimes and disappearances. On the front shelf sits Ambrose Bierce's cane and top hat, found in a dusty little cantina many years ago in Mexico. Below it is Amelia Earhart's favorite pilot cap.

And below that, a deck of Bicycle playing cards, complete save for the nine of hearts. Unmarked except for a small spot of what might be either dried blood, or beef gravy. Innocuous looking, yes, but this deck is connected to a strange disappearance which occurred in this very city, not long ago. . . .

FULL MOON SHIFT

Roy Graham

A full moon shift at Grimmanti's Bar and Restaurant begins like this. At midnight, we unbolt the carved Nordic oak door and welcome our first customers down the narrow stairwell. You are most likely not one of our customers unless you're the sort to wear an onyx mask to dinner, paint your hands bright red, or regularly spend two hundred dollars on a meal for one. If you were, though, you would pass through the cramped foyer to see our restaurant open like the main chamber of a colossal cave, tables covered in black cloth, set with wide ivory plates and solid silver cutlery as far as the eye can see, the bar stretching infinitely East and West and the high ceiling invisible—the meager candles and oil lamps are unable to penetrate the darkness, which rises like heat.

I, Armando Maldonado de Torres, am one of the proud servers at Grimmanti's. If we are doing our jobs well, you will seldom see us. We will appear to greet you, take your order and ask if you would like us to grind salt or pepper onto the plate. You will not see us bring your food or the check. These things will simply appear in front of you, a wonderful surprise punctuating the end of a perfect cocktail or a particularly amusing dinner story.

To work this sort of magic requires an excellent sense of timing, a Houdini-like capacity to wield misdirection in one's favor, and a general aura of nobodyness, the ability to become an unimportant though mobile part of the background. Many of us unwittingly trained for years to gain such abilities.

If you are very lucky, our proprietor—not the eponymous Grimmanti, who died twenty-four years ago on his one hundredth birthday, but Jove, his one-time apprentice—may visit your table himself. He will flash a silver smile to rival the knives and ask about the tenderness of the meat, the vintage of the wine, the agility of his waiters. Jove is lord and master of this place, you will come to understand, though he has chosen most magnanimously to break bread with you this evening.

The food will be excellent, of course, but there are many places one can get excellent food in New York City. What you are paying for here is an experience: a sly stirring in darkness, at the edge of your vision. The music playing from invisible speakers that recalls your childhood home. The faint smell of ozone, and the prickling rise of neck hair, as if every patron of Grimmanti's were on the verge of being struck by lightning and reduced to ash.

Tonight, though, is a full moon shift, and though I know I'll make out like a bandit in tips, I'm also scared. These shifts happen, predictably, once a month, thanks to a particular quirk or superstition of our manager, a redheaded Northern California transplant everyone calls Rooibos. She writes out our schedules by phases of the moon. I normally work First Quarter to Full Moon, with a break over Waning Gibbous and then back for Last Quarter. Nobody knows why she does it this way. Or maybe everyone does, and it's just too late for me to ask. I think it has something to do with her belief in shamanism and elemental spirits, but it could be merely a standardizing system, like military time.

Full moons aren't just the busiest shifts to work, they're also the weirdest. Last month, Primo the chef was pouring a chipotle glaze onto a rack of lamb when he dropped the bottle. It shattered on the tiles, and the dark, pungent sauce splayed out in an anatomically-accurate rendering of a human skull.

"¡Mierda!" he shouted, leaping away from the spill and crossing himself. "¡Ahora voy a maldecido por semanas!"

I grabbed a rag to be helpful, but when I reached toward the spill Primo smacked the back of my hand with a wooden spoon.

"Ow! What the hell?" I cried, cradling the smarting hand.

He started pouring salt from a three pound Morton's box in a circle around the chipotle skull. "Steamed mussels for table seven." He jerked his head at a plate next to me. "Getting cold, idiot!"

So tonight will again be the sort of shift where anything might happen. By ten business is still relatively slow, only the inner tables occupied. My head is beginning to droop; I haven't gotten much sleep lately. When Rooibos taps my shoulder I actually jump, smashing my hip on a bar stool. I should have gotten used to this by now. She's always silent as a ghost, as if her relentless yoga-rattery and gluten-free veganism have let her transcend the clumsy human form altogether.

"Armando, please calm down," she says. "You're scaring the customers."

"I don't think that's possible."

She ignores that and hands me a small black flashlight. The metal cylinder is cool. LEDs sit under the lens like Swarovski crystals. I accidentally click a rubber-covered switch on the back and the laser-bright beam shoots up to blind me.

When my night vision comes back, Rooibos is giving me a disapproving look. "I would save that, Armando. In case, you know, you need it."

"What's it for?" True, Grimmanti's is always deep in darkness, the staff swimming through it. Even the glow of my cell phone seems diminished here, as if cowed by the great umbral presence. It would've made sense to be given this light five months ago. Instead I was left to bumble through the gloom, like a crab at the Abyssal layer of the ocean. By now I've gotten used to it.

"Keep your voice down, but, like . . . there's something in the walls tonight."

"Oh." I stifle a yawn, the curse of the graveyard shift. "A rat-kind of thing?"

She tilts her head and looks thoughtful. "Hmm. No. Probably bigger."

I stifle a second yawn, but feel uneasy. "By what margin exactly?"

Rooibos shrugs. That's disconcerting; she usually has an answer to newbie queries. "Just shine that thing around during any off-time you have tonight," she says. "In between taking care of tables, of course."

"Just shine it around like, what, a cat burgler?"

"To break up the really dark spots. Jove says it's fond of darkness. Whatever's in the walls, I mean. Okay? Great. I knew you'd help out."

"I still feel very unprepared for this whatever-it— " I start to protest, but she's already gone. So I slip the flashlight into the pocket of my black slacks, next to my favorite deck of cards.

* * *

Unlike some of our staff, I was not raised behind the bar or in the kitchen here at Grimmanti's. I had merely responded to a job ad on Craigslist.

SERVER NEEDED!!!
MUST BE WILLING TO WORK VERY LATE NIGHTS.
AT LEAST TWO YEARS NYC RESTAURANT EXPERIENCE REQUIRED.

True, wait staff in the City wasn't exactly on my list of qualifications, since I'd arrived here only recently, but I had by then discovered resumes are merely ink on paper, formed into words that can say anything you want them to. For safety's sake I located my fictional cuisine alma mater, Los Tacos de los Lobos, deep in Spanish Queens to discourage actual investigation.

I was late for my interview by half an hour, though not due to laziness or poor planning. Those are cardinal sins for an aspiring stage magician. I'd flogged those traits out of myself long ago.

My first problem had been that Grimmanti's Bar and Restaurant didn't have a street address. It was seated somewhere in the wild brick yonder of Alphabet City, where gradually the numbers diminish like endangered species, and you begin to find 701 somehow following 344 seven blocks later. I had been emailed a set of old-fashioned directions which read like advice for finding some back-country yard sale.

Left at the bent stop sign. Right at the dinosaur graffiti. Stay the course past the abandoned cupcake shop. When you smell the East River, turn all the way around and walk fifty more paces.

And so on.

Grimmanti's had no awning or sign, just a heavy, narrow oaken door set like a worn filling between an auto repair shop and a smoothie bar. Both were closed, of course, since it was two in the morning. The email had said the owner wanted to see me during the hours I would actually be working. That an afternoon interview would be a poor representation of what I might be like if hired.

I opened the door to see a staircase descending, lit by one dim light bulb hanging from the ceiling of the landing like the lure of some blind deep-sea fish. Beyond the foyer, the restaurant was emptier than I would ever see it again. Later I suspected it had been cleared out specially for the interview, which is a confusing and horrifying thing for a New York restaurant owner to do.

"You're thirty-three minutes late, son," said a voice devastated by cigarettes, or maybe Southern California forest fires. It had come from the farthest-most table of the three dozen filling the restaurant's main antechamber. "Do you think that bodes well for your employment?"

All things considered, the comment seemed unfair. I'd left my diminutive apartment in Harlem with two hours to spare. At one point in the directions given me, I had to take a taxi three blocks, tell the driver my worst fear, then tip him with a photograph of me taken on my seventh birthday. I was two months behind on rent, though. If I didn't get a job in the next several days and pay what was owed I was going to be evicted, so I was willing to jump through a lot of hoops just then.

"It took a while to find the place. Sorry," I mumbled.

He grinned unexpectedly. "Yes, it is rather difficult the first time. But the trip gets easier, don't worry. Please, have a seat."

I sat down across from him. The lights seemed too low, especially in the corners of the room, and as far as I could tell there were only three present: me, my interviewer, and a shadowed figure behind the bar doing something possibly alchemical involving hand-blown bottles of various colors, shapes, and sizes.

Even after I sat down the interviewer appeared a head shorter than me, yet gave every impression of a gigantic individual, as if everyone had always been too polite or scared to tell him otherwise. He carried himself like a supernova on the verge of exploding and taking out the whole star system with him. His name, I would learn later, was Jove. Nobody would ever tell me whether it was first or surname.

"So, Armando. Why do you want to work at my restaurant?"

Well, that was easy: I desperately needed money to stay in New York, and I had to remain here if I was to ascend to my destiny on the world stage. I'd already conquered the infantile performing magician's scene in the most illustrious societies of New Mexico. To sharpen my skills, I needed to surround myself with real magicians. The elite illusion-jockeys of New York City brooked no comparisons, outside of Vegas and maybe a couple people in LA.

I didn't say any of that to him, though. Obviously. "Because it's an institution, sir. One I have often admired from afar. The grandeur—"

He held up a hand. "Please cut the bullshit. My time on this Earth is preciously short. You'd never heard of Grimmanti's before you sent your application—which, by the way, was falsified with great care and enthusiasm, and for that I applaud you. Now, what is it you really want to do? Few young people intend to wait tables their whole lives."

Overly cynical, shockingly perceptive, or maybe just a standard speech? I had no way of knowing. But I decided the best course of action with an omniscient entity was total honesty. "I want to be a magician."

He snorted. "What, like Aleister Crowley?"

"No. Like David Copperfield."

He spread one palm in generous acquiescence. "Okay, son. Let's see some magic."

I remember waiting to see if he was kidding. He was not. Jove, I would come to learn, rarely joked about anything.

Fixed by those penetrating blue eyes, I'd already gotten the impression he would be difficult to misdirect. Quickly I inventoried the materials at hand. A candle on the table. Some change in my pocket. And a single card. "Deepest apologies, sir, but I can't do my finest trick without cards."

Like a magician himself, with a flourish Jove produced a fresh pack, still wrapped in plastic, from under the table. Weird. They were blue Bicycles. Standard deck, thank goodness.

I unwrapped the pack and did some tricky shuffles. Basic stuff for any card shark, but it bought me time to force the nine of hearts to the top with a few careful cuts. I held out the deck and Jove took the top card. "Don't show it to me," I said. "Burn it."

I pushed the lit candle on the table towards him. Without hesitating, he dipped one corner of the card into the flames. In that moment I planted my own nine of hearts, also from a standard blue-backed Bicycle deck, in the folded cloth napkin on my side of the table.

Yes, I always carry around a duplicate for just such a moment. No, I wasn't expecting to do magic at a job interview, but it never hurts to have one good trick at the ready.

He reached over the table, now covered with oxidized nine of hearts debris, and handed me what was left, a charred corner of card stock, which I put on my tongue like a tab of acid. I pretended to roll it around in my mouth, then unfolded the napkin and spat into it. The trick was technically long since complete, but I wanted to indulge us both.

Finished, I slid the napkin across the table. When he opened it, he smiled. Not with visible surprise, only a look of contentment. "One more question. Can you keep a secret?"

"No man or woman is better at keeping secrets than a trained magician, sir."

"Excellent point. Clean up this ash. You're hired."

Jove made me take an oath of secrecy that very day: Don't tell anyone where you work, bring no one here, don't file taxes. Not unlike the Magician's Oath, the promise already binding me not to reveal the secrets of any illusion to a non-magician. I was an experienced oath-taker and secret-keeper before I'd found Grimmanti's.

Now, as customers filter in, I work the eastern half. Junebug, the other server, takes the western. My first table is a two top. A woman in white with a man in dark suit. He says, "We'll have the three course meal." That was a relic of an old menu that no longer existed, well before my time.

"I'm sorry, sir, but we no longer offer the three course option." I have no idea what it once consisted of, but I get at least one order for it per shift, and always sense relief from Primo that he no longer has to prepare it.

My diner clicks his teeth in distaste. They appear a little too sharp and numerous. "A simple beef steak for two will suffice, then. Bloody and rare. Very rare."

"Of course, sir." I nod as I jot it down. "And would you like something to drink with that?"

The woman with him, who's wearing what looks like a torn antique satin and lace wedding gown, languorously assures me, "The barman will know our order, my dear, as he always has done, as he always will."

"Very well, then."

I move to the next table, snapping my light on and shining it surreptitiously at the inkiest corners whenever a portion looks too . . . sheltering. The occasional blue-white flare in the dark tells me Junebug is also breaking up the darker parts of the room in between her tables.

Our job, a smoking habit I stole, and maybe the shared camaraderie of the constantly endangered, are the only things she and I have in common. She swims calmly as a tiger shark through the reef of tables, moving with predatory certainty. I bump into people, tables, dense patches of air. If one of us finds whatever is in the walls, I do hope it's Junebug. Not out of pure selfishness or raw fear, but because I genuinely believe more in her ability to slay monsters than in my own.

The first month here, I hid my sleight of hand practice from her. Coins I'd vaporize and then make tangible again would vanish back into the tip jar. Whole decks of cards shot up my sleeves if she turned my way. But I don't do magic at work anymore. It seems less impressive now.

We meet back at the fire escape after an hour or so and climb outside. It's winter in the foreign kingdom of Alphabet City, and as usual Manhattan's snowplows have not touched the nameless side street Grimmanti's sits on.

Junebug offers a cigarette and I produce a light with a little flourish. Old habit. In our work shirts, thin black button-ups, we have about the time it takes to smoke two-thirds of our Marlboros before hypothermia sets in.

Junebug taught me how to survive my first shift: which customers to look in the eye, which to only speak to in a whisper. Safe places to check your phone where Jove, Rooibos or something much worse will not find you. How cigarette breaks were mandated by the unwritten restaurateur's code, and a great excuse to get some breathing room, even if those breaths were full of nicotine and tar.

Across the street, at the 24-hour diner, a spindly kid drags a bucket of mop water out the door and tips it into the street. Hot gray streams course out, carving creeks through the iced-over street, steam rising off the union in great waves.

Between drags Junebug glances over at me. "You keep rubbing your eyes."

"I haven't been sleeping well."

"Late shifts tend to do that. Rooibos told you about the flashlight thing?"

"Yes. She did."

She shook her head. "This place is so fucked. I never had to worry about shit like that when I worked for the Cuban bistro."

"I thought you liked it here."

She shrugs. "At first. Now I'm looking for something else. Stay anywhere long enough, you get tired. The same old shit every night. Feel like I've been here a hundred years, you know?"

***

These days my airport farewell to sister, mother and father (the latter the only one who was crying) felt as if it had taken place in a parallel dimension. The eldest son embarking to meet his destiny in New York City, home of Copperfield, Blaine, the legendary Houdini. So it was goodbye to red mesas at sundown, to our nice two-story home in Portales, New Mexico. Goodbye to the happy coughs of hot, dusty summers.

With my savings, matched by my family in a tremendous display of faith and generosity, I put down a deposit on an apartment in a corner of Harlem where people sold mangos heaped on cardboard boxes on the street. I didn't venture farther than the end of my block for almost a week. At first, homesickness and fear kept me inside. Then real sickness, and a sharper, less-wistful kind of terror. I'd apparently picked up a cocktail of pathogens from the plane trip. Fever hit with the mercilessness of an extinction event, like a dinosaur-killing comet. For days I shivered uncontrollably under a blanket, huddled flush against the dirty radiator despite the early October warmth. I practiced lifts from a deck of cards when I had the strength. Sleeping day and night, imagining I was dying. Wondering how long it would take anyone to discover my body in this Marianas Trench of humanity, a high-density zone of life and death in which I was an undetectable hiccup.

Days later, feeling better, I found half a loaf of bread in my fridge. Over a plate piled high with dry toast, I read a letter which had appeared in my mailbox some time during the fever.

An invitation to the Harlem Shadow Society, a collection of local illusionists boasting alumni as renowned as William Caligrio and Brother George Malcolm. No petty tricksters these, but real artists of the craft. Leon Severino, my master magician and instructor, had recommended me for membership. I burst into tears. Who would have guessed that the owner of El Humo y Espero had such connections?

I was still a bit fever-mad during my entrance audition three days later with the Shadow Society. Which only strengthened my performance. Deftly, my trained fingers acted on memory—the flourishes, reversals and forces, the deck scything through the air, rippling like water—while I stared in rube-like amazement at my own tricks, like a spellbound child. They accepted me as an initiate on the spot, with full access to their tomes of knowledge, their combustible colored powders, their collected decades of experience.

Full dues, too. Payable by cash or money order only.

***

Though there are no windows here, the full moon is now dead center over the restaurant. I feel it like a change in altitude. Things have gotten odder. For example, my second table pays with a little heap of what looks like pirate doubloons. I jangle the large, heavy coins in one hand. A nice weight to them, so if not real gold then an excellent facsimile. I count only five, and have no clue as to denominations, but definitely get the sense change is expected.

I'm about to call Junebug over for advice, but she's busy leading a disoriented woman with mother-of-pearl-colored hair to an empty table. In fact, someone I know, though the last time I saw her was in the full light of day, and the hair was then snow-cone blue.

Marienne Dumont Archibeque, if that's her real name, is an odd one even by Shadow Society standards. She believes herself a reincarnation of both a Mesopotamian queen and a Roman general. She studies stage magic, though not out of any desire to perform. "So I can recognize trickery and distinguish it from true sorcery," she once told me.

She turns and spots me, blinking drowsily, and shrugs up around her shoulders a fur coat that would be the envy of any Inuit. She's teetering on silver stilettos. "Ye gods, Armando? I can't believe my eyes!"

"Hey, Marienne."

She reaches out and touches my face. As if to confirm I'm real, not some sly illusion.

I lean away. "Uh, how are you?"

"Never mind me! What about you? Where have you been all this time?"

"Oh. Well, I guess it's been a little while since I've stopped by the Society."

"A little while? The elder magicians nearly voted to write your name out of the Book of Shadows. They thought you were dead!"

"What! Didn't anyone stop them?"

"Oh, Armando, none of us could stop those dinosaurs from doing anything. The Society's theirs. You know how it is." She looks down at the tablecloth, as if embarrassment has pierced her fog of . . . whatever. "Besides, the rest of us thought you weren't coming back, either. It's been so long." She trails off, then zips back hopefully. "But they haven't done it yet! All you need to do is attend a Shadowmoot before they pull the trigger."

Indignation wells like bile in my mouth. "They were going to kick me out for missing a few meetings? People have lives to live and bills to pay!" Not the least of them the Society's own exorbitant dues.

Marienne leans forward. "Oh, not me. I'm so glad you're alive, Armando. The only person in my echelon I really liked. The rest were all stuck up. You, though, so humble! And for one so young, with such great talent! That entrance exam, your take on Fearson's Aces . . . I've never seen a more brilliant interpretation of that trick. Cross my heart."

She's rambling now. Even so, that takes the rug out from under me. Marienne was one of the judges during my exam. My bitterness of a moment ago now seems petty, childish. Stupid tears well up behind my eyes. "Um," I say, wiping them away as discreetly as possible, "Darn the smoke in here. Do you want to order something?"

***

In the kitchen I pass her order to Primo. "Gnocchi with pesto."

He frowns. "How did she get in here?"

I shrug. "Who knows. Maybe an accident? She seemed clueless." Though it's pretty much impossible to stumble accidentally on this place. She acted as if she'd been drawn in by some gravitational force. "Maybe to talk to me. Not that I invited her."

Primo isn't listening. He's muttering and cursing, trying to rehang the door to the meat locker. It appears to have been torn from its hinges by some tremendous force. There's a bloody smear on the floor that leads from it all the way to the main ventilation shaft.

"A whole side of beef," he mutters, grunting as he hoists the door into place again.

When I finger the flashlight in my pocket, my sweaty fingers stick to it. "Man, the health department is going to hate that. Primo, um, listen. Do you ever hear anything in the walls? Like, something really big."

He slots the bolt into the door hinge and bangs it a couple times with the tenderizing hammer. Then wipes his sweaty mustache and at last turns back to me. "Gnocchi with pesto, you say?"

***

Waiting to pick up the order I flip through the clipboard hung near Jove's office door and check the hours on my timesheet. Marienne said it's been months since I last attended a Shadowmoot, but that can't be right. Is Grimmanti's, on top of strangeness after strangeness, now stealing time from me as well? Stretching my days and hours like in the old Irish fairy stories? As if one day in the restaurant equals a hundred on the outside.

There's no dilation of time evidenced in my notes, though. Just three months of work between now and my last time off to go to the Society, or really to interact with any other human beings at all, for that matter.

Initially I'd liked that Grimmanti's seemed a sort of pocket dimension, outside of time and space. It felt appropriate for a magician. Lately, though, I've been too exhausted to seek gigs at birthdays and bar mitzvahs. In my dreams I no longer fly nor go on strange adventures. Instead I repeat the same figure eight through my tables, serving hunched, faceless things. I wake in the late afternoon, and barely practice anymore. I spend my days off sleeping, eating, building myself back up for the next shift. Grimmanti's is not a job but a vortex, a great black hole sucking my life into its lightless depths, to be compacted into a single atom of purpose that is not my own.

I knew then I had to escape. But Jove probably would not take my resignation well.

Just then, like a demon invoked by the thought of his name, he enters the kitchen behind me. I know by the way the door practically explodes inward. Primo busies himself more fervently boiling gnocchi. But I turn to face the boss, who in a tailcoat tuxedo (it is a Saturday night and he is exceedingly traditional) looks like a prohibition gangster heading straight from a speakeasy to an escape tunnel to the East River.

He scowls at me. "Armando. You should know I am severely displeased."

I didn't. But experience tells me to wait for the details before speaking.

"I was very clear when I hired you. I said under no circumstances tell anyone about this restaurant or share directions. You weren't even supposed to file taxes. You understood all this."

"Sir, I didn't tell Marienne anything, if that's who you're speaking about."

"Do I look like a holy fool, son? I saw you cavorting at the table. Did you simply want to impress her?"

"No! It's a coincidence. She just walked in."

"We don't have walk-ins. Only regulars." He pinches the bridge of his nose and closes his eyes. "Regardless of *how* she arrived, your friend is too . . . young to be in here."

"Too . . . ? But she's about thirty, I think. Maybe a little older?"

He ignores that. "There will be trouble if she stays too long. Or eats the food. Or wanders off. And I won't be able to stop it. Understand this: your girlfriend's fate is now your responsibility, Armando."

Not my girlfriend, a fellow magician. Of course I don't say this either, but think it mightily. I turn away to leave.

Jove puts a surprisingly gentle hand on my shoulder. "Son, you've got to understand. My customers can't exactly go to Chipotle. There are only so many neighborhood institutions like this left. They expect . . . a place where they can be themselves." He falls silent after that, but still grips my shoulder, so I can't leave.

"Sir?"

"The world's getting smaller. The darker corners all being rounded off." He sighs. "All I know is, they deserve to be served well, somewhere."

Back on the floor the murmurs of the early crowd have lycanthropically shifted to the hoots and howls, the braying and laughter of full mooners. My tables are all very hungry tonight. I feel eyes on me as I weave through, blue and brown and black and gold, many luminous in the dark, but I hurry by without stopping. When I get to Marienne's spot, she is gone.

Junebug is ping-ponging between tables, collecting orders and delivering drinks from the bar: tall smoking multicolored concoctions, or ancient-looking bottles accompanied by heavy crystal shot glasses. I grab her arm and yell her name, though even I can't hear myself in the din.

She flinches, turns, then recognizes me, all in mute mode.

I move closer until my lips almost touch her ear. "The woman who was sitting here . . .the, uh . . . sorta normal-looking one. Did you see her get up and leave?"

"Oh, her. Yeah. Asked me where the bathroom was," she shouts, then shakes off my hand and sidles past, sliding between two tables to take the order of a third.

She probably heard the fear in my voice, a tightness and quiver common during my training period. I don't blame her for leaving me to solve my own problem, though. I only feel sorry for making her have to take over the eastern half of the dining room, too.

***

When I reach the back of Grimmanti's it's even darker there now than earlier. I've never been inside the women's restroom, of course. The first time I went looking for the men's I got lost for an hour and wet my pants. Since then I usually dash out to pee at the diner across the street. It's much quicker.

I click on the smooth black flashlight, remembering Rooibos' warning, and swipe its beam around randomly, carving swathes of visibility into the shadowed halls and ink-black corners. The walls back here are unpainted plaster, the color and texture of curdling cream.

Somewhere behind me the muted, mingled roar of Jove's midnight patrons is reaching a howling apex. What's really troubling me, though, is much closer. Something is rattling and banging at the floorboards underneath my feet. Steam pipes, maybe, or a subway train passing. Or a monster struggling to break through planks and plaster. Nothing here can be deflected with the nine of hearts in my pocket. It's hard to misdirect an audience you can't see.

And frankly nor do I want to see even a slice of it illuminated in the thin beam of my pitifully small flashlight.

I'm still pretty sure I can find my way back to the floor to save Junebug from the wrath of my hungry customers, and maybe even keep my job. I like Marienne, but we've met only a few times, months ago. She isn't family, and more acquaintance than friend. I suppose I press forward anyhow because just by coming in here she reminded me of what I had once known through to my DNA: I am not a waiter. I was meant to stand on a larger stage, before the world. Or at the very least the MGM Grand in sunny Las Vegas.

I follow an impossible number of turns, sliding a hand along the uneven left wall the way one might do if trapped in a labyrinth. Though I don't like to think too much about that old story right now. Labyrinths have blind corners and minotaurs. It's all too easy to picture some muscular claw bursting forth from the plaster and grabbing wrist or ankle . . . but so far so good. I turn a corner I don't remember and see, miraculously, a door with a flat slice of golden light spilling from underneath, marked with a large female symbol. At the same time, the subterranean rumbling and thumping increases until the fillings in my teeth are shaking.

I take off running, seeking the cover of the ladies' room, hoping to the Holy Ghost that Marienne is there. That the monster in the walls is not only old-fashioned but also a gentleman. I wave the flashlight wildly behind me, running full-tilt through darkness. The whole dining room out front is screaming with rage or thwarted hunger as I slam into the door and tumble though.

Back out onto the main floor of the restaurant. I've somehow gone in a wide, endless loop. And though I'd expected the floor to be ugly chaos without me on duty, things seem fine. In fact oddly celebratory. All the patrons are banging on the tables with fists or spoons or glasses, excitedly and in unison, chanting a name again and again.

It must be someone's birthday.

But when I listen a little closer, they aren't chanting a name. Instead, in unison, they're all screaming out an order.

"Three Course Meal!"

"*Three Course Meal*!"

"THREE COURSE MEAL!"

In the dimness, over various cheering, howling and snarling forms, I see a flash of opalescent hair and gasp. It's Marienne, eyes closed, suspended limply in the air above a table cleared of dinnerware. The pale woman in the ripped antique wedding dress stands atop it, along with her dinner companion, the dark-suited man with too many teeth. He's tucked a cloth napkin into his collar as a bib. She doesn't seem to worry as much about the state of her dress. Unprotected, it dirties quickly.

After his first bite, the toothy man is pulled off the table by a woman with shiny onyx skin who squirms underneath Marienne to try and catch in her mouth any wayward drips. Then an enormous . . . thing . . . in a tuxedo throws someone over the bar while fighting through the crowd, breaking a whole shelf of bottles all at once. Part of the bartop lights up with a carpet of blue flames. A shelf of expensive liquers explodes, one hand-blown bottle after another.

The light from the fire transforms the scene into a Boschian nightmare. I can only make out brief vignettes and disco-strobe flashes, like flipping through Polaroids printed in Hell. Above it all, Marienne spins slowly above the table like a levitating magician's assistant, a horrifically damaged prop long past living.

But there won't be enough to go around.

The air reeks of sulfur and copper. Someone is laughing shrilly and far too loud. Atop each other the diners climb, ascending a hill of horrors to reach their favorite meal.

Just as my legs give out underneath me, a hand seizes my shoulder. Someone holds me up.

It's Jove. "Armando," he growls, turning me around so I face away from the bloody, frenzied tableau. "Clock out, son. You'd better go home early tonight."

***

Magicians, more than any other professionals, know the potential of the things we possess to disappear. Wallets, keys, board game pieces. Memories, money, people. In 1983, David Copperfield, foremost conjurer of the modern age, made the Statue of Liberty disappear. This is called in the trade a Vanishing. A cage full of doves evaporates into some nether realm, for example, along with gallons of milk poured down stacks and stacks of newspaper. The vanishing of Marienne Dumont Archibeque was significantly less public. Copperfield magicked away the statue in front of a live audience, and he brought it back afterward. But I feel certain my poor colleague from the Shadow Society will not be reappearing any time soon.

Neither will Grimmanti's. At least not for me.

A few weeks after that final shift, I stopped by the place. Or rather, tried to. In the spot where it had always stood there was no tall oaken door. Just a smoothie bar and an auto shop, huddled a few feet closer together than I remembered.

It was late, and dark. I went home as if in a guilt-ridden dream. One from which I suspect I have never quite woken.

* * *

The Shadow Society welcomed me as if I had never left, though, and I've redoubled my practice. I remained silent on where I've been, and what happened, even as the elders crossed Marienne's name from the Book of Shadows, shaking their heads. Lucky for me, magicians can appreciate a secret. My silence is clearly a betrayal, yet I doubt anyone, even the Society, would believe my story.

The strangest thing is, despite it all, I still feel a strange loyalty to Jove and the others. They spent their nights drifting, as I did, through that nether realm of vanished doves and milk: the late shift, the five A.M. subway riders, the ones who leave for work with only the light of the full moon to guide their way.

If you believe clothing makes the person, the Bazaar offers an unending supply of sartorial selves to the Invited. Down the largest aisle, the great broad way of the main concourse, stand most of the clothing booths, tents, and shops. Tables piled with Russian fur hats, Victorian gaiters, Italian countesses' bejeweled purses, handmade Edwardian shoes, like-new hair shirts, and the entire collection of Oscar Wilde's favorite cravats. Or you may peruse racks hung with items like medieval saint's robes, red satin can-can petticoats, Buffalo Bill's own fringed leather coat, and of course the usual pre-distressed designer jeans broken in personally by European supermodels.

On one partition hangs a piece of ordinary-looking formalwear: a man's size 40 tuxedo in fair condition. But I can't really recommend it for a trip to the opera or dinner at the club. Unless your social calendar after that is quite, quite empty. . . .

WHIRL AWAY

Carol MacAllister

After twelve weeks of daytime TV, cheap beer, and generic frozen pizzas, Sammy's stomach gurgled and sloshed like the stagnant water in his clogged kitchen sink. So did his thoughts. How quickly he'd lost his job at the Manhattan ad agency! How lightning-fast his social status had fallen, while his grand lifestyle had plummeted on a greased parallel slope straight to *Pariah*. No one called. No one texted. Former colleagues unfriended him daily on Facebook, at least until he could no longer afford DSL.

"Cripes, I'm forty and already circling the drain," he moaned.

He'd never been big on saving, and there wasn't much to liquate. Long-divorced . . . at least he had no dependents. He'd bought all those bespoke suits and tailored shirts, taken the trips to Cancun. Picked up the tab for expensive drinks in clubs. A severance package kept him afloat the first two months, and now he was drawing New York State unemployment. But there'd soon be an end to that, and then what? The dismal prospect of looking for another job had inspired him to downsize further. He moved from the leased beachside condo to Vagabond's Rest, a motel complex converted to low income housing.

At first he checked the online job sites very morning, only to discover even minimum-wage gigs selling nuts and bolts in hardware stores or flipping burgers were swamped with applications from college grads. Even Walmart had cut back, firing half their elderly front-door greeters.

Gotta do something before I end up living under a bridge like a fucking billy goat. So he went downtown to the federal building and applied for Section 8 housing. He was assigned immediately to a place in The Bronx: The Wayside Boarding House. A rundown brownstone, its most memorable feature was the multi-generational colonies of German cockroaches living in the bathroom down the hall and a pervasive smell of dirty socks. Aside from one geezer who was always parked in front of the common room's TV, the other residents never seemed to emerge from their rooms.

But things did pick up a bit after that. An extension for unemployment came through. and the next day he got an actual call. He shifted his cell phone to the other ear. "Who's this?"

"Ed! Ed Myers from the agency. How you doin', Sammy? Wasn't sure if you kept the same number."

"Yeah. 'Bout the only thing I got left now. What's up?"

"The asshole new owners gave me my walking papers three weeks ago, too. But I got a lead and thought of you. Something that might work for both of us. There's a reception hosted by this start-up media group. Upper Eastside penthouse, Sunday night. I'll text the address."

"Hey, sounds good. Thanks!"

"Some other guys from the agency should be there too. Oh yeah, one more thing. It's formal. You'll need a tux. But hey, you still got that fashionista wardrobe, right? See you then."

Sammy hit END glumly. He'd sold off all the good stuff to raise cash. His formalwear had gone to a trendy consignment shop in Brooklyn. Then again . . . a rental should do. There was a place a couple blocks away. He went that afternoon and put down a deposit on a classic black tuxedo.

Saturday morning he picked it up and with the old spring back in his step returned to his ten by twelve box at The Wayfarer. Unzipping the garment bag felt like opening a gift. That fine tailoring . . . so much like the one he used to own. "Nice!" he told it. "You're gonna get me out of this craphole, if only for the night. But who knows. Better times may lie ahead for us both!"

That evening he buttoned the tiny onyx shirt studs, fastened the black bowtie and gold satin cummerbund, and straightened the suspenders. But when he picked up the jacket something fell out of the pocket. He bent and picked up a business card. Cut from heavy linen cardstock, it had an engraved gold border and an embossed mask in the shape of a quarter moon. COMPLIMENTS OF THE NIGHT BAZAAR, it read in heavy black Old English caps. Scrawled on the reverse in elegant India-ink calligraphy was his own name:

Samuel James Holden, Esq.

As he caressed one edge a tingle shot up his fingers. A sharp electrical pulse snapped them open and the card flew from his hands, turning transparent. He gasped and caught it in mid-air. Suddenly it was solid again.

"What in the Hell!" He tossed it onto the nightstand. Maybe the previous owner had left it when he turned the tux in. But . . . it was *his* name.

Whatever, he decided, and dropped into the old armchair, the only seat in the room. As he sat waiting for his taxi to show, he had time to think. Was this really a good idea? He was no longer part of the old crowd. They knew he'd been let go. What would he say to them now? His stomach knotted. Sweat beaded on his forehead. *I can't face those people. What if they ask where I'm working now, what if . . .*

He snatched up the half-empty bottle of whisky he'd left next to the chair last night, downed a mouthful, then slumped back into the cushions. A taxi horn tooted. Once, twice. Then a third longer, pissed-off blast.

Sammy just sat in his rented tux and took another slug of Old Grandpappy.

A flashing neon sign hung outside his second-story window, advertising *The Whirl Away*, a bar next door. It came on as evening approached. The flickering green and red neon meant to catch the eye of passersby annoyed the hell out of Sammy. Window shades, heavy curtains, a moth-eaten blanket from the bed, nothing ever blocked out its colorful pulsing glare.

Now his drunken stare tried to take in the words. An inner voice kept time as the memorizing strobe repeated, *Whirl Away, Whirl Away, Whirl Away.* The sign sent green and red streaks skirting along the walls and crawling over the ceiling, as if he was caught inside a kid's kaleidoscope. He closed his eyes to shut out the dizzying flashes.

"*Sammy?*"

He flinched and sat up, looking around again. "Who's that?"

A whispering seemed to surround him, but when he looked around he was alone.

"Sammy?" the voice repeated, and several more joined in. The whispers seemed to be trickling in through the window. But that was crazy, he was on the second floor.

"Who's that! What the hell d'you want?" A belch rolled up from his gut as he squinted around in the dim strobing light. No one answered.

When he braced his hands to lever out of the sagging chair, both hands gripped not polyester tweed but thick velvet. "Hey," he mumbled, "This isn't my chair."

The room brightened suddenly as if someone had shoved up a nonexistent dimmer switch. Incredibly, a uniformed waiter stepped out of Sammy's tiny closet, walked over to his chair, and bowed. Sammy drew back, aghast, as the server extended . . . a tray of hot hors d'oeuvres.

"Care for one, sir?"

"What . . . what's that stuff? How did you get in my room?"

The waiter moved the tray closer and said more firmly, "Sir, please help yourself to some grilled pineapple chicken. Take one."

Sammy stared down wide-eyed at the artful arrangement of skewered chicken and fruit, surrounded by parsley. The mouthwatering sweet-and-charred aroma urged him to pop one in his mouth. "Mmm." It was delicious. He reached for two more, dripping sauce on the pleats of his rented shirtfront. Too bad, he thought. But I haven't had food like this since. . . since . . . but where the heck am I?

Across the room now hung a huge banner printed in red letters, *Gala Youth Fundraiser*. And he was no longer in his dumpy shoebox, but a grand ballroom. Formally-attired men and glossy, slim women chatted in groups, swilling wine and laughing. A brunette in a black cocktail dress smiled at him.

He nodded back. *Who the hell are these people?*

Then things got even weirder. A small orchestra struck a up a popular tune. The melody pulled everyone onto a dance floor polished smooth as ice. As Sammy sat gaping, a woman with a stylish asymmetrical cut extended a gloved hand. "Care to dance?"

My God, she's gorgeous, he thought, rising like the reanimated dead as she led him out onto the floor. She smelled deliciously of tea roses as they danced to the slow music. Just as he was working up the nerve to say something witty, harsh discordant chimes drowned out the music.

"What's going on?" Sammy asked.

His partner only shrugged and kept dancing.

He glanced around the ballroom. Was he the only one who'd heard that piercing ringing? The chimes continued striking, louder and louder. No one else seemed to take any notice. Was it all in his head? Not a church tower outside or a grandfather clock inside, since the harsh gonging had already gone on well past twelve strikes. His brain was throbbing. He felt dizzy, as if he might throw up. He dropped his partner's hand and stumbled off the floor. He made it to the rows of chairs set against the wall and collapsed into one.

As he stared out, gripping his aching head, the party before him simply faded away. Faded, faded . . to black.

He woke seated in his ratty old chair, as if he'd never left it.

Some dream. Everything seemed so real. It was a nice escape, but . . . I better cut back on the cheap booze and greasy fast food.

He stood shakily, fighting vertigo as if he'd just stepped off a merry-go-round. An inviting scent drifted up from the fine pleats of his dress shirt. He scratched at an orange stain and licked his tacky finger. "Mmm. Pineapple chicken."

But how could that be? Obviously the formalwear place hadn't done a good job of laundering the shirt after it was returned by the previous renter.

The next afternoon, when he took back the tux he noticed a brochure lying near the register.

GALA YOUTH FUNDRAISER

Holy shit. It's the same party I dreamed I was at last night! But wait . . . what's with the dates? The event had taken place last week.

Maybe I saw this before and that's why I dreamed about it, he decided. But it had seemed so damned real.

His old colleague Ed had never called back, but who could blame him? Sammy had wimped out, a no-show.

Then two weeks later a former agency client called to invite him to another black-tie affair, with a twist. "A formal cook out," the guy explained. "Sort of a pop-up event, that's big now."

Sammy grinned. The client apparently didn't realize the agency had let him go. Well, he wasn't about to enlighten him. And he wouldn't make the same mistake this time. He had to seize the day, or be trapped in boarding-house purgatory forever.

Back to the store to reserve another tux.

On Friday he picked it up. Took a shower in the tiny mildewed bathroom at the end of the hall, fought the biggest roaches for a clean towel, then got dressed.

Already he was feeling the same panic, though. *If Stevens finds out I don't work at the agency anymore, it'll be tough to explain. I'll look like a loser. A fool.*

Dressed and ready, he sat and stared out the window. His booze money had gone for the tux, so there was no bottle to ease his annoyance now as the bar's sign flashed through the dim room: *Whirl Away. Whirl Away. Whirl Away.*

His head throbbed in time with the words. He didn't bother to call a taxi this time. Just closed his eyes, hoping sleep would come fast.

The floral scent of an expensive perfume tickled his nose. With a yawn, he woke, and saw he was seated in a balcony, first row. Some sort of theater? The place was filled with well-dressed people filing up and down the aisle below, as they were ushered to seats. On the stage rows of chairs fanned out around a podium. Each sat behind a black metal music stand. *Good grief, I must be at the symphony. Looks like Stratton Hall. Guess this is the dress circle.*

Musicians stepped on stage and took their places. As Sammy eavesdropped on the conversations around him, the orchestra members tuned their instruments. The sparkling gems and well-cut gowns of the women, the men's bespoke formalwear, all impressed him. *Yet I fit right in!*

At the end of his aisle a server in tailcoat and white tie offered glasses of champagne. He took one and sipped, pinky extended.

At last the maestro stepped onto the platform, borne on a sea of muffled applause.

The woman seated to Sammy smiled at him. "Oh dear, you don't have a program. Please, take mine."

The heavy linen pages she handed him were bound with a black grosgrain ribbon. He leafed through it, but didn't recognize a single selection. He quietly slid the program under his thickly cushioned seat and sat back sheepishly.

He enjoyed most of the music. Though familiar songs a person could hum along with, like the Boston Pops symphonies or Broadway show tunes, would've been better. But just as the final selection began, a clock loudly struck the hour. Was that part of the program? The chimes grew louder and louder. He covered his ears with both hands and glanced around. No one else seemed bothered. How could they not hear it?

The room grew darker. "Wait," he whispered, "I'm not ready to go."

The woman next to him glanced over. "Pardon me, did you say something?"

But the hall was already fading away. Sammy slipped into the void, as before, to linger briefly in darkness. Again he woke back in his room.

Next day when he returned the tuxedo, the petite Asian woman behind the counter smiled at him warmly. "Many thanks for returning this so quickly. We've had such great demand. Two weddings coming up this weekend. And three funerals. Not all the tuxes came back from last Tuesday's symphony yet!"

Symphony . . . that's where I was last night. So how could it be Tuesday, what the hell is going on?

But he could hardly tell her that. She'd think he was loony. "Oh really? Huh, too bad. Some folks have no consideration." He shook his head.

Gloomy skies and ceaseless rain made the next day seem endless. His tiny room shrank to claustrophobic dimensions. The TV in the common area hadn't worked for two weeks, so he slept all afternoon. By the next day he felt like a muskrat in a trap. If only he could escape like before. But there was no money left to rent a tux.

He wondered, What if I put on my best clothes and sat and just waited. Would it start up that traveling thing again?

One way to find out. He put on his sole remaining suit, a worn pin-striped single-breasted wool blend, with a red silk necktie. Then sat stiffly in the same, the only chair. God, it was hot. The rooms weren't air-conditioned. After an hour or so he dozed off, sweating in the dismal humidity. He dreamed a bee kept flying right at his face and woke up swatting at thin air.

Nothing there but flashing colors from the neighboring bar's sign, the insistent hum of neon outside the open window. *Redgreen. Redgreen.*

Redgreen. He'd sat like a lump all afternoon and gone nowhere. Yet he'd done everything the same, except . . . no tux.

So that must be what made it work.

Over the next two weeks he skipped beer and pizza to save money. Late in the afternoon he went out to the formalwear shop again. Their cheapest model, a 1980 basic black polyester with cigarette burns on the cuffs. He rushed home, dressed quickly, and eagerly sat down to wait. As evening approached, the room grew dim and the bar sign flickered to life. *Whirl Away* pulsed through the dark.

His diaphragm fluttered as he throttled the armrests. *Where will I end up? Who cares. Any place is better than this dump.*

When he heard the murmur of conversation he opened his eyes. He was seated with nine other guests at a round table covered with a white cloth. The banquet room was packed. Waiters scooted between tables, carrying platters of fried chicken, macaroni salad, green beans, and roasted potatoes.

A highly perfumed woman was seated to his right, wearing a red dress with fake rhinestones trimming the neckline, her blonde helmet of hair sprayed firmly in place. She flashed a coquettish grin and pointed to his mixed green salad, then passed the rolls. "Here's the dressing, too. Would yah like some buttah?"

"No, thanks." Is that accent for real, he wondered. Maybe she's putting me on. "Got to watch my waistline."

A waiter in white apron and black t-shirt leaned in from the left. "Care for some wine?"

"Sure. Do you have a list?"

"Yeah. A short one." The waiter smirked. "Red in the jug, or white from a box?"

Sammy grimaced. "Anything else?"

"Bud, Coors, Heineken?" He jerked a thumb at the far back corner, where another man was pouring drinks at a portable counter. "Anything else you can get at the cash bar."

"I see. Thanks." Sammy glanced around, wondering what this affair was all about. Large red, white, and blue posters were propped on easels up front, near a dais. ELECT KOSLOWSKI, they said, below a close-up of a lantern-jawed, gel-haired guy. Red, white, and blue crepe paper streamers and balloons gave the room a Fourth of July vibe.

Ah, I get it. A political gathering.

The head table was set up as if for a wedding reception. Supporters waited to shake the hand of the man on the posters, congratulating him on getting elected, Sammy supposed. At least he enjoyed the meal—greasy, but still better than anything he'd eaten at home in a while.

His hair-sprayed friend batted her lashes and scooted her chair closer.

"So," he asked, "Did you work on the campaign?"

She toyed with a loose tendril that curled like a fat yellow caterpillar in front of one ear. "Yeah. I passed out bumpah stickahs and pens wit Mr. Koslowski's name." She held Sammy's gaze and laid a hand on his thigh. "So what'd youse do?"

He nearly choked on his apple pie. "Oh, y-you know. Phone calls, that sort of stuff." Really, up close under all the makeup and hair spray, she wasn't half bad. Maybe—

Just then a clock chimed. He flinched and dropped his spoon. "Sorry, excuse me." He reached down to pick it up and his elbow knocked the water glass. It tumbled off and fell into her lap.

"Shit," she gasped. "Dat's cold!"

As the chimes boomed louder, Sammy gripped his ears. "Stop it, stop it," he moaned. "Not yet!"

"What's wrong wit ya?" the woman asked, frowning.

But he was already slipping into darkness. He clawed at the table's edge, trying to hang on a few moments, but it was no longer there.

He woke back in his dank room, morning sun streaking in through the grimy pane. He'd enjoyed the escape, however brief. Mid-day, as he walked back to the rental store, he noticed a campaign sign tacked to a streetlight pole. Chris Koslowski had run for councilman in the election three days earlier.

Each trip he'd taken, each event, had happened *before* he'd attended it.

They're like . . . re-runs.

But how did that work? Could some sort of residue from the last event it had attended linger in the tuxedo's fabric, to be activated by the flashing neon of the Whirl Away sign? It sounded insane. Scientifically absurd. Sure, he was no rocket scientist, but . . . what else could it be? When he wore that tux and sat in that chair he went into some sort of trance, and got to relive the event.

Two more tuxedo jaunts seemed to confirm the pattern.

Or maybe it's only me, he thought. *What an amazing talent. Who knew I could do this?*

It did seem that the less expensive the rental, the more economically the haunted tuxedo traveled. It was at a wedding reception in what looked like a high school gymnasium decked out with plastic palm trees and wading pools that he finally grasped this.

His suit this time was an ill-fitting older style in a cheap polyester blend. Still, he was happy to hook up with a nice looking woman who seemed to take a shine to him. One that went well with the sheen of his suit's cheap fabric. They slurped down margaritas mixed in a large plastic garbage can, dipping cups in for refills like everyone else. The DJ played selections skewed toward the Jimmies: Buffet and Cliff. He and his partner danced to the slower tunes.

"Like to get together afterward?" he asked.

She nodded shyly. "Sure."

When the band took a break they went to the buffet, trays of pizza slices and pans of meatballs and ziti. When the paper plates were all tossed away, a lighted disco ball suddenly flicked on and spun, throwing lightning-bug flickers. The DJ hollered, "Everybody's gonna get down tonight!" Now Seventies disco music blasted from huge speakers.

After that things grabbed Sammy by the balls. His ill-fitting polyester tux turned unforgiving as his partner dragged him out to the concrete slab to reenact old disco routines. The thin polyester grew damp and clung to his sweaty body. The pant legs bunched at the knees, making dance moves awkward. The tux coat felt like a straitjacket. God, he couldn't breathe!

Sammy clawed at jacket and shirt, trying to loosen them. A few studs popped off and hit the floor.

"What the heck are you doing?" his partner shrieked.

"Wait," he said.

She shoved away his sweaty hands.

"Just a cheap rental!" Sammy yelled, to be heard above the wailing BeeGees.

"How dare you? Weirdo!" She slapped him and stormed off.

He dragged off the dance floor, thinking back wistfully to the more stylish tuxes he'd used to rent. They'd always taken him to upscale affairs. This time he actually welcomed the familiar gong that heralded his escape. Mortified and more than ready to go, he concentrated on the ear-splitting sounds, to hasten that slipping into the void.

As before, when he forced open sleep-heavy eyelids he was seated in the tattered old chair. He glanced out the grimy window and shook his head. *If only this tux hadn't been so threadbare.*

Next morning, he carried it back to the shop. A black stretch Hummer nearly mowed him down as he crossed the street. The limo reminded him of when he'd owned his own tailor-made clothes, suits and tuxes and sport coats galore. *The good old days. Look at me now.*

Every once in a while he did find a good deal. But old, mismatched outfits created disappointing escapes that were difficult to control. One, a bowling banquet, turned into a brawl. A horse show filled with has-been hookers turned into a hair-pulling match. A fiftieth anniversary party at Leisure View Senior Complex bored him to tears.

Sammy felt even more despondent. He glared out at the flashing sign one night and thought, *That's what I really want. To whirl away and never come back to this dump.*

Shuffling over to the bed he bumped into the nightstand. Wait a minute, he thought. What if I still have a few bucks stashed in the drawer? He whipped it open. Inside was nothing but a paper rectangle. He snatched it up. Oh, yeah, the card that had fallen out of the first tux's pocket.

A tingle burned through his fingers just like the first time he'd touched it.

What the hell's a Night Bazaar, and who needs it? My whole life's bizarre.

He tore it up and tossed the pieces out the window. A few bits blew back in like desiccated snowflakes, to scatter under the bed.

Next day he returned the tux, planning to kick his rental addiction. Time to stop dreaming. Get some kind of job, even if it was standing behind a counter at a convenience store.

He turned into the alley that ran alongside the formalwear shop, a shortcut home. Halfway down it, though, a young man stepped out of a side door. The back of the store, perhaps. "I seen you come in a lot, amigo. You lookin' for to rent a nice tux tonight, cheap?" he asked.

Sammy halted, frowning. He'd just resolved to give up haunted tuxedo traveling, but . . . "Nice? How nice? And how cheap?"

"Classic Seventies number, with vest. Vintage collector's item. A little worn on the inner seams, but still lookin' good. You like baby blue?" The guy talked out of one side of his mouth, like he'd seen too many gangster movies on Netflix. "Ruffled shirt, rhinestone studs, da works."

Sammy thought it sounded dated, but then again, retro was back in style. All that BoHo-SchmoHo stuff. "How come you have it? And how much? You work here?"

The Gangster of Formalwear grinned. "Part time. Main job's at Davidson's. Funeral parlor, driving the hearse. I work here nights. In the back, pressing suits. How much you got on you?"

"Five bucks."

"Done. Meet me here tonight, at closing. Seven." The fellow glanced nervously at a woman walking a Corgi past the alley entrance. "But you gotta promise to return da suit, same place, tomorrow morning before we open. Got it? I don't want no trouble."

"Okay, sure." Sammy handed over five crumpled bills. "Whatever you say."

At ten to seven he headed out. When he got there, no one was in the alleyway. But a plastic garment bag hung on a rusty length of rebar sticking out of the brick wall. Light blue fabric was visible through the plastic. He grabbed it, looked around to see if anyone was watching, then strolled nonchalantly back to the boarding house.

In his room he unzipped the bag and laid everything out on the narrow bed. "Hey. Nice!" He fingered the light blue ruffles, the navy cummerbund, the rhinestone studs. "Huh. Looks like what I wore to high school prom. A fun time. Wouldn't mind getting lost back in those days."

Lost. The idea gradually took root. What if he ignored the clock when it struck? If he just didn't listen, maybe he could get out of here for good. Stay wherever it took him.

"Wow!" He told the ruffled shirt, holding it up to his chest as he preened in the cloudy mirror over his dresser. "You and me are leavin' town in style."

He felt a pang of guilt thinking of the presser at Davidson's. He'd promised to return the tux. But at least the guy had a job. No, two. If he was stupid enough to take chances making money on the side, well, too bad. He'd just have to play dumb, or come up with a story to tell the owner.

Sammy pressed his lips together tightly as his shaking fingers fumbled with the tiny studs. Finished, he took one last look in the mirror, then went to sit in the chair, to wait for the moment the flashing sign came on. Tonight it seemed to take forever.

Whirl Away. Whirl Away. Whirl Away.

After a couple seconds he felt weightless, as if he was descending in a Ferris wheel car. The colors spun into his room, around the walls, across the ceiling.

This time the process seemed to take longer. *Must be this old tux. You pay five bucks, you get five dollars' worth. At this price, I might end up at a formal yard sale.*

At last it came. The usual transitioning darkness closed in. But then . . . nothing. He wasn't moving. He drummed his fingers on the armrest. Tapped his feet. Tried to stand but fell back into the chair. All around nothing but pitch black.

He lifted both arms and his hands brushed across some satiny fabric. It was soft, smooth, inviting. "Oh my." He smiled. "Must be a ball gown. Or a fancy cocktail dress. What a hoot if this tux really did take me to a prom!"

Faint music came out of the dark. Not a song he recognized, though.

A slow number. Then voices rose in song, but so slow and lugubrious . . . nothing like a dance. *Cripes. Must be classical stuff. Hope it's not opera.*

The voices grew louder, nearer. Then it hit him. *Hey. They're not singing. They're sobbing.*

A deep monotone was mumbling some dolorous chant. Perspiration trickled down both sides of Sammy's face. The close stale air made breathing difficult. When would the event begin? He was so hot and uncomfortable. The suspicion grew that he wasn't actually sitting, but lying down, though it was hard to tell in the dark. His heartbeats thumped in his head. The tuxedo grew sodden. All sense of direction deserted him.

He fumbled again in the dark, feeling for a light switch, a wall, anything to orient himself. Only that soft plushy fabric. It felt tufted, with buttons. A *fancy Victorian sofa, maybe.* He imagined fresh-faced girls in high-waisted gowns throwing him seductive glances from behind fans. How far in the past could the magic take him? He held his breath. The lights would come up any minute. Then he'd know.

Nothing.

"Darn monkey suit! Why's it screwing up this time?" He tried to shout it into action. "Whirl away! Whirl away, you bastard." But he felt breathless. The air was so thick and heavy his curse came out more as a whispered plea. "Something's not right. I'm no place at all."

The chimes sounded, but different this time, booming out more like a pipe organ. His plan to remain wherever the escape led had lost its appeal. "Whirl away, whirl away. Come on. Come on."

He focused, trying to hear the chimes. But where were the familiar booming strikes that had always heralded his return? Again came several pipe-organ blasts. "It can't be over yet! I didn't go anyplace," he muttered. A soft thud shook him. Maybe the stupid tux was finally shifting into gear.

Then a voice came again, deep but faint, saying, "Ashes…ashes, dust to…."

Now he had a terrible feeling he knew where he was. Not the formalwear shop, where his tux supplier worked part time. But

Davidson's. The funeral parlor. *The guy's day job.*

"Let me out! Let me out!" He pounded on the coffin's bolted lid. Wedged his knees up and pushed hard against it. His screams were absorbed by the tufted padding.

"Help me. Help!" *Can't anybody hear? Agh, never mind. I can get out of here myself. All I have to do is take off this tux. Then I'll be back in my room, party over.*

By wriggling around like a contortionist he managed to slip one arm out of the jacket. Barely able to raise the opposite shoulder, he worked the other arm partway free. But as he twisted in the tight space the jacket twisted too, binding his arms behind his back.

I can't freakin' move.

Why was this happening? What had he done differently? Only torn up the business card for that Night Market thing. The scattered bits settling like early snow under the bed . . .

The fabric tightened as he bumped up and down, jerking from side to side. His raking fingers shredded the satin lining. His nails caught on buttons securing the tufting and broke. An explosion of polyester burst from the ripped seams, covering Sammy, filling his eyes and nose and mouth. Choking him breathless.

There'd be no return of this rental tux. No hope of getting back to that boxy old room.

Sammy had finally done it. Simply whirled away for good.

There is much exotic entertainment to enjoy at the Bazaar. This includes authentic folk dancing, spirits, and foods from Eastern Europe and many other locales. In the Romani section, for example, the Invited will find mandolin music, traditional dancers, good charms and bad spells, lovely embroidered shawls, grilled meats, rich red wines, even an after-dinner hookah.

But be sure to speak softly and politely while you sojourn there. Honor and obey the customs. Some of the vendors are not only proud of their origins, but still staunchly believe and even practice much older ways. Such a people might be all too easily offended.

Then it would be simply a matter of time before your sins came back to haunt you, in ways even I would prefer not to contemplate. . . .

OBEY

Isaav Skinner

Sara was beginning to suspect it had been a mistake to go out at all tonight. Her planned trip to do research for her urban fantasy story was already going wrong, thanks to Rick. And they hadn't even arrived at the stupid bazaar yet. She hated confrontations, but there was no way to put it off much longer. She had to get rid of her boyfriend.

"Who is this pussy?" he was saying now. About Luca, the graduate teaching assistant from the writing workshop. The one who'd generously offered to get her into a secret urban bazaar in the first place. And holy shit, where had Rick gotten the stupid wife-beater shirt, with OBEY printed across the front? She pulled her arm free of his grip as they followed Luca between two parked cars on 123rd.

"If he keeps eyeballing you," Rick called after her, "I'm gonna kick his skinny Gypsy ass."

"Kick it *after* he shows us the party," his friend Gabe piped in from behind them. "'Cause I'm planning to hit on some Gypsy ass tonight!" He laughed so hard his fat cheeks quivered.

"God, Rick, your mouth. Try not to be such a racist. Please don't call them that." Why did he have to measure dicks with every guy she said hello to? "I told you. Luca's the TA in my Eastern European Lit class. Besides, I think he has a girlfriend."

"Sure it isn't a boyfriend? That goatee would make a primetime cum-swabber." He grinned at Gabe and raised one hand.

"Ha! *Cum-swabber*. Nice!" Gabe high-fived him.

"You both make me want to puke." She rolled her eyes and wheeled in midstride to face them. "We're not going to a keg party at your frat house now. So try to act less like apes, if that's even possible."

Rick looked stricken, and she felt bad for being so harsh. But in the next moment he frowned and turned away, back to laughing with Gabe.

She glanced ahead, worrying, but Luca gave no sign he'd heard the taunts. They were supposed to be going to the bazaar alone, but Rick and Gabe had showed up at her dorm just as she and Luca were leaving. Reeking of cheap beer, demanding to crash the party. She should've broken up with him then and there, but was afraid he'd take it out on Luca. What could she say? Rick was still her boyfriend, for now, and she was to blame for it.

That *for now* attitude always drove her father crazy. *For now* didn't exist in his vocabulary. Neither did any idea why she, according to him, was wasting her time and his money getting an English degree. He was a lawyer. *He'd* never wasted time with serial girlfriends or ambiguous degrees. He'd known he was going to marry her mom in tenth grade, at the same time he'd decided to go into law.

Well, too bad. For now she wanted to write and have a little fun before she turned into a funsucker like her father. And Rick *had* been fun, at first. Much nicer when they were alone together. But she didn't want to commit to anyone she really, truly liked, because fate always seemed to steal those people away. Whether he believed in it or not, *for now* had kicked her father in the teeth when Sara was five and his *forever* wife drove over a patch of black ice and wrapped her minivan around a sycamore. Little Sara had walked away with a bruise on her forehead. And her father had never been able to bring himself to replace her mom with another woman.

She flinched back to the unpleasant present at a heavy-metal guitar ring-tone. Rick pulled out his phone, angling it away from her.

She fell back and gazed at the screen. "Who's Misty?"

He shrugged. "Oh, you know . . . just a friend from class. But I don't think she has a boyfriend."

"You're an ass." Tonight, after the bazaar, when Luca was out of the way, she'd finally dump Rick. No more excuses. She sped up to catch Luca. "So tell me more about this bazaar."

"Our family's been part of it for centuries. It's, like, a reunion of a bunch of Roma who get to pretend they're still in the old country. Me, I'd rather go clubbing, but Grandma would curse me if I didn't show up."

She laughed, but he didn't, so she quickly stopped. "Oh, um . . . really? But why?"

"I'm supposed to meet and marry a nice Romani girl, like every other man in my family has for the last two hundred years." He shrugged. "What better place to be introduced to one than the Romani section of an old-fashioned bazaar?"

She laughed. "I get it. My dad makes me go to his company picnics so I can meet and marry a nice young attorney, and give birth to two-point-five lawyer grandchildren. As if!"

He grinned. "Then tonight we'll drink to your future ambulance chasers, and to my shiftless but musically gifted offspring."

"Deal. I hope this bazaar will help with my story. Especially the ending. Did you think my characters were a good choice? The girl who falls in love with an Italian duke living in Brooklyn, but he's really a murderer, I mean. There aren't any Romani in it."

"The theme of forbidden love." His dark eyes gleamed like sapphires in a jeweler's display case. "To write love, first you've got to feel its pain." His hand brushed hers. Probably an accident, but her breath caught anyhow. She glanced back, but Rick and Gabe were staring at some passing women.

As they turned down an alley, though, Rick sped up and shoved between them, jabbing an elbow into Luca's side."Hey bro, is it true you Gypsies will sleep with anyone, even your own sisters?"

"Oh my God. Shut *up*, Rick! I'm so sorry, Luca. He's just insensitive."

"*Whaat?*" Rick turned up both palms. "I saw it on History Channel."

Luca smiled. "Only on the coldest nights, my friend. Lucky for me, my sister is very beautiful." He winked at Sara, and walked on ahead.

Rick stopped in the street, jaw slack. "Holy shit."

Sara shook her head and hurried off after Luca, not bothering to look back and see if Rick was following.

They turned down another narrower, even darker alley. This one smelled of dead fish and rotten eggs. When they emerged onto the next street, the only people out were a few homeless guys on cardboard mattresses, and women in platform heels and pleather skirts. They passed a boarded-up tattoo parlor and crossed a weedy, overgrown lot. At the far end a rundown, boxy building was cordoned off with sagging chain-link fencing and yellow *NO TRESSPASSING* and *CONDEMNED* signs. Half the windows were broken out, the others covered with graffiti-tagged pressboards. This place made Rick's dirty frat house look like the Hilton. She ought to snap a picture on her phone and text it to her dad. *Having a nice night out. No lawyers in sight. LOL*

"We're supposed to party *here*?" Rick screwed up his face as if he'd smelled something worse than the stinking alleys.

"Just a façade, bro," Luca assured him, smirking." To keep out uninvited guests."

They ducked under a *KEEP OUT* sign and squeezed through an opening cut through the chain link. The dented steel door was unlocked. Past it electrical wiring hung like vines from the ceiling. Twisted rusty rebar bristled like insect feelers from crumbling pillars. Sara wrinkled her nose. If she wanted spooky atmosphere for her story, this looked like a good bet.

Luca guided them across a concrete floor littered with smashed cans and shards of glass, past a door hanging on one broken hinge. Then into a stairwell lit only by a flickering red bulb. A man lay slumped on the second floor landing, toothless mouth gaping, snoring away as if he lived there.

Rick snorted. "That your brother, Luca?"

"Distant cousin." Luca shrugged. "Twice removed."

Three more flights up, a huge guy stood with crossed arms at a doorway that must lead to the roof. A forked beard hung to his chest, the ends braided and tied with black ribbon. Tattoos of roses, knives, and buxom girls covered his chest, crawled down his tree-trunk arms, slithered up the sides of his neck, and capped his shaved head.

Luca greeted him in a sharp-sounding language Sara had never heard him use before. The guard eyed them and scowled. Luca turned back to Rick, grinning. "*This* is my brother. You wanted to ask him something about our sister, right?"

The big man cracked his knuckles and grunted, eyes narrowing to slits.

Rick sidled behind Sara. When she tried to step away he gripped her arms, holding her in front of him like a shield. "Uh—come on, man. I was only—uh—uh—"

The guard's scowl morphed into a toothy grin. He guffawed and high-fived Luca.

"Just having a little fun, my friend." Luca inclined his head at the rusted door." Come. The bazaar's waiting."

"Asshole," Rick muttered.

Sara's turn to snort. Oh, yeah. Tonight she'd definitely end this stupid relationship. Forever.

The big man hit the crash bar. The scents of sweet pastries, roasting meats, and some sort of perfume—or maybe incense—wafted out into the stairwell. Her mouth watered. She stepped through and into to a scene out of an Indiana Jones movie. Tall torches flamed against the night sky. Merchants were dressed in jeans and loose white shirts, or embroidered robes. Some men were naked to the waist in bloused trousers and boots. The women wore fluttering scarves and long embroidered skirts. Wooden carts and curtained stalls displayed rolls of shimmering silk, gold and silver jewelry, strange-looking porcelain dolls, gleaming curved knives, vials of neon-colored liquids, countless brass and carved wooden trinkets.

A crowd was gathered in a half-circle around a shirtless man covered with green tattoos. The implants bulging under the skin of his arms, chest, and back made him look eerily like a crocodile. The crowd cheered and jeered as one after another he flung six flaming torches twenty feet into the sky, juggling them deftly as they fell again.

"Shit. What the hell is that?" Rick muttered. When she turned to look he pointed at an ancient-looking woman with waist-length gray hair. She was hunched on a stool before a brocade-draped tent. Large gold discs weighted her earlobes. Her bony fingers gripped the end of a chain that hung to her feet in loops and disappeared under the tent flaps.

"Don't get too close, man," Luca warned as Gabe stepped nearer, staring.

The chain suddenly jangled. A creature the size of a toddler, covered head to toe with curly black hair, vaulted out through the flap. It landed on all fours and hissed at them, rearing to bare pointed teeth.

Gabe stumbled back. "What the fuck!"

Sara watched, paralyzed, as the creature lunged and bit his calf, then clawed its way up his jeans with talon-like fingers.

"*Babik*!" The old woman whipped it with the loose end of the chain. The furry little demon yelped and fell back, whimpering. "Nyet, nyet, Babik," she crooned, reaching down and petting the shaggy head. It hissed at Gabe again, then curled up at her feet, licking the coarse hair on its arm like a sulking cat.

"Wh-what the hell?" Gabe sputtered. "That fucker fucking bit me."

Luca tossed a thick gold-toned coin into a basket beside the woman. "It's dangerous to get too close to things you don't understand."

A troupe of strolling musicians approached and Sara got out her pocket notebook. They were classic. Just what her story needed. She'd recovered herself enough to scribble details: the largest man's round, hairy stomach, which protruded beneath an orange vest. His violin, a child's toy in those huge, meaty hands. Beside him a teenage boy with a shaved head and an eye patch twanged the strings of a teardrop mandolin. The oldest, an old man with skin creased like a worn, soft wallet was playing a wheeled cimbalom. His long, wispy beard brushed the strings. He swung the padded hammers with a flourish, producing the tinkling sound of water flowing over river stones.

Three dancers in gem-studded halters and sheer, flowing yellow skirts glided up to spin and swoop, twirling bright green scarves. The waists of their wrapped skirts barely clung to swaying hips, dipping far below pierced, jeweled navels.

Sara scribbled faster, barely able to keep up with all the details.

"Whoa," muttered Gabe. "I think I'm in love."

Luca tossed coins into the basket in front of the cimbalom. One of the dancers grabbed Gabe's hand, another captured Rick's. They draped scarves around each man's neck and ground their hips against them, gyrating to the music. The third dancer, a tall woman with long black hair and full red lips took Sara's hand, gazing at her longingly.

Sara stiffened, trying to pull back. This was a little too weird. She only wanted to observe, not participate. "Oh, no . . . no, thanks, I don't—"

"Roma princess," the woman cooed. Her breath carried the sweet, musky scent of roses. She pulled Sara closer and whispered, "*Khel*," in her ear, breath warm and soft as the breeze from a butterfly's wing.

Suddenly Sara's hips began swaying as if they had a mind of their own, in perfect time to the notes from the mandolin. Her hands gripped the soft chestnut-hued skin of the dancer's curvy hips and moved in sync with them. *Okay, enough*, she thought. *Now let go, step away, and write it all down*. Instead, her right hand dropped the pen and slid under the sarong to cup the smooth muscular cheek of the woman's ass, caressing the soft flesh there.

The dancer smiled and stroked Sara's face with silken fingertips, then kissed her neck.

"No . . . I'm not . . . I can't even dance! *Stop*," Sara gasped, feeling both panic and overwhelming desire as the woman blew hot breath on her neck. When she tried again to pull away, her belly cramped as if with hunger. Her breath came in heaves. "Please . . . don't . . . please. . . ."

A hoarse whisper in her other ear. "How about a Gypsy sandwich?" Rick pressed into Sara from behind, running his hands up her hips, waist, the sides of her breasts.

"Stop it!" She gritted her teeth and managed to rip her hands off the woman, then turned and shoved him away. She staggered away from the circle of dancers, toward the dimmer edge of the torchlight.

Luca followed and touched her shoulder. "You okay, Sara?" He handed her the fallen pen.

She drew a shuddering breath. "What the hell just happened? I mean—she whispered something, and I turned to Jell-O. For a second, I wanted—I would have actually killed to—"

He shrugged. "Here the patrons tend to revel in suppressed desires."

"No, it's not just that. It was more like . . . did she *enchant* me?"

He considered. "Hmm. Well, Romani women are very talented. Only the strongest can resist their charms."

Sara glanced back toward the troupe. Now Rick was pretty much humping the dancer as she gyrated, shimmying against his chest and groin in slow, sensuous sweeps.

"And his mind would be pretty weak," Luca said dryly.

Sara gritted her teeth. "That walking hard-on doesn't need an enchantment."

Luca looked surprised. "I thought he was your boyfriend."

"Sure. When one of us gets the urge for a drunken booty call. We met on Tinder."

"Then why stay with him?"

"You sound like my dad," she snapped, then added, "Sorry. Rick isn't *always* a dick. Once I read him one of my stories and he actually cried. He's a lot worse when his buddies are around." She finally looked right into Luca's dark eyes. "But no. I'm not exactly in love."

"Excellent!" He grinned and held out an arm. "So we can work on that story ending together. How about some wine?"

She glanced back at Rick, who was now the sandwich filling, pressed between two of the dancers. He looked oblivious to anything else, including her. "Sure. Why not." She took Luca's arm.

He led her past a stall where a fortuneteller wrapped in orange and yellow scarves shuffled an ancient-looking tarot deck. They stopped at a circle of ornately-carved, chest-high wooden tables. A cheery, round little woman came over, lugging a heavy clay jug. Luca grabbed two pewter goblets and pressed another of those foreign-looking coins into one of the woman's pudgy hands. She filled their goblets with a thick blood-red liquid.

"To forbidden desires." He raised his cup.

"Um, sure. Forbidden desires." She touched the rim of her cup to his, then brought it to her lips, inhaling raspberry and cinnamon and something musky. The warm, sweet liquid bathed her tongue in honeyed fruit, cardamom, cloves and other tastes she couldn't identify. It was fantastic. She swallowed half the cup quickly. Writers drank a lot, right?

"Whoa! Slow down." Luca pulled her goblet away. A bit of wine trickled from one corner of her mouth and dripped onto her shirt.

"Shit!" She rubbed at the dark spot. "This is new."

Luca ran a thumb lightly over her lips, then cradled her cheek. Her head felt light, as if she'd been out in the sun too long. The torchlight seemed too bright. Her knees wobbled and she grabbed his hand. "Uh oh . . . think I better sit."

He guided her to a chair. "I should've warned you. Roma wine is strong."

She sat back, closing her eyes so she wouldn't have to watch the torches spinning in slow circles. "Why'd that dancer call me a Roma princess?" she murmured.

"There's a wildness in your eyes. You have the look of one."

"Really?" She giggled. "But I'm Irish. Although my Aunt Ginny did run off with her hippie boyfriend about a hundred years ago, to live in a van and play the tambourine."

He laughed. "See? The life is in your blood." He traced small circles in her palm with one finger.

Her heart fluttered. She suddenly felt shy and wanted to pull the hand back, but he held on. Without opening her eyes she could feel his face close to hers. She actually stopped breathing when his wine-scented breath softly kissed her lips.

"*Luca*!" shouted a harsh voice.

He flinched and snatched his hand away.

Sara opened her eyes. An old woman with a straw-like mane of white hair was standing beside their table. A half dozen big gold hoops jingled in her thinly-stretched earlobes, brushing the shoulders of a flowing black cloak.

"Grandmother!" Luca leapt up, almost knocking the table over.

The woman's steely-black eyes shifted to bore into Sara's.

She tried to glance away, but couldn't. A dull ache slowly grew in the center of her forehead. Only when Luca stepped between them could Sara break the locked gaze, feeling suddenly weak.

Luca grasped the old woman's shoulders and kissed both cheeks, then straightened and said stiffly, "Púridia, this is, um, one of my—uh—students. Sara."

Sara nodded, eyes riveted on the table top. "Nice to meet you, ma'am." She didn't dare look up again.

The old woman said something in that same sharp language Luca had used before. Sara didn't get the words, but that icy tone breached the language barrier.

Luca laughed hollowly. "Sorry. My grandmother understands English very well, but she won't demean herself to speak it."

They talked rapidly back in forth in Romani. Luca's face reddened. He stammered, looking more and more like a scolded boy than a twenty-something graduate student. The woman said one last thing, jabbed a gnarled finger into his chest, then turned and hobbled off.

He gazed after her for a moment, then sighed and sat across from Sara. He kept his hands in his lap, and now he was staring at the tabletop, too.

"Well, that sounded pleasant," she said.

"Sorry. Púridia's very. . . traditional. It isn't personal."

"I get it. I guess. Maybe I'd better find Rick, and—"

"No, please don't leave." His dark eyes turned pleading. "There's a lot you haven't seen yet. My grandmother may act like it, but she doesn't actually rule the bazaar."

Sara snorted. "No, just you."

"That's not fair. I have to respect the old customs, even when I'd rather not."

She sighed. "You're right. I shouldn't have said that. And I really do get it. I can just imagine what my father would say, if . . . oh, never mind. I should go."

"Wait. There is one more thing I want you to try. Get out your notebook."

He left before she could object, disappearing into a nearby tent. He returned with a three-foot silver vessel divided into four teardrop-shaped bulbs. A metal bowl twisted into the shape of a thorny rose sat on top. Four black and white hoses spiraled from the lowest, largest teardrop, wrapping the base like vines.

Sara gaped at it. "What the heck is that?"

"This, Roma Princess, is a peace offering. The finest of Romani hospitality." He pinched up some leafy substance from a cloth bag. It smelled of cherries, turned earth, and . . . copper? He pressed this into the bowl of the hookah, then used tongs to drop a glowing coal on top. He handed her one hose. "Inhale. But take it slow."

She'd never even smoked a cigarette. Wouldn't her father just stroke out if he saw this. "I should really . . . oh well. When with a Roma, I guess." She drew in only a mouthful. The blood-red liquid in the base bubbled thickly. A smoky grape flavor coated her tongue and throat. Instead of making her cough, it gave a strange sense of calm. When she blew the smoke out, the tenseness from the confrontation with Luca's grandmother flowed away. This experience she didn't need to write down. No one could forget such strong sensations.

Luca closed his eyes and inhaled deeply, then slowly exhaled, smoke streaming from his nose in straight, white lines.

She giggled. "You look sorta like a dragon."

"You like the hookah?"

She nodded, taking another drag deep into her lungs. A bright tingling rippled down her arms and legs. This time as she exhaled the colors of the bazaar flared brighter. Every stitch of the satin tents, every nail in the wooden carts, each separate flickering in the torch flames. It grew so sharp she had to close her eyes. Still she heard the flaps of the tents fluttering, golden hoop earrings jangling, the distant flow of the cimbalom coursing through her like a rushing waterfall. "Is your grandmother still around?" she whispered.

"No. She went back to her tent, on the far side of this part of the bazaar."

"Good." She stood and held a hand out. "So you can dance with me before I go."

Luca leapt up and led her from the table to the edge of the torchlight. In that dim region they swayed slowly, her head cradled on his chest, his arms enveloping her, the scent of smoky, tart cherries on his breath. She leaned away to touch his face, seeing a miniature version of the torchlight dancing in each of his dark irises. "Did you put a spell on me, too?"

"No. I think you put one on *me*." He kissed her neck and caressed her shoulders. "I'm thinking of a new ending for your story right now."

She smiled but then thought, *What if Rick sees us? Things might get ugly*. "No, wait." She pushed his hand down. She'd break it off with the jerk boyfriend later. Then she and Luca would have all the time in the world. No need to rush things.

Luca ignored that and cradled her face in both hands, leaning down to kiss her deeply. As his tongue flirted with hers, she felt the same overpowering desire as she had with the gypsy dancer. An urge to rip her clothes off and let him take her right there on the rooftop. Never mind all the people everywhere.

She pulled back again. "Sorry, but . . . we'd better not. I need to end things with Rick first. He might be a cheating prick, but I'm not." She kissed Luca's cheek and turned to step back into the full blaze of torchlight.

A familiar voice yelled, "*What the fuck*!" Someone grabbed the back of her shirt and jerked her backward. "What do you think you're doing, Gypsy-boy?" Rick let go of Sara and punched Luca's face. The slighter man staggered back and fell.

"Stop it, Rick!" she screamed. "Wait! Just wait! I need to tell you—"

He ignored her, and kicked Luca's ribs. She heard a sickening *crack*.

Sara broke free of Gabe and jumped on Rick's back, but he shrugged her off and kicked Luca again."Come on! Get up, Gypsy bitch!"

Luca lay still, eyes closed, one cheek pressed to the gravel.

"Stop hurting him!"Sara lunged at Rick again, but someone grabbed her from behind and wrapped her in a bear hug.

"Relax," Gabe hissed, breath sour with beer, wet lips grazing her ear. "It's just a party, babe."

Rick kicked at Luca's head and it bounced off the gravel.

"Oh my God! Stop it, Rick. *Please*! You're going to *kill* him!"

Rick lifted his foot again but suddenly froze, the heel of his Nike inches from Luca's bleeding cheekbone. "What the fuck?"

The old woman stood across from him, her grandson between them, long white hair glowing ghostly in the moonlight. She flicked one hand as if shooing a fly. Rick flew back ten feet, skidding to a stop at the edge of the rooftop.

Púridia turned toward Sara and chanted something.

"I'm sorry," Sara sobbed. "I didn't know he'd—"

Rick shoved up again. "Out of the way, Granny!"

The old woman ignored him. She pressed a hand to Luca's forehead, still chanting. Luca jerked. His eyelids fluttered. The woman held one hand under his broken nose, letting the blood pool in her palm.

"Te del o bengandetute! Te del o bengandetute!" She closed her fist on the blood. *"Te del o bengandetute!"* Suddenly she straightened and flung the blood in all three of their faces. Rick's, Sara's, and Gabe's.

"Ow!" The drops that flecked her skin burned like hot grease. She had a flash of the old car accident. The blood that had gushed from her mother's neck. The horrible way it had sprayed back on Sara and the cloth baby doll she used to carry everywhere, back then. "Oh God, no," she moaned, feeling sick.

Rick drew a hand across his face, smearing it with Luca's blood. "You dried-up old bitch!"He drew back a fist to punch the old woman.

But two huge men, one the tattooed bouncer from the front door, stepped up on either side of her, glowering.

This is my fault, Sara thought. For not speaking up. My fault for making excuses for him. For selfishly enjoying rubbing Rick in my father's face. For not getting rid of him earlier. For thinking he was ever a good idea in the first place.

But now she could start to fix it. All she had to do was speak up. Apologize. Do the right thing. This was real life, not a story.

She pulled free of Gabe again. "Come on, Rick. Leave them alone. Let's go."

"The Gypsy bastard had his dirty hands on you, Sara!"

She sighed. "It wasn't—Look, I'm sorry, everyone. But it's over now. Let's just go."

"Yeah," Gabe muttered, rubbing blood from his eyes. "This is some screwed-up shit."

Sara pushed at Rick's chest until he fell back a couple paces. All three turned at last to leave.

But of course Rick couldn't let it go. "Granny won't be there to save you next time!" he yelled over one shoulder. "When I see you again, I'm gonna rip out your throat!" He threw off Sara's arm and stomped off.

Luca sat up, grimacing. She glanced back at him and mouthed, *I'm sorry*. Did he even see her? He looked dazed, only half conscious. She bit her lip, turned away, and followed Rick and Gabe back out through the rusted steel door.

* * *

The vibrating tenor notes of a mandolin rolled through Sara's body, softly, slowly. A haze obscured everything, like the view through a gauzy scarlet veil. She moaned, thrashing amid a tangled mass of greased bodies. Writhing as unseen hands groped her breasts, caressed her mouth, pulled at her hair.

The mandolin's tempo quickened. The hands grew rougher, more demanding. She arched her back, dug her nails into someone else's soft flesh as the song played like a carousel picking up speed, until the notes blurred into an angry wail. Two shadowy faces drew nearer. One bit her breast.

She screamed and lashed out, clawing at her attackers, biting back. Thick, salty blood filler her mouth and gushed over her lips as she let out a choked scream.

***

She opened her eyes and groaned, "Oh my God!" Her head nearly split in half as daggers of light stabbed in through the bedroom window. She was in her dorm room, near Morningside Park. How much had she actually had to drink? She pressed both palms against her temples to hold her brain still, and rolled over. The clammy, sweat-soaked sheet felt like sandpaper on her raw nipples.

Luca. The bazaar. Rick beating, almost killing him. Dear God, was he all right?

The walls spun like a tilt-a-whirl. She lunged for the plastic can beside the bed and retched until her eyes ached. When the nausea finally subsided, she sat up and grabbed the phone.

She scrolled for Luca's number, then hesitated, thumb poised a hair's breadth from the call button. His shining eyes flashed in her mind. Then his beaten face. Would he even want to hear from her? She tried to lower her thumb to send the call, but it wouldn't move. She gave up and scrolled to Rick's number instead. If she hadn't made clear she never wanted to see him again, she'd make sure of it now. Her thumb moved easily this time. After four rings, his voicemail picked up. "*You know what to do, bitch.*"

Ugh. How had she stood him this long? "What the hell happened last night, Rick, a buffalo stampede? Never mind. We need to talk. Call me."

Another wave of nausea. The red haze clouded her vision. She winced, turning away from the window. From somewhere soft notes plucked on a mandolin drifted to her.

Where the hell is that music coming from?

She got out of bed and stepped up to the window, blinking against the harsh light, watching with detached fascination as her hand shoved the sash up and knocked the screen out. It clattered to the pavement five stories below.

Wait! What are you doing? she asked herself.

The mandolin music played louder, faster.

She lifted her left leg over the windowsill and pushed it out into the open air. The other leg followed. She sat on the sill, its thin aluminum edge biting her naked thighs. Her bare toes scraped a two-inch concrete ledge. The only thing, five floors up, between her and the concrete sidewalk below.

No. Stop!

Instead she ducked to pull the rest of her body out. But her forehead smacked the top of the window frame and she fell backward, slamming the back of her head on the floor.

Everything went black.

***

When Sara woke again she touched the back of her head and winced. Her fingertips came away bloody. "What the hell? *Oww*."

Had that been some sort of drunken flashback? She pushed up on her elbows, then staggered to her feet and backed away from the window, into the bathroom. In the mirror over the sink her chin was stained red with dried blood. Flecks speckled her chest. More was crusted under her fingernails.

"What the fuck?" She frantically scrubbed face and chest, then stood panting, gripping the cold porcelain of the sink, afraid to look in the mirror again.

A pair of nail scissors lay on the back of the toilet. She picked them up and ran a thumb over the sharp edge. Beads of crimson welled. The phantom mandolin played again. She lifted the small, gory blade and licked it, looking into the mirror. Smiling as she watched herself press the sharp point to her throat.

"No!" She threw the scissors against the wall and clamped her hands on the cold porcelain again, so hard the muscles in her palms cramped. "Stop it! Stop it! *Stop it*!"

The mandolin song faded.

Her stomach roiled. She dropped hard to her knees beside the toilet. When the retching subsided to dry heaves she rose and splashed water on her face at the sink. Then she went back to the nightstand to get her phone. Again, her thumb hovered above Luca's number, but she couldn't make it press the icon. "What the hell is going on?"

She called Rick again. *"You know what to do, bitch."*

Had he drugged her or something? "Answer your damned phone, you fucking asshole! Something is *seriously* wrong and you're going to tell me what happened last night after we left the . . . no, never mind. I'm coming over."

She yanked on jeans and a gray hoodie, then rushed from the room. Out into a cacophony of car horns and sirens and jackhammers. A young woman holding a small boy's hand walked past. The child pointed at Sara and burst into tears.

Sara glared. "Jesus. Never seen a girl with a hangover before?" But her heart slammed against her ribs and pounded between her ears. The child's cry was a blade piercing her brain. She wanted to slap him, to pound his stupid fat little face into the pavement to make him stop. "Can't you shut that kid up?"

The mother gaped at her, snatched the little boy up, and hurried away down the street.

Sara bent and gripped her head. "Wait! I'm sorry! I—I didn't mean to say that."

The mother glanced back with a look of absolute horror and broke into a run, the child bouncing on one hip.

Sara staggered over to lean against a light pole. Passing pedestrians gave her a wide berth, or glanced over warily and then shied away.

What is happening to me?

A homeless man in layers of filthy shirts and jackets approached, pushing a rusted grocery cart laden with black garbage bags. "Got a dollar, Miss?"

"What?" Her eyes locked on the pulsing jugular vein half-obscured by locks of straggling white hair. Blood rose to pound in her head again. She reached toward him, fingers splayed, imagined herself ripping out his throat. She could almost taste the salty copper of his blood.

"S-sorry, Miss," he stammered, back pedaling, dragging the cart with him. "I-I don't need it." He turned and ran off down the street, abandoning the cart on the corner.

She pressed her fingertips against her eyelids, wanting to claw the image of the homeless man's bloody neck from her head. *Stop it! Stop it! STOP IT!*

After a minute or so she took a deep breath and moved on, keeping her head down. A crowd was gathered on the sidewalk outside Rick's building, gawkers jammed three deep against yellow police-tape. Two uniformed cops and a detective-looking guy in a wrinkled suit stood beside a big green dumpster.

She stepped up behind a man in an orange vest and yellow hardhat and tapped his shoulder. "Excuse me. What's going on?"

"Sanitation worker found a body in the dumpster. Throat ripped out. Musta pissed off the wrong dude."

She stared at him. "The . . . the throat?" *No. That had just been a bad dream.*

She clawed her phone out of her pocket and hit *RICK*. The muffled notes of a heavy-metal guitar sounded nearby. The detective reached into the dumpster and pulled out a ringing phone. Sara shook her head, staring down at *RICK* on her screen. At the tiny picture of him with his middle finger raised.

She turned away and shouldered through the crowd. A metro bus rolled down the street toward her. Beneath the rumble of its tires a mandolin played. She imagined the studded black tires rolling over her body, crushing her ribs, her skull.

Yes, that was the only answer.

She stepped out into the street, gauged the speed of the bus, then took another step.

A hand grabbed her shoulder and yanked her back onto the curb. "Be careful, kiddo, you're liable to get hurt."

A handsome fortyish man in a dark tailored suit stepped around in front of her and laid both hands on her shoulders. "Say, you OK?"

She imagined throwing him under the wheels of the bus instead, watching his body explode inside that expensive pinstriped wool shroud.

"Oh my God! Get away from me!" She knocked his hands off and sprinted away.

A stocky young man leaning against a sign at the next street corner turned listlessly to look at her. His eyes were swollen slits in a pallid face. Three raw scratches ran from his forehead, over his nose and lips, and stopped at his chin.

She slowed to stare at him. "Gabe?"

His eyes widened until they seemed to shake in their sockets. With a guttural cry he skittered backward, away from her, falling over a garbage can.

"Gabe! It's Sara. What the hell's wrong? What happened to your face?"

"S-stay away, you . . . you *freak*!" He crab-crawled over spilled trash.

She was on him in a flash, grabbing his arm as he levered himself up, spinning him around to face her. "What happened to Rick?"

He blubbered, clamping both hands over his face like a terrified child. "Please don't kill me!"

"What're you talking about?"

"I'm sorry! I'm so sorry!" He dropped to his knees, and clasped his hands like a penitent in church. "I'll do anything you want. Just don't—"

The red haze obscured his face. She watched her hand lash out and slap it, hard. He fell back between two parked cars, helpless as a cockroach on its back. Exhilaration streamed through her. No . . . hunger.

"I'm sorry! I'm sorry!" he wailed, flailing.

She bent, grabbed his shoulders and picked him up as if he weighed no more than a toddler. Then she threw him into the street.

Tires squealed. The metal rack extending from a garbage truck exploded through his head in a spray of brains, flesh, and bone fragments.

Sara stood watching. A shiver of pleasure washed over her. Gradually the red haze dissipated. *Oh, no. No, no, no, no, no!* She backed away.

A woman screamed. A crowd shuffled over to gather behind Sara. "What happened?" someone gasped. "What did you do?"

Her hands shook as she pulled up the hood of her sweatshirt and slinked away.

"Somebody stop her!" a man yelled.

She sped up and dashed around the next corner. On the curb ahead a man was just stepping into the open back door of a taxi. She shoved past and jumped in.

"Hey!" he protested.

The driver, a thin bald man, turned his head to look at her. She glared at the vein pulsing in his neck. "Just drive. Now! Up . . . uptown."

"Jesus!" He flinched as she slammed the door. "You all right, Miss?" he asked, pulling away slowly from the curb.

She picked up her phone again. She could call her father. Yes, call him and tell him to . . . to what? She buried her face in her hands and sobbed. No, that wasn't the answer. This was her problem. She knew where she had to go to fix it.

She got out in the Bronx and walked the last five blocks, getting lost, retracing her steps. An hour or so later she finally stood in front of the condemned warehouse. Taking a deep breath, she squeezed through the gap in the fence and climbed the stairs.

No stalls or carts or tents were set up on the roof. No dancers or jugglers or musicians strolled through a crowd. A few scraps of colored paper blew aimlessly back and forth. Otherwise there was no sign the bazaar had ever been there.

A dark figure sat on an upturned crate at the far end. Púridia, Luca's ancient grandmother, wrapped in the same thick black cloak, sitting there with her eyes closed. Long, coarse strands of white hair lifted on a breeze like wisps of smoke. The woman's lips moved soundlessly, as if she were praying. Or perhaps casting another spell.

Sara rushed over to her. "Please, tell me," she begged. "What's happening to me?"

The woman reached into her cloak and withdrew a long, curved knife. The blade gleamed in the sun. Sara stepped back. But Púridia only turned the blade away from her, and offered the jeweled hilt instead.

"What is *that* for?" Sara asked warily.

"The blood price to be collected." The woman was still speaking in Romani, but somehow Sara understood the words now.

"A b-blood price? What do you mean?"

"You must pay the price for trying to kill my grandson."

"But that wasn't me, it was Rick and Gabe!" *Gabe . . . I killed him. I killed Gabe. Oh my God.* "I tried to stop them. I didn't want anyone to hurt Luca!"

"Two blood prices have been collected. A third remains unpaid."

"What do you mean?" She stepped back. "Did *you* kill Rick?"

The old woman smiled and shook her head. *"It is not for me to collect. I only play the music."* She picked up the teardrop mandolin lying at her feet and plucked a few slow, soft chords deftly with her gnarled fingers.

The entirety of Sara's dream came back. The writhing bodies, the coppery taste of blood. The red stain on her chin that morning. She dropped to her knees in the gravel and pointed a trembling finger. "You cursed me. You threw Luca's blood on me and cursed me and made me kill them!"

"Enough, Púridia!" shouted someone behind Sara. When she turned to look, Luca stood a few feet away. His left eye was purple, swollen shut, his lower lip split, bristling with black stitches.

"Oh, thank *God*!" She leapt up and threw her arms around him, but shrieked and recoiled. It felt like she was hugging a burning griddle.

Luca looked pained. "You can't touch me ever again." He lowered his gaze. "It's, um, part of the curse."

"What's happening to me, Luca? Am I going insane?"

"You shall not taint our family with your whorish western blood."

Luca gritted his teeth and rounded on the old woman. "You can't do this, Púridia. It's not her fault!"

"Yet it has been done."

He stalked through the gravel to face her. "Then *undo* it!"

"*What is called down in blood cannot be undone. She must pay the price.*"

"But she's innocent!" He stepped closer, reaching out to grab hold of his grandmother. She raised one hand and he froze.

The crone's lip curled. "*She watched that monster try to kill you. Then she left and lay with him. With both of them.*"

Sara covered her face. "*What?* No, no! I mean . . . oh God, I can't remember." Hot tears rolled down her cheeks. "Believe me. I didn't know what I was doing. I was under a spell, for God's sake!"

"Tepochinenpengelazhav. *May you pay for your shame.*"

"What shame?" Sara screamed. "What is this blood payment you want?"

"*Only one price will wash away the shame you brought upon my family.*" The old woman stroked the blade of the knife in her lap.

"No. I won't!" Sara wheeled and sprinted away, across the roof. She raced down the five flights, hit the crash bar on the first floor and burst through—right back onto the roof.

"Wh—what the hell—"

She ran down the stairs again, pushed through the door, and stepped back onto the roof. Down the stairs again and again and again, trying every level, emerging back on the roof each time. Blisters rose on her heels and soles, burst, and bled through her socks. Her thigh muscles screamed as if searing knives had been plunged into them. Finally she collapsed, unable to go on.

Still the old woman waited. Luca stood by looking stricken, but not moving to stop her.

Sara crawled the length of the roof, gravel gouging hands and knees, and held up bleeding palms." Here. Is this what you're looking for?"

The old woman scowled. "*That will not satisfy the price.*"

She hung her head, too exhausted to fight anymore. "Then just kill me and be done with it."

"*The fee is not for me to collect.*"

"Then who? Will you make Luca kill me?"

"You must obey. Collect the fee, and do it properly this time." She plucked at the mandolin again.

"What do you mean?" But she understood now. The attempted leap from the dorm window. The bloody scissors in the bathroom. The bus on the street." You crazy old bitch. I'm not going to kill myself!"

"Then you will know no peace. You will kill without mercy, but not without regret. Pay now and spare the innocents whose blood will still not sate your lust."

She spat in the old woman's face. "Shove the stupid curse up your ass!"

Luca closed his eyes and shook his head. His hands trembled. He really was terrified of this witch, his own grandmother.

The old woman closed her eyes and began the chant again. A keening wail pierced Sara's head. Suddenly she was no longer on the roof. She was strolling amongst the scattered debris of a jetliner crash, salivating at the roasted-pork stink of burnt corpses. Then walking barefoot atop the backs of bloated bodies in a mass grave, leaving a trail of darker prints in dusty-white spread lime. The scene shifted again. She sat, small and trapped in the broken glass and twisted metal of a car smashed against a tree. A bloody baby doll lolling in her lap.

With a cry she was flung back onto the rooftop, writhing in sharp gravel, tearing her own hair out in clumps, clawing at her ears until they bled. *Have. To. Stop. The. Pain.* She took up the knife in trembling hands and unzipped the hoodie to bare her chest. She pressed the sharp steel point to her skin until a thin trickle of blood ran between her breasts.

"Don't!" Luca lunged and ripped the blade from her fingers. He swung it in a long arc. The old crone shrieked as the blade sliced through her neck. A gout of blood erupted. Her head rolled off her shoulders and thumped to the gravel. The eyes stayed open, wide and blank, still glaring.

He dropped the knife and knelt beside Sara. They clung to each other, trembling. His touch still seared her, but now the pain felt welcome, cleansing. Like it might even save her. "Oh my God. Thank you! Thank you! Thank you!" She kissed him again and again, sobbing.

"It's over." He squeezed her tighter. "All over now."

The wind shifted and she caught the smell of blood. Hunger swelled within her, hollowed her belly. *Empty. Hollow. Have. To. Fill. It.*

She snatched up the blade and pressed the point to Luca's chest.

His eyes widened. "What're you doing?"

"Get away," she whispered. When he didn't move, she screamed, "Get away! Run, damn it. Obey me!" She rose and swung the knife, then jerked it back, grimacing with the effort it took. Sweat ran down her face. "Don't you get it? It's *not* over. I'm still cursed."

"But you can fight it!" He took a step closer.

"Stay back!" She swung the knife and he stopped. An image of driving the blade to its hilt in his chest flashed in her head. She shivered with pleasure, then gagged. "I—I *can't*!" She saw it all again. The ditch full of genocide victims. The crash-mutilated bodies. The hunger sharpened, driving itself like a spear into mind, belly, soul. She saw the bloody cloth doll again, her soft fabric baby with the round, lifeless eyes. The way all the eyes she ever saw from now on would end up looking if she didn't somehow act to stop this. To end it.

"No, I can't." But even as she said the words she was dropping the knife, scrambling up onto the low wall. "This is how the story really ends," she told Luca.

And before he could change a word, she stepped off the ledge.

Have you noted this long ebony table of circus memorabilia? The prices are quite reasonable. Some of the items are every bit as spectacular as the opening parade of Barnum & Bailey's. An event you may have witnessed in your youth, eyes wide, mouth agape and greased with popcorn.

My own former employer, The Incunabula Brothers Shows, was where I learned to ride with real skill. And then, to ignore pain. But there were acts even more dangerous than the equestrian show. The fire-eater, for example, who risked self-immolation every night.

Walk past the carved torches and dented spurs jumbled here, the framed posters, the embroidered-velvet-and-mirror elephant caparisons, all the way to the darker end of the table. Where something small sparkles and gleams, throwing off enticing beams.

It is a sharp-featured, triangular mask, made of tiny inlaid prisms, fitted together by some long-dead master of mosaic work. Quite lovely, no? But think hard before you lift it to try on. When one assumes a new face, even once, sometimes it becomes impossible to go back. . . .

EMBER AND ASH

Corinne Alice Nulton

Between the grinding, uneven ticks of the old pocket watch stuffed in Asher's pillowcase, he saw his brother die again and again, in an endless loop.

Sixteen years earlier, when the twins had been barely two, the Incunabula Brothers' fortuneteller had suggested putting the rusty old timepiece near Asher's head to mimic the heartbeat of his brother, once both boys could no longer fit inside one crib. Neither would stay in any bed long without the other—at least not until Madame Vera had offered their frantic, sleepless mother the battered watch that so many years later still managed to force its gears to gasp out every little tick.

In the middle of the night Vera had heard their exhausted mother crying hopelessly. She'd come to their caravan and scooped up Asher before he could run, enveloping him in the prickly wool shawl she kept her arms hidden beneath. "Remember, they came into the world holding each other before you ever held them," she had explained, bouncing baby Asher on one knee. He'd giggled, then nearly gagged on the fumes of the strong, musky patchouli she wore. His brother pulled at the hem of Asher's pajama pants, wanting *his* turn. Asher had scowled and kicked him away. But when Aiden wandered off he'd scrambled down Vera's leg, the one that had been lamed, running after his brother to keep him in sight.

"Ouch!" Vera had gasped, smiling ruefully at their mother. "Ugh, you see, separating them at this age is as hard as trying to separate parts of yourself. They see themselves in each other, like mirrors. If it must be done, you must do so gently."

So for sixteen years the old watch had been a calming, steady reminder that Aiden was in the bunk above. Or that he'd merely sneaked out into the tent of his latest girlfriend. Or was practicing for some new act out under the stars. Regardless, Asher's other self had always been somewhere in reach. Their Airstream trailer, still painted with the fiery red letters of their father's old act, "Fire Cleaver," had cramped them together for most of their lives. They'd learned how to walk, how to pick pockets, how to con Oldman Jackawitz into letting them hold the baby tigers, how to gently pick up their new baby sister, how to live without a father, how to juggle fire like him, how to compose a mystical act, all in tandem. The watch was the sound of his brother's heart when it otherwise couldn't be heard.

But tonight, between the raindrops pinging off the trailer roof like bullets, the timepiece ticked a metallic screeching. Too similar to the sound of a Harley's metal carapace spinning and sparking as it slides along a concrete pavement, ripping a leather jacket to shreds and dragging the exposed flesh of his brother behind, as it spins and spins.

The suffocating stench of burnt rubber and bloodied, abraded skin filled his lungs. Each night Asher ground his teeth, hoping at least in his imagination that this time his brother would break free from the bike. For with each tick, both boy and machine moved closer to the wheels of the speeding tractor-trailer until they disappeared in a sudden fluid-y crunch and rush of wind that vanished with the passing freighter—leaving a splash of blood, a wave of flattened parts from both vehicle and human. Gone. At least until the next tick when bike and boy would crash again, leaving Asher not just brother-less and twin-less, but self-less.

Their separation had not been a gentle one. The clockwork sentry seemed a mocking reminder of that. At last Asher snaked one arm under the pillow and flung the pocket watch up against the far wall. Then he held his breath to listen.

No ticking.

He sighed with relief.

"Ash-Ash?" called a sweet little voice from beneath the covers, huddled between pillows in the upper corner of his bunk.

Oh shit. He'd forgotten Ember. He whispered, "Go back to sleep, kiddo. Please."

It wasn't that he didn't adore his five-year-old sister. He just could not stand the endless barrage of unanswerable questions.

Instead she yawned and mumbled, "When's Aiden coming home?"

"I told you, love. He's not. He's dead."

"Oh." She always acted surprised, like it was the first time she'd heard it, though she'd been told a thousand times in less than a week. "Then when can we visit him?"

"Can't, love. It's not that he just lives somewhere else. It's that he's—he's—" Asher flinched, for the damned watch had suddenly started ticking again, and again he saw his brother crash and spin. "—dead."

She snorted. "That's dumb."

"I know. Right." He sat up and started cocooning her back up in the blankets, but she only squirmed out again, to wrap her arms and legs monkey-like around Asher. Maybe some part of her had finally realized that their brother really was gone. Maybe that's why she clung, wrapping those pudgy little arms with deep folds and elbow-dimples around him so tightly. Why she tucked her head of wispy red hair so snug under his chin, in order to hear his heart beat while she slept. He almost didn't mind how sizzling hot it grew under her sweaty, restless little body.

Asher held her tight, too. He hoped they'd entered an era where the questions would finally end. And started to drift off himself, until he heard her whisper, "Aiden better come home soon. He promised me a tea party."

Asher groaned into his pillow.

The questions were unbearable. His mother had escaped, as usual, between whiskey bottles number two and three. The poor woman had already lived in a permanent state of drunken stupor for three years after their dad left. He couldn't even imagine how his brother's death would now bewitch and curse her. He'd have to get used to handling the five-year-old's questions all by himself. To combing her hair and feeding her.

And he'd have to find a new way to support them all. The lives of the twins had blurred together in synch with their scorching sarcasm, their shared face, their matching black skinny jeans and steam-punk vests and boots, their taste for burnt coffee. All as seamless as their magic act. Where, after several dangerous fire-eater tricks, one brother vanished into flames just as the other walked out of a second blaze at the climax. It suggested that the two were actually one boy—disappearing and reappearing within the fires to do other, even riskier stunts.

"Some fancy vanishing act," Engleram, the bitter old trinket-seller had belittled it, curling a whiskery lip. Yet the crowds roared for them night after night, regardless of where the circus played.

Well, Asher certainly couldn't perform that now. He couldn't *actually* do magic. So how would he support the family? His stomach churned at the thought of working solo. He peeled his sleeping sister off, stood, and then froze. There was a lump huddled in the upper bunk—had it all been a bad dream? Was Aiden really back somehow?

Gently he lifted the blanket for a peek: Tousled blond hair. Laddered black tights.

No. Just Eliza, the acrobat, the blond vixen. Aiden's girl—though not his girlfriend. She lay knotted and wrapped in the sheets as if they were the same elastic bands that suspended her from the peak of the tent. Her flawless little body could glide like a dove over an audience, but she played with boys as if they were mice, catching their tails under a falcon's talons.

But why was she here now, in his brother's bed? To feel close to him, maybe. Did she miss her favorite plaything, then?

Pft. . . serves her right, he thought and shook his head, half tempted to dump her out onto the floor. He didn't, for fear of waking the five-year-old again.

He slipped from the back room of the trailer, wedging through the jammed pocket-door into the larger living space where more carnies sprawled on couches and pallets, snoring and tossing. That was the thing with vagabonds, carnies, and circus folk. No boundaries. No privacy. His mom lay among them, head cradled in Vera's lap. The fortuneteller sat regally upright, face lost beneath the shadow of her cloak. As Asher tip-toed closer to step over them, her cane swung up between his feet, nearly tripping him.

"Where you going?" she whispered from under her hood.

Startled, he fired back, "Somewhere I can pee without ten people listening!"

"Stay," she hissed, lifting the cane to tap his chest this time.

He limbo-ed beneath it, moving faster than she could rise and follow. Hissing back, "Or else what? You'll feed me to the lions?" He chuckled at his cruel joke. He knew the rumors about her husband, after all. Who didn't? Hurting her made his own wounded soul feel less lonely. Another common circus trick.

"Asher!" she called after him. Several carnies muttered and turned over, grumbling in their sleep.

He didn't dare look back as he darted out into the crisp night air. He kept running until the tents, trucks, and trailers blurred into a river of gaudy circus colors pocked with ripples of rust, holes, and chipped paint. Only halting when he reached the glittering sign that read, "*Time Trinkets*: Collectible History and Other Rare Items to Improve Your-Story."

He snorted at the cheesy catchphrase. If hurting Vera, his second mother, had felt so revitalizing, no doubt seeking revenge on the decrepit Engleram, who'd always sneered at the brothers' act, would cure him altogether. He slipped under the curtained doorway into the dark, still tent. The old man's labored breathing was audible in the adjoining plywood annex.

Asher veered off toward the display counter. For the first time in his life there was no one to keep him from jumping behind it and fingering the oddities. Giant gems, chipped goblets, the top half of an orangutan's skull, assorted fossils, the mounted, taxidermied head of a two faced-goat, various-sized crystal balls, vintage mathematical instruments, arrays of clocks, jars and jars of grossness—one with a bug-eyed fetus. Every sort of glittery trinket and bauble, and the big black box engraved with skulls the old man had told him held the dread Black Plague. Even now he didn't dare touch that one, though petting the double-faced goat had been a childhood fantasy.

His brother would be so jealous.

At the thought, Asher caught his reflection in a prismed mosaic box on the top shelf. He imagined for a second it was his twin smiling back at him. That Aiden was once again within reach. He stood on tiptoe to glide his fingers over cool glass tiles, to touch his brother's hand. The image in the glass didn't follow his motions. No hand met his. The eerie stillness jolted him back.

"BOO!" Eliza tapped his shoulder, her lips brushing the words in a puff of hot breath against his ear. But he'd been frightened even before she touched him.

He pushed her away and returned to examining the glass-covered box.

She wasn't used to being ignored. Her fingers tapped irritably against the display case of jewels. "Whatcha doing? Get lost on your way to take a private pee?"

"Nope." He was suddenly reminded of his mission. How great it would be to wash the old trinketeer's treasures in the lasting stench of his urine. He undid his fly. "This is the spot."

He waited for her to gasp and turn away. Instead she merely stood there, pressing her half-exposed chest against the glass case, head tilted like a cat as she sized him up, waiting for his pants to drop. Annoyed, he snapped, "What the hell do you want, Eliza?"

"Not you." She shook her head, gaze still riveted on his crotch.

Blushing, Asher quickly zipped up his pants.

She giggled. "Oh, relax. Vera sent me. Told me to keep you out of trouble."

Asher rolled his eyes. "Perfect."

"Oh! How cool. An urn to keep snakes in!" She pressed an ear to a gigantic pottery vessel, curved and smooth as an ostrich egg. "I think I hear something moving in there."

"Dare you to stick your arm in!" Asher snapped. Perhaps a bite from some tame garden snake kept by Engleram would make her leave.

She smiled at the challenge, flashing big hazel eyes at him from under long blond bangs. "I *am* quite the charmer, you know."

As she bent over to peer into the neck of the vase, he leapt to grab the glass box from the top shelf. But as it toppled into his arms, along with a silky, folded black cape, he realized it wasn't a box after all. It was a mask. One he now remembered from childhood. The lines of glass triangles reflected and distorted the viewer like the curved belly of a spoon, washed in the little rainbows beaming from the corners.

"Ahhh! It bit me!" Eliza teased. When he didn't react, she spun to look at him. Her eyes widened. Real fear trembled in her voice. "Asher . . . oh God, put that back, Asher. That was the old shape-shifter's face!"

"I know what it *is*." He and his brother had all but memorized the chilling performance. The mask always sat upright and still as if propped up by a stick with the cape concealing it. As soon as the tent was jammed with an audience, the cape would shift this way and that until at last a person unfolded from it like an accordion. The face would mold into that of an old man, or young child, or pregnant woman, or shift between the tragic faces of soldiers of lost eras, aristocrats from the Dark Ages. Faceless demon-like creatures would appear with the features of cracked porcelain dolls. Shape after shape, person after person would fold themselves in and out of the cape, babbling a bit of verse, doing the occasional joke or trick. Then his or her face blurred on into that of the next individual.

"That act used to give me nightmares," Eliza muttered. Then, as if unwilling to own any weakness, she added, "Though I know now it was just an old trick and all."

"Was it?" Asher was searching for his brother again in the various shards of glass, expertly fitted, that made up the mask. What if it wasn't an act, but really a way to channel the dead? What if he could wear it and let his brother share his body? He would have him back! His sister could have tea! His mother might stop drinking!

Eliza punched him as if she could read these thoughts. "Don't be dumb. It was a scam. The act ended only because the guy ran away one night."

"Or . . . ." Asher animated the mask with one fist inside it, and glided it over to Eliza's face menacingly. "Maybe it ate him! Num-num-num!"

"Stop it!" she hissed, pushing him back.

Her shrill cry must have stirred the sleeping old man next door. The snoring from the annex halted abruptly. Engleram mumbled in Romanian until his English finally switched back on. "Ummm . . . gaaa . . . 'ello? 'elllo!"

Asher gave a deep bow and gestured to the doorway. "You're the charmer, remember? Here's your chance."

She punched him once more before ducking into the adjoining room. "Hello? Sorry, sir. It's just . . . Vera sent me for some of your wonderful tonic. Asher's mom is ill."

Her lies were always as sweet and easy to swallow as poisoned honey.

The moment she left his sight, Asher slammed the mask onto his face. It probably wouldn't work, though it had been the most memorable act of the circus. If nothing else, perhaps he could invent a new solo act with it.

The cool glass engulfed his face. An icy chill bit at his spine as the cape slipped over his shoulders. Shivering, he whispered, "Aiden?"

Suddenly he felt his eyes, his cheeks, his nose being sucked up against and then into the mirrorlike facets. The glass wasn't balancing on his cheekbones, but *inhaling* them. He grabbed at the edges, stabbing his palms on sharp corners of the triangles, trying to rip it off as it swallowed his nose, his lips, his shaggy bangs, his ears. Only his eyes did not feel the horrible suction, which seemed to be ripping up skin, blood and bones, pulling them through the narrow slits.

He thrashed desperately, flailing at it, bashing his head off the glass display case until it shattered, trying to free his disappearing self. But the back of his scalp caved inward, into the mask, his skull cracking with a horrible, final *crunch*. His limbs, his joints, his bones disassembled and curled like a squeezed accordion, compressing into the glass face. Even his feet were sucked into the prisms like limp strands of spaghetti.

Imprisoned, but he could still see out somehow. Could still watch Eliza and the old man halted in the doorway, frozen and staring as the cape hid and the mask swallowed what was left of Asher. Clearly, he realized, the former shapeshifter had not abandoned the mask, but had been absorbed into it, as he himself was being eaten. He blurred like a slithering smudge over the glass, until only the shadow of his body was framed in one of the many reflective panels of the mask.

Yes, he could see out. But he could not control the inhuman creature slowly reaching dead-branch limbs out from under the horrible face of the demon—he gasped, remembering and realizing, *I am a part of it now*— and he felt the glass morph into the cracked porcelain doll face with three rows of a needle-toothed smile. It flashed this at Eliza for a single moment before she too was suddenly *in* the smile. All that had made the acrobat beautiful was inhaled by the ravenous monster.

The old man scrambled this way and that, but as soon as the girl went limp and fell, the creature turned to him. It ate him much more slowly, with gusto, the needle teeth ripping first into his soft beer-belly. He had plenty of time to scream and curse and struggle before finally falling silent.

Then it was over. The creature folded back in, and Asher's body folded out, though the mask was still fused to his face. He rolled around screaming, soaking the cape in the blood and fleshy bits left on the floor as he wrestled with it.

"Ash-Ash?" A tentative little whisper.

Ember stood in the raised door-flap of the tent, her favorite stuffed tiger tucked under one pudgy arm.

"Stay there!" he yelled, just as the mask sucked him up and changed into the form of a six or seven year old boy.

"Come play with me, Ember!" the boy called, holding out both arms.

She shuffled forward, then stopped, wrinkling her nose when she stepped barefoot into a puddle of wet, sticky blood. "Where'd Asher go?"

Had she been there the whole time? Had she followed Eliza out and stayed hidden until now? Oh God—he looked around. The gore stretched to every corner of the tent. Even in the dark, it was clearly a bloodbath. Asher wanted to push his little sister back out so badly, to cover her eyes and tuck her back into bed, but he was helpless. He had no control.

The little boy acted like he hadn't heard her question. "Let's have a tea party, Ember. I hear you love tea parties!"

Did the monster have access to his thoughts, too? Oh God, no!

His sister took another step forward, craning her neck to look right and left, calling, "Ash-Ash, you still here?"

The little boy quickly folded back up into the mask, and the porcelain demon took his place. Crawling slowly over the ground on all fours on thin, skeletal limbs. His arms and legs dragged through the leftover bits of the corpses he'd just made. In his head Asher screamed for the monster to stop. Instead it followed Ember deeper into the tent, the glittering needle smile inching toward her. Just as one tooth grazed a feathery eyebrow, there came the familiar, suffocating sent of a spicy old perfume.

Vera.

"Away! Away!" The fortuneteller burst into the tent, throwing her cane at the monster. She scooped the child up and cradled her in one arm, while her other hand scurried spiderlike through the many chains around her neck, pulling out a scapular, a pentagram, a vial of a dirt-like substance. She threw these things at the beast one by one, but nothing deterred it. Instead it seemed to feed off the old woman's panic, coiling like a snake, standing on its back limbs, allowing that shining, broken face to tower over and grin down at Vera.

She teetered on one good leg, struggling to balance both herself and the weight of the child without her cane. As the face loomed closer she dropped her remaining amulets and with her free arm groped across the nearest wall shelf, as if some miracle might be kept up there.

He watched her finger brush the narrow metal bars and sharp vents of a space heater, the kind the carnies kept for those cold nights under canvas. The gas-canister variety with the little blue flame. Without taking her eyes off the demon she twisted the dial as high as it would go. Then dragged it off the shelf and threw it at the creature's scabby legs, which ignited even more quickly than would the dry, dead branches they resembled.

Clearly, the monster did not like fire. With a prolonged hiss it folded back into the mask.

Asher managed to leave his own glass panel then, crawling out while the monster was occupied licking its wounds, and the fortuneteller rocked the wailing child. The mask still adhered to his face, but at least he could move his arms and legs again."Vera?" he sobbed. "Vera, what the hell did I do? I didn't mean. . . I don't know what happened!"

"Oh, Asher." She shook her head and shifted Ember to one hip. Then she broke off the arm of a coat rack, holding the tip over the still-smoking heater, which was scorching the rug it had fallen upon. "I told you to stay in tonight." The flicker of light igniting from the end of the makeshift torch obscured her expression in the darkness, but a sound like tears broke her voice.

She *had* told him, hadn't she? But he hadn't listened. He tugged at the mask again. "Why can't I get this thing off? Help me, Vera, please!"

She held the flaming coat-rack arm between them, apparently still not trusting the shape that appeared to be Asher. "How? You are not yourself any more. The mask takes your soul and fuses it with the other victims, the other shapeshifters who have worn it."

"But one's a fucking monster!" Asher screamed. "And what about my face. Is it gone?"

"It too is lost, blended with the other faces trapped in the mask."

The noises of the waking circus came faintly from nearby tents outside. The growl of a stretching tiger, the cursing of the less-than-cheerful clowns wandering only half-conscious until they found their morning coffee. Out there the sun would be rising, throwing rosy beams through the movable city of tents, caravans, cars, and trucks.

"Go now," the old woman hissed. "You must leave us, and never come back."

"No!" Ember cried harder in Vera's arms.

Asher wanted to touch her, but didn't dare tempt the monster to come out again. He heaved back a dry sob that scoured his throat. Vera carried the child away from the door, so he could pass.

In the open air, the three looked at the black smoke encircling the tent. Slowly the smoldering rug would grow into flames, burning the canvas walls and the remains of the nightmare.

Vera added in a gentler tone, "At least for now, Ash. Until you learn to control your new . . . selves."

He nodded and looked up at her one more time before letting the mask mold him back into the little boy. "And what happens then? Do I get to come back?"

Vera seemed to grow taller as his own body shrank. She shrugged sadly, and raised the torch higher, casting its flickering light over herself and the child. "I wish I knew."

***

In the decade that followed, Ember wore her brother's pocket watch on a chain around her neck. She fell asleep to the grinding lullaby of each ever-slowing tick, wondering if or when it would finally stop. The watch came in handy for timing her stunts. Not long after Asher left, she started picking up matches and clicking stray Zippo lighters, studying how fire worked. By six she'd mastered the Human Candle and the Moonshot. She continued to practice until she, like her siblings, like her father, had mastered the art of flame. Her mom was a vague figure still smothered by her own grief, drowning in alcohol somewhere in the background. Vera was Ember's second mother.

"Behold the Little Matchstick Girl!" the ringmaster would proclaim as she blew kisses from center ring, flames spurting from her rosy lips in the direction of the audience. The crowds still remembered, still asked about her brothers' twin act. Oddly, though, their collective memory had somehow condensed the two of them into the figure of a single boy with great fiery talents.

Of course she argued with everyone who would listen that she'd lost not one brother but two, even though they shared the same face. One had died in a crash. The other had died in a black cape. One had lost his life. The other, his face. Those she confided in, and they were few enough, rolled their eyes at the second story. The child obviously had an imaginary friend, or simply a strange method of grieving. Perhaps she'd spent too much time with that storyteller, that card-shaper of too many futures, Madame Vera.

Sometimes Ember, too, wondered if it had all been a nightmare.

Her doubts were finally doused in an abandoned parking garage, where the camp set up one night in New York City. She had to alter her act since the garage had a low, steel-beamed concrete ceiling, and juggling fire was harder when the ground quaked with the rumble of traffic above. Still she caught the torches, doused them, and took a low bow, her red bangs brushing the cracked concrete. Coming up slowly, she caught a glimpse of a little boy out in the crowd.

The same child she'd seen that horrible night long past, when she'd lost Asher. Funny he'd known to come on the one night she could not swallow sky-high blue flames and exhale them back out over the crowd. No doubt the fire was what had kept him away all these years. That, and the clock, all the while ticking like a failing pulse over her heart.

As the applause dwindled and the audience shifted their gazes to the other ring, the boy stepped out and approached her. Cautiously, she extended the torch as a barrier between herself and the demon, just as Vera had years before.

Looking hurt, the boy shrank into a smaller girl with huge blue eyes. She whispered, "Please . . ."

"Away! Scat!" Ember hissed, shoving the torch close to the toddler. Annoyed, or perhaps merely distracted, the creature turned toward a drunken teen girl, one clad more in tattoos than in clothes, staggering towards one of the sex-service tents. The mask glinted like the sun catching sharp steel, once, twice. It flashed the porcelain monster's face as it grinned with needle teeth at the passersby. Then it morphed into a tall handsome figure. Her brother, Asher—the boy who'd mirrored Aiden so perfectly. She saw both boys were there, two in one, each superimposed over each other.

She tensed as the torch burned out and her eyes readjusted to the darkness. But the demon was gone. She absently clicked her favorite lighter, wondering if she dared follow.

No . . . on second thought, maybe not.

She felt relieved the beast was gone. And relieved, too, that not all of her brother had vanished. Not yet. He was in there, still struggling, still shifting endlessly among his myriad selves.

Not far from the entrance to The Traces, the private fae alleys where the Kindly Ones hold sway, remember to browse at a timber-sided shop called Fibula and Femur. All that might be forged from tooth and bone —responsibly and sustainably harvested, of course —can be found here. Wind chimes of ancient finger bones strung on red ribbons. Soup bowls hollowed from the brain pans of prehistoric cave bear skulls dug up in Sherwood Forest. Delicate backgammon dice carved by talented wood sprites from the toe bones of thousand year old unicorns.

I come here often. Not to buy, but to visit a particular skull which resides on a pedestal in the back room and is not for sale . . . so far as I know. One of my oldest acquaintances.

Lean closer, and you may hear him speak, and feel the words like a sudden hot breath against your temple.. . .

THE LEAST DETAILED PLANS OF A GREAT AND COMPLICATED APPARATUS

Edison McDaniels

I. The Neander Valley

The twenty-foot fall from the bluff killed the tiger, but it did not kill Cree.

Lean and sinewy, powerfully built as any ape, he had been running and climbing and punishing his body for twenty rains. Beneath a protuberant brow his large, wide set eyes appeared ever attentive. His skin was thick, leathery, and largely hairless. The sun had parched it an earthy burnt ochre.

The hard landing did break his left arm just above the elbow. It also fractured his skull. He lay unconscious, a pool of blood congealing under head and arm, until his people found him. Beside Cree lay the tiger, spitted on his spear. It had passed directly through the animal's powerful heart. His people gazed in awe at this mystical stroke of fortune and skill, then dragged them both back to the dwelling place, a cave in the low hills on the edge of the valley.

A shaman examined Cree by torchlight, chanting hard guttered consonants and soft vowel sounds, *ka-ka-ka* followed by *ti-ti-ti* over and over again. Then she pulled on Cree's arm until the exposed bone slid back under his leathery hide.

When he didn't wake by dawn, the men carried him to the mouth of the cave and turned him onto his side. They pressed his lower gut until he pissed, then fingered his hole until he shat. They turned him onto his back again and the shaman, the lone woman present, parted Cree's dirty hair. She found a deep wound just above his right ear.

This shaman, whom the clan called Raha, had seen many more than thirty rains and thus was one of the elders. She was slightly built, with a palsied arm and one leg shorter than the other. The gash in Cree's head bled anew as she poked it with a horny nail half again as long as its finger. A small boy of perhaps ten rains squatted in the dirt nearby, watching. Raha eyed him, grunted loudly, and pointed to a wooden bowl. The boy scurried insect-like, one skewed leg bent outward and fused to ninety degrees at mid-thigh. He carried the bowl back between his teeth as if he'd been born to such tasks. The shaman motioned with a clenched fist that he should crush the contents.

He sat back and worked a stone pestle between his thighs. Dung beetles and giant ants wiggled and snapped pincers as he crushed them to a gloppy paste. At Raha's bidding he held the bowl up so she could spit in it.

The men gutted the tiger and added the animal's stomach juices and bowel gruel to the bowl. The boy worked the mixture industriously to a thin paste and handed it to the shaman.

Raha sniffed once, grimaced, and grunted approval.

They laid the unconscious man in the dirt. Several men held Cree's head as Raha took up a sharp stone. Cree pissed as she incised the side of his head to enlarge the wound. She checked the bleeding by packing it with black dirt from the dark inwards of the cave, having learned from long experience that too much bleeding never ended well. Next, she rocked the sharp edge of a stone chisel back and forth against Cree's skull. Carving a crevice, deepening it until she broke through to the white soft meat below. She repeated her efforts in three more places—grunting and sweating all the while—finally prying out a square of bone the size of a large beetle.

Raha swept long bony fingers into the hole and under the edge of Cree's skull, sinking the one with the clawlike nail in to the second knuckle. A large clot pushed out and dribbled free, and the convoluted gray surface of Cree's brain came into view. The shaman spat and wiped her own forehead, hand trembling with fatigue. She filled the hole in the skull with as much paste from the boy's bowl as it would accept, and wrapped his head in the hide of the tiger he'd so remarkably killed. Later, she made a necklace of the beast's eyeteeth and hung it around his neck.

Many days after that Cree regained consciousness. His arm gradually healed even more crookedly than his head. He would always have a beetle-sized divot in his skull to remind the people of how sacred he now was. He wore the tiger's eyeteeth as a trophy, and aged very slowly, living another three score rains, an impossibly long time. He outlived every one of the people present that remarkable day, outlived even their children, and most of their children's children. He even outlived Raha.

When his spirit finally fled his body, the people washed and wrapped his mortal remains in the hide of the very same tiger whose yellowed eyeteeth still hung around his neck. This high honor was made greater yet as hundreds of dung beetles and other insects were wrapped in the hide with him. Thus reduced in time, his holy bones and sacred skull were buried under the dirt at the back of a cave in what would later be called the Neander Valley of Germany. There they moldered undisturbed for one hundred thousand years.

II. Jolly Frye, M.D.

In Maryland in 1881, three days after his twenty-first birthday, Jolly Frye completed a two year program of study at the Baltimore College of Medicine. The first year he'd been ranked third in a class of twenty-two, but by graduation stood first of the nineteen remaining. A feat less difficult than one might assume, since the second year was merely a repeat of the first year's lectures. By then he'd run his hands through the decomposing entrails of exactly two cadavers. The first being the remains of a person of low character who had died incarcerated in Ravenstown Debtors Prison on the banks of the Chesapeake. The second, procured from the local hospital, was a fat unfortunate little man whose girth reminded Jolly of a woman seven months gone with child, and whose skin was as yellow as summer grass. The poor fellow had died with pale chalky stools and a water-filled belly. That is to say, from an inflammation of the liver, if such could be judged by that pocked, shriveled organ.

A doctor fresh from schooling is like a loaded gun. Or perhaps, more aptly, a horse yet to be broken. For a new physician needs nothing if not to be broken himself. What the young Jolly knew coming out of Baltimore Med was a little pharmacy, a bit less anatomy than grasped by his butcher, and still less of the conundrum that is the body at war with itself. He was akin to an engineer who has been privy to the least detailed plans of a great and complicated apparatus, yet has rarely beheld the device himself. Jolly had some rudimentary inkling of how the body worked, though only in the theoretical. He had studied disease in its many manifestations, but from afar. He was book learnt but lacked practical knowledge.

His most interesting possession was an ancient skull, bronzed with a patina of age, given him by an ancient professor of surgery named Otto Chadwick. The German—he spoke English with that over-articulated 'Veek for Week' accent—had learned his surgical arts in the abattoirs of European masters long before Jolly had been born. From the Neander Valley of Germany, he was a small, delicate man of impeccable dress, with an affinity for string ties. He had come to the States during the late war as a mercenary soldier. A bullet to the head had stroked his dominant arm at Petersburg in 1864, though he'd miraculously recovered and stayed on after the North's victory. Despite the apoplexy and coarse tremor that ensued, this otherwise useless hand and arm moved with unequaled grace during surgery. Indeed, Otto Chadwick was the most skilled surgeon in Baltimore for the fifteen years immediately following the Civil War.

Professor Chadwick was not only apoplectic, but perhaps prophetic. Not a few claimed he was mad, being nocturnal by nature and prone to long rants if disturbed unaccountably in his office or especially while operating. He spent his days with a single-minded fervor behind the knife, often berating himself and those around him for the mildest perceived slight. His nights unfolded in the seamier parts of Baltimore, where he lived alone in a large home with only a youngish widow woman he referred to as 'my housekeeper' for company. In the summer of 1881 Chadwick presented Jolly with a small tightly-wrapped box at the end of his second year of study. The attached note read: *I am done. This will bring out the best in you, my boy—and the worst as well, I fear.* The professor died the evening of that graduation day of a brain hemorrhage. Thus the cryptic note was never explained.

Also unexplained—and largely unmentioned, at least in polite company—were the soul-less cretins discovered in the professor's basement some weeks after his death. They numbered a half dozen or so, for accounts of the matter were vague and shadowy. His housekeeper claimed to have had no knowledge of their presence. A big-boned, intemperate woman, salacious and alcoholic, she was confronted on her doorstep by a crowd of respectable citizens.

"Tainted," one official said, shaking his head as he watched the mob.

"Stained by the devil's work," said another.

Then a neighbor woman shouted, "Witch!" and events deteriorated from there. The drunken woman was spared the pyre, but only by the thinnest margin, run out of town at the point of a pitchfork instead. The cretins themselves scattered to the countryside. Or perhaps were destroyed with the burning-down of the house. Rumors abounded.

The newly minted Doctor Frye had no use for scandal or rumor. He had known the professor just well enough to accompany him on three or four of his nightly rounds, an experience of which he never spoke afterward. He had no idea why Chadwick would present him with a gift, let alone make it a dying wish. He discovered upon opening the box that he was the new owner of a skull. Jolly, an eager student of both medicine and anatomy, was amused.

He examined it, noting the curious presence of a hole above the right ear. An irregular square somewhat larger than a two-bit piece. He could drop a walnut through the opening with no trouble, and the nut would rattle around the braincase, falling out when he turned it over. Probably a battle wound, though the skull looked too old to have belonged to a veteran of the Late Unpleasantness. A certain feeling emanated from it as well, something less than holy. In Jolly's hands the bony orb seemed infused with the spirit of the dead German.

This last idea sounded mad, but he couldn't shake the notion. Nor could he manage to part with the skull. He tossed it away into the littered alley behind his house that evening. The next morning it was back on the table in the dining room. Jolly felt certain he hadn't gotten up in the night to retrieve it, though he'd found mud smeared on his sheets that morning. He couldn't explain this, and was no longer amused.

The next week he went so far as to bury the thing in the countryside. He managed a single day of peace before he inexplicably found himself bent in the dirt, digging the bone up with his bare hands, by torchlight. He hadn't felt able to breathe in its absence, as if it was himself he'd buried in that hole. It took a week to pick the dirt from under his fingernails.

After that the skull went into his medical bag, where it remained without further incident. The bag went everywhere with him.

Dr. Jolly Frye was well studied in lung fever, thanks to an unusual abundance of cases in Baltimore. This dire inflammation caused the patient to have difficulty breathing and a wet, phlegm-riddled cough. It required the most immediate attention, first giving an emetic—tartrate of antimony or pulverized ipecac were the usual. Tincture of Virginia snake-root, swallowed every half-hour in teaspoonful doses, induced free perspiration. If a rapid pulse supervened, it was better to substitute tincture of veratrum viride, three to ten drops every hour, which sweated one even more effectively. A mustard plaster of the chest was moved elsewhere as the skin became sore, the better to excoriate a wide area. The bowels could be opened with a preparation of salts of magnesia, then the patient given flaxseed or slippery elm tea by mouth. The diet was reduced to Indian-meal gruel, very thin. With these careful modern attentions, in most cases the fever finally abated. Then the patient, now feeble and low, was dosed with tonics compounded of gentian and a lesser amount of nitro-muriatic acid. This last served both to bring the unfortunate soul around and to guard against a relapse.

At the Baltimore College of Medicine Frye had also attended women through the travail of childbirth, at least a dozen at the same sordid hospital as had housed the fat, very dead man with the corrupted liver. Jolly had watched half of these unfortunate females die of puerperal fever within days of confinement. He noted with interest that all who died had given birth at the hospital. Those lying in at home had lusty babies and rarely took sick—and even then were likely to recover if the physician could bide his time and occupy himself in pursuits distant from the ailing. These observations were the first practical bits of medical knowledge he took home.

Thus prepared, Dr. Jolly Frye moved West to hang his shingle in St. Louis. The bag ever accompanying him, he practiced general medicine and a little surgery. He saw toothaches, earaches, stomachaches, and migraines. He attended a large family overcome by charcoal fumes, saving only the youngest, who owed her life to Jolly's sudden inspiration to paint her face with cider vinegar. The notion—really more of a hunch—had come unbidden, like a hot breath at his temple. It had felt as if his head would explode had he not tried it. Such notions, which he referred to as his *imperfect work*, came occasionally as he progressed in learning and experience.

Men were thrown from horses. Wagon wheels collapsed under loads too heavy, rolled over and crushed their drivers. Drunkards stumbled from tawdry places and fell in the street. The good doctor also became adept in the use of the Nelaton probe for finding bullets, though extracting them remained a fraught undertaking. In these cases and more, Dr. Jolly Frye excelled. He saved folks others could not, though at times even he could not say where his curious—even miraculous—ideas came from.

"It is my imperfect work," he would sometimes murmur when pressed. Slowly this imperfect work took on the ardor of obsession.

He also married, then found he couldn't abide the smell of her cologne. His new wife was not lusty enough. He wanted licentiousness and she was not of that order, either. She hated the way he carried his bag everywhere, even to dinner or the theater. She tripped over it on their wedding night. It was the last thing she saw before sleep and the first thing on waking. When after their second year together she insisted she did not want it inside the house, they divorced.

Ten years on, a young boy in town was kicked silly by a horse. Jolly plastered the child's head and waited. The boy lay an entire day unconscious. Afterwards he suffered sudden, violent paroxysms. Jolly prescribed a strengthening liniment, waiting for his imperfect work to speak up. But the fits continued one or two a day for weeks and the hot breath at Jolly's temple did not come. The boy—insane or epileptic or both—at last succumbed. It was like that sometimes. Jolly could not control the notions. They came unbidden, and would not be commanded.

The boy had left a scar on the doctor's psyche, however. Watching him writhe so violently, pissing and shitting himself day in and day out, had been hard. More than once Jolly had thought to end it, but he'd really wanted to save the poor sufferer. Perhaps, for his own sanity, had *needed* to save him. But need, it seemed, had nothing to do with his imperfect work.

Now, fifteen years after leaving Baltimore for Missouri, Jolly had another itch in his craw. The medical bag he carried was gaining weight. Or perhaps it only *seemed* heavier, and he was getting older. Possibly the heft of the thing at the end of his arm was an effect of the rheumatism, but he doubted that, being fit as a fiddle otherwise.

It was the goddamned skull.

Slowly, inexplicably, it had become part of him, like an extra appendage or a growth. Yes, a tumor, he decided. A diseased piece of flesh he'd have cut out of one of his patients. It festered, but never quite fulminated. Instead, it gained weight. And like an abscess kept growing, pushing aside all in its way.

Or perhaps it was Jolly's obsession with the skull that gained weight. No matter. He prescribed a change of venue as he might for a consumptive seeking a sanitarium, and packed his bags and headed farther west, all the way to the Pacific coast. Perhaps fresh salt air would lighten his load.

San Francisco in the late 1890s was a lively place with no shortage of cattle, money, guns, whores, and card games. All of which meant no shortage of work for enterprising physicians. And Jolly was above all enterprising. He not only wanted, he needed to save people. He set his sights on Chinatown, a particular den of iniquity. The stories he heard would curl teeth. A man could get lost in such a place.

He found the Gold Coast abuzz with Pasteur's revolutionary germ theory, which had recently been validated. Listerian antisepsis and its carbolic acid spray was all the rage.

By then Jolly had begun to call the skull Chadwick. Sometimes he had the insane idea it was ranting a lecture at him in something akin to German, just as the old professor used to do. It went to The Gold Coast as well, in a black box at the bottom of his medical bag.

That bag which never left Jolly's side.

III. Chadwick

Jolly was not prepared for Chadwick's first words to him. One Saturday afternoon he was in his private clinic near the waterfront, leaning over the near-lifeless body of a young man who'd fallen a dozen feet from a roof somewhere out in the city. Unfortunately, he had landed on his head, face first. A two-foot piece of iron stake protruded from the socket where the left eye had formerly looked out. The impaled man was breathing slow, laborious, agonal breaths. He might survive an hour, two at the most.

—If he can survive an hour, he can survive a day. Und if a day, then a veek.

The words came unbidden on a hot breath that filled Jolly's head like water rushing uncontrollably over a cofferdam. He straightened, hands held up before him, searching the room over the tops of his spectacles. As he had already known, he and the impaled man were alone. Jolly felt certain his patient hadn't spoken. In his professional opinion, the man was unlikely ever to speak again. Aside from that, the voice and its accent were familiar.

"Who's there?" Jolly asked.

—*Me und you. Uns.*

"Who is . . . me?" Jolly hazarded, not sure he wanted an answer.

—*Chadvick.*

Jolly would have thought it a jest, except no human joker would have been able to get inside his head. He wasn't so much hearing the voice as feeling it. As if a window had been flung open, one that had not existed a moment before, and he was looking out on a totally new vista. Or rather—and this felt more to the point—someone else was looking in on him. And that person could see *everything*.

Though he had probably never in his life wanted to do anything less, he turned his head. On the floor beside the door sat his black bag. *Jolly Frye MD* was stamped in inch-high gold letters near the top. The clasp, which Jolly hadn't opened that morning, was now undone. The dark mouth of the bag yawned wide. "Damnation," he muttered.

—*Ve must vent the pressure, quickly.*

In Jolly's head it sounded—or felt—like German. Just as he thought this, the bag twitched. He took a cautious step toward it.

The man on the table was growing duskier with each passing second. His long thick hair was probably black but so full of blood Jolly couldn't be certain. The patient made a choking sound. His Adam's apple bobbed up and down, then began to shake in a seizure. The medical bag twitched again, this time with an audible rustle. Jolly ignored the convulsing man and took another step toward the bag. He could see the inner contents near the top now. The smeared newsprint of *The San Francisco Chronicle*, folded and tucked into an inner pocket. Behind it, a sheaf of papers in a loose-leaf binder. A worn copy of *Saxson's Surgery Principles for the General Specialist*. The top of his wooden instrument case with its clasp still appropriately fastened. The gleaming bell of his stethoscope.

And the bronze patina of the curved top of the skull.

"What in hell . . . I did not take you out of your box." Then Jolly realized he'd said *you*. Not *that*. Not *it*. "Chadwick?" he added unwillingly.

—*There is no time. Ve must act quickly.*

Jolly leaned over the bag. In its depths he could make out the rest of the skull. The box that had held it was now black dust in the bottom of the bag, as if it had corroded away. The hole in the cranium, on the right side just above the ear, was now silhouetted in red.

Blood red. As if it were bleeding.

"Jesus Christ," he whispered.

—*No. Chadvick.*

And that was how it began.

IV. A God

From that moment on Chadwick guided him.

The first order of business was to gather up the impaled man on the table and move him to the operating theater, maintained in Jolly's private clinic for his more affluent patients. Most of his work was done at the public hospital, of course, but an incision opened in such a den of filth was likely to fester. Jolly preferred a patient's dining room to that hell hole. Of course, home surgery was simply impractical with modern Listerian antisepsis. Nobody wanted carbolic acid sprayed all over his furnishings. The stuff ate into everything. It killed bugs, but tarnished silver. And hands. Every surgeon and surgeon's assistant in town had chemical dermatitis. Jolly's hands eternally itched. The outer skin turned black and peeled incessantly.

Moving the man was no problem. Jolly discovered his arms now possessed twice the strength of the day before. An animalistic vigor flowed through his extremities as he gathered the patient up and carried him across the hall. He laid him face up on the operating table, adjusting his head to maintain the airway. The impaled man went from dusky gray to not quite pink with his next few breaths.

Jolly set the skull on the table too. Was Chadwick looking at him, at both of them? He thought so. The skull had no eyes, of course. But something had changed. Not merely the fresh blood lining that hole, but the bony eye sockets themselves. Jolly had once seen an ape, some years earlier at the Philadelphia zoo, with a bulging brow ridge. The skull's forehead seemed to mimic that ape now, its missing eyes shadowed under powerful, primitive prominences.

The skull of a caveman. The thought came to him in the exact manner of his imperfect work—as a hot, unbidden breath against one temple.

Inside my temple, he corrected. *Or no. Inside my head.*

No time to dwell on such insanity. He quickly set up the Listerian apparatus to spray carbolic acid over the surgical site, and retrieved knives and trephine drill from his bag. He took off his sack coat, rolled his sleeves to mid-forearm, and reached for the spike impaling the man's eye.

The very goddamn structure of Chadwick's bony *face* morphed into indignation. One side of the mouth, both upper and lower jaw, skewed upward as if made of molten lead rather than solid bone. It had no lips with which to bend words, but it bent them nonetheless.

—*Leave it. Ve must vent the pressure. There is no time. Ve must act now, without delay.*

Jolly hesitated just long enough to take in a fortifying breath, then tied the man's long hair back and made a quick slice with his knife. On the right, behind the hairline. He cut to the bone in one fell swoop and tied off the temporal artery before it could bleed much. This was all *so easy.* Why hadn't he seen it before? He laid bare the skull by pulling aside the skin and temporalis muscle. When he picked up the drill Chadwick's liquid bones actually *smiled.* Trephining the skull, always so laborious in the past, now seemed as easy as ligating the artery. He knocked out the final bit with a chisel and small carpenter's hammer. Less than twenty minutes had passed. Incredibly, the impaled man's chest still rose and fell.

A thin mist of carbolic acid filled the room, renewing itself periodically from the spray apparatus. Jolly's hands tingled and itched.

Once he had the skull vented, he pushed a finger inside and curled it around to extract the clot of blood Chadwick told him was there. Out came a reddish-gray glob, blood mixed with brain matter.

"He's a dead man." Jolly's shoulders slumped.

—*Not at all.*

The disembodied voice of the dead German echoed in Jolly's head, underlaid by something else. Ka-ka-ka ti-ti-ti? The sounds were decidedly not German. In fact, no language Jolly had ever heard, and there were many spoken in the saloons and alleys of San Francisco.

—*He vill live a day. Ve must collect a few incidentals.*

They left the man in the theater, brain still open to the air. Chadwick said they wouldn't be gone long. Jolly had always been a practical man, a conscientious physician, so he covered his still impaled patient with a sheet. Before closing the door he glanced back. The white linen drape looked for all the world like a winding cloth.

He and Chadwick were gone an hour. First they stopped by an apothecary. In Chinatown he carried Chadwick inside the herbalist's shop, a bulge under his jacket. The owner, a cadaverically thin Asian with a pencil mustache and wispy hair possibly thinned by years spent smoking his own root concoctions, seemed nonplussed by the doctor's request.

"Yes, of course I have cockroaches," he answered in response to Jolly's question.

"We—that is, I—would like a handful."

A nod. "Desiccated, no doubt?"

Jolly looked down, pulling his jacket open a tad before he nodded back.

The herbalist moved slowly behind the counter to a large glass jar on a shelf. He opened it and pulled out a handful of dried roaches.

Jolly hesitantly stepped forward. "That appears to be *blattella germanica*."

"I am impressed, kind sir. It is a rare man who knows his roaches."

Jolly glanced under his jacket at Chadwick, whose stony face performed that liquid contortion again. "I actually need *archimylacris eggintoni*."

"Ah, a very good choice indeed. But *b. germanica* is as close as you will find, I fear."

Jolly's own face now contorted. "But . . but I must have *a. eggintoni.*"

The proprietor shifted his weight and sighed. "But *b. germanica* is a very able substitute, whatever your need. Of this I assure you. Besides, *a. eggintoni* is no more."

"How's that, you've run out?"

"It is, how do you say, extinct. For over 50,000 years."

They left without the roaches, after Chadwick explained in a hot burst that desiccated cockroaches lacked 'vital spirit.' The waterfront was infested with vermin of a most vital sort, Jolly decided. Back in his clinic they searched the damp cellar by candlelight. He had never seen so many roaches; *b. germanica* was everywhere.

—*Von't do.*

Yet it was all they had. So Jolly mixed the drugs and herbs to a gruel, as directed, using his own spit as binder. He stepped on a large cockroach—he couldn't have said it was *b. germanica* or *a. eggintoni*; to him they were all the same—then another and another, and scraped them off the floor. He added the crushed insects to the gruel, which become a noxious paste. Chadwick gave the instructions, after listening intently to that unfamiliar foreign cry. The instructions would not have been intelligible without his translation. Or that, at least, was Jolly's sense of it, for all of this sordid business took place in his head, his hands obediently doing the bidding of those two voices.

—*Ka-ka-ka ti-ti-ti.*

Only gradually, with the ranting of that foreign tongue pinging off his brain, did Jolly understand he'd made a hole in his patient's skull not to take something out but to put something in. After a moment's hesitation he filled it with the roach paste and sewed the flap closed, feeling not one hope in a hundred this wound would ever heal. The man could not possibly survive.

But the following morning, a Sunday, the patient's pulse was stronger. At Chadwick's insistence, Jolly pulled the stake from the impaled eye. There was no bleeding. He half-carried, half dragged the man, since he no longer had the unnatural strength of the day before, to the cellar. Still not convinced the fellow would live, and not wanting others to know of this experimental treatment if he died.

He watched his patient carefully. Within a week, the wounds were healing. The fastest recovery Jolly had ever seen, especially considering the severity of the original injury. He was ecstatic. *What modern miracle have I discovered?*

Weeks passed. The man rose from his bed but didn't speak. At first, he merely huddled in a corner and shat himself, growing pale and sallow from lack of sunlight. He failed to thrive, yet did not die. The one remaining eye must have been keen, though, for as the weeks passed into months the remains of rats and the occasional cat or dog appeared in the cellar room. This patient reminded Jolly of a primitive, with the withered flesh and coarse sinew of a reluctant cadaver.

Why does not he die? Jolly asked himself this several times a day for years. Feeling ashamed of what he'd created, yet also fascinated. He was a man of science, living in the vaunted modern age of Listerian Antisepsis. Since the days of antiquity, man had tried to incise the human body. Nearly always the result had been the same: the fester of infection, the specter of death looming large.

I have changed all that. The impaled man should have been dead several times over. That he was alive, withered or not, was no small miracle.

What else could he conclude? Chadwick must be a god.

V. The Question

Why does he not die?

The question tortured Jolly between visits to his women. A different one every night. As a young man, his sexual needs had been few. But approaching fifty he became obsessed. Or perhaps possessed. The devil was in him and he couldn't help himself. It wasn't just that his need for release had increased. He'd developed certain proclivities that disturbed him.

For one thing, a taste for meat so rare as to be nearly raw. He didn't even like scorch marks. He wanted his meat to bleed, just as he wanted his women—

No. Some things one could not contemplate. What he did in the gray hours after midnight he feared would someday be the death of him. Certainly the death of somebody. He lacked control. Or rather Chadwick did. That goddamned skull.

Why does he not die?

Two and a half years after the impaled man had left his operating theater for the cellar, another unfortunate came within Jolly's grasp. A nameless boy dropped unceremoniously on the doorstep, appearing leper-like or possibly plague-ridden. He labored to breathe, drooling like an imbecile with his neck so twisted that his gaze was fixed nearly behind himself. Jolly immediately recognized a festering meningitis. Chadwick, presumably watching from his usual spot on the shelf beside Frye's medical bag, concurred. Though the lack of eyes always made it difficult to tell for certain where Chadwick was looking.

Jolly knew what was called for, or what Chadwick said, anyway. But he couldn't bring himself to do it. He had brought one man back from the brink only to revive a creature with a subhuman mien. So he left the boy twitching on the floor and withdrew to his private library. Of course he took the skull with him. Chadwick insisted upon it. Chadwick always insisted.

Drapes drawn, Jolly stood in the darkness of his library and fingered a half-empty shot glass. In the flickering gaslight he gummed a mouthful of whiskey and stared down at Chadwick. Sometimes the burnished bone alongside the hole in that damnable skull gleamed as if made of polished rosewood. It appeared so now, infuriating Jolly. He could see his own eyes staring back at him in the bone's high gloss—like casket wood, that shine. They reflected listless and unfocused, much like those of a bloated man he'd once stuck in the gut to drain off the wretched bile that was killing him.

"You misbegotten son of a whore." Jolly slammed the glass down on the library desk.

Chadwick did not flinch. At least so far as Jolly could tell.

"Goddamn you! I can't do it. I won't. The man—he lived but does not live. He breathes, but there is no fire *here*. Inside. How is that possible?"

Jolly snatched up the glass and pressed it to his forehead, looking to the ceiling. As if some answer might be written there by a God he'd never trusted, nor cared to. When none came, he downed the remaining whiskey and chucked the glass toward the skull.

The jigger knocked Chadwick off the shelf. He tumbled through the air, taking long enough to hit the floor that Jolly had time to imagine himself tumbling in just such a manner. He gasped and dove to catch it, but the skull struck the floorboards inches from his outstretched fingers. It broke into a half-dozen jagged shards.

Jolly lay on the hardwood stunned, not quite whimpering. After a brief instant of regret—*What now?*—it dawned on him that this was what he'd wanted. Wasn't he now *free?*

"Yes, yes. Thank God. Free." He levered himself up and leaned back against the bookcase, spine pressing an upright edge. He took a deep breath and exhaled. But if he was, why then didn't he *feel* free?

From somewhere nearby came a low, ululating howl.

Jolly muttered under his breath, "What the hell was that? A wounded animal? Yes, no doubt. Some unlucky cur caught under a carriage wheel." His voice quavered with desperate hope.

But it came again, far too close. Not some dog in the road. The sound was long, dirge-like, and not merely nearby. It had come from directly beneath him.

"A stray has taken up residence in the cellar." But even as he said this, Jolly knew that wasn't right. No dog could live long in that black place. *Why, the only thing down there is . . is . . .*

"Something is now moving *down there.*" He *felt* it in his spine, through the faint vibrations conveyed by the bookcase. Sweat slicked his back and armpits.

A thump came on the stairs.

"Oh God. No." He looked at the door. *Closed, thank goodness.* Had he locked it, though? He didn't know. Would it matter? He didn't think so. He stole a glance at the fragments of the skull. Were they quivering, or was that a trick of the gaslight?

I must put Chadwick back together. Right now.

He crawled to the scattered bones. The thumps continued up the stairs, closer and in time with each beat of his heart, which he felt severely in the depths of his chest. Jolly collected the fragments so clumsily his fingers seemed to belong to someone else. The pieces of bone felt foreign, not at all familiar.

The thing that was ascending—Jolly couldn't bring himself to think of it as a man, not anymore—must be at the top of the stairs now. "It's on this floor." His voice trembled at the exact pitch of a terrified child lost in the dark. He fumbled with the shards of bone, trying to fit them together again. His hands, which had done so many difficult tasks over the years, couldn't manage this one simple thing—the only thing that mattered at that moment.

He pressed two curved pieces together and Chadwick's left eye socket suddenly stared up at him. Another jagged piece slotted in. Soon Chadwick had half his face and base of one ear back. But the thing was coming down the hall now, sounding off-fettle as it dragged one foot and clumped the other heavily with every other step.

Jolly's crotch grew sodden with piss; the room turned rank. Moaning, he groped at the two parietal bones—large, mostly flat with broad curved contours—and pushed them together over the top of Chadwick's skull, recreating the braincase. The skull looked of a piece now, but didn't *feel* complete. Jolly held it up before him. Chadwick seemed to leer back, though with only half a leer.

"Your lower jaw. Where the hell's your lower jaw?" He held his breath and stole a glance at the door. The knob was slowly turning. He spied the jawbone under the fainting couch, lunged to curl his fingers around it, and pulled it to him. This bit all but reattached itself.

The door had opened far enough for Jolly to see that he did not want it to open any farther. A grimy gray-hued hand with ragged nails gripped the edge. It swung in another inch or two and then . . . stopped.

—*That hurt*, Chadwick said.

"I-I'm sorry. It was an accident. One that will never happen again."

The door closed with a snick of the latch. The thing shambled and clunked its way back down the hall, back to the bowels of the cellar.

Back to hell, Jolly thought but did not say aloud.

—*Ve have more vork to do, you und I,* Chadwick said.

Jolly nodded emphatically, if not enthusiastically. If the words had come like a hot breath before, they scalded now.

Back in the exam room he looked at the failing boy. Emaciated, filthy. No longer did he convulse. But waves of fever came off him like heat from a coal stove. Jolly touched one bony arm. Skin dry as parchment. He pulled the eyelids up. The listless child stared past him. Not quite the glazed-over death stare, but close. He might have been blind for all Jolly could tell. Yet perhaps here was a chance to make history. To use science. The boy was certainly dying, so . . .

—*Ve must vent the pressure.*

Jolly picked up Chadwick in one hand and cradled the child, who seemed to weigh nothing, in the other. In the theater he set up the carbolic acid sprayer, selected a knife, and pulled a trephine drill from his bag. The room filled with corrosive mist. The thing in the cellar guttered something inhuman and unintelligible. Jolly's hands tingled and itched.

But Chadwick guided him. The insanity that followed was not for any but the stoutest and hardest of heart.

VI. A Wasted Bunch

The nameless boy fared no better than the impaled man. He did confirm Jolly's supposition that something in the revolting paste was, if not life affirming, at least death defying.

Three years passed. Five. Then seven. The imperfect work which Jolly had once told himself was in the name of science more and more seemed to serve obsession and madness. But it continued, like the thing in the cellar. Always under Chadwick's perverted guidance. Their animating spirit lost, his patients survived. They were in fact goddamned indestructible.

Jolly toasted his imperfect work in bars across the waterfront, unable to get them out of his head, let alone his cellar. A wasted bunch, no soul to speak of, a corruption of the human condition. Most physicians are haunted by the patients they have lost. Jolly saved his and was haunted all the more. Their number in the cellar increased by one or two each year.

He couldn't bring himself to kill them. Indeed, he didn't know if it was possible. Besides, they were his creations. He had pulled them back from the brink. Did not every doctor dream of such triumphs—if not in reanimating, then surely in staving off death?

The creatures came and went at odd hours of the morning, always under cover of darkness. They trapped rats and mice and insects and sucked the essence of life from them like milk from a mother's teat. They roamed alleys, molesting trash heaps, plundering chicken coops and cattle pens. On the blackest nights—Jolly soon grew to loathe the dark of the moon—they came out in packs. Sometimes they took entire cows, but more often only parts, leaving the dying, bleating animal to be found by its master in the morning. Some even dug up fresh graves. Jolly feared more the day when they might seek a fresher two-legged meat.

Rumors abounded. The neighborhood was said to be haunted. Unmentionable things moved in the shadows. The number of strays around Chinatown fell to nil. Whatever problem the rest of San Francisco might have with rats, the blocks around Jolly's clinic had none.

Sometimes the police investigated, but never in any serious manner, not at the edge of Chinatown. Jolly's clinic sat on the borderland between it and the rest of the waterfront. Once a mosquito-infested, inhospitable swamp, the last part of San Francisco to be drained and occupied. Given to the Chinese precisely because it was felt by the city fathers to be near uninhabitable. Two problems solved in one swipe of the pen. The prolific Celestials were as hearty as the rats living in the sewers and considered as filthy by the white residents. But they would be largely out of sight, thus out of mind. Perhaps the insect problem would soon abate too.

The city's leaders preferred the Chinese to the mosquitoes, but that was as far as it went. They had no interest in policing them inside their own pestilential community. The transgressions which abounded there were not the city's most urgent business. Officials couldn't be bothered with myth and innuendo. The Chinese, a superstitious lot, came to them with tales of half dead horses with missing legs. Of pets vanishing in the night. Of grave robbing. Mere apocryphal things.

And so the people took to burning their refuse, and learned to keep cherished pets, even livestock, close indoors. At night neighbors shuttered their windows against the occasional disturbing sounds coming from within the boarded-up windows under the white doctor's clinic. The noises of wild animals feeding, of death abroad on foot, of things best ignored by civilized souls.

The sounds of Chadwick's people.

VII. Mad Dog

A primal lust whispered in Jolly's ear as a disembodied breath of hot air. *Fuck her again*. He'd shot his wad twice already, and still did not feel satiated. *I don't need you for this. This I could have done with my wife.*

Of course the woman on the bed was not his wife, for he had shed her long before in Baltimore. Half his age, this one smelled of boiled eggs and the lye soap used downstairs in the laundry. He preferred the stink of the pig pens and horse stalls in the alley.

He looked over at Chadwick and a renewed urge filled him. Lust flared up his spine like a lit fuze, intent on boiling the very skin from his bones. He thought, or perhaps only imagined, Chadwick was looking back. It was of course difficult to tell where the gaze of an eyeless skull fell, precisely. Jolly pushed into the woman again.

The warm air that blew across the low San Francisco hills and into the open windows was redolent of salt and sardines. The pungent smell of boiled fish guts mingled with dried herbs wafted up from the Chinese kitchens at street level. Roosters crowed and chickens clucked in nearby pens. Somewhere out in the Bay a distant steam whistle pierced the night, shrill and caustic and haunting.

Jolly's breath came once again in quick, short gasps. Sweat slicked his armpits. He pulled the woman closer and ground himself against her. She had black hair, which he liked. She exhaled a breathy, sultry tone each time he thrust. The thin bed complained loudly as they bounced up and down.

"You cheap whore." The words were for her, but they could describe him just as well.

Another breath of hot air, a sharp and then sibilant sound like ka-ka-ka ti-ti-ti repeated several times. Jolly looked down on the girl under him. How docile she was even in the midst of all his pounding. He covered her lips with his, grunted and looked over at Chadwick. He spat in her face. No reaction. He bit her shoulder hard and she came alive then, flailing and thrashing. She punched his face and he fell back, reveling in the iron taste of her blood mixed with his own. He spent himself in his hand.

Finally satiated, Jolly rose and dressed. He looked at the girl on the bed, at the blood seeping from her bitten shoulder and cursed himself. He'd gotten carried away, but it wasn't his fault. The whore was only half his age, and still had barely managed to keep up.

"For your trouble." He tossed a silver dollar on the nightstand.

"You crazy," the girl muttered. "Like mad dog."

"Probably." He looked in the mirror, prodding the bruise on his cheek. "Thanks for this, it did help." He wiped blood from his lips and mouth with her petticoat and tossed it on the bed beside her.

"Mad dog," the girl spat again, scowling.

"All men are mad dogs, missy. Some merely more honest in their acts." He turned out the oil lantern and picked up Chadwick. The weight of the skull was lead in his hands. He left via the front stairs, as always, and decided a stroll through the crowded, winding streets of Chinatown would be reviving. The stench of piss and horse manure in the gutters kept him moderately aroused the whole way home.

VIII. Apocalypse

When the apocalypse did come, Jolly was with one of his girls. Not a Chinese this time. His proclivities were too well known in Chinatown by 1906. No madam who valued her stock would let him through the door. He'd come to appreciate the baser instincts, and the Chinese were too proud a people to fulfill his needs. He preferred a common street whore who rarely bathed or complained. They gave blood, if not freely, then wantonly. At least, that's what Chadwick claimed.

Feeling the skull's hot, grotesque breath ever at his temple built up a black steam within Jolly. An overheated boiler will blow, but his girls were the vent. His, because he ruined them. A single night touched by that black steam, and they were left boiled bags of skin and bones. Scalded, so to speak. Jolly's recollections of these escapades had become increasingly clouded. Some days he lost time. Others he fell into a stupor and could barely recall his name. Was it Jolly, or Chadwick? With each passing day he felt less the former and more the latter.

On the morning of April 18, 1906, while fucking his latest wench, he caught her upper lip between his teeth and tore it off as a jackal might rip into its prey. The wash of blood was exquisite, her screams primal. Hot liquid spilled across his hands to lubricate their way around her neck. He squeezed tighter. The whore's eyes bulged. She writhed under him as no woman ever had before. He felt the strength of two—no, ten—men. Her neck snapped like a piece of dry kindling and she went limp against his hardness.

Yet Jolly knew none of this by then. The long transformation was complete. Inside, whatever part of him remained wasn't enough to light a match. The eyes that peered out now from his bony orbits possessed a depraved lust the late physician could never have mustered on his own.

Fully awake at last, Cree breathed deep just to feel Jolly's lungs expand, to take in great satisfying drafts. It had been so long, so very long. On the table beside the whore's bed, the skull—Chadwick was only the most recent of a thousand names—glowed a bright burnt ochre. Cree tested Jolly's face, opening and closing the eyes, raising the skin of the brows, tensing the muscles that moved the jaw back and forth. On the bedside table Chadwick's bony features liquefied like molten lead to mimic those movements.

Cree loosed an ancient howl, a thousand thousand years in the making. He spoke in ancient tongues—*ka-ka-ka ti-ti-ti*—and at last spent himself over the dead whore so cataclysmically the room began to move, then to shake violently. Soon its walls shook with a force even greater than Cree's.

"No! Not now!" he shouted in Jolly's now-familiar language. "I am so close! My people need— "

The windows shattered and he was showered in glass, an arm and half his naked torso pin-cushioned with shards. A jagged seam opened in one wall like a rip in the fabric of the world. Through it he saw buildings tumble like a child's blocks, cobble-stoned pavement crack into canyons. Smoke filled the room, rising from the floor below along with the stink of burning wood and horseflesh. The ceiling collapsed and the dead woman beneath him plunged through a hole in the floor, as gravity took them both. The madam's whole painted palace toppled in on Cree.

It took many hours—most of a day—to dig himself out from the rubble. He found Chadwick amidst the debris, intact. The skull might wash out to sea, but even then Cree's borrowed body would find it in time. They hadn't been together for 100,000 years by chance.

Now he searched Jolly's mind for help. The physician was still there, though small and obscure as a rat in the fetid bowels of an ancient ship's hold. Thousands of years before, Cree had learned that when he leaped to take control, it was best to leap into a shaman. Professor Chadwick, who had found his skull on a shelf in the dank confines of a shuttered medieval leper asylum, hadn't been one. But he'd had a useful knowledge of anatomy. A wonderful grasp, in fact. But Jolly had trumped even that. He was a true healer, what they called in this place a physician.

Cree ignored the squealing rat's protests. He queried Jolly's knowledge and inventoried his battered body. The left arm was shattered, useless. Blood leaked from both ears. A large glass splinter was embedded in one eye. Cree cursed. His host was now half blind. What to do?

The small, weaselly voice, all that seemed to be left of Jolly Frye, MD, squeaked, "Pull the splinter out."

Cree took hold of the glass gingerly and tugged. The hot jelly which eyes are filled with ran down his cheek. Jolly's legs wobbled before Cree braced and stiffened the knees. He reveled in the hot excruciating jolts, having not suffered severe physical pain since being burned alive at the stake five hundred years before. Though shamans made good hosts, witches did not.

Without pain, there is no master, he thought. *Pain is good.*

He followed Jolly's instructions to bandage the eye with a strip torn from his shirt, but did so hastily. He must go find his people soon.

Cree scooped up Chadwick and worked Jolly's legs up and around the burned out avenues of Chinatown, toward the waterfront. Smoke and steam clogged the air. Bodies lying in pools of blood-colored mud clogged the streets. He found no clean water. His strength waned, but he had to find his people. He'd waited so long to bring them back together, and now it was almost done. His back hurt. The pain became more exquisite the farther he walked.

That inner voice spoke up again. Now it sounded less like a rodent. Jolly had climbed out of the ship's hold and onto the deck. "You've hurt your back, too. Busted it, most likely. Walk any farther and you'll be paralyzed." Jolly the rat chortled at this prospect.

"Don't ever laugh at me!" Cree used Jolly's lips and breath to form words, but they still held that same awful cadence, the same sense of water rushing endlessly over a cofferdam, that had nearly driven the doctor insane over the years.

"How can I not? Look at you, you're pathetic." Jolly said, his old voice steady now, without that awful droning cadence.

The waterfront was unrecognizable save for the gray roiling sea beyond. The clinic a mere pile of bricks and timbers. But the cellar was still beneath it, and Chadwick's people trapped inside. No, Cree's people.

Jolly's boot kicked in one boarded window. Pain stabbed Jolly's back and ran down both legs. His face grimaced.

Cree smiled at the small pleasure of that shared pain. He peered inside the cellar window. A dozen bodies floated in muck. Drowned. All dead.

Their shared face contorted again. He gritted his teeth and bit back a howl of grief. Chadwick's molten bones mirrored the look, his burnt ochre shading to black.

Jolly the Rat only laughed.

Cree, weeping from Jolly's eyes, raised a hand and slapped Jolly's face. "I said, don't laugh!" He slapped him again, again, again.

"You sob like a child. How pathetic," Jolly managed to spit out between blows, along with a broken tooth.

"My people are dead!"

"Not so fucking indestructible after all, eh?" Jolly slurred through battered lips. His body danced and flailed like a puppet tangled in its own strings. Laughing and hollering one moment, sobbing and slapping and shouting the next.

"Shut that infernal hole!" Cree screamed.

"They look like bloated cows. Bet they swim better dead than alive."

As he laughed, Jolly's head pounded with pain. Maybe he was about to have a stroke. He reached up with his broken arm and felt fresh blood trickling from one ear.

The pain spun Cree's excitement higher. He rocked their battered body back and forth. "I said shut up!"

"Want peace and quiet? Then get out of my head!"

The pain was becoming less bearable now. It simply had to explode, like an overfilled balloon. Cree rose taller on Jolly's feet. "I will make you stop." He gazed back at the bodies floating in the cellar, drifting on a secret tide, stinking of raw sewage and decaying flesh. A painted sign floated past. JOLLY FRYE, MD. Cree turned away to search the road, a mass of mud and fallen birds and broken crockery. A dead horse lay on its side half a block away. Two mongrel dogs tore at its flesh. Beyond them a building smoldered, black columns of smoke rising.

Cree set Chadwick on a rock and scanned the buckled, ruined road. Twenty feet down, the remnants of a stone wall pushed out of the ground like broken gray teeth. Cree stared at it thoughtfully.

"Go ahead, do it," Jolly rasped. "Get this hell over with."

Cree took off running toward the wall but slipped in the mud just before he reached it. Still he managed to ram Jolly head first into the stones with enough force to knock their brain unconscious.

When Jolly woke sometime later, he felt boneless. In fact he could feel nothing below the chest. "Well, now you've done it. I told you my back was broken." He propped himself up against the gray stones to keep from sliding down and drowning in the mud. Maybe a lung had been punctured, as well, by a broken rib. He spat blood. "I'm still here. Ain't shut up yet. We're both pathetic now, you and me."

Cree did not answer.

The pain, intense and unrelenting before, had dissipated so completely Jolly could barely recall it. Perhaps his tormentor had also departed? There was the blind eye to remind him, though. And two useless legs. Not to mention Chadwick, staring at him from the rock a bit down the road. Although it was always difficult to tell this for sure.

"Wish I'd never studied medicine," Jolly mumbled.

Chadwick didn't answer either. The once-molten features had solidified into . . . what, exactly? A grimace, or grief? The bony sockets looked even more empty than usual.

With his last bit of strength, Jolly tossed a stone. It struck the skull and toppled it off the rock. Chadwick landed sideways in the muck. The square hole in the braincase above one ear, fashioned so laboriously with a stone chisel a hundred thousand years before, slowly began to fill with mud.

The fae and I have a long and sometimes pleasant shared history, though we don't always agree on procedural matters pertaining to the Bazaar. Immortal creatures can be difficult to deal with. But they can also be helpful when paid in a coin they like.

And they and I both have a great love of horses. This set of spurs on a table in the tent next to my own booth used to be mine. One is cast in steel, the other carved of mother of pearl. The glittering green powder that glimmers on their surface is Faerie Dust, most likely of the Mermaid Scales variety. Instead of polishing it away, I leave it there as a reminder of my lost daughter— and the night I finally found her again.

CUT 'N SHOOT ALLEY

Aphrodite Anagnost

Wearing her favorite oxblood velvet tail coat and breeches of the same hue, Madam Vera led her leopard appaloosa, Lord Byron, to the freight elevator of a building near Central Park East. They stepped in and she turned to press B2, almost losing her balance as the elevator cab lurched, then began its descent. She bent to slip a finger into one boot where the seam had rubbed her calf raw. It was sore, yes. But many great horsemen crippled by falls could still ride much better than they walked.

A sticky-sweet aroma wafted up the shaft and into the elevator. "Ugh." She wrinkled her nose. "Cotton candy." It had been her dead husband's favorite snack, a scent that would forever evoke the night Mal had shot her lover. God, how she hated cotton candy.

At last the doors slid open. Byron knelt so Vera could mount. As she took her seat a mysterious optimism spread through her body, warming it like hot buttered rum. Perhaps this would be the night she spotted her lost daughter in the crowd. If horsemanship was in Rose's blood she might come, called by the displays at the Night Bazaar's equestrian exposition.

Vera walked Byron to the entrance of the enormous underground stadium. Salty roasted peanuts, the coconut oil of popped corn, the smell of cumin-rich New York System gaggers with the works—and, unfortunately, more cotton candy—all weighted the air in the arena. But such frivolity was part of every riding exposition. The rubber mulch spread over the concrete floor of the arena still emitted the scent of antique sneakers. The space was a subterranean replica of Madison Square Garden, one third the size of the original. And its coliseum a literal cakewalk, with fancy kiosks between the bleachers specializing in tortes from thirty-six countries.

As they trotted into the ring from the shadows the audience cheered and applauded. A Lipizzaner had just dumped his rider. The young man was on his knees, gripping one shoulder and grimacing. Medics rushed out to carry him off on a bumping gurney, wheels squeaking. The riderless horse reared, then cantered around the course taking the jumps until a groom ran out to lead him away.

The audience stood as one to applaud Vera, and she inclined her head to acknowledge the accolades. She would pay them back with an exemplary performance.

A white linen-covered banquet table set for twelve stood in the center of the arena under a steel airfoil fan the size of an elephant's ass. It tick-tick-ticked like a metronome as the breeze from the rotating blades bent the flames of a glowing row of a dozen candelabras. Particles of straw beneath the table glittered like pixie dust.

Years ago, this same jump had caused her near-fatal fall, when her husband Mal Incunabula had deliberately ignited fireworks during her performance. Back then the young Byron, barely four, had startled and taken off too soon, too far from the jump. His forelegs had clipped the tabletop and he'd landed in a scramble, mane on fire, pinning Vera beneath him, crushing her pelvis. The limp that remained was her daily reminder of failure.

Tonight she meant to do it right. She touched the faint burn scar on Byron's shoulder. "Let us go, you and I," she whispered.

They proceeded in an easy canter. After a touch of the spur, she folded flat over the horse's neck as his withers rose. Keeping her seat low, her torso in aerodynamic unity with Byron, she slowed the jump down in her mind—her great signature trick. Byron jerked his legs up tightly, flying, hovering over the burning candles for what seemed like forever. She'd tasted flight before, and never wondered how it felt to be a bird. This was so much better. Lighter, more mysterious, like the airborne dance of a bee.

Byron landed gently on the forehand without breaking a sweat. The crowd thundered applause, roaring, "*Vera, Vera, Vera!*" They stood on tiptoe, craning to catch a glimpse of the triumphant pair.

Noble head high, Byron's ears pricked. His shoulders seemed to levitate as he reared backward until nearly sitting on those powerful spotted haunches. Vera lay back along his croup, pulled out her tortoise shell combs, and let cascades of long red hair mingle with the heavy black tail. She waved to their audience as she stroked him gently. Then Byron walked off stage on his hind legs, just like a man.

She would pay for this grand entrance in agony later, perched all night on a chair in her tent, studying the leaves to advise desperate migrants and CEOs, all worried for different reasons, wondering if the great stone wall separating Mexico and the States would ever come down. . . .

She squeezed a cramp out of her thigh. Her joints said rain was coming tonight. She left it up to Byron to find the stable, for he knew his way around every Bazaar. A horse felt his way through the lively, throbbing flesh. The human brain was far less reliable.

At the rose-gabled barn entrance, Byron bowed low. She slid off, then flexed each knee, one at a time, to test the damage. Painful, but she'd stood much worse than this.

"Madam." A young man reached out to take the reins. He had the hair and demeanor of an English schoolboy, the square shoulders and posture of a trained rider. And, she noted, the full lips of a skilled kisser. "I'm Boris, senior groom with the equestrian circus." He bowed over her outstretched leather-stained hand, his thumb caressing the callus where a gold band had once choked her finger.

She combed through her hair with both hands, making a part at the famous piebald spot.

He blinked, then rubbed his eyes with the back of one hand. "Oh, my. You actually *glitter.*"

"Do I? Um, thank you. I must have picked up some pixie dust in Cut 'n Shoot Alley." Could this specimen, young enough to be her son, actually be flirting? Surely not. She blotted her forehead with the sleeve of her carmine tailcoat.

"It's an honor to host you and the famous Lord Byron, Madam Vera."

She smiled faintly, then limped around her horse, patting and massaging, loosening the girth. Byron sighed in pleasure as she stroked his face. Vera's swan-neck spurs, strapped so low on the boot heels the tips touched the ground, clanked as she walked to the tack box to pull out a cooling blanket.

Boris began the customary examination of the hooves, then felt up each leg, checking the joints for heat and swelling. "What unusual spurs you have," he remarked as he threw the rectangle of green lightly over Byron's back. "Is one made of mother of pearl?"

She nodded. "I lost the right one long ago. So I had the left cast, and a steel mirror-image made."

He raised his eyebrows. "I've seen the same spur before."

She laughed. "Doubtful. These were custom made for me."

"Well, ma'am, no offense, but I have seen *one* other." He unbridled and haltered Lord Byron, then pulled a linen from his belt to wipe out the horse's ears and nostrils.

She frowned. If so, there could be only one other. "Saw it where?" she demanded.

He peeled back the cooler, and slung the saddle onto one hip, then redraped the fabric on the horse, poll to loins. "At Gotham Curios, by the time-travel ticket counter. That one-armed preacher with the missing ear and scars on his face—you know, the guy on the 7000 Club?—he sold it there, then went over to the travel agent. That shop opposite the mermaid burlesque."

She frowned. "What kind of scars, exactly?"

"Old-looking ones. From big cats. I heard he was once the ringmaster, long ago, in a famous circus. 'Til his own tigers tried to eat him. Rumor was he didn't feed them. They say now he's a great prophet, because he survived the attack." Boris shrugged. "Anyhow, that's the legend. Haven't you seen the 7000 club? Evangelical TV for a New Age—"

"No. " She shook her head. "I never watch television."

"Huh. Well, I don't go in for that literal interpretation stuff. But it's interesting . . . faith, I mean."

Her throat closed. She shivered from a sudden cold sweat, a redoubling of nausea. How could it be that after she'd fled the circus Mal *had* survived? And become a wacky celebrity, no less.

"Anyhow, someone bought the spur. Right away," added the groom.

She tried not to seem too interested. "Really. Who?"

"A girl . . . well, young woman. I saw her in the tack shops. She looked a bit like you, especially the hair." He tugged at his own unruly brown forelock. "Perhaps you have a younger sister?"

"Er, no. A coincidence." She turned away to wish her horse goodnight, blowing into his nostrils where the moist flesh was the color of rose petals. Byron's breath was sweet alfalfa, which he liked to pocket in his cheek like tobacco.

"Madam Vera," said Boris abruptly. "Would you be interested in selling your spurs?"

"They don't even match. Why would you want them?"

"Because . . . they're yours." He blushed. "For a thousand prewar Deutschmarks? I'll take excellent care of Lord Byron. Here, the horse is always king. And you, Madame Ecuyere, queen." He handed the lead rope to a female apprentice. "I will treat him as my own."

She drew up, offended. "You certainly will, even if I don't sell the spurs."

"Of course! Beg pardon if I implied otherwise. Fifteen hundred, then? That's all I have."

"Very well." Selling the spurs felt like selling a hand or a foot, but she might need ready cash if the buyer he'd seen had been Rose. She would have to hide her from Mal, if he was here too. She'd looked for her lost girl for so long: in the cards, the tea, the coffee, the stars, even the I Ching and the runes. But the answers had come too easily, and therefore were never credible. It's bad luck to delve into your own future.

"I will treasure the spurs, and always use them in the most delicate manner." He lifted his shirt, revealing a money belt. Counted out heavy engraved bills and some English pounds to frost the top of the stack, handing over notes so flat they looked ironed.

She opened her coat, pulled up a shirt tail and zipped the money into her own waist wallet.

He blushed again, and ducked his head. "And now you must kiss me."

"I beg your pardon?" She bristled, then recalled that kissing *was*, in fact, the custom for sealing any transaction worth over five hundred Deutschmarks. Oh well. She drew in a deep breath. He smelled clean and manly, like sawdust and boot blacking. He slid both arms around her waist and pulled her close, then gathered her hair away from her face. He kissed her throat, breath warm against her skin. His lips were soft, and tasted of salt. His hands moved up her back, kneading, massaging, and came to rest at the base of her neck. He looked into her face. "Such gorgeous violet eyes."

She closed them abruptly. No. There was no time for this… this…*flirtation.*

As he brushed a chaste kiss across each eyelid, an erection pressed against her belly. She pulled away. Passion and rage—that's how she'd lost Rose to begin with.

Boris sighed and stroked her cheek. "I shall take wonderful care of Mr. Byron. When you come back, please . . . stay awhile." His face had relaxed back into boyishness.

"Perhaps. We'll see." She bent and unbuckled the pearl spur. "They're yours now. Never misuse these. A spur's touch should be fleeting as a butterfly's wing."

* * *

She took the short-cut down Cut 'n Shoot Alley, through the uncensored part of the Bazaar. *Adult Guidance Advised* flashed neon green on a Times-Square sized sign at the beginning of a brick road painted yellow. Inside The Chapel of the Order of the Rose Cross, one of the three-sided stick-built cottages on the alley, a monk in brown robes and rope girdle swung a censer of smoldering frankincense. A congregation in medieval and Renaissance costumes, as well as jeans and tee shirts, knelt and murmured prayers.

Vera was about to enter for blessings when the Amazonian red parrots next door began their warm-up. This house-cat-sized quartet interspersed caterwauling with select operatic phrases. Their conductor tossed out sunflower seeds until the squabbling birds finally agreed on "Somewhere Over The Rainbow."

They sang in harmony, then all shouted, "Bravo!" congratulating themselves. The conductor motioned Vera over with a sweep of his tapered baton. "Please, come and meet the divos."

"Thank you, that was beautiful." She stuffed five dollars into the birds' tip jar. "Breathtaking, in fact. Miss Garland would be envious. I've got to run to open my own booth, but I'll be back! Carry on, Maestro." She nodded to the parrots. "And gentlemen!"

She started to pass the RV home of the fairy dust and pixie powder vendors, but slowed, drawn by a magnetic pull. The doors weren't open yet, but from inside came muffled explosions, the smell of pyrotechnic residue. The fae were doing real chemistry in there.

Next to Queen Mab's Fairy Dust stood an unpainted outbuilding much like a goat barn. Its digital sign, though turned off, read *LOVELOCK RANCH, NEVADA*. Probably still setting up. The door hung slightly ajar, its hefty deadbolt engaged but not in the striker plate.

Vera stepped closer, curious. The gap showed a desk with a cash register, a coiled bullwhip, and a brass table lamp with plastic shade. Just beyond it a middle-aged man reclined in a vinyl Barcalounger, face in shadow. The circle of light illuminated an oilskin duster draped over the chair, a black string tie, undone, and gray hairs curling from the open neck of a white starched shirt. His trousers were pushed to his ankles. A slender woman in a crimson bra and matching thong squatted, elbows braced on the seat as her head bobbed in his lap. He clutched her long red braid.

Vera stepped back. Each nerve howled to escape, so she ran. An icy numbness trickled from the crown of her head to her toes. For the first time since she'd dismounted, no part of her hurt. All sensation had seemingly departed. She automatically followed the yellow-painted brick lane to the red canvas Punjabi-frame tents, the Middle-Eastern themed street scene whirling around her.

"Get over it," she chided herself. Just a blow job between adults, after all. But . . . that red hair. Could it really be Rose, working in a brothel?

Her fortune-telling booth was a brocade tent set up between Goldmine Gentle Dental Recycling and Guardian Time-Travel Leisure Company. The dentist, a former NASA engineer, stood outside the booth. Her tooth hobby had become a profitable operation. She had short pink hair and wore a white cocktail dress instead of a doctor's smock.

"Heard your act was simply brilliant," Dr. Gentle told Vera. "Oh, and I believe you're due for a whitening."

"Swamped tonight. But business will probably be slow next week at the Salt Lake Bazaar, " Vera said as she hurried past. "And if I have any clients in need of your services, I'll send them right over." A dental patient could have his mouth mined of precious metal and the cavities filled with safer, more comely ceramic. Gentle Dental also bought jewelry, candlestick holders, and sterling flatware.

Limping again from the strain of the *aires*, Vera almost tripped on the single step up to her Fortuna booth. The auras of customers already waiting in line appeared to her as color wheels radiating emotions.

"Come," she invited the first inquirer, a middle-aged man, and he followed her inside the tent. He requested Darjeeling. This pleased her. Its leaves are drawn to each other and always formed plenty of symbols. "You may leave your payment there when we are finished." She nodded toward the heart-shaped obsidian box with a slot in the top. "And if you are wearing computers, watches, or other electronic devices, please turn them off. They interfere with my Mojo."

The man shook his head. "I'm free of digital devices." He sat at the small round table, anxiously smoothing the creases out of its blue velvet cloth, a finger tracing the constellations embroidered in gold thread.

"So you're a college professor," Vera said

He beamed. "Yes! How did you know?"

It wasn't the tweed jacket with suede elbow patches, or the polka-dotted bowtie, or a bespectacled face framed by unruly gray hair in need of cutting. These days, professors tended to look more like hipsters, or Steampunk rockers in tight black pants, rather than members of a stuffy Ivy League club.

"A fish, swimming upward toward light. There, in the middle," she said. "With a crown—this puts you at the highest level: tenured professor in a competitive graduate program." She looked up to see a smile, the perfect teeth like pristine moonstones. So, a nonsmoker. "And I see a horse, my totem animal, which always means success."

"Really. Are you sure?" The crease in his forehead deepened. Perhaps he was one of those high achievers who could never relax enough to have fun. No wedding band, no tan line to indicate a missing one. He looked slightly underfed, so probably not married.

"Really, sir, I see only positive symbols in the cup. However, there is one thing." She tilted her head to get a different perspective on the shapes in the bottom: a crab under the Eiffel Tower. Prostate cancer? That didn't feel right. There was a dolphin nearby—Ah. So, a vacation. Next to the tower, en pointe, stood a Renoiresque ballerina.

"Do you have a lover, sir?"

"Well, I don't know yet," he said. "I am in love with a woman. She owns a business."

"A ballet school, in France?"

He gasped. "How did you know about Lily?"

"It's here in your cup."

"Hmmm," he squinted down. "All I see is soggy brown shreds."

"Tell me both your birthdays." The crab still disturbed Vera, but fortunately the ballet teacher had been born under a Cancer sun. "Her school will fail. See the cross? She has faced many trials, but you will not drift apart. And the bird by the handle? She will be calling soon and join you after a safe journey. You will declare your love with a bouquet of Belle de Crecy roses, and settle down together in a Connecticut farmhouse made of stone."

The man followed her every gesture and word. "I see. But what is your advice now?"

She smiled. "Go next door. The dentist has a lovely rose-gold ring to sell you. And do give my pen back. You're a shameless pickpocket, sir."

"Sorry." Despite getting caught with the vintage Mont Blanc, the professor slid the pen back across the table only a little sheepishly. He put down a handsome tip, fanning out five fifties.

"For that sum," she said, somewhat mollified, "I will give you additional advice. Stop stealing. Otherwise you will soon be knifed in an alley and bleed to death internally in the Cornell Emergency Department, leaving your future child to grow up without a father."

He gasped. "My. . . my . . .?"

"And now, good night," she said firmly, steering him out the door.

Hovering on the air outside was a faint burnt-bone stink from the dentist's drill next door. By now a long serpentine queue had formed, waiting on Vera. The next ten readings went quickly, except one for a Starbucks franchise owner who'd forgotten the combination to his in-home safe. She provided several numbers, but with no way to test them the reading dragged on for twenty minutes. She did succeed in conjuring up his sainted grandmother's old phone number at last. And so, finally happy, he left.

By the time the midnight fireworks began, she'd filled the heart-shaped box and stuffed her money belt so full it barely zipped. She thought again of Rose, who might even now be nearby, and surrounded her with protective white light.

After two more customers she got up to stretch and check the tea stash. Shelves of exotic leaves were stored in bamboo boxes—from the extravagant Da Hong Pao brushed with goats' milk, to the bittersweet sencha, with its fresh green taste of just-picked leaves. Farmed botanical drawings from tea labels lined the wall behind her table. She'd just turned away from the curtain to put the kettle on to boil when someone entered and sat so hard the chair springs squeaked.

Vera glanced over one shoulder. "Boris! Is Byron all right? May I pour you a spot of tea?"

He shook his head. The handsome groom's eyes looked bloodshot and pouchy.

"My darling, how long have you had that vile headache? Here, drink this." She poured a cup of twig tea and stood behind him, laying hands on the crown of his head, fingertips circling down the jaw to both shoulders, anesthetizing the spasms with her magnetic touch.

He inhaled deeply. "Malvoleo, the Incunabula brother who lost an arm."

Her hands froze in mid-massage. "Yes?"

"He came to the stable two hours ago and punched me in the head with his robotic prosthesis. Then braced one foot on my chest and ordered me to turn over your spurs."

Oh, yes. Vera could easily imagine that familiar boot heel pressing into Boris's sternum, threatening to burst his heart. She'd felt it and Mal's fists more than once, herself. "I am so sorry. Are you badly hurt?"

"I'll be fine. My assistant struck the knave down from behind with a poacher's spade. Then I punched his evil face." Boris appeared rapt, recalling his pugilistic triumph. "The fool spat out a mouthful of broken ceramic caps. I let him crawl around the feed room floor and gather up whatever pieces he could find in the straw."

"Oh dear. That sounds so . . . pitiful." Vera smiled.

"Malvoleo was moaning, still unable to stand," said Boris. "So I told him about the dental shop, then came here to warn you."

"The tigers knocked him off his stool once," she mused. "One bit off his left ear, then with a single swipe smashed his face down so hard his teeth cracked to bits. Thus the caps. He was merely a moron with a stool. No idea how to use it."

"And how is that?" Boris looked intrigued.

"A good trainer uses the four poles under the seat to confuse the tiger. The cat becomes indecisive, uncertain. Looks for guidance from the handler."

Boris sniffed. "They say Malvoleo was the best before the accident. But I tell you, no animal in my barn could abide him. Byron kicked his stall door and turned his tail to it. The barn cats all leapt up into the hayloft, hissing."

"Mal loves the whip. And all animals hate him," she said. "They can smell bad energy. It smells of cotton candy and bitter almonds."

"And now he's a famous televangelist!" Boris gulped the hot tea gratefully. "Necromancer, more likely. But prophet?" He shook his head. "No way I'd let him near *my* soul."

"You're absolutely right, Boris." Mal could never succumb to the divine. He only wanted to dominate it. And to kill.

Mal had murdered the one man she'd loved, put her in the hospital near death, and stolen their daughter away. No matter how she'd begged, he would never tell her what he had done with Rose.

"Anyhow, big cats can't be tamed," Boris was saying. "I prefer horses, who love to work for a kind trainer."

"As do I. Oh, but you're bleeding," she said.

Boris rubbed his right fist, then spread the fingers. Rivulets of blood had dried between the knuckles. "Not mine." He grimaced. "From the bastard's mouth."

"Is your hand paining you? I can fix that." She prepared a bowl of parsley tea, and soaked a long thin rectangle of cotton in it. She carried the basin to the reading table and rubbed the crusted blood away.

"Got him square in the jaw." Boris flashed a savage smile. "Justice feels great."

"I'm sure," she said, wrapping his hand in the infused bandage. "Yet it is so seldom attained."

"We offered to let him take a shower. Bought you some time. Thanks for your kindness. Now I must go." He took her hand and kissed the ring finger.

"You are always welcome here, Boris. I owe you a great service some day."

He had just left when Vera heard the drapery whoosh open yet again on its brass rod. She did not look up from filling the kettle with spring water. "Welcome. Please close that behind you." She turned then, and almost dropped the pot.

A young woman sat at the small, round table. Like most of Vera's customers that evening, she was studying the zodiac signs stitched on blue velvet, fingering the gold threads. But her hair . . . her face. Vera might have been looking at her younger self. Faint ligature bruises marked both the woman's wrists. She reached into the cuff of one Frye boot and pulled out a wad of cash.

"No," said Vera. "Please, put that away. Gratis for you."

The girl looked surprised. She hesitated, then obeyed. "I want a cold reading, Madam Vera."

"Certainly. Tea or cards?" She took a large pinch of salt and circumambulated the table, sprinkling protective crystals as she walked.

"Tea, I think. What's the best?"

"I prefer Lapsang Souchong. Not the most exotic, but this one's fine. Black. Smoky. Sweet."

The girl nodded. Vera spooned an ample portion of coarse leaves and sticks into the bottom of a thin porcelain cup, and carried it to the table. "Remove all technology, please." She presented the seagrass pannier. "And be sure to turn it off."

The girl unbuckled a vintage tank watch, then pulled a phone from her pocket, setting them carefully in the basket.

Vera closed her eyes and whispered, "Guide us to higher consciousness with pure hands and deep vision." She stared into green eyes familiar as her own, searching for the depth of Rose's intuition.

Vera's chest grew warm, then hot. Rose's cheeks reddened. Soon her face shone with sweat. She opened her blue velvet coat, then unbuttoned the neck of her black blouse, fanning herself. Vera glimpsed a crimson bra strap. She closed her eyes for a moment, then reached out and turned over a large hourglass.

"Sorry. Are you in a hurry?" Rose frowned. "Or just expecting someone in particular?"

Vera felt crushed. Foolishly she had hoped for immediate

recognition, an emotional reunion. Clearly that wasn't in the cards, or the leaves. "Not at all. I do have to slip out later, for an appointment." To see Mal, one last time. And finish the bastard off. Then she would visit the time-travel agent. Perhaps take a short vacation on an unspoiled Caribbean Island in the 1950s, where men wore their manners as well as their white linen suits.

She pushed the saucer toward Rose, the delicate cup handle turned to the girl's left. "Drink, please. Savor the taste of each steeped leaf. And concentrate on your question."

There came to her ears a faint, repetitive plea, as clearly as if it had been spoken out loud. *I can take no more. I know what I want.*

She wanted to reach across the table and take her daughter in her arms. To explain how, after the accident, while Vera lay in the hospital hovering between this world and the next, her lover had spirited away her baby. The plan had been, to a relative in England for safekeeping. But he'd been murdered before reaching safe haven there. Then Mal had visited and given her a tonic laced with cyanide salts, poisoning her into a coma. And when she woke, Rose was gone. And perhaps hardest of all, she would have to tell her how later, in a delirium of revenge, she'd fed Mal, Rose's father, to his own hungry tigers . . . or at least had tried to.

But she held her tongue. The amends of a lifetime can't be made in one night.

"This tea is delicious." Rose sighed, a hint of pleasure pulling up the corners of her lips. A pair of mysterious dimples appeared. Mal's gift, perhaps his only one, to his daughter.

Otherwise Vera might have been looking at her younger self. The long body was a bit narrower. The Cupid's Bow of the upper lip made irritated and pouty from the exact same unconscious habit of licking it. The way she now gulped more tea heartily, and winced at the bitter dregs.

"Swish the cup left in a circular motion, three times," Vera instructed. "Concentrate on your question. The most important one, that is."

Rose set the cup down with a trembling hand, the porcelain ringing when it bumped the saucer. Vera leaned to peer into the sodden leaves.

She felt a headache coming on. "Turn the cup upside down quickly, then rotate it left three times. Continue to think only of your question."

The tea reflected reality. The first image, the hummingbird, meant Rose had secrets. Next to it she spied an old wolf . . .a cruel lover more than twice her age.

Rose glanced into the cup too, then closed her eyes and took a deep breath. "Um. Maybe I should mention I'm in sort of a violent relationship." She pulled her sleeves down self-consciously to cover the bruised wrists. Crossed and uncrossed her arms.

Vera scrutinized the slag in the cup. Worms, which meant secret foes. A hunched woman carrying a large sack. A man with a stick. A whip encircling the porcelain bottom. She looked deeper into the settling leaves. The whip had an extraordinarily long lash. "He hurts *you*."

"What?" The girl scowled and rubbed one wrist. "Okay, yes. Sometimes we fight."

Vera pushed the cup away and examined the saucer. More worms: coming misfortune. The treachery of a nearby foe. The whip slashing its way through the shambles. "No one deserves to be abused, Ms.—?"

"Just Rose. But I'm no victim. I hit back. Sometimes even throw the first punch."

"I see. Do you think he's afraid of you?" The same man who'd trapped Vera had trapped Rose. Did he know she was his own daughter?

How could he not. What a sick, sick bastard.

"No." Rose licked her lips. "I don't think so."

Vera had planned his demise so carefully, seemingly perfectly. The tigers were frantic to get out of their cramped cages after a long harsh winter, and made vicious by Mal's miserly rations. The caretaker had given them only half as much meat that morning, at her request. Before Vera left the Incunabula Circus forever, she'd paid the man a healthy stipend to keep quiet. Mal had entered the cage with a crowbar but still they'd mauled him, going for the limbs to get at the marrow. They had dined on him, but apparently not to death. Time to finish the job.

The girl straightened into a cold regal posture.

Vera understood this healthy response to shame. "Are *you* afraid?"

She clenched her fists under the table, imagining the countless ways she might now rid the world of Mal for good. This was the Bazaar, after all. As a last resort she could hire a hashishin.

"Um . . . sort of. Sometimes." Rose coughed. "I mean, I'm in no real danger. I've got things under control. It's verbal abuse, mainly."

"I see." Vera returned to gazing down at the tea. "I see a man, indistinct and pale, carrying a cross over his right shoulder. He's following a serpent."

Rose leaned in to look down at the leaves and sticks. "The man with the cross . . . is that a preacher?" She hesitated, biting her lip. "Once I was afraid. He pressed my face into a pillow. Sat on me and held my neck. I couldn't breathe."

Rage caused Vera's mouth to water, her nails to dig deep into her palms. *I will kill the bastard this time, or die trying.*

Rose blinked hard, as if holding back tears. "That time . . . well, I packed. But I couldn't leave my horse."

The blood was certainly true. "So you have a plan?" *Like perhaps cooking the evil shit in an oven.*

"I'm going to ship my horse first, then get a ticket to any place and time that practices obscene discrimination against amputees." Rose laughed bleakly.

"Ah, how nice. Such as where?" Vera tried for a light tone.

"Haiti, if I want to stay close. Afghanistan would be awful for him. Maybe Russia."

"Well don't go to any place and time that would also be awful for you." Vera reached for one of Rose's hands and squeezed it. "The past cannot stop you from achieving any goal you desire. It has no power over you. Get rid of your . . . this man. And live your life."

Rose yanked her hands free. Now the words spilled out in a flood. "Did you know he used to be in the circus? He survived a tiger attack. He tied my wrists together, tight. And made me do things . . . here at the Bazaar. But he's a preacher, so now he says he's sorry. Now *I* have the power. Maybe I don't need to be in such a hurry to go."

"Second thoughts are sometimes overrated." Vera leaned over the table earnestly. "Go with the first."

Rose stood and paced around the tent. "I could do anything right now."

"Well, hold on. There's more." The sodden leaves and sticks were taking on the shape of past events and those yet to come. "A ladder and several lines of dots, much like the dividing line on a road."

"He travels a lot for work," said the girl thoughtfully.

"The leaves, your life . . . Rose, these are *your* leaves. It's *you* who will travel the circuitous route. And who will return. Without him."

"OK, I get it. I'll go see the agent."

Vera leaned back as if to study a Van Gogh from a distance. The view on the porcelain saucer was clear as a starry night. A large white M framed the entire scatter of leaves in negative space. "His name is Mal Incunabula, correct? He was my husband. And I . . . I'm your mother. Or have you got that figured out already?"

Rose sat abruptly, staring down at the saucer, teeth clenched, fists gripped so tight the knuckles stood out whitely. "One arm I could overlook. But that horrible Mad Max claw he attaches to it . . . ugh. Please don't tell me he's my father." She swallowed audibly. "I'm hoping . . . was there someone else?"

"There was." Vera reached out and cupped her cheek, treasuring its reality, its warmth. "But Mal is your father. I'm sorry."

Rose bolted up, face contorted. Looming over Vera, whose turn it was now to stiffen in shame. "You could be wrong! Have you thought of that? Seems like you've got a vendetta against someone, but the man you're after can't be the same Mal! You're fucking crazy. And I'm leaving!"

"All right. I won't stop you. But he will destroy you if you stay. You won't be able to stand him or yourself." Now she saw the floating Ophelia in the dregs. Every memory of Mal, of her kidnapped, abandoned girl ensnared by the selfishness and pain that looped back on itself, rendered her furious.

"Oh really, Madame Vera? Well, where were *you* when I was raised as a Cavendish on the Isle of Wight?" Rose looked away. "Sometimes I wish I could go to sleep and just not wake up."

"Never say that. Take care, for yourself. Always." She lowered her voice so no one waiting outside would hear. "When you were still a baby, I took a fall in the arena. First I was in the hospital. Then back home, but so weak . . . 'A tonic,' he said. I drank it, and the lines of my palms turned blue, my fingernails spotted white. I grew even weaker. One morning, I began pouring these health tonics into a potted jade plant. It died, and I got better. After that, it was I who fed him to the tigers. An unfortunate miracle he survived."

"Mal the Miracle Man, Healed by the Living Waters. Living by Reckless Devotion." Rose cried one tear, which dripped onto the embroidered scales of Libra on the blue cloth. "So he knew I'm his daughter?"

Vera smiled without humor. "Oh, yes. And I'm going to kill him for it. He tracked you, purchased your spurs and then seduced you. He tried to beat up a man to get mine. It's all here in the leaves. Scissors. A quarrel. Violence. A separation of lovers."

"How could you have been so stupid?" Rose cried.

"Shhh." Vera pressed a finger to her daughter's chapped lips. "I was eighteen. Same as you. Young girls are his specialty."

"A few hours ago, Madam . . . Mother . . . I was watching your capriole, and suddenly had to sit down. My arms and legs ached. A muscle in my neck coiled like a serpent and I was paralyzed there in the stands. I went to the Taxidermy Pub and downed a shot of Flaming Scorpion vodka, but it didn't help. So I visited the blue-headed fairies up Cut 'n Shoot Alley. A cute one with butterflies hovering around her shoulders blew green dust in my face. The pain disappeared. She sold me a dram bottle. She told me whoever is pure of heart and inhales the glittering powder will be healed. But deceiver, beware. Breathe the dust of mermaid scales, and he will die."

"What a lucky find," said Vera.

"I've got the power, because he feels guilty. And the powder as well." Her daughter rose from her chair and turned to leave.

Vera frowned. "Where are you going now?"

"To kill him."

"Not without me." Vera pulled open the curtain to address her remaining clients. "Thank you all for waiting so patiently. Rest assured I have something special for each of you. But in the next ten minutes, a rain storm of significant proportions will be dumping buckets over this tent."

Someone in the crowd booed. The line tightened and bunched up like a crouching tiger.

Vera held up a hand. "But don't worry. It will only . . . I repeat, the storm will only affect *my* tent via a shimmering cloud."

"But why just your place?" asked a gentle, soft-spoken young woman with an aura so strong it not only appeared orange, but smelled of fresh-peeled rind.

"Extemporaneous magic gone haywire. Organized to burn out over my tent as a squall."

"Are you saying it is not safe to partake of your services?" asked a fiftyish man in double-breasted blue suit and thinnest of silver silk ties. He cradled a briefcase as one would a cherished infant.

"Very safe, sir. It will pass quickly." Really, for a master of the universe, he seemed quite unfamiliar with physics. She sent a deep blue vibration of trustworthiness. He staggered back a step, then regained his balance. She flooded the whole crowd with the same wave.

"Say, where can we get some good grub?" croaked a chain-smoking priest. She recognized him from the Chapel of the Rose Cross, way up Cut 'n Shoot Alley. Even his complexion was yellow, matching nicotine-stained clubbed fingers. "And some strong delicious drink?" he added.

"I recommend the honey-sweet Krupnik and a poppy pastry in the Lithuanian tent. On my tab, everyone! Take your time. They do some fierce Cossack dancing over there. Come back when you're tired."

Everyone in the queue was so easy to read. Finding Rose had ignited Vera's senses. But she didn't want her daughter doing anything to feel guilty about later. Such as murder. The poor girl needed to hold onto whatever unstained virtue she had left, or end up sprawled out on some psychotherapist's sofa for the next ten years. Or in prison. No, Vera would find a way to get rid of Malvoleo, before Rose could poison him with the dust.

She clapped sharply to regain the attention of the crowd. "We'll break for two hours, until the cloud lifts. Those who have waited shall receive, for the fee of a single reading, both the cards *and* the tea. Unless you prefer Turkish coffee."

The cloud was already drifting toward them, illuminated by starlight, surrealistic as a goldfish flying out of a clock. Billions of tiny droplets of water shone like tiny colored lights, an artist's rainbow palette floating on thin air. Up the alley Rose and the dentist were huddled, speaking in hushed voices between the two shops.

"Are all men complicated?" Rose was saying.

"No, not at all." The dentist smoothed a crease out of her short white dress. "Why, do you have a rotten one?"

Vera stood watching them. She smelled cotton candy and sulfur, and heard the heavy drag of Vibram soles scraping pavement. She rushed across the street for a half-shot of Krupnik, to dull the ankle pain so she could travel faster. Her affliction wouldn't delay a dual task: to keep Rose from the sin of killing Mal, and to do the deed thoroughly this time, herself. She slammed down her glass and slinked through alleyways, headed to Queen Mab's House of Faerie Dust.

There were other forms of magic at the Bazaar complementary to her own. She felt sure Mal would be happy to get Rose into a back room at Gentle Dental. And that she would play along in order to blow the lethal dust in his face. So there remained little time to save her daughter's soul—well, better late than never.

Vera bought a skateboard from an elfin teenage vendor, and used her good leg to push.

When she reached Mab's the doors to the silver bullet-shaped RV hung open. Flickering dust and intense waves of heat were spilling out. All the fairies were busy helping other customers. Except for one, whose feet were soaking in an extra-large goldfish bowl filled with hungry koi.

"Top of the evening, Madam," she said in a Dublin accent. The smallest of the group, a real pixie of a fairy, blue right down to her skin and dragonfly wings, which lay unfurled to dry under a heat lamp. She wore a gauzy aqua sheath and smelled like fresh rain.

"Good evening." Vera sat next to her. "I need to speak with the most experienced dust magician here. A very serious matter. Life or death."

"Yes, I know." The fairy laid a finger aside her nose. "Say no more." Lifting her feet from the fishbowl, she pointed to a door past shelves of canisters. "After you."

Inside, the fairy held open the door to a private consultation room with sofa, desk, and two armchairs. Eerily similar to an attorney's office but for the forest-elf secretary out front, and a unicorn on break who was drinking out of a tinkling fountain of stacked stone bowls.

"Oh. So you are the specialist?" asked Vera.

"We are all dust specialists here." The fairy smiled. "Only my closest friends know my real name, which is not Queen Mab, of course. But I can help you as the resident mistress of potions. This is my shop."

Vera wasn't used to trusting a person who wouldn't reveal her true name. But she could also tell the fairy was being truthful by the steadfast blueness of her aura. And time was running out. "I've never sought help from a mythical being before. But there's some fairy dust in the hands of a person close to me. She means to kill an evil man. I mean to stop it."

"Oh. But why?" The blue fairy looked puzzled. "After all, the dust cannot kill any being except the truly evil. Which one might see as a good deed, no?" Her wings flitted. "Now, let's get down to business. Your daughter bought the dust from me, so why are you here?"

"How did you know she's my daughter?"

"Please. How could I not?" Mab widened her big blue eyes and jabbed a finger in the direction of Vera's piebald spot, shaking her head. "You're as line bred as a snow leopard gecko."

Eerie flute music trilled in the background. This fairy seemed very old, predominantly good, but with a trickle of darkness. "I want to protect my daughter from a problem begun before her birth. So it is mine to correct. That's why I'm here." She would take whatever help the fairy offered. Mal would soon be arriving to get his teeth fixed. He'd always been vain about his perfect smile.

"Take this." The dram bottle the fairy pressed into Vera's hand was chilly against her palm. "You want an antidote. The dust can't be undone. But this may lessen the power of your daughter's spell. Yet you still *want* the man dead, so . . . I make no promises about the outcome."

"I don't want a sin to weigh on her soul. I'll do whatever must be done. Later. When she's not around."

"Very well. Blow the powder in his face. Or, if you can, shove it up his nose." The fairy shrugged and furled her blue wings. "When it's over, you'll know."

Vera inclined her head. "How can I repay the debt?"

"Five hundred deutschmarks, or eight hundred gold rubles. We also take major credit cards, Euros, and PayPal. No dollars, please."

"Oh my. That's steep." In fact, a third of what Boris had given her for her spurs.

Mab smiled. "And I'm powerful."

Vera could not argue with that. Nor would she. It was unwise to anger any fae, but especially the blue ones. Disgruntled water fairies could raise hurricanes, even tsunamis. She quickly handed over the crisp bills.

"Thank you, Madame. When we meet again, you may call me Berrystream. As my friends do."

"Thank you, er . . . Queen Mab." She bowed respectfully. "When we meet again, I will indeed." She took the bottle and packed it into her waist wallet.

On the skateboard, the trip back to her end of Cut 'n Shoot Alley took mere minutes. She slid to a stop in front of Gentle Dental and went inside. She recognized the man sprawled in the dentist's reclining chair by the boots with heavy Vibram soles, and the titanium robot of a prosthesis hanging off his left shoulder.

Rose was arguing with the dentist. "But that chain around his neck is mine!" She wagged a finger at the pink-haired woman, then pointed to the silver one around her own neck. "Only two like it in existence. Both of them mine!"

The pink-haired dentist shook her head and pressed a nitrous mask over Mal's nose and mouth. "He is my patient," she snapped. "He needs four crowns and wanted to pay in silver. His canines are cracked to shit! I can't both concentrate and catfight with you, as much fun as it is." She frowned and replaced the mask with a rubber thong stuffed up his nose, and turned away to adjust the flow on the oxygen and nitrous tanks the hose was connected to.

"Fine then!" While the dentist was preoccupied Rose ran to Mal and yanked the tubes out of his nose. She opened the dram of fairy dust and crammed clumps of powder up his nostrils, then emptied the bottle onto her palm and blew the rest in his face. "Hurry up and inhale, Miracle Man," she said. "Come on!"

He was breathing through his mouth. Rose clamped her lips over his and exhaled. Then put the nasal cannula back, letting oxygen carry the pixie powder straight to his brain.

Vera frowned. How to slip in there unobtrusively and appear helpful?

Dr. Gentle turned back around. "Young lady, the man is here for new caps! Are you insane?" She held freshly gloved hands up like a surgeon. "I knew I shouldn't have given my hygienist the night off."

Rose backed away from Mal's head. "Sorry, Dr., uh, Dentist. Please continue with the root canal."

"Caps!" The dentist corrected, rolling her eyes. She sat back on her stool and studied the surgical tray of various curettes and blades. A bite block and a bone file. Floss.

Vera stepped into the back room, between them, and cleared her throat. "Pardon me. I was a medic in the cavalry. So I can relieve the young lady of any duties she might find unsavory. . . .

"Terrific! Come here and manage the patient's anesthesia. He's asleep now, but this bothersome girl—"

"I'll handle them both," she told the dentist. "Rose, a good deed? Go to Flavors of Lithuania. Purchase a bottle of Krupnik for later. And a half-dozen poppy seed scones. Then we can talk."

Her daughter frowned but nodded grudgingly. She unfolded her map of the Bazaar. A calico cat strolled in and wound his way around her boots in an infinity whorl. A tuxedo cat came to sit in the doorway.

"Go on now!" Vera urged, as if the girl were a puppy. "Oh, and why not pick up sardines for all these loitering cats. For some reason, Cut 'n Shoot Alley is crawling with felines tonight."

Rose clenched the crumpled map and curled her lip at Vera. Who turned away blandly to straighten Mal's oxygen tubing, taking care not to clear the shimmering dust from his nostrils. She nudged her daughter. "Run along. I can handle things here. Bye!"

With one scowl back at her, Rose turned and ran off.

Vera rolled up her sleeves. "How else may I be of service, Doctor?" She cradled Mal's face, which felt clammy and in need of a shave, and centered it.

"If you could simply monitor the patient while delivering the nitrous? Turn the red dial up to one if he starts to wake. If the light on his finger monitor glows yellow, turn the oxygen—that's the green dial—up to three."

"Certainly." Vera nodded and sat on the stool at the patient's head. The dentist continued the tooth salvaging procedure. Vera supplied more nitrous as Mal coughed, sniffled, or wiggled his nose. She kept the valve open until his ear stubs stopped twitching. Finally his body relaxed. Beads of sweat rose on his forehead.

She patted it dry, and noticed it was covered in tiny gray hairs. Hmm. Mal was without a doubt a bad man. She'd never seen him as vulnerable as he was at this moment. He looked somehow . . . smaller. His clothes oddly baggy. His skin saggy. And that dose ought to have been deadly, by now, surely? Though subtle, fairy potions generally had an immediate effect. And if perchance he'd somehow acquired a speck of goodness, then inhaling the mermaid dust should have caused his arm to grow back, and his ear cartilage.

She slipped one hand under the sheet and felt for the attachment between stump and prosthesis. Despite the sedation, his shoulder rose to meet her hand as she touched it, much as a pet might react to attention. She could fit three fingers between the fuzzy arm stump and its high-tech hardware. His body was indeed shrinking.

Just then the hair on Mal's arms stood on end. His jaw grew even slacker.

"Lovely. It's going well." The dentist looked delighted. "Now hold the nitrous and increase the oxygen to three, please." Leaning in, she buried her instruments in Mal's cavernous mouth.

"Will do!" Vera emptied the antidote bottle onto her palm. She rolled two cotton swabs in the dark purple glitter and stuffed them into Mal's nostrils.

The dentist looked up, mask foggy, one eyebrow raised. "What was that?"

"Just clearing the nasal passages with a little, um… saline and iodine. Snotty fellow. I learned this trick in the cavalry."

"Well, I'm on the final fang." The dentist chuckled. "Find me another mask, Madam V. Under the table. And a new pair of gloves, please."

Vera rummaged through the supply rack, finding both items between stacks of orthodontic rubber bands. Now was her chance. The dentist was focused on donning the tight gloves. Assuming Berrystream's instructions must be followed literally, she blew the remnants of dust onto Mal's face. His lips wiggled as if he were about to sneeze, then subsided.

The dentist snapped one glove friskily. "Okay, I'm ready for action."

But now even the hair on Mal's head and chest looked strange. It was getting shorter, thicker, as though his brains were sucking the strands back into his head. A fine coat of hair covered his face, the hue gradually deepening to a blue-gray.

Vera checked his pulse. His palm was clear of growth, but one of his nails snagged her knuckles, leaving a spot of blood. "Heart rate's ninety. Strong and regular," she assured Dr. Gentle. The poor dentist was bent over in an L shape on those tall white spike heels, working away.

Mal's prosthesis fell off and clattered onto the floor. Vera stared down at the lump of titanium and Kevlar at her feet. It seemed to have the all the parts of a Leatherman tool about the wrist, plus fingers. The tip of one contained a USB drive. Had these all been hooked into his nervous system? Ugh. What insane biotechnical department would give a sociopath a device that was clearly part weapon? She lifted the neckline of Mal's ridiculously-oversized hospital gown to check on his stump. It was smaller, and quite fuzzy now.

The dentist squinted, shook her head and peered back down into the mouth, then closed her eyes and shook her head again. She sighed and turned back to the stainless steel tray, lifting the remaining porcelain cap with dental forceps. "His left canine really *is* too long, damn it! I'm going to have to grind this down to make it fit."

Mal's mouth had been one of the first things Vera had noticed the day she met him, back at circus school. His lips had drawn her, so soft, pale and pillowy-looking. But now they were thinning before her eyes. Especially the top one, which was developing a split in the middle. And darkening almost to black.

The dentist seemed to have all but forgotten her patient, who was transforming, shrinking on the gurney. Instead, she was fixated on the last crown on the tray, attacking it with a drill, spewing bone dust. Rose was probably divvying up the fish amongst the stray cats of the Alley, and perhaps hitting the vodka. Which is what Vera wished she were doing right now. She pressed two fingers to the side of Mal's fluffy neck. Pulse one hundred forty and regular. His skin was hot and blanketed in blue-gray fur. His eyes undeniably yellow.

He rose suddenly in the dental chair and stood on all fours, arching his back, hair puffed out like a Halloween cat's. Had he stopped shrinking at seventy or eighty pounds, Vera would have been worried. But he'd deflated to the size of a large common house cat.

He stood on the gurney a moment, gazing at Vera, and gave a slow, languid blink. She did not return the approving gesture. Then, with a writhe of the tail, Mal hissed and leapt off, scratching the back of her hand on the way down.

"Come here, you little shithead!" She grabbed him and wrapped him in the fallen hospital gown he'd shrunken out of, and squeezed all four paws together until he resembled a fur-lined purse. She swaddled him in the gown, reached for a pair of orthodontist's rubber bands, and deftly snapped one around the base of each testicle. "There. That'll fix you."

He used her lap for a springboard to jumpstart his escape from Gentle Dental. No doubt he would become the new feline Pied Piper of Cut 'n Shoot Alley. He was that sort of fellow.

Vera cleared her throat. "Doctor?"

The dentist, who had been intent on stuffing the last cap with cement by means of a tiny spatula, looked up.

Vera smiled. "I really admire your focus. It's remarkable. You don't get distracted by anything, do you?"

"Where'd my patient go?" Dr. Gentle mumbled through the surgical mask. She dropped the little spatula.

Vera shrugged. "He kind of went . . . poof."

"Oh dear." The pink-haired dentist winced. "Do they do that here often? I think he's that televangelist who survived the tigers. It must have something to do with that." She tapped the prosthesis, looking professionally nonchalant. But then of course she was a NASA scientist. "And he left his arm. Hmm. Looks like a light metal. Interesting attachments. Say, is that a lighter? Check out this little hack saw. If he doesn't come back, that's worth some money."

"You should keep it," said Vera. "After all, he left without paying."

"But I didn't get the last tooth in. What am I supposed to do with this?" Dr. Gentle held up the cap.

"Save it. He might come back." Though she knew he would not. Plenty of feral cats out there needed leadership, even if it was bad.

"Forget it," said the dentist. "This tooth is toast. Cement's dry." She tore off the mask, the gloves, the gown. "We're done."

"Here's a tip. He must've left it." Vera handed over a wad of bills pilfered from Mal's wallet. If there was anything else good in there, she would give it to Rose.

Who was just coming in the door, folding the map, a creased brown paper sack tucked under one arm. "I got a little lost. Not sure why. But I fed some fish to a bunch of stray cats. Then they all just suddenly took off down the Alley." She froze when she saw the dentist headed to the back room, carrying the robotic arm, muttering, "These are some of the very same materials we used on Apollo 21!"

Rose waited for Dr. Gentle to close the door behind her, then whispered, "He's dead? Where's the body?"

"Not dead. Even better. Transformed, and disappeared."

"To what, and where'd he go?"

"Catalina? Katmandu?" Vera shrugged.

"Seriously?" Rose scowled. "You actually let him go!"

"He's a cat now," said Vera. "Not a tiger. Not a bobcat. A plain old kitty. Come on, let's go back over to the booth so I can finish with my customers. Then I can explain everything over a glass of Krupnik."

They cut through the line that curved again in front of her tent. "You were right about that Lithuanian place!" hollered a guy who worked at the time travel booth. Dozens of watches hung off his trench coat. "That was a honey of a vodka! Got any strong tea in there?"

"I really need coffee," said the chain-smoking priest, grinding a butt under one boot heel.

"I'm a busy man. Let's see those cards!" yelled the businessman, still cuddling his briefcase.

Like a bunch of drunks at a fiesta, thought Vera.

"Water's already boiling," called Rose. Vera closed the curtain and stepped inside.

"I'm looking forward to a scone before I hit the time travel agency," said her daughter. "And some of that honey vodka."

"We can drink to the present." The girl might still be running, but she would no longer be chased. Clearly Rose could take care of herself now. Vera set out the cups and the cards.

When her daughter sat to pour the tea, Vera saw herself reflected in Rose's green eyes. Her own face in miniature, faintly lined with anger, as if the muscles had set that way from too much practice. How wonderful it had felt, all those years ago, to hold the baby. That delicious sweet, powdery aroma, so addictive she used to wonder if she'd hallucinated it. Yes, they'd been robbed of a past, and all things considered, perhaps there would not be a future. And yet . . . who knew?

Vera lifted the steaming cup Rose had handed her, for a toast. "No past. No future. There will only be just now. Agreed?"

After a moment Rose nodded, and raised her own cup. "No past. No future. To now."

In the stall known as Antiquities Out of Time, you will find many wonderful oddities, curios, and mementoes, though some may not seem impressive at first glance.

Take the small mirror hung on the display wall, over there. A square frame of plain walnut inset with silvered glass, the size of a small window. Clearly it is very old, for the glass at some angles seems to refuse to reflect one's face, and the varnished wood has darkened nearly to black with age.

But sometimes, of course, a door is not just a door . . . and a mirror is in fact a window. . . .

DENKRAAM

Mau VanDuren

How strange it is to visit this city I used to know so well, whose language I speak fluently, and whose culture is my own. Yet thirty years on, I felt like a stranger. Tickets for trains, busses and rail cars used to be bought where you got on, from a person, paid for in real money. Now they must be acquired online or from a kiosk at the railway station, plastic only. Even the money was changed, the trusted Gulden no more. Now I had a pocket full of Euros—who ever came up with that name?

I arrived by train at Central Station, by far the best way. No traffic to fight through, no parking to hunt for. And it put me right in the midst of the bustling city center.

The area north of the station used to be an old working class neighborhood with narrow cobblestone streets and small row houses without modern plumbing. Instead each tiny back yard had an outhouse furnished with a barrel replaced once a week. All that charm had now been obliterated to make way for a glass and concrete convention center.

On the islands in the Amstel River, gray shoebox apartments stood where stately red brick warehouses used to brood. Still, the old city was pretty much as I remembered it. Even the single row house surrounded and dwarfed by the Victoria Hotel remained, a stubborn reminder of its erstwhile owner who had held out when the neighbors all sold their homes to the developers.

Along the canals spicy whiffs of marijuana still blew off the terraces of small cafés. And cash still ruled in the bars and among the prostitutes of the old red light district, the "Walletjes." But the women seemed younger, more artificially enhanced. Now they were mostly of East European descent. I'd read in the newspaper not long ago that the single remaining Dutch sex worker was seventy-three years old and about to retire.

I'd rented a furnished room online via AirBnB, in a house in the middle of the Walletjes, on the OudeZijds Achterburgwal. One of the oldest canals in the city, it was lined with tall, narrow patrician houses. Most were only one or two windows wide and leaned against each other in one direction or another. If you took one away, the lot would tumble like a row of dominos.

My room, three steep, narrow flights up, had once been an attic at the rear of the house. The sole window was too high to see out of, and faced south. The hazy October sun projected a bright square on the opposite white wall. Sparse, but a perfect location for my investigation into the disappearance of a stranger. And a strange murder whose victim had been the daughter of an old friend.

I had met Sjoerd Schokker during my first case for the Order of Colfax. He'd just been promoted to detective in Drente and was investigating a murder at a hunnebed, a Stone Age burial site made of huge glacial boulders. He found me sneaking round the site investigating an entirely different matter, and arrested me. I protested and produced identification, though I'd left my passport back in my room. "The criminal always returns to the scene of the crime," he had told me firmly. But during the interrogation he found out I was American, which did not fit the killer's profile, and also noticed and recognized the small runic tattoo on the inside of my wrist that indicated I worked for Colfax.

He let me go, and together we'd solved the murder of an eighty-six year-old Catholic priest. Soon after he transferred to Amsterdam. I had not been back since.

***

My next stop was the Bureau of Police. The modern three-story orange box that had replaced the nineteenth century office and jail of the city constabulary certainly clashed with my memories. I showed my identification to the sergeant at the front desk. "I am an insurance adjuster assigned to the case of one Fiet Loos." The uniformed woman made a quick call, then led me up a black granite staircase straight to the office of Inspector Sjoerd Schokker.

"Mozes," Schokker said matter of factly, upon seeing me hovering in his doorway. "Come in. I thought it would be you. Insurance adjuster, really," he added, tutting disapprovingly.

He rose from his chair and stepped around the cluttered desk to greet me. We shook hands while he studied my face from under bushy brows now gone white.

"Hello, Sjoerd," I said. "Different times call for synchronized vocations." I'd never expected we would work together again, not under these circumstances.

He shrugged and retreated to his chair. Sjoerd's hooked nose and unruly white hair, his stooped stance and feigned hesitant manner reminded me of his vintage TV colleague, Columbo. Minus the cheap unlit cigar. But now he looked depressed as well.

Once seated, I began to explain. "My client hired me to—"

He frowned and held up a hand. "Hold on. Client, did you say?"

I hesitated, but Schokker was always out to connect every possible dot. He wouldn't go on until I explained. "I mean The Order, of course."

He put his finger to his lips, leaned back and looked up at the ceiling. "Hmm. The Ancient and Illustrious Order of Colfax."

"You remembered." Of course he had. Schokker never forgets. "They asked me to investigate a disappearance here. And the murder of

Fiet may be connected to it. Which is why I am here now, my friend."

His face grew dark at the mention of his daughter's name. The laugh lines around his eyes faded. He reached into his jacket pocket and pulled out a bent cigarette. That explained the smell of stale tobacco in his office, though he had not smoked when I knew him before. "A disappearance, really? Was it anyone I should know of?"

"If you can tell me what you've discovered so far, maybe I could help," I said.

"And what would you expect in return?"

"OK." I shrugged with feigned reluctance. "Maybe we can help each other."

"Agreed." He tucked the cigarette between his lips, produced a lighter, and soon was puffing thick blue smoke.

"The Order hired me to look into the murder as a possible lead. They want me to find this missing . . . person."

I mentioned neither the name of the disappeared, since the killer had many, nor the fact that this so-called person might not actually exist. "The one I seek has been involved in murders and disappearances of others. Colfax thinks that he or she is not only jumping ahead of us from place to place, but . . . from time to time." I waited for Schokker's reaction. Surely he wouldn't believe that right away, but we could at least consider the concept.

"From time to time," he repeated slowly. "You mean to say, an actual time traveler?"

There is no such thing, of course, but layman's terms would be easier to understand than explaining the real mechanisms involved. "Yes."

The policeman chuckled, but it was not a happy sound. "As clear as mud, but it covers the ground—to paraphrase an old calypso song."

I couldn't help smiling. Schokker had accepted the explanation, for now. "The order believes there's a possible link to a watering hole called Café 't Mandje."

He leaned back in his chair. "Yes. An odd aspect of the case, that vanishing sailor."

"What do you mean?" I hadn't heard of any sailor being involved.

By now smoke fogged the office. I coughed, and Schokker turned to open a window behind his chair. Smoking was still ubiquitous in this country. Although banned from public places, diehards always managed to find a way.

"My daughter. . . the victim . . . was last seen in the company of a sailor wearing a dark blue jacket and pants, striped shirt, and a dark woolen cap." He propped his elbows on his desk and tented his fingers. "At Café 't Mandje that night they were seen leaving together. But we have no idea who he is, where he came from, or where he went."

"Most peculiar," I agreed, although I had my suspicions. Otherworldly ones.

He abruptly rose, pushing his chair back, its wheels squealing in protest. Clearly there was something else bothering him. "You know," he said, "I ought to simply take you to where she was found." He crushed out the butt roughly in an ashtray concealed in his top drawer, as if it had somehow displeased him. Then I followed him out.

* * *

St. Olav's Chapel was at the end of the Zeedijk not far from Café 't Mandje. It had been built by Norse seamen in the early 15th century in honor of their king. Only the small red brick archway still stood. It had since been incorporated in the wall of a hotel. On the short walk from the orange box we mixed with the multitudes walking to and from the Central Station—young and old, a rainbow of colors, heads uncovered or covered with hats, turbans, caps, and hijabs, clothing ranging from decency-defying miniskirts to abayas.

"A shame," Schokker mumbled.

"What is?"

"That it's all been privatized." He pointed at the station. "Now it's delays, outages, and steep price increases."

Public transport, a long-time priority in this small, densely populated country, used to be state run and affordable. Schokker added bitterly, "Mass service industries were better left in the public sphere. At least politicians are responsible and accountable to voters."

"Agreed. Not all change is good. At least your work is still public," I added.

"But for how long?—Ah, here it is." Schokker pointed at the ancient gate where the body of Fiet Loos had been found. I had never met Fiet, though I'd seen her Facebook profile. In the photos there she was dark-haired, smiling, a pretty young woman with rosy cheeks that needed no makeup. One who liked cute cat videos and historical quotes about famous women. In crime scene photos taken here at the gate she had lain on her back with her head against the door. Her legs extended, feet crossed and out in the street. Staring up, face white as chalk, vacant half-lidded gaze looked slightly puzzled. As if she'd just caught a glimpse of another world in the sky above the cobblestone street that was to be her final stop in this life.

The gate was of red brickwork that arched over a heavy dark oaken door. Sizeable forged iron hinges hung from thick bolts anchored in the small old bricks, which were stained by centuries of soot and pollution. As was the wood, which was also somewhat splintered. This was all that remained of the 15th century chapel.

"And nobody noticed her until morning?" I asked. That seemed odd.

"Not until dawn when the sweepers came," he said tightly. "Though plenty of people walk by here any time of day or night. Probably thought she was drunk . . . or maybe shot in the arm, if you know what I mean. No blood, you see." He turned away abruptly.

"No blood," I repeated softly.

"Correct. There was a wound to the neck. She died of exsanguination." Now he sounded angry. He spread his hands to encompass the pavement. "So where is it? All that blood."

"She might have been killed somewhere else."

"No," he said impatiently. "She was assaulted here. And died here." The last words came out on a sigh. "We found one of her earrings there." He pointed to the lower left corner of the door. "The other was still attached to her earlobe."

"Could it have been planted?"

"No." He scowled at me. "There was a splinter caught in her hair.

It came from there." He pointed at a spot about five feet up the face of the door.

"And how many punctures in her neck?" I was almost certain now the killer had been a vampire or some other such creature.

"Just one," he said. "Why do you ask?"

"Never mind. You wouldn't believe me."

"Try me. I need answers." I detected a hint of desperation in his voice.

I hesitated. Then again, why not just tell him? Worst case, he'd laugh at me and reject the idea. "I had been hoping for two punctures."

"I thought you'd come up with that. It might seem a logical conclusion, if one actually believed in such things." He waved it away, looking scornful. "In any case, there was only one hole. The killer—let us say for now the sailor—brought a large needle, a tube, and some sort of vessel. Then the . . . the body was drained. Like an animal at a slaughterhouse." He pinched the bridge of his nose. "But why, that's the nagging question. An illicit transfusion? Organ snatchers? We may never know." He jammed his fists in the pockets of his jacket so hard I feared for the seams.

I looked at the old door. "What lies behind this?"

Schokker frowned at the timbers and shrugged. "Nothing much. Just a brick wall. And of course the hotel."

"Does it open?"

"I don't think so. No reason to. It's merely a decorative architectural feature now."

I stepped up and inspected the handle, a large forged iron ring looped through a thick black bolt. No doubt there was still a latch on the other side. I tried pulling and then turning the thing, but it wouldn't budge.

"What are you thinking?" Schokker asked. "The sailor couldn't have gone through that."

"Most couldn't, but ours just might have. There has to be some way to open it."

"I suppose . . . yes, to get to the wall for repairs. Hmm. Maybe we can find out. Let's go to Café 't Mandje this afternoon," he suggested. "I'll ring you around five."

***

That evening we walked the short distance from my temporary home to the Zeedijk. The streets were filled with tourists parading up and down the canals, taking photos or strolling past young ladies in revealing outfits silhouetted against the dim, warm red glow of a room. And of course a well-positioned, inviting bed.

We turned into a side alley and came nose to nose with an exquisite woman standing in the open doorway of her own paradise of eroticism. Heavy black eyeliner accentuated bright lion-gold eyes. The contact lenses stood out in that pale face, though they were almost overshadowed by the blood-red lips. Her fangs were long and pointed. The scant white lace lingerie looked straight out of the latest Victoria's Secret catalogue. Perhaps they should do a Halloween issue . . . or maybe they already had.

"Hello," I said. "Are you by any chance a vampire, Miss?"

The question might sound superfluous and entirely too forthright, but in my profession it was prudent. If she was truly a Night Traveler, then she would understand the danger she was now in, faced with a possible slayer. If she wasn't, then the older man in the rumpled black suit was merely a possible client looking for an exciting role-playing sex encounter.

I was of course ready to defend myself, the hand inside my jacket gripping the silver handle of my wooden dagger, made of hundred-year-old *palo santo*, or "holy wood," harvested by nuns in Mexico. I never took chances with vampires.

She smiled, revealing more of the clearly fake ivory. While she caressed my shoulder she briefly turned to look at Schokker. "Oh, hello, Inspector." She apparently decided she had nothing to fear from him, and turned back to me. "Naughty man. You guessed." Her mocking smile seemed calculated to lure me inside. "Come into my place, and I will show you a whole lot more."

Actually it is easy to imagine the attraction of sex and pain to some. The girl on top, your throbbing penis inside her warm body while she holds your balls in one hand and sinks those pretty polished fangs into your willing neck. The anticipation of the act was the ultimate lure.

But I banished those thoughts. Not why I was here. I had never married, and tended to avoid long relationships, but still at that point was feeling not a little guilty and embarrassed. Real vampires are so much easier to deal with than the pretenders.

"Come on," Schokker said. "We have things to discuss. Work to do."

I was happy to move on. "Thank you, Miss," I managed. "Afraid I took you for someone else." Not a lie, and in any case I didn't want to disrupt her solicitations. She had a living to make, after all. She smiled, I nodded, and we walked on.

"You liked Tasha?" Schokker inquired, peering at me closely.

"What? Oh. Well, she is rather intriguing," I admitted. "In an academic kind of way. And that is the ideal profession for a female vampire."

My skinny friend snorted, perhaps thinking I'd made a joke. But I was dead serious.

"They are much better off now than before," Schokker said. "No more pimps, no more wanton exploitation."

I looked at him quizzically. "You really think so?"

"So the papers say. Independent entrepreneurs now, regulated by the state." He grimaced, but I had no clue why. Perhaps he disapproved? Anyhow, it explained why she hadn't been afraid of a policeman. "Some do well and then go back home after five years or so. Buy a house, get married, start a family. Others never escape," he added bitterly.

Was he thinking of someone in particular? I kept the question to myself.

We arrived at a small two story building inconspicuously set in a long row of shops that followed the curves of the old Zeedijk. In the large front window dangled artifacts of all kinds: 1950s toy cars and trucks, vintage ladies' hats, a tin rocket ship. Through the hanging collection I caught a glimpse of a small bar to the left, and a dim nook farther back. The door stood open.

Café 't Mandje was the hot spot in my investigation, so I followed Schokker inside. While he greeted the bartender I let my gaze roam the walls, the ceiling, and finally over the customers. Yellowed posters and psychedelic stickers, faded color and black and white photos of well-dressed, cross-dressed, and half-dressed people hid most of the original plaster. The ceiling also functioned as a repository of artifacts large and small. More model airplanes, boats, trains, and cars dangled on strings with hats and neckties strewn among them. The room smelled of beer mixed with strong perfumes. I don't like scent, especially on men. Often the user applies way too much, offending my olfactory system well after the air has cleared.

Most of the clientele looked middle-aged and nondescript, but the younger ones did not hide either sexual orientation or preferences. Two lesbians sitting at the end of the bar near the window were a study in black. Their Mohawks, their eye make-up, even their lipstick. They cradled each other's heads as they kissed slowly, intensely. A group of older women was seated around a small table in the far corner, all dressed in jeans or knit pants and loose T-shirts. Their hair was uniformly short, so initially in the dim light I'd taken them for men. A young, apparently straight couple and a few men were laughing and joking in the other corner.

The bar was five stools long with a sixth fitted in at the end. The long rectangular mirror behind it was obscured by a great collection of liquors, primarily the many brands of Dutch jenever. Think vodka with a subtle wheat flavor, sometimes a gentle hint of juniper.

Schokker handed me a draft Heineken and pointed at the barkeep. "This is Martin. " Then he pointed at me. "And this is Mozes."

We raised our three glasses with the requisite chorus, "Proost!"

Martin was a sturdy looking fellow in his mid-thirties. Clean shaven, inquisitive brown eyes, light brown hair so short it was almost crew-cut. "Interesting place you have here," I told him, raising my glass to take in walls and ceiling.

He smiled. "This was the first civil liberties bar in Amsterdam, Mozes. Tolerance has been our motto since 1927." With that he turned away to serve some new customers.

"Founded by a woman, a lesbian herself," Schokker added. "Here, let me show you something." He walked over to a tiny tabletop bolted to the wall with a chair set on either side. Immediately above it hung a small mirror. Once we were seated I noticed there were a few more such arrangements around the cramped establishment.

"These mirrors used to allow the clients to check each other out, to make eye contact without being too obvious." The policeman chuckled, though with little humor. "People are less circumspect these days. Nobody worries about being discreet now."

The history of the mirrors was interesting, but I needed to discuss my true purpose. Leveling with him now might prove helpful. "Sjoerd, let me fill you in a bit more on my reason for coming."

He inclined his head. "Please do."

"The person I want to find, the one who disappeared, in fact never existed." I leaned back in my chair to observe his reaction.

He raised his eyebrows and curled his lip. "OK . . . and so the murder never happened? How nice."

"Certainly the killing was real enough." As I weighed how best to explain, and how much to divulge, the barkeep arrived with more beers.

"Martin," Schokker said, glancing up at him. "Join us a moment. You may want to hear this."

The bartender sat down, a useful move considering the mirrors. He probably knew more than anyone else about the goings-on in the café.

I repeated what I'd told the policeman, then added, "With an ordinary disappearance someone is born, lives a life, has friends and relatives, but one day loses all contact. This kind of case is rather different. A whole life has vanished as if the person had never existed."

Schokker frowned. "But how is that possible, Mozes? If someone never existed, then how could we even know of such an individual? "

"Precisely." I nodded. "This conundrum is what The Order of Colfax specializes in. They know such things, and like to investigate them. They have done so for as long as recorded civilization."

Martin squinted as if he knew something, too. In such cases I find silence is the best policy. "This has something to do with the sailor who killed Fiet?" he finally blurted, then glanced warily at Sjoerd. The inspector looked not just sad, but racked with pain. I did not need to ask to know what he was thinking.

Martin bit his lower lip. "There was something damned odd about it. The papers say they still don't know what punctured Fiet's—her neck. And there was no blood on the ground." He paused and again glanced tentatively at Schokker. Who still said nothing. "She must have been moved there."

"Or sucked dry," I suggested.

Martin nodded and looked down at his hands, which were clasped on the table. He said nothing else.

The policeman stood. "Well, I still have work to do. Good night." He abruptly turned away and left.

"Poor Sjoerd. On top of his grief, he probably thinks we're loco," I said. "These things are hard to understand for most folks. No imagination, no beliefs anymore."

"But it's more than that," the barkeep said thoughtfully. "She was his daughter, after all."

"Yes. Of course. I never met her."

"They adopted her as a small child." He fumbled with his glass. "His wife died soon after. He had little time for the girl. Not that he disliked her, not at all, but . . . his job was always demanding. I bet he is guilt-ridden now."

"Tell me more about Fiet. Her last name is different than her father's."

"She changed it. I think she didn't want him to know, well, what sort of work she was doing." He clenched and unclenched his hands, looking down at them still. "Fiet was the sensitive type. Should never have entered the profession."

"She was a prostitute, then."

He nodded slowly. "A misleading word, like whore or harlot. Terms which don't represent their real function, their value in society. I prefer sex hostess." He looked up again. "They're more like social workers. Many have regular clients. They help solve personal problems. But they get no credit for it. Only disdain."

Clearly Martin knew many in the profession and sympathized. He seemed to harbor strong feelings for the victim. Had perhaps even loved her.

"I can still see her sitting here at this table." His gaze narrowed and darkened. "Last week, with that sailor. She in your chair, he in mine with his back to the bar. So I couldn't see him very well."

So Martin must've been the witness who'd said they left together. "They came in as a couple?"

"No. Matter of fact, I never saw him come in at all. He was just suddenly sitting there with her."

"Did they leave together?"

"Yes. Don't know where they went after that, but the next morning she was found at St. Olav's, dead."

"Ever seen the sailor before?"

"No. He came back the same night alone, though. It was late by then. Sat down again right here. Later I noticed he was gone again. Who knows where he went after that. The police can't find him anywhere. As if he went up in smoke." Martin leaned back and folded his arms, daring me to do better.

Just then I thought I detected some movement in the little mirror. I turned, but saw only the reflections of legs and feet at other tables. I felt sure that wasn't what I'd caught a glimpse of before. "Things aren't always what they appear to be," I told the barkeep.

His gaze moved from me to the mirror and back. "You saw something in there?" Before I could answer he added, "I often wonder about them. Mirrors. Whether they show what we want to see, instead of . . . know what I mean?"

I nodded. "Like you said, it takes imagination and belief. They do bring illumination sometimes." I got up. "Better go find dinner somewhere. How much for the drinks?"

* * *

Later that evening I walked back to Café 't Mandje hoping to grill Martin harder and perhaps find out more about the mysterious sailor. Had the man spoken at all, perhaps with a Norse accent? Not much to go on, but it might show some sort of ritual connection to St.

Olav's Chapel. I'd also been thinking about the mirror. That I'd spotted something other than the usual reflection hadn't appeared to surprise the barkeep. I should've asked more then, but I don't work well on an empty stomach. And I don't have the devils of regret and grief to endlessly drive me, unlike poor Sjoerd.

When I entered the bar, though, Martin wasn't there. Instead a lively young woman with a wild spiky coif and large silver earrings shaped like bear skulls tended to customers. I ordered a beer and sat silently on the sixth stool at the end. This early after dinnertime the place was quite empty, so I downed my beer and stood up to pay and leave.

"Wait. Martin just called. I told him you were here," she said. "He wants to talk. He's on his way."

I sat again and ordered a second beer. Soon the barkeep rushed in and dropped onto the stool next to me, out of breath."Imagination and belief," he said. "Remember? Well, there *is* something off about that mirror!"

I turned to look at the tiny table, its small mirror. "Off in what way? I thought I saw some sort of movement, a dark flash, maybe even a face, but . . ."

"It all has to do with the *denkraam*."

I frowned. Not a term I knew. "And what is that?"

"Your mind's . . . well, frame. The larger your *denkraam*, the more it can contain. The more you can know, and see. My father taught me that."

My turn to look incredulous. I had heard of a similar concept, but never deemed it possible. "Explain."

He took a deep breath. "My father was a writer. He spent a great deal of time in the mists of Ireland and the fjords of Norway, doing research for his books. Maarten Toonder was his pen name. The sagas and mythology provided inspiration, he always said. In that mindset he discovered the concept of the *denkraam*, one frame for each individual mind. He's the one who named it that, in fact. A thinking frame."

"I have never heard it called that before, but . . . go on."

"Everyone has a frame with its own specific limitations. Very few people know this, though. And, as with most things, you can't work with what you don't know exists. But that is perhaps just as well. You can get lost in these frames, especially if you step into someone else's."

"Hmm. I suppose a thought frame could be possible. It makes a certain amount of sense."

"Years ago my father taught me how to open my *denkraam*. What I saw scared me to death. So I quickly closed it again. I was young then." He actually shivered. "But last night, after our conversation, I tried again and it opened!"

"What did you see this time?"

"A weird sort of marketplace. Inside there." He pointed at the small mirror.

"But what does that have to do with Fiet's murder? Let me have a look at that thing again." I rose to go inspect it.

He grabbed my arm. "Wait. Not now! Too many folks about. Let's come back after closing."

* * *

Café 't Mandje closed at two in the morning, but life went on full force in the sex tourist neighborhood, I noticed as I walked back to the bar. Men in suits were still negotiating with near-naked women in doorways. Some curtains twitched shut as others slid open and another satisfied client exited. Most appeared to be young men having the ultimate experience, ready to take the memory home to their towns and girlfriends, no doubt expecting to duplicate it. I silently hoped they would learn good sex is actually a two-way street.

I worked my way through a throng of young men cheering another who had just exited one house. His beaming face communicated his success. Paid sex on a dare, no doubt. In my day the saying had been, "You have to learn on an old bicycle." Meaning older bikes had an inherent knowledge that improved your riding experience before taking on the newer bicycle . . . or perhaps, less benignly, was it that old bicycles had little value, so they could be banged up and then discarded? Never having visited an older prostitute, or any, for that matter, I cannot say.

I was early but Martin was already there, our eagerness to investigate clearly mutual. He flung open the Café door and we again sat at the tiny table.

"OK," he began. "I will now try to take you into my *denkraam*." His expression was dead serious. "First, you must do this." He put both hands over his face, the fingers spread, the tips pressing against his temples, and his thumbs braced on his chin.

"Ah, the old Vulcan mind-meld, Mr. Spock," I mumbled. The move had instantly lowered my confidence in Martin's *denkraam* concept.

He frowned. "What?"

"Never mind. What next?"

He closed his eyes. I followed the example.

"Now concentrate. Empty your head of all thoughts," he whispered. "Focus on a small empty spot in your mind. Once you see it, imagine this spot is actually a tiny window. Concentrate harder. See if you can get closer to it. Then, let the window grow."

I tried hard to concentrate but . . . no window.

"Once you can see something through the glass pane, slowly open your eyes," Martin added.

I still saw no frame, let alone a pane to look through. But I kept my eyes closed, determined to pull this off.

"And then, inside the room, look into the small mirror there."

He suddenly stopped talking. The room was silent.

"Martin? Wait a minute." I still saw no window. "Give me a moment to catch up!"

No answer.

I slowly opened my eyes. Martin was not in his chair. I looked around the room. Not behind the bar, either. I glanced up at the mirror, which was empty and dark. Some sort of joke, perhaps? But where had he gone? He couldn't have left so quickly, not without me hearing footsteps on the old wooden floor, or the opening and closing of a door. Unless he'd actually succeeded in finding his mind's open frame.

I looked again at the mirror. Now there was no reflection there at all.

I stood and inspected it all around the edges, then felt the surface of the silvered glass. I again saw my own reflection, where I could have sworn it hadn't been a moment before. I must've been mistaken, then. Sometimes a mirror is just a mirror.

Still, I sat again and placed my fingers on my face the way Martin had. I closed my eyes and emptied my mind as best I could. That took a while. I concentrated on an imagined point far, far away.

Nothing. And Martin did not spring back into the room to laugh at my antics.

Could this be how the sailor disappeared? But then there was the door at St. Olav's. I had to get that to open, too.

Martin would no doubt turn up when he was ready. In the meantime I called Schokker's cell number, and was not surprised to find him still at work in his office.

* * *

"That lever's up here somewhere," the policeman said as he shone his flashlight around the arch above St. Olav's door. "There!"

Good Lord. It was at least nine feet off the ground.

"Here. Let me give you a leg up." I stepped close, stood with my back against the timber and linked my hands, palms up. Schokker leaned on my shoulder and stepped into them. He was very light. Grief had thinned him even more.

There came a soft click and a grinding of rust over rust. We both tumbled through the gate as the door opened behind us, and then swung closed.

There was no brick wall behind the old door. Instead we found ourselves sprawled on the ground in sunlight so bright at first I could make out very little. Except that it was hot, very hot. I heard screaming and the thuds of blows, the smack of punches landing on flesh. We were in the middle of some sort of struggle. I squinted as my eyes adjusted to the light, and saw that Martin and an older man dressed like a sailor were across a small public square, fighting.

"The sailor!" shouted Schokker. He rushed over and leapt upon the man, grabbing him around the neck. The sailor jerked free and bolted down a nearby alley. Martin staggered a step or two in the same direction, breathing hard, but didn't pursue him.

"What happened?" I asked.

He turned to me, face bloody. "Oh boy, am I glad to see you. And not a moment too soon! That bastard jumped me. Nearly killed me, too."

"Is he your vanished sailor?"

Martin wiped his bloody face on one sleeve. "One and the same. "

"Here, let me help." I pulled a handkerchief from my pocket. He had a few impact cuts on his cheeks and chin. I cleaned these as best I could without antiseptic or water.

"Martin! What happened?" Schokker demanded from behind us.

"He must've recognized me from the bar," Martin said. "When I tried to talk to him, he punched me in the face. "

"But where are we now?" I hoped he knew. I saw stalls stocked with Nordic-looking wares. Elaborately knit sweaters with silver clasps at the neck, fancy cheeses, strings of sausages, baskets of berries, silver runic jewelry. All bathed in bright midday sun. It was so hot, no wonder few people were about.

"Looks like a market square," Schokker said. "But where, Norway?"

I looked around. Behind us, set into a wall, was a small, rectangular window about the size of the mirror back in the bar. "Did you come through that?" I jerked a thumb back at it.

"I think so," said Martin.

I went over and discovered the window was still slightly ajar. But I didn't trust it to stay that way. I found a train pass in my pocket, folded it several times, and jammed it between latch and frame. "We just better remember where it is, if we hope to get back."

"Wait. You didn't come through that way?" Martin asked.

"No. The gate at St. Olav's." Schokker gazed around. "Weird sort of place, this."

Martin and I hunted for some sign here of the chapel's door, too. But unlike the connection between window and mirror, we found nothing to indicate its presence.

"Let's see if we can find the sailor, at least, before we try to return," I suggested.

As we walked toward the stalls I looked around. The Scandinavian market was in a town plaza but the buildings surrounding it looked northern Mexican, like a film set from "The Magnificent Seven." The tough, bald actor Yul Brynner could enter at any moment in those long trademark strides. The sparse poverty of the town contrasted sharply with the richness of the goods in the stalls. Outside the market in the bare, scorched square a few bedraggled chickens scavenged for bugs or crumbs. The sign that hung on thin chains above a closed wooden door read CANTINA SECO. Not the most inviting name for a bar.

I had once read in one of The Order's books a mention of an out-of-place market like this, but the details were sketchy. The so-called unexpected always pops up with reasons of its own, though. I was certain of one thing. The sailor who had played an important role . . . The Order hadn't mentioned him before I left. Recent events certainly made him a good candidate for the disappeared killer. But it occurred to me that we were all of us members of the disappeared, now we had come to this place.

We turned down one of the aisles between the stalls. The sharp smell of cheese mixed with the musty odor of mold. An occasional salty waft of dried fish filled my nostrils. A stall with rubber and leather footwear smelled of sweaty feet. A table with onions, cabbages, and spices produced alternating aromas of frankincense, myrrh and cloves, not quite masking the pungent underlying stinks of rotting meat, human waste, and naphthalene. Yes, the market looked as if it was mothballed. But who would leave such rich foods, luxurious fabrics, exotic spices, and expensive housewares unattended, to wither or rot?

Walking up and down we encountered only a few people. All appeared in a hurry and they all ignored us. Some were dressed in western clothes, but others wore thawbs, kaftans or saris. I even spotted a kimono, and a woman from Bolivia in the traditional tall bollard hat.

"Gentlemen," a voice called from a draped alcove. An old woman sat at a small table on a low cane chair. An embroidered cloth covered a round object on a velvet cushion. Her face was tanned and lined, but the eyes were bright and full of life. She was dressed like an old-fashioned fortuneteller in a carnival: long colorful skirt, flowered shirt, tall boots, and a red bandana over long, graying red hair.

"I see an aura of danger. Stronger with you." She pointed at me. "And *you* have been in a fight." Her finger arced to point at Martin.

Well, that was hardly a big revelation, considering his battered face.

"That's true," she admitted, as if she'd read my thoughts. "But I can anticipate your future. You might even be able to change it." Her smile exposed teeth with a few gaps. Yet there was still a radiance about her, as if a younger woman actually inhabited that aged body. The result was disarming. She was protecting the fragile innocence of a sapling with a rough bark exterior. "The Bazaar is not necessarily safe for Outworlders," she added.

"Outworlders?" Martin stroked his battered chin. "What do you mean by that?"

"Those not of here." She shrugged.

"And where precisely is 'here'?" Schokker asked.

She swept an arm to encompass the whole market. "Here is Everywhere." The arm came down. "And Nowhere."

The policeman and I looked at each other. Our turn to shrug. His critical look said, *Crazy as a bedbug*.

"It can be terminal," she suggested. "What stops, and yet never left." She squinted around at each of us. "You must beware!" She raised both eyebrows, rearranged her skirt around her booted legs and looked away. "You don't believe." She sighed. "Very well. Suit yourselves."

"We're looking for a sailor." I described the man. "Have you seen him?"

She smirked. "A sailor, you say? They come a dime a dozen here."

"This one is tall and strong as a gorilla. About a decade younger than me."

She looked at me more closely. "Why would I tell one who doesn't believe me anyway?"

"I apologize, madam." Better to try honey. "We had no intention of insulting or doubting you. It's just that we're out of sorts after a hard and rather unexpected journey."

"Out of sorts, indeed." She paused. "Seamen come here all the time, willingly or not."

"Ours seems to come and go willingly, leaving death behind," I said.

"You must know him!" Martin insisted.

She looked at him with narrowed eyes. "Did he bring you here?"

"Maybe," Martin said. "That is, I think so."

"Hmm. You had better be certain. If he did, he directs this scene. As in a film. You're all just the actors." She appeared to reconsider that last statement. "Well, up to a point."

I turned to Martin. "Could it be that we ended up in his *denkraam*?"

The barkeep frowned. "Instead of you being in mine, we're in his?"

She turned to Martin. "He was the man who attacked you."

He nodded, though this had not exactly been a question.

"Then you're lucky not to have been terminated," she told us. "In the Outworld he's a vampire, you should know. Here he is not permitted to bite anyone, but he is still very strong."

Martin nodded, pressing a hand to his swollen jaw. "I noticed."

I slipped my right hand inside my jacket, found the silver handle of my trusted holy-wood dagger, and pulled it out. "Will this work here?"

Her left hand stretched out, palm up, facing the dagger. She withdrew it quickly without touching the wood, and shuddered. "It is old enough, and powerful. The Colfax. I thought so." I started to speak, but she held up a hand. "Yes, your weapon will be effective."

"Thank you." I tucked it back inside my jacket. "Tell us where we can find him."

"There are only two places where creatures like him wait out the heat of day." She pointed back where we had come from. "The Cantina, or the whorehouse."

"Where? I saw no whorehouse." I looked around for some sign of one.

"It is inside the hotel."

The scents from the bazaar grew stronger. The naphthalene, the underlying rot. "Is this place being mothballed, madam?"

"Better not dillydally." She closed her eyes and lowered her old head, the action eerily reminiscent of an automaton in a booth I had seen once as a child. Clearly our audience had ended.

We thanked the old lady and started to walk back down the aisle toward the Cantina Seco. Martin followed my gaze around the stalls. I paused and turned back to ask the woman if our currency would be accepted in this place. She was no longer there.

"I'll be damned," Martin drawled.

"We all will be, no doubt, if we don't hurry," said Schokker.

The market was entirely deserted now. Most stalls were empty of wares. Some had disappeared altogether. The mid-day sun pounded on our shoulders and bare heads. We found the unpainted, weathered pine door of the cantina closed, presumably to preserve whatever coolness remained. Martin gripped the heavy ring that served as a handle. He pushed, then pulled. The door didn't budge.

"Try turning it," I suggested. With a click it now opened on a dark interior. Unable as yet to make out the furnishings, I followed my friend inside. Once the bright sun was behind us, the room slowly resolved into a primitive bar made of three beer barrels topped with rough boards, and four rough-hewn tables, their legs still with bark attached. And . . . hold on . . . a variety of gilded Louis Seize chairs with red velvet seats and backs, ornately carved. One of these held a man slumped in sleep, his head on his folded arms supported by the table top. A wide sombrero lay next to him on the floor like a tourist souvenir.

"Buenos tardes, señores," said the barman, from his station behind the crude bar. True to form he was polishing glasses with a white cloth. "Bienvenidos. What would you like?"

"We're looking for someone," I said. Though it appeared our suspect wasn't here.

"Would the señores care for something more exciting than mere liquor?" a female voice came from a corner. She was plump, with an attractive face, but the brutal sun had not done her skin any favors. Her blouse was low cut, putting sizable breasts at risk of losing cover. Her black hair hung long and straight down her back. It was impossible to guess her age.

"You have cold beer?" Martin asked the barman.

"We need to move on to the hotel," protested Sjoerd anxiously, though he made no move to leave. As if someone else was indeed writing the script for us.

"Si señor. Three cervezas." The proprietor reached behind him and produced three bottles of Noche Buena, popped the caps and handed them over the bar.

"They're warm," we all complained in unison.

The barman shrugged. "Warm, cold, it's all a matter of relativity. Outside it is hot, in here it's only warm, and the beer is cooler yet. Wouldn't you agree, señores?"

"I guess." Martin took a swig. I did, too. The man was right. All relative, and it wetted my dry throat nicely.

"When you have quenched your thirst, señores, you will find me waiting," the woman said. "One at a time or all three together, is all the same to me. Together costs triple, of course." She rose and strolled away, turning into a dark corridor. A sign above it read THE LAST CHANCE HOTEL.

I turned to the barman. "We're looking for a sailor. Seen one today?"

He smiled with brown teeth. "But, señor. What would a sailor be doing in the Chihuahua desert?"

"What's a Scandinavian market doing here?" I countered.

His eyebrows rose above wide innocent eyes. "What kind of market?"

"The one outside. On the square!" Sjoerd shouted.

"There is no market in this town!" The barman pounded the boards of his counter.

Martin rushed back to the door and threw it open. The square was empty save for a lonely, round stone well.

"I told you so." The barman came over to stand next to us. "Things come, things go. We come and go. You too come and you . . . well, no matter." He turned back to the bar.

The sleeping man at the table woke, staggered to his feet, and nearly fell over his chair. If you discarded the tan, the moustache, the wild black hair, and the Mexican costume, he might have looked like a

Pennsylvanian farmer of German stock, big bellied and blond.

"Time for fun." He belched loudly, took a few more unsteady steps, and fell flat on his face. At the crash, the plump woman darted from the corridor. She grabbed the man's arms to hoist him, straining hard, bending lower and lower until her right breast popped from the low neckline of her blouse. She ignored this minor inconvenience and started dragging the man into the hotel.

"What about the sailor?" I pressed the barman.

He shrugged. "I don't know where he went. He appeared with the market."

Sjoerd shook a fist. "Tell us what you know about him, right now!"

If the man was intimidated, he didn't show it. "Señor, nothing you see here is as it appears."

Before I could ask what that meant, the drunk spoke from the floor near the hotel entrance, where the woman had paused to rest a moment. "He's telling the truth. We lead a very strange life. Today you find us speaking Spanish and drinking tequila. We dress in Mexican garb, have a tan to match, and live in a Chihuahua town. But it's all an act we are forced to play. As long as you are here, we will be here. But if you leave and come back another time, we may be Inuits, and butchering seals for dinner."

Martin glared at me, incredulous. "What do you make of this?"

"Could it be," I said, "that this place is controlled by one particularly strong *denkraam*? Not yours, obviously. But someone else's. The vampire sailor."

"Vampire, you say?" The large German sombrero man frowned as if puzzled. "Is that what he is?"

I nodded. "Yes, and a killer. You know him, then?"

"He comes and goes with the market," the woman said. "No matter who or where we are, it comes and goes as well."

"He once told us that if he ever doesn't return, we will terminate. Just . . . disappear. That we are all merely of his making. But who could credit such a thing?"

"Sir," I asked the sombrero man, who seemed quite sober now,

"What is the first thing you remember? Where are you from?"

He sighed. "It is such a long time ago, I hardly recall. But we all came here just as you. One moment we were elsewhere, and then just . . . here."

The barman broke in. "My original name was Farid. I'm from Lebanon. At least, as far as I know. And this," he pointed at the woman, "is Miriam. She's from Amsterdam."

"I believe I was called Stephen," the sombrero man said slowly and thoughtfully. "From Buckingham County, Pennsylvania."

"Amsterdam, really?" Martin said to Miriam. "From where and . . . um, when?"

"Zeedijk. I remember there was war. The Germans came." She looked down, the lovely plump face suddenly drawn and pale.

"You mean Nazis?" Sjoerd asked, and she nodded.

"How did you get here?" Now that I knew her name I could see the hints in her features. She must be Jewish, a dangerous condition back then. Even in the Netherlands the SS, the Gestapo, and some among the local Dutch police were merciless in their pursuit of Jews.

"The owner of the café was hiding me in a back room. When the Nazis came I had to make a quick decision. I met the sailor there. He said I was lucky because he liked me, though he would have sucked me dry if we'd stayed in Amsterdam. He said I would be safe here. That he'd lost one of his fangs in a fight, and he was under orders not to drink from people here."

One fang. One puncture wound. I glanced at Sjoerd. His face was white, teeth clenched. "Orders? From whom?" he demanded.

She shrugged and looked at her feet. "An old Romani woman, I think."

"How did the sailor bring you here?" I asked. "Through a mirror?"

When she nodded again, Martin cried, "You must be kidding! From Café 't Mandje? The owner was Bet van Beeren!"

"That's the one!" the woman confirmed, bouncing on her heels with excitement. "Do you know her?"

Martin shook his head. "I work there now. I'm sorry to tell you this, but . . . Bet is long dead."

"Oh." She bit her lip. "The Gestapo took her?"

"No, she survived the war by those same quick wits. She lived to be quite old, but I never met her."

Miriam looked perplexed. "Then . . . the war is over? How long have I been here? What year is it now?"

I told her.

"No! Seventy-five years, truly?" She started to cry.

I realized now I'd read about her disappearance years ago in The Order of Colfax's archives. A cold case, but once considered high priority.

"One vampire tooth, one puncture wound. It looks like we've identified our killer." Feeling pleased, I turned to look at Schokker.

He was no longer beside me.

"Your friend has gone to the hotel," said the barman. "And he looked very angry."

***

The Last Chance Hotel looked much like the Victorian brothel set I'd seen in a London production of *The Threepenny Opera*. Mack the Knife would have felt at home. The lobby was hung with long red velvet drapes trimmed with golden fringe, held back from the windows with gold-tasseled cords. Women wore corsets and lacy pantalettes, or satin thongs and lace bras. Some were draped in scanty Chinese robes. They sat or reclined on chaises longue, doing each other's hair, polishing their nails, mending underclothing. A few were singing and giggling, entertaining men. Clearly our vampire sailor must've seen a similar production at some point in his life. Whenever that had been.

At a desk in the center presided a stern-looking madam in Mexican peasant blouse and lace mantilla, a black antique cash register in front of her. She was arguing with a customer, and now I saw it was Schokker.

We drew closer. "I'm not leaving without her," he was telling the madam.

She shrugged. "Fine. Then you aren't leaving. I will run a tab for you." She went back to counting a stack of bills.

"Sjoerd," I called. "We must go. The market is already coming apart, rotting and fading."

He shook his head. "Not now. Not when I've just found her."

He pointed at a young woman sitting on a brocade-upholstered bench, reading a novel. I gasped.

It was Fiet Loos, alive and well in a black miniskirt and white peasant blouse, her thick dark hair swept up and secured with a Spanish comb. Not the pale, drained, murdered young woman of the crime scene photos. This was the very much alive Fiet I'd seen on her Facebook page. A smart young woman just beginning to make a life for herself, with both good and bad choices, like all of us. Perhaps headstrong, but wise and persistent enough to make her own way. Even without benefit of a mother. Even despite a distracted, over-worked, inattentive father.

Sjoerd gazed at her longingly. "You see? Here, somehow, she still lives. I have another chance. "

I glanced at a far corner where the sailor hunched at a table, hands over his face like a man entranced. "No, Sjoerd. He's changing the *denkraam*. We have to go."

"Then I'll take her with me," he insisted.

I grabbed his arm. "That will do no good. Your daughter is dead in our world."

From overhead came a loud *crack*. A thin rain of plaster trickled from the ceiling to baptize our heads in fine white dust. "If you stay you'll be trapped in his next twisted *denkraam*. He's changing the location."

"Then so be it," he said stubbornly. "I won't abandon her again." With that he tore his arm from my grasp and walked over to Fiet.

She looked up, smiled and closed her book. Sjoerd dropped into the chair next to her and took her hands in his. He was weeping, but his face radiated peace and joy.

"No time left," I told the others. "We must go back through the mirror now, quickly. If I understand things correctly this place will change as soon as the sailor decides exactly what world to think up next."

"Damn! You're right." Martin clenched his fists. "Should we just kill him?"

It was tempting, but I didn't know for sure what effect it would have on the residents here, or on us. "Then Miriam and Stephen might die, along with any others who have been here a long time. We must go now. Follow us!" I told Stephen and Miriam.

Still Martin hung back. "But what about Sjoerd?"

"We can't make him leave. He's chosen to stay here with Fiet."

We left the cantina, running across the courtyard to the wall with the window in it, the one Martin had entered through. I pulled at the frame. The cardboard I'd jammed into the latch fell out, and it opened.

Miriam stepped up, took one look and said, "I can't fit through that."

Farid the barkeep had no such qualms. He climbed up and dove in, legs and feet disappearing through it. Stephen and Martin followed. I looked back once, to see if Schokker might've changed his mind. Perhaps he would still come.

The light in the town square grew darker.

"Miriam, please! Go now!" I begged.

She hesitated, then shook her head and stepped away. "Don't you see? I can't! In that world, I'll be dead." She turned and ran away.

It was probably true. She would've been gassed, surely, by the Nazis. At least here she had a chance, even if her fate depended on a vampire sailor's twisted whims.

A heavy cloud obscured the sun. The well on the square started to fade. Grass was pushing up through the dry hard dirt, growing right under my feet. The wall around the window wavered and shimmered, morphing from mortared stone to hand-hewn timbers. The sailor was thinking up the fine details of his next *denkraam*.

I leaped for the open window then.

Someone grabbed my ankle. Without looking to see who it was, instinctively I whipped out my holy dagger and thrust it backward, hard. There came a shriek of pain and rage.

And then I was through.

***

I found Martin sitting at the tiny table in Café 't Mandje. The mirror reflected only the small table and the legs and shoes of other patrons. It was just a mirror.

"Miriam refused to come," I said.

"Who?" Martin frowned, looking puzzled.

"Miriam, your friend from the cantina!"

He shrugged. "OK, but ... where's that?"

I thought I understood. They had only ever met there, in the sailor's world. He had no memory of her in his world. And she was still an unwilling actor in the changing scenes, having chosen an uncertain life over certain death. While here ... it was as if they'd never met. My Colfax training allowed me to retain her memory ... though for how long, I wondered. Much of what the Order did and how they did it was still a mystery to me. My department only covered disappearances. Knowing things that had never actually happened was one of their specialties.

My cell chimed. I took the call as Martin went to order two beers from the bar. I texted an answer and hung up.

"My investigation is done," I informed him when he returned. "I told my employer I have solved the case."

Just then the young woman with the spiky hair came up and cheerfully greeted us. She set three frothy beers on the tiny tabletop without spilling a drop. "I didn't see you come in," she said apologetically. "So sorry for the wait." She hurried off to wait on another table.

I turned back to Martin. "You were right. The sailor was indeed the killer who disappeared."

He looked up from his glass. "Sailor? What sailor?"

"The disappearance I came here to investigate," I reminded him.

Martin nodded. "Right. Linked to the murder of Fiet. So we're looking for a sailor?"

"Well ... yes. " Better to go with that. Easier than explaining it all right now. There would be time later, if need be. I lifted my beer and took a long draught.

It was interesting to experience how reality might have changed. I worried that with the thrust of my dagger I might've accidentally killed

Sjoerd. Because if not, shouldn't he be here? On the other hand, if the holy wood had killed the vampire, Sjoerd might still be trapped in the sailor's world with Fiet. Or would he be here in that case as well, since that meant the sailor had never existed? But I had been unaware of these trying contingencies until just now. Colfax had seen to that. I wondered how much they knew about our adventure. Probably everything.

"Tell you what. Forget the sailor." I told Martin. "The old fortuneteller, she was interesting, though, wasn't she?"

He blinked and looked at me blankly, as if thinking, *Good god. Is he off his rocker now?*

Of course. If the vampire-sailor had never existed, his *denkraam* hadn't either. Therefore our whole adventure in the marketplace had never really happened. Even to me.

It was frightening. Now I was the anomaly, the only one who still had recall. Although already it seemed harder to bring back details. And what about the Mexicans in the market square? And Miriam. This meant she'd never met the sailor. He'd never saved her and taken her there. So had she been murdered in the gas chambers after all?

Suddenly depressed, I turned to Martin. "Remember I told you about a disappearance?"

"Yes." He folded his arms and leaned back in his chair.

"And that the person who vanished might never actually have existed?"

He hesitated. "Um . . yes. I think so."

"Well, he did and then he didn't. No, don't even ask. It will be better that way. Just know that the case has been solved."

Martin squinted. Probably I had just confirmed to him that I was indeed truly nuts.

I chuckled. "Life. Time. Space. It can all be so very complicated."

A shadow fell over the tiny table. Martin and I looked up. Our glances snagged first on a pair of long legs in a black satin miniskirt, and rose to take in a sheer white blouse, and then finally lifted to contemplate Fiet's pretty, smiling face.

She stood there with Sjoerd, beaming at us. So very much alive.

"Mind if we join you?" she said.

These small, charming faerie statuettes, dressed in short leafy skirts and silky scarlet stockings, are the most popular item in the Fae for a Day Shop, a daub-and-wattle cottage at the farthest end of Cut 'n Shoot Alley. But only a privileged few of the Invited will be permitted to pass beyond the watchful primrose hedge which guards the border between the main Bazaar and the private realm where the Kindly Ones prefer to dwell, only mingling with humans on their own terms.

Though perhaps "privileged" is not the most accurate description for a mortal who encounters faeries in the Upper World, and through that chance meeting earns the dubious benediction of a rare, transformative gift. . . .

THE KINDLY ONES

Naia Poyer

Dodging elbows and sludge-puddles on Seventh Avenue, Miller peeled a yellow sticky note from the envelope holding his first paycheck. Through clouds of tobacco- and meat-scented smoke, he read:

> *So glad you're my* EMPLOYEE *now . . . congrats on adulthood! Don't spend it all in one place. . .*
> *(I hate it when grownups say that).*
>
> —*Stella*

He sucked down air that smelled like sewer, and didn't care. He had a job. And the spare room in his friend's Harlem apartment. This was better than he'd expected life to get for a long time.

His reflection rippled across a mirrored bank window. The profile sleek. Not thin, but . . . right. Handsome, almost.

A jangling caught his attention. At the bank's entrance camped a homeless white man wearing a dirty gray skullcap. A steady stream of passersby stepped over his outstretched legs, ignoring the pathetic jingle of coins against Styrofoam cup. Wrapped in an unseasonable puffy white windbreaker, he looked like a pile of dirty snow the spring had failed to melt.

Miller's heart plummeted. He had only a couple weeks of homelessness under his belt, and had only had to sleep outdoors once. Still, that rock-bottom feeling was too familiar.

In his pocket were twenty dollars from Stella, the last of his pre-paycheck loan. But with that first paycheck in his hand, no matter what, he was better off than the guy on the corner. He pulled out the cash, soft from use and warm from riding next to his thigh.

As he approached the man, Miller tried to look bigger. As if just noticing the cup, he paused, leaned down and tucked the rolled-up tens into it. The breeze caught up one; he snatched it from the air and shoved it back in. His cheeks were burning. The homeless man sat still, eyes hidden beneath the cap. His head looked oddly lumpy. Up close, a hot puff of body odor escaped through the T-shirt's neck. His sweat smelled like a rotting leaf pile.

Then the man spoke. "Why, thank you, Miss." His breath smelled like compost. "Of all the girls walked by today, I've seen prettier, but you got the biggest heart."

Miller stiffened with anger.

"Girl with a heart like yours deserves looks to match." The guy continued. "Girl as kind as you should be the fairest lady in New York."

Probably the man was just ignorant, just trying to be nice. Miller told himself this for eight blocks as he scowled and kicked the pavement, but it didn't make him feel any better. The paycheck became a sweaty wad in his fist.

***

"Asshole," Stella growled at the wad of mochi she was punching on the kitchen counter. "Did you tell him off, at least? I woulda shoved a live pigeon down his throat. Wait—no. Very, very unfair to the pigeon. Probably I'd just curse him." She waved toward her living room altar—one of three in the tiny apartment she let him share—a mish-mash of anonymous deities and stockinged faerie statuettes.

"Nah, I just . . . it wasn't worth it," Miller muttered, mashing the adzuki bean filling but without Stella's enthusiasm.

"You said, like, he didn't even really look at you. And your voice is so low now, how could he make such a mistake unless he was trying to?"

"That part was weird," Miller admitted. "I just assumed I fucked something up."

Stella grimaced and strangled the lump of dough. "Listen. You are not the fuckup here. It is not your responsibility to trick people into being decent. Go back and tell him he was wrong. Do it nice, or do it nasty. But don't keep letting others tell you who you are."

She lowered her eyes to the mangled mochi. "Just, obviously . . . do it during the day, with plenty of people around."

Miller swallowed. "Yeah."

***

In Stella's cheerful blue-and-yellow tiled bathroom, Miller pressed a razor to his left cheek. Then he squinted at the mirror. Something was wrong.

The meager stubble that had been there this morning was gone. The beginnings of a beard he'd waited on like buds in spring. The cheek was smooth, and even softer than he remembered.

The razor clacked loudly onto the sink's porcelain lip.

"What the actual *fuck*."

***

Three days later, his face was still hairless. And now his chest scars hurt. He made it through a five-hour shift at Muffin Hunter/ Bean Gatherer—Stella's coffee shop—hoping customers mistook his grimaces for smiles. Then he went home and ripped off his t-shirt.

The slanting scars beneath his nipples were still a dark plum, but they looked shiny and strained. His fingers brushed his right pectoral.

"Ow, fuck." It was sore and puffy.

This was not good. He fumbled the phone twice dialing the doctor.

* * *

Two days later he was on the examining table, paper crunching under his ass. "It's even worse than when I called," he whined, hating the wrongness of his voice all over again. A poster across the room showed a stock-illustration blonde looking weirdly sassy while examining herself for breast cancer. Miller looked away.

"Could they . . . I know it's a stupid question, but . . . can they grow back?"

"No, no," Dr. Nguyen reassured him, stepping up to the exam table. "That's extremely unlikely. I mean, yes, not all the breast tissue was removed, so a small amount of growth could occur, but . . ." She took a look at Miller and paused. "This much, this fast . . . is . . . unusual." She laid a cool gloved hand on his chest, and he flinched. "It doesn't appear to be an infection, though. And your scars are healing well."

Miller bent his head to see. The pink scars had definitely grown thinner and lighter since yesterday.

"We can up your hormones," Dr. Nguyen said, less confidently than Miller had hoped.

* * *

On the ride back he reflected that, till now, everything had been going very well. So naturally it was time for a mystery illness. The new prescription rattled in his pocket every time the R train screeched to a halt. He felt deformed. He'd tried wearing an old binder to hide the resurrecting breasts, but the pressure made him cry.

He gripped his knees and stared at the backs of his hands. Hang on—was it just his imagination, or was the skin on them . . . lightening? Miller's mother was Puerto Rican, with a rich dark complexion; his father white enough to tell Lutheran-dad jokes. They were both assholes. They were great together. But the point was, Miller had never looked this pale in his life. His brother had often passed for white, but he. . .

He shook his head hard. Not gonna think about Derrick. This stress is what's making me sick.

A weary-looking man was working his way down the car, pasting fliers over ads featuring grinning college students. SUNDAY FUNDAY! the fliers read. As he taped, he kept muttering loudly, "Why you not smilin', bitch, why you not *smilin'*? Bitch, why you not *smilin'*. . ."

Miller had woken up that morning to bloodstains on the sheets. His period had come back. He had no idea how to stop this backslide.

So he was on his way now to yell at a homeless man. You know, to make himself feel better.

***

The guy wasn't in his usual spot, which had been newly graffitied. **HATE IS STRONGER THAN LOVE**, spelled the artful splashes of paint.

Fair enough, Miller thought.

He finally found him a block away, in front of a 7-Eleven, legs blocking the doorway. A pantsuited woman tried to step over them, decorously ignoring the person they were attached to. He rattled the cup loudly between her legs. She yelped and ran away. The guy sat back and laughed like a stalling engine.

Figures, Miller thought. I *would* give all my cash to the shittiest beggar in Manhattan. The man didn't look up when Miller got there. Just reached between his feet to pick up the stump of a cigarette, and lit it so quickly Miller saw neither match nor lighter.

Smoke trickled between yellow-brown teeth. Still without glancing up, the guy said, "I'd been wondering when you'd drop by to offer thanks, Camilla."

A surge of acid burned Miller's throat. "What did you just call me?"

"Your true name." The man chuckled, pushing up his skullcap for the first time to reveal shiny little black eyes and—shit, were those stubby *horns* curling into his greasy hair?

Miller felt he couldn't comment on *that* without sounding crazy, so he stuttered, "A-actually, it's called a birth name. I don't know how you found out mine, but—"

"Oh, you poor, sweet girl. The Kindly Ones are not taken in by your deceptions." He flicked a knobby finger at Miller's flat chest, his short haircut, the sneakers he wore a size too large.

"Dunno what you're talking about, but the last guy who called me 'sweet girl' got his ass kicked." Lie. Miller had never confronted . . . anyone, really.

The man shook his head, button eyes crinkling at the corners. His skin glowed dully, though not with health. He shone like a dim and hideous Christmas angel on Satan's front lawn.

"Human deceptions," the man said, "which those such as I can always discern. Illusions, disguises." The voice of a man who rasped *Help me out*? more often than *Hello* had been replaced with something smoother, more courtly. "Oh, I understand your motivations. Such a one as you, so nobly born, fallen on hard times, must take precautions—"

"I—*nobly born*?" Miller snorted. "My parents are rich stupid lawyers from Jersey who kicked me out! I'm not in hiding, I'm just a dude. Also, fuck you!" His heart was racing so furiously he barely managed to gasp out the words.

"Camilla." The dead name sucker-punched Miller again. "I know of your inner turmoil. I am a faerie—and just as importantly, a feminist! Thus, in return for your earlier kindness, I made you a gift. You shall become the most beautiful woman in this fair city of New York!" The horned guy smiled like a magician sawing someone in half. And maybe it was only a windblown leaf, but just then a tiny green bud seemed to blossom from the tip of one horn, then vanish.

"Tell me you didn't just say what I think you said."

"In this day and age, such pressure is put upon women like you. Those not born with the requisite . . . charms and graces. You are taught to doubt, to hate yourself." Miller guessed he'd gleaned this insight from a *Cosmo* left on a park bench. "But now you can be what you never thought possible. With your beautiful nature, plus my generous gift, you will be the perfect woman. The kind even faeries will long to possess."

"You absolute bastard," Miller spat out. "You're telling me you magicked my tits back? Made my beard fall out and my . . . made me bleed, as a *thank-you?* Because you're a fucking *faerie?*"

"Indeed!" The vagrant's face lit up with a beatific grin.

Out of words, Miller leaned down and grabbed one of the faerie bum's horns. It felt smooth yet heavy, like a conch shell worn by the current of centuries. He yanked hard, just to see that arrogant face feel pain.

He got his wish. The faerie twitched, face a spasm of surprised anger. A jolt of pain shot up Miller's arm. He let go and cradled his wrist. It felt bone-deep and fizzy, like the afterache of a bad electrical shock. The hair on the arm now appeared lighter and finer, the bitten-down nails grown long and lustrous.

The last time his arm looked like this had been nearly five years ago. Leaning by the window of his mother's car, fingers savagely picking at the vinyl as she'd lectured, *Stop it, Cammie! It doesn't kill you to wear a dress one day of the week. You can't make everything about your . . . obsession with being* special.

Now, unable to tear his gaze from those perfect, shell-pink nails, Miller whispered, "You can't make me the most beautiful woman in New York City. Whatever you do to me, I'll never be a woman."

"We'll see." The faerie closed his eyes and leaned back against the brick wall, smiling like a pleased cat.

"What the hell do you want from me?" Miller yelled.

Flecks of spit hit the faerie's cheek. He opened one eye. "Your dramatics weary me." He hadn't seemed this pale and drained before Miller touched him. "As thanks are out of the question, you may fetch me some manner of restorative elixir. When I've recovered, we may perhaps discuss compromise."

"Okay," Miller said. "*That* I can do."

He entered Stella's coffee shop into a gust of warm air. Whenever someone complained about the lack of air conditioning, she would silently point to a poster behind the bar: THINK OF THE FUCKING BABY TREES. "You're early!" she shouted now over the din, already handing him two iced coffees to chauffeur to customers. Sweat shone on her collarbone. Her long bleached dreadlocks were roped into a ponytail that slapped her shoulders as she worked.

"Actually, I'm here to buy. I'm, uh . . . getting coffee for the guy who misgendered me."

"What! That is exactly the opposite of what I told you to do!" She smacked down her silver scoop like a gavel. "Did you chew him out first? Did he apologize?"

"Not exactly. Turns out he's a faerie, and he's cursed me with boobs and beauty."

"Well if that ain't a shitty thing to do to someone who just paid for your heroin." She scowled and poured steamed milk into a Christmas tree mug.

"I need advice, Stella. How do I deal with a gender-essentialist faerie douchebag?"

"Well, once I hit one in the face with a bag of rose quartz and told her to fuck off back to Brooklyn. But I sense this situation is different." She thought for a moment. "Faeries love cake. Shit's like paranormal crack to them."

"Great!" Miller grinned. "Let's work from there."

* * *

"Oookay. Here you go." Miller handed a large triple-shot birthday-cake latte to the faerie, who removed the insulating sleeve and tossed back half in one scalding gulp.

"It tastes of . . . cake," he said dreamily. "And of . . . the Indies."

"Yup." Miller shrugged. "That, uh, sure is where the magic beans probably came from."

The faerie examined the crude runes Stella had written on the cup and hidden beneath the cardboard sleeve. "Your wizard is clearly an excellent chemist. Though quite illiterate."

Damn it, Stella. Spell of Binding, my ass.

"It occurs to me you know not how to properly address me, mortal lady," the faerie said. "For now, you may call me Horn."

"Wow. That's so . . . original. If you hung out with drag queens you might think up a better name."

Horn hissed like a creepy lizard. "I've had enough of queens to last me an eternal lifetime. And *you* shouldn't talk of originality, Ca-miller."

"Ooookay then." Miller backed up a step. "So what about that compromise you mentioned?"

"Ah, yes." Horn licked a palm and polished his horns, an act far more disgusting than dapper. "There is an otherworldly event tonight in this city that never sleeps. I should like an escort. What better companion than the most beautiful woman in New York?"

Miller snorted. "And why would *he* want to be your date to some trashy faerie rave?"

"Accompany me, and you might learn the true merit of my gift. But if you attend the Night Bazaar, and by dawn your resolve still holds firm, I will take it back."

"Easy as that?"

"Of course. I'm not an unreasonable . . . man. And experience can change a person."

"Wait, isn't the Night Bazaar some pop-up hipster craft market in Brooklyn? Why there?"

Horn waved a dismissive hand. "I assure you, this is no bazaar you would know of. For it is one few mortals are privileged to attend. And never ones who think sweater vests are cool. Will you go, then, shorty?"

"Holy shit, never use slang again." Miller narrowed his eyes. "Especially not that kind of slang, if you're gonna go around bleaching people's skin for beauty purposes." He heaved a defeated sigh. "But yeah, I'll come along to your racist faerie shindig. Because, wow. I've certainly never been asked out quite so persuasively."

"So mote it be!" Horn held out a spittle-dampened hand for a shake. "I don't need your number. I shall find you and send directions."

Miller made a gagging sound, then turned and walked away.

***

He arrived at the designated corner—a still-ungentrified area of the meat-packing district—five minutes late, defiantly wearing a blue sweater vest. In its tiny pocket was a 7-Eleven receipt with the cross streets written on it. A pigeon had nearly dashed herself to pieces trying to deliver it through the glass pane of Miller's window.

Stashed in the pocket of his corduroy pants was one of Stella's sassy, stockinged faerie statuettes. A *spiritual anchor*, she had told him. *Imbued with the power of my home and hearth. Plus, faeries hate iron, and the wings are probably at least . . . steel?* But whether or not Stella's 'magic' worked, the stark contrast between the sweet figurine and the nasty vagrant faerie was enough to remind Miller to be cautious. Behind dim streetlamps, the skyscraper across the street seemed to suck and destroy light instead of reflecting it. Or maybe it was just very, very dirty. Yet its windows shone with the clarity of calm black water. They were all tilted slightly open to reflect a black sky full of stars. The dark tower loomed twenty stories above its neighbors, and Miller could swear he'd never seen it there before. He glanced at the pink-gray clouds concealing the actual stars above, and swallowed hard.

He thought Horn was late too, until a whole row of streetlamps shuddered out one after another, ending with the one he leaned against. The faerie materialized from behind a parked car, where he might have just been squatting the whole time. He touched a nearby meter, then snatched the quarter it spat out. Tossing the coin high in the air, he caught it in his mouth.

Miller frowned. "Here I got all dressed up, and you didn't even try."

The faerie still wore the dirty windbreaker and skullcap. The breeze wafted his sweat-stink of rotting leaves. But his posture was erect, and the grime on his face now resembled makeup for a masque. He turned a calm smile on Miller, and extended one dirty, cracked hand. "Shall we?" he slurred, the quarter tucked under his tongue.

They crossed the street, passing a group of young men with loose ties flapping over their unbuttoned shirts. One dropped a beer can and immediately tripped over it. "Hey, fags!" another yelled.

Miller stiffened, but Horn ignored them. He approached the building in slow, dignified strides. Miller realized he was gripping the faerie's sleeve, though he couldn't remember taking hold of it. He wanted to let go and run, but his eerily perfect nails dug into the dirty coat with a will of their own.

"Whatsa matter, fags? You scared?" One of the men broke off to follow them, to drunken laughter and wolf whistles.

Miller struggled to let go of Horn, but couldn't. It felt like the shame-filled way he used to cling to his brother when people laughed at him. *You think you're a boy, bitch?* They'd yell, and Derrick would sneer and say nothing to defend him.

They wouldn't reach the black double doors before the drunk caught them. Miller tried to drag Horn along faster, but the faerie only gave him an eerie smile. "Do not fear," he said. "The event is by invitation only."

They reached the doors and Miller grabbed at one. What he held was shaped like an arched metal handle. But it felt damp and gritty, and shone oil-slick, as if made from the very asphalt of the New York streets. He hauled it open and lunged through.

A scream erupted outside, followed by panicked shouts from across the street. Miller turned to look, but now only Horn stood behind him. The faerie closed the door, one eyebrow quirked. "It is rude to follow where you have not been invited."

Horn seemed different now, and not just because of his improved posture. The moldering leaf smell had intensified, cut through by a sharp animal musk. The windbreaker had tightened and brightened, molding to his body. It now looked ceremonial, almost military. At his waist hung a slim oak cane, unsupported by any belt, twisted like a living branch. His horns had grown larger, more lustrous . . . this time, without the aid of saliva, thank God. They curved gracefully, nearly meeting at the back of his curly-haired head. His face had become dignified: the dark irises now shone green, and his pale skin was smooth and clean, though his weirdly proportioned facial features were still unsettling.

Miller started toward a window to look out and see what had happened to the drunk, but Horn headed him off with a touch to the cheek that brushed an eyelid. Miller jerked away, but too late—his eyeballs ached deeply. What had Horn's touch done to him this time?

Silently, stiffly formal, they approached the sullen gold cage of an antique elevator. Horn jerked the folding grate open with a clatter. Otherwise the building seemed empty of life. Miller stepped into the elevator car, starting as he caught his reflection in the mirrored wall. His eyes had turned from golden brown to an electric blue. The elevator started to lurch down. He turned from the reflection, deeply alienated, and with his new eyes watched through the grate as the oily stone of the elevator shaft grew darker and darker.

They arrived at the sub-basement with a loud clunk. For an instant Miller saw only a vast darkened storage space through the grate. Then Horn dragged the cage's door aside, and the basement erupted with light and sound.

It was as if a junk shop had been granted independent city status. And then, immigration had begun. Tents, stalls, and flimsy bark huts leaned together to form narrow lanes where people crowded shoulder-to-shoulder. Yelling, laughing, shoving, buying, eating, singing. Some were costumed, others were not. Harlequin clowns and hobo clowns drank with birthday clowns. Elephant heads were perched atop Regency gowns.

Miller watched a tinfoil robot purchase an antique unicycle. A stubbly man in Adidas who could have been his high school gym teacher came up and tried to sell him a pouch of psychedelic mushrooms. The overall effect was of a Ren Faire where no one had quite agreed on the time period—or universe. Beyond the stalls and tents hung a hazy green light.

"So, stupid question. Are these all . . . faeries?" Miller asked Horn skeptically, watching the mushroom man wander off. Definitely not his gym teacher; too nice an ass.

The faerie's laugh sounded like a hunting horn. "Of course not!" His cane swatted the calves of a harlequin as she elbowed past. "Privileged acquaintances of the supernatural. We don't share space with hoi polloi. The Kindly Ones rightly claim the nicer real estate."

* * *

The basement seemed infinitely vaster than the building it crouched beneath. It was unclear if this was by magic or structural design, but Miller didn't want to give Horn the satisfaction of being asked. He'd seen enough "Doctor Who" to keep his mouth shut around smug immortal guys.

But he sighed involuntarily as they wended through an alley, Horn's sights fixed on distant tree-tops. Swaying gently without wind, branches swept the too-high ceiling, leaves fluttering from silver to green-blue and back. The closer they got, the sweeter the air smelled. The streets were growing quieter with every step toward the forest.

"Memories, gentlemen?"

Miller turned to see a lady in a red cardigan smiling at him. She looked like a youthful grandmother sitting and playing a chunky Gameboy. Her table was piled with toys and knick-knacks, all Nineties' things Miller had owned once. "No thanks," he said, but mustered a smile. She'd called him a gentleman, after all. And he had pleasant memories of every item on her table. He picked up a deck of cards.

Horn frowned as if disturbed by the things laid out there. "We are late," he growled. "And put *that* away." He pointed to an item that, to Miller, seemed to be nothing but a deck of Yugioh cards.

"Going beyond the Traces?" the vendor asked, voice rising slightly. Miller shrugged and set the deck down. Horn's hand was hovering by his lower back. He walked away, fearing another touch.

They emerged from the alley to be confronted by a sloping wall of mounded dirt, topped by a border of yellow-and-white primroses. The flowers branched outward as if snatching at them.

"Is there an entrance to this garden?" Miller asked, looking for a gap in the floral riot.

"You can enter the 'garden' wherever you like," said Horn, lip curling.

"Stop trying to scare me," Miller told him. "I am scared—but only of meeting more people as annoying as you."

The faerie's smile widened. Miller felt the sharp green eyes watching as he scrambled up the dirt slope and kicked at the bushes.

***

They emerged into a forest clearing. The thick canopy he'd seen from afar belonged to fewer than a score of trees, each with generous green-and-silver foliage. Built into their lower branches were platforms draped with banners and ribbons, connected by rope bridges. Miller momentarily mistook the chatter of beautiful voices from above for calling birds.

Horn scanned the area, apparently looking for someone or something in particular, then shook his head in disappointment. Then he grabbed the rope ladder at the base of the nearest tree and offered a hand.

"I got it, dude," Miller growled. The ropes were white silk, woven with glints of silver. They trembled as Horn started up after him. "And I hope you know, if you're staring at my ass down there, that makes you gay."

"Hello!" an excited voice trilled before he even cleared the platform. A taloned, beringed hand shot out and dragged him bodily onto the planks. His knees scraped the ragged wooden edge, leaving skin behind.

"Ouch, Jesus!" Both knees were bleeding through rips in his corduroy pants.

"Oh dear. I'm so sorry," chirped the slender woman who'd just hefted all 160 pounds of him. Her hair was a cloud of gold, her face downy with golden fur. "Let me staunch that." In her hand was a red silk handkerchief, embroidered in gold. Her fur-lined lips came close to Miller's ear. "I smell other blood on you. I will trade generously for your Flow—"

Miller grabbed her wrist, the handkerchief inches from his knee. She meant his period. It still hadn't stopped, and somehow the creature could tell. "No. Thanks. I'm good," he said through gritted teeth, skin crawling.

Stella had made him repeat a mantra over and over: *Take nothing. Trade for nothing. Give nothing away.* And then she'd added darkly, *Even a loan shark wouldn't survive a Faerie market.*

A flash of memory: his brother Derrick, reading him a poem about two sisters at an otherworldly bazaar. *We must not look at goblin men, we must not buy their fruits / Who knows upon what soil they fed / their hungry thirsty roots?*

The inhuman woman frowned as if reading his thoughts and pulled free from his grip. She crumpled the rust-red handkerchief in her fist.

The ball of cloth nearly hit Horn's head as it appeared at the top of the ladder. "*Aon scéal*, handsome," the woman said. "Get this one a draft to drink. She's duller than a bag of dead mice."

"*Diabhal an scéal*," Horn replied wryly. "So I've noticed."

Miller huffed and got up to look for a way to the next platform. As he passed the woman's table he noted other merchandise—scarves, gloves, eye masks, silken restraints—all dyed rust-red and embroidered with golden hair. He touched a silken cuff, then reeled back as a dizzying jolt of lust and fear shot through him. Thank God he hadn't taken the handkerchief.

Miller swayed across the rope bridge to the next tree; Horn followed, pleasantly greeting each merchant they passed. There were people made of cobwebs, long-legged spiders walking upright, and shimmering vapours that danced—literally—to techno music. A well-dressed being with bead-black stalk eyes tried to speak to him from a chitinous mouth that opened and closed like double doors. Its hisses and clicks meant nothing to him.

"Ugh, a primitive." Horn rolled his eyes as the creature's mouth frothed with effort. "Fishmen shouldn't be allowed. This is not a seafood market." Miller followed him but craned to look back. He could discern no emotion on the crablike face as foam spilled down the front of its green silk shirt.

Beneath a dead spot in the overhead warehouse lights, a faerie with translucent skin and pulsating blue organs tried to pull Miller into a dirt ring of glowing fungi surrounded by silent onlookers. He tried to politely decline. She listened patiently, her visible heart pulsing rhythmically, then reached out and yanked down his pants. She had him on the ground, half-naked, before he knew what was happening.

"Shit!" he shouted, grabbing at Horn's ankle as she tried to drag him past the glowing toadstools.

"If you don't want it," Horn said with casual amusement, "simply say 'no' three times."

"No! No! No!" Miller scrambled away and grabbed his pants. "That's too fucking many! Why can't you people listen the first time?" He yanked them on without bothering to find his underwear, the onlookers still blandly watching.

Miller hovered near the exit bridge and glanced back at the see-through faerie. Her organs glowed faintly, like phosphorescent shrimp in a saltwater tank. Then he noticed Horn watching him, and blushed.

"You have a longing for women," Horn said. It wasn't a question.

Not just women, asshole, thought Miller. *But I don't want you getting any ideas.* Really, nuance was lost on faeries. Horn only seemed to pick up on extreme emotions and medical technicalities. Miller touched the faerie statuette in his pocket.

"Hurry, we're to meet with someone," Horn said impatiently. They descended a long rope ladder. Miller dropped to the packed earth, turned around—

—and touched noses with a beautiful being. Her nose was long and slender, skin an earthy autumn red, eyes big and dark. Brown hair flowed down her back, sleek as a seal's pelt. Large velvet ears pricked up and swiveled toward him as he stammered, "Oh. Uh, hi!"

"Hello," replied a girlish voice from a mouth that was unexpectedly wide and full of small pointed teeth. Her pink dress was cut low to bare shoulders freckled with spots of white. He couldn't tell what animal she reminded him of. She had the grace of a deer but the alertness of a bird dog.

"Lhi," Horn kissed the girl's head. "How I've missed you!"

She nuzzled his cheek in response, humming in primal delight. Her narrow philtrum split her top lip in two, like a cat's.

"Pet, meet Camilla."

Miller didn't bother to correct him this time. "Pretty lady," Lhi said, and his heart skipped a beat. Had he been pretty, as a girl? He'd never thought so. But Lhi seemed to. Her eyes darted with a pure animal intelligence. Unlike Miller's, Lhi's body was her whole self. It was everything she needed, and displayed exactly what she was.

A hunter.

Horn pulled Lhi aside, fishing in his pocket and mumbling something about "a gift."

Miller looked down, sick with doubt. He hadn't felt this uncertain in years.

A root curved around his sneaker. Collected in the crevice, and strewn all over the ground, were hundreds of red berries. Looking up, he saw they all came from one enormous tree. It had not one thick trunk, but dozens twined together like sinews in an arm. High above, moonlight winked through the tear-shaped leaves and clustered white flowers—though the moon should have been hidden by dirty clouds and twenty-odd floors of building. "What's that?" Miller immediately felt like a drunken moron. Clearly it was an enormous fucking tree he had somehow failed to notice till now.

A branch acknowledged this point with a slow swish.

"Oh," said Horn, "just a big old bitch of a tree." He crushed some berries underfoot, leaving a bloodlike smear in the dirt. The leaves above shivered mesmerizingly. Miller sat down abruptly on a hard loop of root. "Ouch," he whispered. His tailbone throbbed.

Lhi dropped to her knees in front of him. "All right?" She extended a long pink tongue and licked him right across the mouth. Her saliva smelled like eucalyptus and burned like menthol. He toppled onto his side, and everything went foggy.

"You'd better have a rest," Horn said from a great distance. Then he and Lhi disappeared. Miller felt dirt and crushed berries under his face. Feet and paws and hooves passed by, but superimposed over them played a daydream where Lhi chased him across the pink night sky of Manhattan. She whooped in pursuit, moving terrifyingly fast. Like a boy on the playground had once chased Camilla to make her kiss him.

Dream-Miller couldn't run fast enough. He slowed, turned, and Lhi smacked into his chest. She made him kiss her. The only word to describe how good it felt was "inappropriate."

* * *

He woke wondering why he was cold and wet. Then realized someone was splashing water on his back. His clothes were stained with water and berry juice. He wriggled out of the soggy vest and rolled over to see what had woken him from the best dream ever.

Cradled at the tree's roots was an enormous clamshell.

How do I keep not noticing this shit? he thought. How drugged-up am I?

The girl swimming inside the shell wore a wig made of bright red yarn. She surfaced and hung her naked torso over the edge. Her cheeks were swelled with water. Miller opened his mouth to complain and got another jet squarely in the face instead.

"Stop it," he yelled, wiping it away. "What is it with you people and body fluids!"

But the cold water was already making him feel less fuzzy. Though he was pretty sure he was still in insta-love with Lhi.

"C'mere," Raggedy Ann stage-whispered, beckoning with both arms in a way that made her boobs jiggle. She needed a nice supportive shell bra. Her skin was snowy-hued, as if the blood underneath was blue.

Miller lumbered over. "Whaddaya want, fishface?" He braced his hands on the shell's edge.

"Oh, nice. Ya know that's a racial slur, right?" She had a strong Long Island accent. Four glistening feet of translucent fin breached the surface, showering Miller with more water. "So what are ya?"

"A guy," Miller snapped.

"Ya mean a human." She laughed.

"Oh, sorry, I thought. . ." His face grew hot. "You're the only non-human tonight to not immediately call me a girl. So thanks for that."

The mermaid narrowed her eyes. "Why would I care? I'm not askin' ya to fertilize my eggs."

"Truth. And your name is. . . ?"

She sighed. "Call me . . . Lorelei."

"Oh. I thought that was just another word for merm—"

"Yeah." She cut him off, sounding like she'd recited this speech a thousand times already. "We don't do names, so ya get Mermaid, Siren, Lorelei, yadda yadda. 'Hey you' is OK too. We're pretty solitary, so it doesn't come up much."

"Why are you here then?"

"Sure not to slum it up with humans, like some of these fucknut faeries. I'm basically just the performing dolphin tonight."

"Huh?" His mind was drifting insistently back to Lhi's big eyes and narcotic tongue.

"Punishment, ya know?" The mermaid tapped her yarn wig. Which, now that she mentioned it, looked like an Ariel costume your mom would make if she hated you.

"What for?"

She made a face. "Messin' around with Herne."

"You mean Horn, the smelly homeless guy? Wait—you *did* that guy?"

"Shut up! Homeless? Get out. He's some kinda nobleman. Still . . . not worth it." She patted the bark of the tree behind her. "His main girl here has me in a tank, and him sleeping on the proverbial couch. Well, I guess the street."

A windless susurrus moved through the leaves above.

"Straight people," Miller said, hoping to sound sympathetic. "So obsessed with controlling each other's . . . eggs."

"Tell me about it." She paused to regard the rough texture of the tree's bark. "She hears us. But she knows she's got me. My dirty mouth isn't gonna change anything."

"Is she . . . up in the tree?"

She flicked droplets onto his nose. "No, moron. The tree is her.

Habundia, witch-queen, possessive bitch extraordinaire."

"The witch is a tree? Then how does she, you know, do witch things?"

"Oh, she's just sulking right now."

Abruptly, the mermaid grabbed the front of Miller's shirt, dragging him into the pool. The shock of cold water silenced him as Lorelei pushed him into the meager shadow of the shell's lip.

"Shh. Herne and his hound are back for ya," she whispered. "Brought you a lovely new gown, I see."

His insides turned even colder than his outsides. Still, a small hot point of light in his chest made him pipe up, "Lhi's there?"

The mermaid's face twisted. "Lhiannan Shee got ya, huh?"

"Pretty la-dy!" called a high voice from nearby.

"Uh-oh." Lorelei winced.

"Pretty lady!" Closer. Miller tried to rise. Lorelei pushed him down till water went up his nose.

"Pretty lady, I smell you!"

"Uh oh. She's got your scent," Lorelei whispered. "Knows your blood." She let go of him and ran a hand over her own arm, where a dusting of iridescent greenish scales stood in for hair. She shuddered.

"Pretty. Pretty. Lady." Lhi's voice held the smugness of a child winning hide-and-seek. She stood above him now. A long-nailed hand reached down to poke his nose. Lorelei had flattened herself against the opposite side of the pool, yarn plastered across her eyes. She started to pull the wig off, but the tawny hand flew up to point at her.

"On!" Lhi barked with childish malice. Wordlessly, Lorelei rearranged the yarn wig. Her face flushed blue. She wouldn't meet Lhi's eyes.

"Sea-scum slut," Lhi hurled at Lorelei's downcast face—the longest phrase he'd heard her use yet.

Miller stood, water sheeting off his body. There were Lhi's glinting eyes, and beyond her, Horn—no, Herne. A grass-colored gown slung over his shoulder. Miller didn't want to get out, but he wanted even less to disappoint Lhi, even after her strange cruelty toward the mermaid. She took his wet face in her hands and dragged her tongue across his mouth again. Stars exploded behind his eyes . . . and other places.

He let her drag him by the hand over to Herne, glancing back only once at Lorelei. She had turned away, stripping bark viciously from the trunk of the tree that was Habundia.

Miller watched Herne draw closer in flashes, as if through disco strobe lights. His sneering face, that awful dress.

Then Herne had him by the nape. His hot breath exploded in Miller's ear. "Time to dress appropriately. We are presenting you."

Then Lhi was pulling off his clothes, and this felt pretty agreeable, but—everyone was going to see. Herne would put him in a dress. And . . . Lhi was going to like him better that way. So maybe it was okay. He closed his eyes and tried not to shiver at the scratch of old chiffon and stiff tulle against his skin.

Lhi was taking off his pants now, forestalling any struggle by licking his inner thigh, knees, anything exposed. And each time he got dizzier, floatier. Cared less.

Everything was exposed now. Pants gone, underwear long lost, no control. No control! Fear began to eat through the toxic bliss. With great effort, he hauled his eyelids open.

Lhi was removing his socks with her teeth, shaking her head like a dog with a chew toy. He had a clear view down her pink dress, where a bit of gray cloth was tucked between her breasts. Another shake of her head, and it fell out onto the ground.

On the dirt lay his missing boxers. Dusty, stained with a small spot of blood.

She's got your scent, Lorelei had said.

You smell like cunt, you stupid cunt, Derrick had said, years ago.

Herne's head was bowed over Miller's shoulder, pulling the scratchy dress up over his legs. Miller reached out. His fingers found a horn and he yanked savagely. As before, a shock of pain ran up his arms, forcing him to let go. Herne snarled with anger, or pain. Both of Miller's arms were suddenly smooth, pink and hairless, with perfect shining fingernails.

The parents had used to send Derrick to Camilla's room to make her get dressed for church. *Big brothers look out for their little sisters,* their mother had always said.

Herne crouched at Miller's side, trying to yank the dress up over his ass. One horn pressed into his ribcage. This produced a horrible pinching of ribs bowing inward, shrinking his waist.

Every time he'd closed her bedroom door behind him, Derrick's eyes took on the cold gaze of a hunter. *You're gonna wear whatever fucking dress I tell you*, he would say.

Lhi pulled a narrow sleeve over Miller's shoulder. It never should have fit, but the biceps he'd worked to build had shrunk to nearly nothing.

Derrick had run track, so he was fast and strong. He'd always caught her no matter where she ran and cowered.

Now Herne was trying to zip it up, but Miller's chest was still too broad. The faerie placed cool hands precisely on the upper ribcage. An awful cracking noise, and the feeling of compression returned.

Miller screamed.

Derrick had held her down on the bed, the chosen dress splayed next to her like a suffering sister. The hunter's objective is to kill. Or to clothe. Sometimes he allows himself to enjoy inflicting pain.

Ah, yes. The excruciating process of being fixed. Miller recognized this pain.

But why was this happening? What kind of faerie had the power of making you girlier, anyway? That wasn't really what Herne did. He was . . . *fixing*. Healing. Erasing the precious progress he could only see as defects in a woman's body.

Did you get her into the damn outfit yet? Miller's mother's voice would shout from the hall. *Oh, stop screaming, Camilla. Christ! It's a dress, not an iron maiden.*

The zipper closed now with an oiled metal snicker. Miller opened his eyes to stare up into moonlit branches. He was on his knees. From above, his brother's face was regarding him with knowing and disgust. But, no—that was Herne's sneer, not Derrick's.

"O Habundia, my Queen, my love!" the faerie called up into the branches. "As you charged me, I've cultivated my heart on the streets of mankind, and it has bloomed and grown. I've even taken in a stray. A tainted boy-girl thing which I am restoring to perfection. I present it to you as a token of our joyful reunion!"

A rustling shivered through the tree's branches. Then they fell deadly silent. Teardrop leaves and red berries dropped like heavy rain, showering faces, blanketing feet. Next came a popping like flattened bubble wrap, as every branch turned from glossy brown to bone-white.

Sharp as gunfire, a crack shot up from the tree's base. Lorelei gasped, dove beneath the water and did not resurface.

Miller gasped too, but was frozen in place. The seven-foot-tall woman who stepped out of the tree's fissure was definitely a Queen of something. She had to duck briefly to protect the enormous crown of antlers sprouting from her head. Nobody in their right mind would make a "nice rack" joke to her and expect to survive.

Her sleek black gown, at second glance, proved to be no dress at all—only her own long hair, scattered with sparkling crystals. Her skin was tawny like Lhi's, but her face more human. Her thick dark brows and pointed nose recalled the Lenape who'd lost Manhattan long ago. Though, Miller supposed, this one could probably look however she wanted. She wore no makeup or adornments, and carried a cane like Herne's, made of the same wood as the tree she'd been moments before. In her large elegant hands, though, it rather resembled a wand.

Herne stepped forward with open arms.

She planted the tip of the wand on his chest to halt him. "I have come down only to speak to you with language. You are a terrible listener elsewise."

"But my love, I did exactly as you—"

"*No.*" She leaned down, digging the tip of the wand into his chest. "You do not change, but only lie. It is a beggar's transformation. I tire of your manipulations. You would understand if you had ever truly listened."

Herne folded his hands around the wand as if praying. White flowers sprouted from the elder wood.

"No," she repeated calmly, though lightning crackled through her voice. She pulled the cane away before the spreading blooms could reach her. "I banished you for a reason, Herne. If you feel insufficiently chastened, I can take away the powers of your horns as well. Go back to the streets above. Torment humans with your . . . kindness. You may rot there—you and your new pet."

Her gaze shifted to Lhi. "But not the old. I shall reclaim my servant."

She gestured expansively to the several dozen onlookers who had gathered to watch and murmur. "Everyone, please continue to enjoy this diverting event! And remember to use safe-sex practices with mortals. Retract excess teeth and all poisonous spines."

"My love, can we not—" Herne reached out.

There was a flash of bone and fur. He hissed and drew back a bloodied hand. Habundia had morphed into a small black jackal, as if she couldn't stand to speak language to him for another second. The beast leapt away, vanishing into the fissure in the trunk, which closed behind it. A locomotive roar filled the air as the tree swelled back to life in fast-forward, tearing water from the ground, funneling it up to the highest twigs. Leaves budded and unfurled with a sound like a factory full of gum simultaneously unwrapping.

Lhi clung to Herne's slack arm and butted her head against his shoulder. "Not . . . stay together?" she keened. He snarled and shoved her away. She curled in the dirt by his feet, emitting a throaty moan.

Miller sifted through crackling leaves, feeling for the soft reassurance of corduroy pants. His fingers found a cold, angular object instead. Loops of metal wings. The faerie statuette.

He squeezed it painfully tight, missing Stella. Through Habundia's branches, the quality of the light was changing, becoming golden with sunrise. "Take it back," he whispered.

"What?" Herne's voice was brittle and distracted.

"Take back your gift. It's dawn. I don't want to be here anymore." He peeled the dress down to his waspish waist.

On Herne's face rose the same expression of disgust and frustrated cruelty he used to see on Derrick's, just before it disappeared beyond the bedroom door. Santa, bestowing a gift no one appreciated.

"You'd be more grateful as a dog," Herne spat, stepping toward Miller. "And I do need a new pet."

Miller braced a hand on Lhi's shoulder to push himself upright, and took a wild swing at Herne. The statuette's head flew off as it smashed into the side of the faerie's contorted face.

Herne screamed and fell to his knees. A brand was burned into one cheek: a fiery, lacy teardrop, the mark of the faerie wing. Which must have been steel after all. Lucky guess, Stella.

Herne's slender cane lay next to the faerie. Miller picked it up and the wood slid away, revealing a long, shining blade.

Lhi grabbed Miller's arm, but he only felt her charm as a sickness in the pit of his stomach now. Like regret.

"I've given you. . ." Herne coughed out, spitting sizzling blood. "My gift!"

"I never asked for shit, old man, except for you to stop hurting me."

Herne cringed against the ground, turning his burning cheek to the cool, damp dirt.

Miller brought the blade down where horn met skull. The left one broke off with a sick splintering sound, leaving a jagged edge. Herne cowered silently, palms over his face, shaking. But Miller wasn't through. He grabbed Herne's wrists, dragging his hands away from his face. They both shuddered at the contact, and familiar bone-deep electric pain rushed up Miller's arm. Damn it—the bastard was still trying to turn him into something else. A faithful hound like Lhi. Fur sprouted on the backs of Miller's hands, and his fingernails felt loose, ready to drop off. He kicked the faerie in the chest. When Herne's arms flew to protect his ribs, Miller brought the sword down on the right horn.

Herne sucked in a breath as it snapped off, more sob than gasp.

For the first time, Miller noticed all the watchers. Faeries, including the transparent woman. But also humans from the other side of the primrose border. How crazed he must look now: two jagged horns gripped in one furry hand, a sword in the other. A sweat-drenched tulle dress hanging around his waist, his chest scars red and inflamed. A hero miscast as a heroine.

He left his pants on the ground. Shrugging off the dress, he let his bare feet carry him to Lorelei's pool. Their gazes followed him: thick legs, tiny waist, no penis, breasts growing back like twin tumors. The weird tips of canine claws growing in under his fingernails. Fine. He was no stranger than any of these things. Herne was a liar, Lhi was a liar.

As he approached, Lorelei pulled off the wig and tossed it against the tree. It hit the bark with a wet slap and slid into the dirt.

He handed her the horn. "Would you heal me?" She nodded as though she knew what that meant. She did cast a nervous glance at the tree, but Habundia's jealousy seemed to have died along with her patience.

He climbed in and stood naked in the cold water, goosebumps rising.

She pressed the horn to his chest and arms. Pain ripped through his body. She slowly traced it around his waist. The ache eased as an invisible corset came uncinched. At last, he inhaled deeply.

As she finished making him right, a howl rose from the primrose border. Lhi's power over him had weakened, but he'd know her voice anywhere.

"I'll be right back," he told Lorelei, and ran naked to the hedge, a horn gripped in one fist. Lhi was clawing at the primrose bushes, trying to follow Herne. But the branches held her back, striking at her arms and lashing her face. She was bleeding and whimpering, trying to dig them up by the roots. Her mouth stained green from biting at branches. Miller wrapped his arms around her. She snarled and flung her head back, trying to bite him too.

He wanted to free her from this awful devotion. Obviously, Herne controlled her mind, just as she had controlled Miller's. He threw her on her back, pinned her arms with his knees. She yelped and strained as he touched the horn to her forehead. Electric power vibrated in the tips of his fingers.

The creature beneath him shimmered and warped. Her outer layer faded to translucence, revealing a network of glowing varicolored strands throughout her body. They wove in and out of each other like tiny sinews. He examined her head, her heart, looking for a colored thread he could pull to undo Herne's warped influence.

He couldn't find one. As far as he knew, the strands all belonged.

Lhi's mewling changed pitch, from rage to pain. He scrambled up, and her face and skin were visible once more. His bare knees had left bruises on her forearms.

"Oh God, I'm sorry. I'm so sorry." He tried to catch her shoulder.

She stood slowly and regarded him with scorn. "We release you," she said quietly. "Leave me now." The last of his longing for her receded. But the remorse stayed.

Lhi scrambled back to the bushes and resumed digging, though writhing, wormlike roots undid her work again and again.

He gave up and returned to Lorelei. "Helped out, did ya?" She raised an eyebrow.

Miller shook his head, unable to meet her eyes.

"Guess you should get going."

"Actually. . ." his heart beat anxiously again as an idea formed. "Want me to get you out of here?"

Her nostrils flared. "How? On that broad manly back a' yours?"

He held up the horn. "No. I thought I could, you know, 'heal' you. I mean . . . if you want."

"Let's hear your proposal," she said warily. With a slap of her tail, she showered him with rainbow drops.

***

Lorelei turned out to be bad at having legs.

"Did you give me defective ones?" she panted, leaning against a chain link fence several blocks from the black tower. The green tulle dress suited her slightly better than it had Miller, but it was still ugly.

"I think you're just not used to them yet." Miller offered an arm.

"I know all about the mechanics of meat stilts! Mermaids are great at science!" She blundered into a lamppost, shoved off from it, and stumbled away to grab the next stationary object.

Miller followed, wearing only his button-down and boxers. He'd given his sweater vest to the drunk who'd tried to follow him into the building. He and Lorelei had found the man on the sidewalk, half-naked, gibbering about a giant pigeon. His torso was covered in long cuts and scratches . . . also, bird shit. Miller could have healed him, he supposed, but didn't. The sweater-vest was scratchy, and that dickhead deserved chafed nipples.

"So. After I heal your fins back and you swim off into the Sag Harbor sunrise, want to see each other again sometime? We could sit around and bitch about faeries."

"Coney Island is nice right now." She accidentally ripped a Please Curb Your Dog sign out of the ground. "Whoops. Just as friends, though. Like I said, not looking for anybody to fertilize my eggs."

Miller nodded. "Yeah, me neither."

Lorelei waved and disappeared around a corner. The wet slap of bare feet on pavement drifted back to him.

He opened the top few buttons of his shirt to the warmth of dawn, listening for the dull jingle of change in a Styrofoam cup. He knew he would hear it again someday. Manhattan was small compared to the Night Bazaar. A man with two stumps of bone on his head was somewhere out there right now, learning to live like a human being.

Maybe.

A curved horn rode snugly in each of Miller's pockets as he walked on, toward home. An electric ache thrummed in his bones. He was already starting to change.

AFTER THE BAZAAR

And now, I fear, we must strike our tents. Pack up the pleasure booths, the tables and stalls of exotic wares. Soon we'll move on to our next venue. Often we depart not a moment too soon, for in the age of cell texts and flash mobs it's hard to keep a party secret anymore. And dissatisfied customers can be unforgiving, even when granted all they wished for . . . and more. We do not fear the local authorities—assuming they could find us—but neither do we care to invite tiresome scrutiny, or be forced to resort to evasive measures.

Nor do we care about online reviews, happy face emoticons, or rankings by stars. The Bazaar is not a chain restaurant or a timeshare resort. We aren't looking for just any clients. Our preferences, as you now know, are rather more specific, and very exclusive.

Still, I hope you enjoyed your visit with us, however brief. A shame you couldn't stay longer . . . but then, of course, nor could we. And if you did not gain entrance this time, well, there is always tomorrow. That is, if you are still here to receive your invitation.

Anyhow, as soon as I report on the accumulated till, the next place of business will call, and I must answer. There is so much to do, even after we're packed. Travel may be broadening, true. But getting there is also a great deal of work when you have such a sizeable entourage. Especially if your destination may involve both Where, and When.

I've heard Venice is nice in the fall. The winding alleys and cobbled lanes run between tall narrow buildings, which lean over the visitor like inquisitive and disreputable great aunts, exuding whiffs of perfume and pasta and old silk scarves infused with faint scents of sewage and mildew. All of it lapped by the watery fingers of a remorselessly-rising sea. I'm just not decided yet on which year would be best for business. Yes, Venice might do well for our next stop . . .

Yours most sincerely, your most humble and obedient servant,

Madame Vera

THE END

(THIS SEASON)

Contributors

APHRODITE ANAGNOST's debut novel, *Memoir of a Death Angel*, was an Amazon Best New Author semifinalist. Her second, *Passover*, co-authored with Robert Arthur, won the Chanticleer Paranormal Book Award, Ghosts Category. Find Anagnost, a country doctor, horse trainer, and equestrian book editor, on Twitter @AphroditeAuthor, on Facebook, and at www.XenophonPress.com.

"Friends of Vera" marks GREGORY FLETCHER's short story debut. His published work includes three essays and *Shorts and Briefs*, a collection of short plays and brief principles of playwriting. Eleven of his plays have been produced Off-Off-Broadway. His awards include the Mark Twain Prize for Comic Playwriting and the National Ten-Minute Play Award. See more at www.gregoryfletcher.com.

ROY GRAHAM is a Brooklyn-based writer and journalist whose work has appeared in *Playboy*, *Vice*, and *Kill Screen*. He spent most of his childhood trying to flex the muscle that would grow his wolverine claws. Roy can be found on Twitter @grayhaem.

LENORE HART, *The Night Bazaar* editor, grew up in a haunted house in Florida. She's the author of *Waterwoman* (a B&N Discover book), *Ordinary Springs*, *Treasure of Savage Island*, *Becky*, *The Raven's Bride* and, writing as Elisabeth Graves, *Black River* and *Devil's Key*. She teaches in the MA/MFA Creative Writing Program at Wilkes University. Find her at www.lenorehart.com, @LenoreHartAuthor on Facebook, and @Elfair on Twitter.

CAROL MacALLISTER earned an MFA from Wilkes University, and has been publishing award-winning short stories in various genres for over twenty years. She's a judge for the International Bram Stoker Awards and a poetry judge for several journals and the NFSPS. *The Blackmoor Tales* is her Lovecraftian story collection. Other works include *Mayan Calendar Reveal*, available in ebook.

EDISON McDANIELS is a neurosurgeon and writer whose stories are informed by medicine, history, and the supernatural. His two novels of the Civil War are *Not One Among Them Whole* and *The Matriarch of Ruins*. Other books and novellas include *An Endless Array of Broken Men, The Touched, Saving King, The Bottom of the Fifth, Juicing Out, The Crucible*, and *Blade Man*. Visit him at www.surgeonwriter.com.

Editorial assistant FAE TYLER MONTGOMERY is a Fantastical Literature and Fantasy Writing major at Swarthmore. She freelances in the non-profit sector, writing and editing for the organizations Business Development Assistance Group and AASuccess. This is her first foray into the world of literature, where she intends to stay, when she's not busy designing clothes for warrior women.

CORINNE ALICE NULTON's "14 Symptoms" was featured in The Brick Theater's Game Play Festival. Her ten-minute play "Flesh" was a finalist at the Kennedy Center. Corinne's short stories have been published in *Cactus Heart*, *Esprit*, and *Ellipses*. She's a recovering coffee addict with a Hermione Granger complex, who keeps the scattered parts of her brain on Post-Its and in the dog-eared pages of Dollar Store notebooks.

NAIA POYER, originally from Virginia's Eastern Shore, currently studies East Asian religions at Harvard. As a queer agender scholar, writer, visual artist, and actor, they hope to contribute to LGBTQIA representation in media and the world in general. Poyer is a professional graphic designer and book designer; they created the cover and interior of *The Night Bazaar*. Visit www.Facebook.com/NaiadBookDesign.

DANIA RAMOS is an author and playwright. Her middle grade mystery novel *Who's Ju?* was named International Latino Book Awards Best Young Adult eBook and was a shortlist finalist for the ILBA Mariposa Award for Best First Book. She lives in New Jersey with her husband. Find her on Facebook at DaniaRamosAuthor, on Twitter @ DaniaDania, or at www.daniaramos.com.

JIM SCHEERS is a recovering serial commuter and author of a novel about 1980s punk, *This is What You Want, This is What You Get*. Visit jimscheers.com or follow him on Facebook at Jim Scheers, Author or on Twitter: @JimScheers.

ISAAV SKINNER is the pseudonym of a novelist who traces his lineage to two Mayflower passengers, a Revolutionary War infantryman, one Vice President and two Presidents of the United States, a Civil War officer, and a D-Day paratrooper. "Obey" is his first work of short fiction.

MAU VANDUREN grew up in a family of doctors, accountants, artists, and musicians, many of whom were killed in the Holocaust, but still speak to him from old photos. His nonfiction work *Many Heads and Many Hands* explores Dutch and English roots of the U.S. Constitution. Learn more at www.governance4us.com and on Facebook at Mau VanDuren.

ABOUT NORTHAMPTON HOUSE PRESS

Northampton House publishes carefully chosen fiction, poetry, and selected nonfiction. Our logo represents the Greek muse Polyhymnnia. Check out our list at www.northampton-house.com, and follow us on Facebook ("Northampton House Press") or Twitter (@Nhousepress) to discover more innovative works from brilliant new writers, for discerning readers of all ages.

CPSIA information can be obtained
at www.ICGtesting.com
Printed in the USA
LVOW11s1247190117
521521LV00001B/176/P

9 781937 99778